Acclaim for LIGHTRAIDER ACADEMY

'Inspired by the Christian fantasy role-playing game *DragonRaid*, the moral and religious teachings in the book are clear. An engaging Christian fantasy, readers will find this an exciting, action-filled read."

— Kirkus Reviews

"James R. Hannibal creates superb stories. His imagination and creativity are literally out of this world . . . Exciting and suspenseful reading!"

— Dick Wulf, creator of *DragonRaid*

"Epic quests, adventures worthy of sprawling maps, awesome battles, talking animals, and heroes who rise to the challenge–I love this kind of fantasy! Hannibal's Lightraider series has all that and more! Definitely worth the read."

— S.D. Grimm, author of the Children of the Blood Moon series and *A Dragon by Any Other Name*

"Hannibal handles genre tropes with skill and aplomb, managing to make a well-worn form seem fresh and new. This exquisite adventure is a great read for kids of all ages."

— Jon Land of BookTrib

"Hannibal delivers an action-packed quest through a world of fantastical creatures and unexpected friendships. A journey of faith and freedom from start to finish!"

— Lauren H. Brandenburg, award-winning author of *The Death of Mungo Blackwell*

BEAR KNIGHT

BEAR KNIGHT

LIGHTRAIDER ACADEMY | BOOK TWO

JAMES R. HANNIBAL

Bear Knight

Published by Enclave Publishing, an imprint of Oasis Family Media.

Carol Stream, Illinois, USA.
www.enclavepublishing.com

ISBN: 979-8-88605-030-1 (printed hardback)
ISBN: 979-8-88605-031-8 (printed softcover)
ISBN: 979-8-88605-033-2 (ebook)

Cover design by Emilie Haney, www.EAHCreative.com
Typesetting by Jamie Foley, www.JamieFoley.com
Map art by Melissa Nash

Printed in the United States of America.

For the real Connor and Aaron.

You are both a daily inspiration.

ARKELIA
Frost Isles
Ras Pyras
The Lion's Teeth
Val Glasa
Ander's Rampart
The Ice Adder
Fell Bay
King's Cradle
Western Sea
Northern Bight
Winter's Bight
Fantasia Sheiling
Misty Wood Lake
Iron Mountains
The Pyrons
Mirror Peaks
Fulcan Plains
Miner's Folly
Miner's Glory
Chasm Vale
Black Forest
Sil Shadath
Darkling Shade
TANELETHAR
The Dragon Lands
Tovat's Pool
Desert of Sin
Blood River
Fading Mountains
Tarlan Plains
Gloamwood
Green Mountains
The Eastlings
The Emerald
The Sapphire
Kezia's Tears
The Westlings
Highland Forest
Blueridge Hills
Eagle Peaks
Maidenwood Grove
Celestial Peaks
Gulf of Vows
Southern Bight
Shark Bight
Gulf of Stars
Dayspring Highlands
The Central Plain
White Ridge Mountains
The Great Sea
Cloud Forest
Many Blessings
Cape Rosland
KELEDEV
The Liberated Land
TALANIA

Fortress
of Valshadox
Sil Shadath
Graywater
Bay
Emen Kar
Barihav
Bezik Hills
Tagamar
Ghost Moor
Fading
Mountains
Gloamwood
Grenton

THE PRISONER
TANELETHAR

FOREST. FOG. DARKNESS. I DON'T REMEMBER WHERE I am. I don't know this place—this place where the creatures brought me the first time I died.

I don't remember my home, my old name. I remember little that is good. Only her face. Her laugh. And it is this, more than anything, that haunts me in this place of ghouls. I remember wanting to protect her. My *purpose* was to protect her.

Yet I'm here, in the dark. And that means I must have failed.

This thought makes me tighten my grip on the curved sword I stole from the barracks' stores—a trainer, blunt-edged and little use against the ore creatures here. An iron orc's hide is too thick for a trainer. But this weapon will make short work of a goblin's mushroom flesh. My body may be weakened after countless days of moldy bread and black water, after so many nights of delirium, but I can still chop through fungal sinew and brittleknit bone with an iron stick.

A wanderer floats past the barracks window, lantern held out with its cloaked arm. I duck, then peek. The sphere of orange light around the creature is small and dim. Sometimes I think those lanterns serve no other use than illuminating the drawn, crumbling faces and empty eye sockets under the wanderers' hoods. All the same, I stay put. I'd rather not get caught.

The moment the wanderer drifts out of sight, I roll over the windowsill. My landing makes not the slightest sound, a skill my body carried over from an old life, though my mind cannot recall its intended use. Was I a hunter? A thief? One day I will learn the answer—if my store of lives holds out.

One, two, three, four. I count my footfalls, running in a crouch. At night, the fog obscures all, both sound and sight. The endless black pines remain shadows until I'm close enough for their needles to prick my skin. Discovering the paces and courses leading out of the camp has cost me dearly. I've lived a dozen short lives—a dozen or more. Each brought me closer to escape, but each death brings me closer to the final sleep from which I won't wake up.

Something screams.

Ignore it.

My first landmark looms ahead. The camp fence is tall, but I loosened a plank on my second venture from the barracks. The barkhides and their masters haven't found it or don't care. The fence is the least of the obstacles penning us in.

A wanderer turns my way before I can push through. Has it seen me with its absent eyes? Or does it move on some predestined path known only to the sorcerers who raised it? Fear wells up, urging me to pull back the plank and squeeze through. I don't want to see the wanderer's face. I don't. But I know better. This is the mistake that ended my course eight lives ago. More wanderers patrol the trees beyond the fence. That night, fleeing one creature, I rushed headlong into another's bony grip.

With a force of will, I turn my eyes to the fence line. An orange glow seeps through cracks. As expected, a second wanderer approaches on the other side, closer than the first.

I time my movements, pulling the plank when one is past and before the lantern of the other gets too close. I'm through. The plank squeaks as I yank it back into place. I freeze and hold my breath.

Silence.

The wanderers continue on.

Tucking the sword into my belt, I judge my course by the fence line and set off again.

A stone path carries me toward the stream. I've died twice on this road, but there's no other route. The overgrowth is too thick in the surrounding woods. I know. I've died there too. Vines burst from the earth to strangle me that night. Spiders kept me company until an iron orc came.

Pink fangs. Twitching spinnerets. Bulbous, pulsating abdomens.

I hate spiders, but not as much as I hate the horned creepers. One crawls onto the path before me and flutters his wings in droning song. His cousins answer from the pines, and I hear their dull voices in my head, threatening to crawl down my throat and set their pincers to work on my innards. I stomp him into the rock with a wet crunch and hurry on.

As soon as I spot a stone bridge–my next landmark–I slow. Only this bridge crosses the stream. Teeth and tentacles once dragged me over its rail into frigid water, yet each life since, I've been tempted to race across. It would be so much faster. Here, in the dark, speed is death.

I turn before the bridge and pick my way through the fading overgrowth to the shore. Three lives ago, I found the rotting wooden posts, ruins of a smaller bridge. They wobble under me as I leap from one to the next. No water sentries come–*valpaza*, as my barracks mate Shan calls them. I land with a quiet *squish* in the muck on the far side.

Another course set, more footfalls counted, and I find the place I call the safe haven. No spiders or creepers spoil the ancient stone circle of its platform. The fog lightens here, enough that I can see the two bright moons through the green haze. I feel I could sleep here in safety.

Should I hold here 'til morning?

No. Daylight brings neither comfort nor escape in this place.

A statue at the haven's center depicts flaming hands forming a figure from clay. I think the figure is a man. Shan agrees with me. He said so yesterday, after I woke from my latest death and described this place. He says the image of flaming hands in the act of creation belongs to the faith of the Maker—a faith the dragons defeated long ago.

Defeated? I'm not so sure.

Jagged slashes of goblin script mar the statue's glistening base. Real fire has blackened the sculpted fire of the hands. But no parts are missing or broken. The fingers show not the slightest chip. If the dragons defeated this faith, why can't they tear the statue down?

Still, Shan knows more—remembers more—than most of us. The constant fear has yet to rip his name from his mind.

I wish I was strong like Shan.

One of the flaming hands captures water from the damp air so that a pool has gathered in the palm. I risk climbing onto the statue's base to take a sip. The water is cool and sweet. If I live again after tonight's death, I'll come back just to get another taste. But now, I must move on.

The second I step off the haven platform, the fog takes me again. Slow steps. Caution. I've only come this far once before. How much farther will I get before death claims me?

A long stone wall lies somewhere ahead, I know, but I won't take the path I tried last night. An easy walk through the lightest overgrowth brought me to an open gate. What was I thinking when I tried to run through? Hadn't I learned my lesson at the bridge? Creatures guard the easy paths, waiting to cut us down. I still feel the pain of the iron orc's halberd in the scar at my shoulder. Perhaps the wall itself is an illusion, a temptation to increase my suffering. Or perhaps freedom waits on the other side—freedom and memory.

I take a new course and use my sword to hack through brush and vines. The crack of every strike makes me cringe. Such noise might bring ghouls or goblins.

"Take me with you."

Oh no.

"You're leaving. I can tell. Take me with you."

The air grows cold. I shiver, but I dare not look. I can feel the apparition floating behind me, taking form from the gray-green fog. One of these cost me my fifth life. She was a little girl, not terrible to look upon apart from the odd angle of her neck, until I took her hand. Then all became horror and fangs. The icy blast of her scream shattered my heart.

Not this time.

"My body is not far," the creature moans—a male voice. "Nor is it buried deep in the soil. I will lead you to the grave. I was a young man like you, once. Strong and able, until the orcs ended me."

"Keep quiet. Go away. I'm no help to you."

"But you could help. You can carry my bones to a place of rest."

"I said, go away!" I hack harder at the brush. Faster. If this creature is here, orcs or wanderers may already be coming. I must reach the wall. The pines press against it. I can climb to the top and jump.

The ghoul drifts to my front, floating backward, unhindered by vines or trees. I wince as I see it did not lie about its age. We are much alike. Perhaps we are the same person. Am I an apparition too, floating here for eternity?

"Please, good sir. Carry my bones, and I'll be your guide. I know the wall by my withered heart. There's a gap where the stones fell—a safe place to cross." The ghoul reaches for me with a desperate moan that borders on a wail. "Please! Help me!"

I sidestep the ghostly hand and make a futile stab with my sword. The blunt tip passes through the creature and bangs into something solid. I hear the *clink* of iron hitting stone.

The wall.

"Out of my way, ghost!"

To my surprise, the apparition vanishes. Did it respond to my command or someone else's?

To complete my escape, I need only climb a pine growing

up against the wall. I believe I can brush away the spiders and creepers that infest its branches.

Before I can jump to grab the lowest branch, a vine wraps my leg.

"Oh, not again."

I speak the complaint out loud. What use is there in staying quiet anymore? I follow it with a yell and take a hard swing. My sword chops the vine away, but the delay has cost me everything. A creature wrapped in a ragged cloak and hood floats from the trees to hang between me and the wall. Not a wanderer. No, something much worse, and much more terrifying. Green flames burn in the sockets of its gargoyle skull. It hisses through long black fangs.

Death has found me again, and this time, I should feel honored. I've only seen one wraith in the camp. A creature of the long past, from what Shan calls the days of the traitor-kings.

The wraith's deep rasp holds a metallic ring. "Where do you think you're going?"

When I fail to answer, black claws emerge from under the cloak and dig into my shoulder. I gasp.

"Asked you a question, I did."

I swallow against the pain. "Couldn't sleep. Too much noise from the creepers. Thought I'd take a walk."

The hiss that follows bears a note of satisfaction. "Spirit, you have. Good. Good. Much pleasure I'll take in cutting it out of your flesh."

The apparition reappears at the wraith's shoulder, along with another. Their human faces stretch into monstrous distortions, and they unleash their icy screams. The wraith's black claws dig deep.

As another life fades, I close my eyes and see only her. She laughs, and in that moment, memory strikes. I understand why I love her laugh so much. It reminds me of our mother.

PART ONE

THE FIVE QUESTS

"Consider it a great joy, my brothers and sisters, whenever you experience various trials, because you know that the testing of your faith produces endurance. And let endurance have its full effect, so that you may be mature and complete, lacking nothing."

James 1:2-4

1

AARON ILMARI
KELEDEV
THOUSAND FALLS OUTPOST

AARON CRINGED AS THE WATCHMASTER POUNDED his long-handled hammer down into the centuries-old timbers. He felt the whole platform shake.

"Cohort! Who are you?"

The line of troops–Aaron included–answered in unison. "We are the watchmen!"

Boom. The war hammer fell again. Wood cracked beneath it. "Who are you?"

"We are the wall!"

Did the watchmaster not see the empty pre-dawn sky and the open sea behind his recruits? Was he not afraid to send this new cohort and half the outpost sliding down the cliffs?

"That's right," the master said, swinging the hammer to his shoulder and pacing before them. "You are the watchmen. You are the wall. The companies of the foothill outposts–from Thousand Falls to the Windhold, from Ravencrest to Orvyn's Vow. These are the last line of defense should war come to Keledev. And you will defend it at all costs." He lifted the hammer high.

Aaron winced. *Here we go.*

Boom.

"Who are you?"

"We are the watchmen!"

Boom.

"Who are you?"

"We are the wall!"

"Never forget it."

Thankfully, the platform survived. With his speech over, the watchmaster laid the hammer aside and broke the cohort into crews for the morning's work. He assigned Aaron and five others the duty of felling trees for the new barricade and sent them to a sergeant for their kit.

"When do we eat?" Aaron asked as the sergeant gathered tools and chains onto a wool cloth.

He wrapped the bundle and shoved it into Aaron's arms. "When you bring me a tree, stripped and ready for the saws." He tilted his head, signaling Aaron to move along. "Next!"

The six trudged in silence uphill through a broad swath of stumps. As Aaron's tehpa often said, early mornings and empty stomachs make for sparse conversation. When they reached the tree line, they paired off to face their foes–stout celestial pines whose lowest branches grew high above the reach of their tools.

The oldest of their crew pointed at him with his axe. "You. Goldenhair. You're with me. Ever fell a tree before?"

Aaron scratched at the short-clipped waves atop his head. He'd never thought of them as gold. "Um. All the time . . . I guess. Lots of Baysilver."

"Baysilver are reeds, lad. Not trees. You must be from the coast."

"My family lives on the Handle, near Rosland Cape."

"That far south?"

"The south is in no less danger than the north if the dragons cross the peaks."

The man let out a grim laugh. "True." He slung his tool bundle across his back as if it weighed nothing and thrust his axe toward the north end of the line. "Over there. I see a good candidate–

ready to give her life for the cause. Quick work means a quicker breakfast. You have a name?"

"Aaron Ilmari."

"Sireth," the man said, setting off toward his chosen target. "Sireth Yar."

Aaron set off after him, ignoring the clear signal that the conversation had ended. "How about that watchmaster, eh? Quite a speech."

Sireth kept walking.

"And the way he kept pounding that war hammer." Aaron cast a glance over his shoulder toward his new home as a volunteer watchman–timber long houses, walkways, and platforms along a series of cliff waterfalls where the western runoff of the Celestial Peaks emptied into the Gulf of Stars. "I thought he'd drop us all into the sea. Does he not appreciate the great age of this place?"

For several more paces, Sireth said nothing, but then he snorted. "Or how long it's been neglected, like all the outposts."

Sireth knew his business with an axe and a pine. To Aaron's knowledge, the whole cohort had arrived the night before, the newest recruits of the Thousand Falls company. None of these newcomers had taken part in the work on the new defenses. But Sireth helped Aaron lay out his chains and hooks where the tree should fall and positioned him on the opposite side of the trunk for chopping. He showed Aaron the proper rhythm for a two-man cut. The two soon settled into their thumping blows, one after the other, and Sireth seemed content with that sound and their breathing alone.

Aaron was not. He needed to talk, if only to cover the grumbling in his stomach. "So, you're older than the rest of us. A lot older."

The grunt accompanying Sireth's next swing was deep and long, approaching a growl.

Aaron coughed. "I mean, I expected all the recruits to be my age. Don't you have a farm to tend? Or a family to care for?"

"My children–Tiran and Teegan–joined the Order. Their mehma passed on to Elamhavar a while back. When the call came, I had no reason to stay in our forest home at Sil Tymest." He held up a palm to stop Aaron's next swings and inspected their work, then waved. "Swap sides. We must keep the cuts even, and yours are not quite as deep."

Aaron didn't argue and let Sireth guide him by the shoulders to the right spot. *Not quite as deep* was a generous evaluation, and Aaron knew it, but this did not deter his next question. Chopping trees was one thing. Fighting was quite another. "Are you not concerned about keeping up with the younger watchmen in training and combat?"

"Older. Younger. My age and yours are not so different when you consider eternity. To the Rescuer and his Elder Folk, we're both infants. And as to combat"–the axe spun in each of Sireth's hands before he landed his next blow–"I have some training already. You forget, most in my generation had not yet come of age when the Assembly disbanded the Order. Many of us had planned to join–had played and practiced at it from the day we could hold a wooden sword. We spent our strongest years still practicing, in hopes it would reopen."

"But it didn't. Not until you had households and children of your own–grown children, at that."

"I'm well aware."

Right. His children. "When did your sehna and behlna take on the initiate's quest?"

"The very first class."

The power went out of Aaron's swing. *Sireth Yar. Teegan and Tiran.* How had he failed to put those names together? "They helped close the dragon's portal. They stopped the invasion."

"For now."

"I take it you share the Order's concern. If the dragons can open one portal, they can open others."

Sireth shot a look at Aaron's idle axe, and did not answer until

Aaron had taken the cue and started chopping again. "That is why we are here, is it not? Last year, one dragon moved ore creatures and goblins to our side of the barrier. A host of dragons might send an army. The Lightraider Order believes that is their plan. My own sehna and behlna saw the preparations."

An army. The preparations. Aaron let the words settle into his thoughts.

He'd come to the barrier for adventure and because the old men of his village had spoken of honor and need. But had he truly considered the cost of his calling? Looking north, he pictured orcs, trolls, and all manner of dragon corruptions rushing down the slopes. A coldness sank into his heart. If that day came, there'd be nothing between this company and the horde but a barricade they'd built with their own hands.

"You all right?" Sireth stared at Aaron's axe, once again idle.

"Hm? Oh yes." Aaron resumed his swings. "I was just wondering. Do you worry? About your sehna and behlna, I mean." He looked northeast up the ever-steepening slopes toward the Order's fortress at Ras Telesar. "Up there, at the academy."

"I'm their tehpa. Of course I worry. But I remind myself they're in the Maker's hands." Sireth raised two fingers to signal Aaron to still his axe. "Ras Telesar may be higher up the barrier, but it's still here, in Keledev, under the Rescuer's protection."

With a sharp *crack*, the trunk gave. Aaron found himself yanked over to Sireth's side. The heaviest part of the pine smashed down right where he'd been standing.

Sireth released him and patted his chest. "I'd say my children are as safe as you are."

2

CONNOR ENARIAN
TANELETHAR
EMEN KISMA

"IS THAT NOT THE BIGGEST GIANT YOU'VE EVER seen?" Teegan glanced back at the creature of root and stone chasing her, Connor, and their new friend Elisai. "He leveled the inn with a single blow."

The giant took one earth-shaking step for every six of theirs. Connor turned his gaze forward again and pointed his crook at the tree line, struggling to find the breath for words. "No time to gawk. Cadet scouts aren't meant to fight giants."

"So you said." Teegan showed far less strain in her voice. She'd always been lighter of foot. "Unseen and unheard. That's our mission." She ducked as a rock the size of her head shattered a nearby tree. "But we couldn't leave Elisai behind."

No. They couldn't. Elisai had opened his eyes and heart to the Rescuer and done much to preserve their lives. Connor would not ask him to spend one more day in this land.

He and Teegan had seen too much in Tanelethar while hiding in bushes or peeking out from shadowed alleys these last few weeks. Connor had watched a goblin wound a child just to revel in her wailing. An iron orc had run a shopkeep through in a fit of rage. And the cadets had witnessed countless subtler evils from the granogs. At the same time, they'd watched men and women selling their spirits–becoming barkhides, constables, and sorcerers–betraying their own and altering their bodies to become part of the dragon's grand war engine.

Connor ducked, gritting his teeth as a big rock whistled past. The giant kept pulling them from his own clay chest. "Can't make it to the hollow tree. Need cover. Now."

A falcon cried above, and Teegan lifted her gaze. "Aethia found some."

"Or she's found a rabbit," Elisai said, lagging behind.

"She knows the difference between a hunt and battle." Teegan's eyes dropped to the spaces between the trees ahead, and she squinted. "Yes. An opening. Small, possibly a cave."

"Please," Connor said, "not another cave."

The notorious Five Quests by which a cadet stalwart moved to the cadet scout rank, hard as they were on Connor and his friends, had been child's play compared to the dangers of Tanelethar. Orcs and granogs in the towns. Goblins in the forests. But the caves . . . Connor had learned to avoid those at all costs. Most were occupied, usually by something foul. On his first trip through the barrier, one particular cave had brought Connor, his best friend Lee Trang, and their guide Kara Orso to a terrifying place leagues away from their starting point–a place with decrepit floating creatures holding lanterns at arm's length as if searching for souls to devour.

A rending of wood behind them drew Connor's eyes over his soldier. "He's taken a spruce for a club. It's the cave or a standoff."

"A standoff?" Elisai asked.

"You'd surely be killed."

Their new charge found fresh vigor and surged ahead. "The cave it is, then."

They rushed through the cave mouth, with Connor coming last, and the spruce crashed against the opening behind him, knocking him off his feet. He stood, brushing dirt and pine needles from his cloak. "Lights, please, Teegan."

She closed her eyes and lifted her head, letting her hood fall back from her red braids, and prayed. *"Mo pednesh Logosovu pyrlas, po mo vynesh kelas."*

Word. Lamp. Way. Light.

The whole cave brightened with a light only Keledan could see. Teegan strode toward a narrow passage at the back, glancing upward as she walked. *"Onoriov, Rumosh."*

The spruce hit the cave mouth again, shedding branches and cones. Dust fell from the ceiling. "What about it?" Connor called to his friend, keeping his eyes on the danger. "Is there another way out?"

Teegan rushed back to him with her voice lowered. "Unlikely. The floor makes a sharp drop a few paces in. And there's worse news. Webs."

"Oh, good." Connor should have guessed. Their lessons had taught them giants and giant spiders often shared territory, thanks to the compatibility of the dragons that animated them.

Elisai rested his arms on his knees, still breathing hard. "Is the Keledan life always this exciting?"

"Not in this way," Teegan said. "Once we get to the hollow tree, you'll never have to return to this place–not unless you choose."

"Assuming we get out."

Connor crept the toward the opening and bent low for a peek. The giant had drawn the tree up again but had not made another swing. "The Rescuer will provide a way. He always does."

"Is he gone?" Teegan asked.

"No."

Elisai shot her a glance. "Can you not hear him in your head? The thrumming? The voice? I hear it as I've heard it for these last three years our town has been its captive." He rocked in time with the rhythm. "*Friend, stay. Friend, come out.*"

Connor heard it too. Song sorcery–rock and hollow wood drumming together inside the creature. The voice followed, softer than the mocktree he'd encountered the year before. But this giant did not call him *friend*.

Liege, he heard it say within the song. *Liege, stay. Liege, come out. Command me. You shall be my lord, and I your mace. What pleasures in destruction we'll see.*

Could he control a giant? Such a feat promised an end to their present danger and a formidable weapon in future raids.

As quickly as the thought entered his mind, a sacred verse pushed it out. Connor spoke the verse out loud. "*Bidagro umirana koth piqodothovu po sornah koth vy serev.*"

I follow your precepts. I hate every false way.

The song ended with an enraged scream.

"Back!" Teegan jerked Connor away from the opening. Clay knuckles crusted with rune-etched stones pounded the cave mouth. The hill shook.

In the quiet that followed, Connor heard a scratching sound from the hole in the back. "Bad things are coming. The giant's song has called to its sister creatures. We can't hide here much longer. But how do you fight a clay creature with no flesh to pierce?"

Teegan unfastened a buckle at the shoulder of her manykit vest, drew a coil of rope free from her arm, and held it out. "With this?"

Elisai nodded. "Yes. I see your mind, and such a plan may work. A great ravine runs down the center of Emen Kisma, through this forest. It lies to our west, not far. We'll have to run fast to outpace the giant's strides."

"And we'll have to choose our moment with care," Connor said.

A green glowing eye appeared at the cave mouth, set in an eye socket of twisted roots and vines.

Liege, come out. Command me.

Teegan flung a dagger straight into the glowing eye. "Go!"

All three raced out as the creature reared up, bellowing. Elisai took the lead. "Follow me!"

The giant tossed the dagger away and gave chase.

"There!" Elisai pointed at a gap between two great pines. "The level ground ends at a cliff. I can hear the river below."

Connor veered away from the other two. "Keep going. I'll distract him as long as I can, and then I'll bring him your way."

If I survive.

The words the creature had spoken in the song gave Connor the inkling that it would follow him over the others. He was right. The giant matched his course and hurled a rock that smashed against a boulder. Debris sliced into his cheek. He kept on running, slipping a flat stone from the stream by the gates of Ras Telesar into his sling. "Rescuer, help us to do this. Help us bring Elisai home."

A cry from above told him he had Aethia's support. The falcon dove at the giant, harrying its pursuit. The slow swipe of its hands stood no chance of knocking her from the sky.

"Thank you, *Rumosh*," Connor whispered.

With their great strides, giants could not well manage a circular course–another lesson from the academy, hard-won by lightraiders who'd come before. Connor used this lesson and Aethia's attack to open his lead and give his comrades time to prepare the trap. Once he'd made a complete turn, he straightened his line and sprinted toward the two great pines Elisai had shown him. Teegan and their new friend remained hidden, but Connor knew they were there and ready.

Gasping, he spoke another sacred verse in prayer. "*Men adveranesh liberaheni. Alerov anamesh recrethanah.*"

Rescue me. In you, I hide.

He dropped to a knee with his cloak and hood covering him and his crook lying in the grass.

The giant thundered past.

A beat later, Connor lifted his eyes and cupped his hands to his mouth. "Now!"

A rope hidden in the grass went taut as Teegan and Elisai pulled on the ends and wrapped them around the trees. Neither could hold on when the creature's leg hit, but the trap was enough to off-balance him. The giant teetered and flailed while the falcon continued to dive at its head. The creature tried to turn, and Connor got his first long look at the full monster. Great hunks of bark covered its legs and forearms like greaves and gauntlets. Rocks formed a breastplate. The root and vine countenance, with its long moss beard and leafy branches like antlers, looked almost pitiable–betrayed.

"Friend," it said out loud.

Liege, Connor heard in his mind.

Connor flung his sling and let his stone fly. The rock sailed past Aethia's flapping wings and dug deep into the clay between the roots at the giant's forehead. The creature toppled backward into the ravine.

The three set off again at a run, keeping a hard pace until they arrived at a hill familiar to Connor and Teegan. As they climbed, a pine sapling at the crest grew into a broad spruce with a framed doorway in the trunk. A lantern hung over the frame, lit in welcome.

Elisai let out a shout of joy. "What a wonder! We've made it!"

Aethia reached the hollow tree first and flew through the doorway. Teegan arrived next. She paused to turn and smile at Elisai and opened her mouth to speak, but she never got the chance.

Liege. Connor heard the bellowing voice in his head. The giant appeared from behind the hill and grabbed the upper trunk of the hollow tree. Roots erupted from the soil at Connor's feet. He shoved Teegan through the door, then held out his shepherd's crook for Elisai to catch. With all his might, he lifted his charge until both could scramble up the roots to the threshold. "Go through! Hurry!"

Elisai vanished into golden light. As Connor fell through after him, he twisted his body and saw the giant opening its wooden maw. What would happen if the giant swallowed the hollow tree while they were still passing through the portal?

3

KARA ORSO
KELEDEV
FOREST OF BELIEVING

A SMALL AND TAILLESS ORANGE *LASHOR*–A PARA-dragon to most folk–crawled out on an oak twig not far from Kara's eye. She sensed concern in the hesitant twitch of his four-legged gait.

"Relax, Crumpet." Kara's whisper might easily have passed for a rustle of leaves. "This is the lightest of the challenges I must face in the coming days–these Five Quests. Watch now. You may learn something."

Her friend Connor had first introduced her to the little gliding creature not long after she'd entered the liberated land of Keledev, and the two had encountered him many times since in their walks in this unlikely high-mountain forest. They'd dubbed him Crumpet because Teegan's falcon had nearly made a meal of him–hence the missing tail.

But Connor was not here now, nor were Dagram Kaivos, Lee Trang, or Teegan. And Teegan's twin, Tiran, if he had made a rare trip out of doors to observe the first of Kara's quests, was not permitted to help.

Kara didn't need help–not on this quest.

A horn blew. Crumpet scurried up the oak, presumably to gain a better view, and Kara set off with silent footsteps.

One tick. After the horn, she had but one slow fill of a water clock's twelve day-vessels to move from one end of the forest to the other, gathering three special items along the way. But what items? That part remained a mystery.

A wooden circle, hung on a spruce, served as her first marker. The guardians had burned the same clue into both sides.

Near a well-known forest haunt

Where warm water lies,

Claim the tinker's favorite tool

Unseen by the tinker's eyes.

"Where warm water lies," Kara said to herself. "Lies, not flows." The forest had a river—the warm, spring-fed tributary known as the Gathering flowed down steep cataracts from the academy's glade above—but its waters also branched out in underground streams to form seven pools. The deer favored the largest of these. She knew it well.

Kara worked her way north to the spot and spied her first target. Master Belen, head of the Tinkers' Sphere, walked the forest path.

Claim the tinker's favorite tool, unseen by the tinker's eyes.

Which tool? Calipers, wrenches, and all manner of devices Kara couldn't name hung from the hooks and loops of Belen's leather manykit vest. Which of them was she to take?

Unseen by the tinker's eyes.

She had to remain unseen while taking the tool. This first quest in the cadet scout rank required stealth through the whole course. She knew that. And the guardians of the light knew she knew. So, why had they added *unseen* to the clue?

Perhaps the clue meant the tool itself was unseen—unseen by the tinker's eyes. Kara kept pace with Belen, moving from tree to tree. Unseen? At his back?

She moved her gaze to the back of his manykit vest and found a chipped lens with a wooden handle hanging from a loop behind his shoulder. She'd seen him use the glass many times, always giving the cadets the same old line. *We must find the source of the problem before we can fix it. You young ones often miss that step.*

The tinker's favorite tool.

Belen moved at a quick pace, giving her no advantage. Not that she needed one. A lifetime of grinding and hammering in his workshop had left the old guardian nigh on deaf.

She matched him step for step just off the path, then doubled her pace and crossed behind. The loop holding the lens hardly moved at her touch. In the space of a heartbeat, she was hidden again, tucking the tool into a pouch on her own manykit.

A good start. Always the encouragers, the guardians had opened the quest by playing to her strength—pickpocketing. Not the most noble pastime, but lifting keys from orc guards or death scrolls from granogs was a necessary lightraider skill that fell within the Rangers' Sphere.

The next two items would not be so easy.

Three younger cadets patrolled the trees, heading her way. Instinct told Kara to retreat, but knowledge held her fast. Movement was how she'd spotted them, and movement would draw their eyes. Kara bowed her hooded head and pressed closer to the spruce. She'd chosen her cloak at the outfitter for such a moment. Its dyed wool matched the general colors of the forest.

Once the younger cadets passed, Kara moved on and found the next wooden marker a few trees away.

Down he comes from Anvil's height,
Guarding lock and key.
Which will you choose? Take only one
To set the captive free.

Anvil Ridge. Kara knew of only two paths leading down from the western ridge, and one was behind her. She made for the other and heard a familiar baying. When the pine boughs thinned enough, she saw Quinton, the academy's big swordmaster, looking the part of an oversize parcelman driving a two-wheeled wagon full of apples. Amos the mule, famous among the cadets for his stubbornness, dragged his burden along at the blazing speed of a tortoise.

Sneaking closer, she saw an iron padlock, unlocked, in the eyelets of the wagon's rear gate. The key, a harder target, sat on the bench beside the big square-chinned swordmaster, tied to a long green kerchief which flopped over the side.

Which will you choose?

The padlock called to her from the back of the cart. A child could lift it free without alerting Quinton, or even Amos–big mule ears and all. And what good was the key if the lock was already open?

Kara took one step and stopped, crouching down again. "Wait," she whispered to herself. "Think."

Just because she saw a lock and a key on the same wagon didn't mean the two were a match. The clue hinted at a captive to be freed. A padlock in her pocket had no use on such a mission. Looking closer, she saw the lock, though loose, held the gate in place. If she lifted it free, the resulting apple avalanche would give her away for sure.

"The key it is, then. But how?"

Kara breathed deep and closed her eyes to let the forest in, just as Dame Silvana had taught her–the crunch of the wagon wheels on the path, the mountain breeze on her cheeks, a small flock of birds chattering in the branches of an oak nearby.

A plan formed. She readied her bow and hurried ahead of the cart. Once she'd chosen her spot, she planted an arrow in the grass and nocked a second.

She drew the string back, listening to the tension build in the bow's recurved ash.

A touch of wind lifted a corner of the cloth. Kara loosed her arrow at the tree full of birds, sending them skyward in a flapping, squawking mass. In the same breath, she pivoted, drew the second arrow, and shot. The green kerchief flew from the bench. With a quiet *thock*, the arrow pinned it to a tree across the road.

The noise of the birds settled. Quinton and Amos drove on as if unaware the key had left them.

Or perhaps the swordmaster had shown leniency. Kara thought she saw him grin.

Once they were out of sight she ran to the key. Item number two. One to go. But where was the next marker?

Kara stole through the brush in slowly broadening arcs–a ranger's search. No wooden disc materialized. Had she missed it? She dropped to a knee in a copse of inkberry to regroup and wait for another cadet patrol to pass. Unconsciously, she rubbed the bronze key between her fingers. A rough texture covered its clover-shaped bow. Was that writing?

A key. A key to a lock. The key to her quest? She glanced down. Tiny, flowing script covered the clover–the stem too. The key was the marker. But in the forest shade, she couldn't hope to read it.

Her hand went to the pouch where she'd set Belen's glass, and when she held it over the key, she laughed–almost too loud. Script came to life under the lens. *Howda'anu koth kolama vadsepah mi kerator ma aneth avah'od.*

All things work together for the good of his people. The items were connected. The first, combined with the second, revealed the third clue.

Imprisoned high near the wandering way,
I await my rescuer's hand.
Beware my guard. Her eyes are keen.
She'll catch you if she can.

She'll catch you. She. Dame Silvana. The guardians had saved the hardest task for last.

Kara steeled herself for the final leg of her quest and continued north. The wandering way could only mean one place–the switchbacks that climbed from the Forest of Believing to the long green glade before the gates of Ras Telesar.

She picked her way with care. It wouldn't do to be caught by a patrol of younger, less experienced cadets. She'd never live it down. But Kara kept a brisk pace. A quick check of the sun's position told her the quest's tick was nearing its end. She had no time to waste.

Next to the switchback trail stood a tall oak, and high in its branches, a cage swung lightly in the breeze. A swallow hopped back and forth on a rod inside. Dame Silvana stood on the path beneath it, leaning on her sword.

Of all the guardians, Kara wanted to make a good showing for Dame Silvana–knight of the way, mistress of the Rangers' Sphere. This was the woman Kara wanted to be. She wanted to be a little taller, perhaps, but like her, nonetheless.

With Silvana's small stature, sneaking across the trail under her nose was no option. And the woman was known to have spotted cadets stealing over the ramparts after curfew from five levels away. So, going around, even a long way down the path, seemed a risky choice as well.

A rustling drew Kara's eyes to a high branch in a tree a few paces away. Crumpet, it seemed, had followed her progress. He geared himself up for a leap and launched from one treetop to another, catching the light wind with the broad flaps of skin stretched out between his fore and hind legs. He wobbled mid-flight, probably a consequence of losing his tail, and landed with a leaf-crunching crash.

Silvana cast a short glance in the direction of the noise, but gave it no more attention than that. Her eyes returned to level and scanned the forest.

Over the top, then. Crumpet had given Kara the answer, though she'd better make less noise.

The trunk of Silvana's oak stood apart, but its long branches mingled with the trees around it. Kara picked one a few trees away with a stout trunk and worked her way to its base. She felt every movement of her body, every shift of the grass and dirt under her feet, as if all were flags and pounding drums to draw Silvana's eyes. But the guardian's gaze never settled on her.

Silvana's own words from Kara's woodcraft training came to her. *To scale a tree, especially an oak, is child's play. To scale an oak in utter silence–that is the mark of a ranger.*

Kara heard nothing but her own breathing.

Here, Silvana's small stature played to Kara's advantage. The highest branches stout enough to hold her were not very high at all. A guardian of Quinton's size might have spotted her.

Don't look up. Please, don't.

She made her way through the mingling boughs to the next tree, then the next. And soon she had crossed above Dame Silvana. Kara hugged the trunk midway up the tree and looked higher, to the swallow's cage.

The bird cocked its head, watching her every move until she'd shimmied close enough to turn the key in the lock. The instant she opened the door, the swallow flew away.

Well, that was a bit disappointing.

She'd half-expected the bird to whisper a secret code in her ear, or at least present her with some kind of prize.

Perhaps it had. Below the bird's post, on the cage floor, Kara found a narrow ring of green agate.

Wasting no time, she took the ring and dropped to a stout branch, arms out for balance, then ran to the northern end and leapt onto a boulder on the second rise of the switchbacks. She held the ring high. "Victory! My first quest is complete!"

"Is it?"

Kara felt the tip of a sword at her back. She turned to find Silvana standing on the boulder with her, no longer on the grass below the tree. "How did you–?"

"The quest is over when I say it is, girl. Or am I not the leader of the Rangers' Sphere?"

With a flick of Silvana's sword, the green ring–a symbol of the rangers–left Kara's fingers.

Silvana caught it. "Tell me, dear. If this was Tanelethar, with enemies closing in around you, and none of your fledgling scout skills could keep you from their grasp, what would you do?"

Another test to finish the quest. But Kara knew the answer. "I'd lean upon the Rescuer. I'd offer a prayer–a verse."

"Yes. Of course." The guardian sheathed her sword and clasped both of Kara shoulders. "But which verse?"

The other guardians gathered on the first switchback. Sacred verses were not Kara's strongest subject. They all knew it.

"Tell me, girl. Quick as you can. In the Elder Tongue, mind you–as always."

Help me, Rumosh.

A verse came to her. "*Men kesoqadoth bi kepachor recrethni, men kemafat ba drachelor.*"

Hide me from the schemes of the wicked, from the swarm of evildoers.

Had she spoken it correctly?

A nod from Dame Silvana told her she had.

"Can I keep the ring then?"

"Why not? It's already in your pocket."

Directed by the guardian's gaze, Kara checked the top left pouch of her manykit and found the agate ring.

Silvana winked. "You're not the only one with light fingers, my dear."

Headmaster Jairun clapped his hands from the switchback below them, his tall staff leaning against his shoulder. "Well done, my girl. Well done indeed. The Quest of the Ranger is complete. One ring is yours. Four more to come. Are you ready?"

"I will be, Headmaster. I promise."

Her stomach tightened with the fear that such a promise might prove hollow. Kara felt ready for two of the other quests, which could come at any day or hour and in any order. But the Quest of the Vanguard frightened her, and the Tinker's Quest–Master Baldomar's forge test–terrified her. She thought of the pity in Baldomar's eyes every time she handed him a shapeless slab of metal meant to be a blade. Pity could not get her through the Tinker's Quest, and one failed quest would ruin everything.

Everything.

4

THE FORGES
RAS TELESAR

SPARKS FLEW FROM RED-HOT STEEL UNDER KARA'S hammer. Sweat rolled down the bridge of her nose. Her arms burned. No matter how hard she pounded the raw metal, it refused to yield.

"I can't do this." She stood back from the anvil and let her arm hang at her side, anchored by the hammer's weight. "I'm not meant to."

By the Maker's grace, Master Baldomar had not started her Tinker's Quest. She'd peeked into the smithy not long after the Ranger's Quest, hoping for another chance to practice, and with a chuckle, Baldomar had promised her at least another day would pass before a quest from any of the Five Spheres followed.

Despite his earlier smile, her words now earned her a hard look.

Baldomar set down the two-toned blade he'd been sharpening. "I'm disappointed to hear you say that, Miss Orso. I thought you'd learned more from your struggles with the Shar Razel."

"That was different."

"How?"

Kara left her hammer by the anvil and took a seat at one of the forge's high windows to let the mountain breeze soothe her cheeks.

Her boots dangled well above the floor. Even after more than a year living in this fortress, she still hadn't grown accustomed to the oversize halls and doorways. It had all been built ages ago, for another race of another time.

Master Baldomar's gaze found hers. "I await your answer." He tossed her a cloth for her brow. "How is this situation different than the Iron Door?"

"At the door, I learned to surrender my will," Kara said, dabbing her forehead. "I let go of my own selfish purpose in joining the Lightraider Order and committed to serving at the Rescuer's pleasure." She had. Kara had gone so far as to tuck the sapphire pendant her elder brehna had given her—the one with the bear wrapped around the jewel—away in a drawer in the barracks. She'd meant it as a symbol of putting all other loyalties aside, even family, to prepare herself for what the Rescuer had in store.

That day, the Rescuer opened the door to his service, and Kara had committed, but she still hoped he'd restore her brehna Keir to himself and her. Keir was all the family she had left. Her parents had died when she was young, and Liam now shared their fate—murdered by orcs while trying to stop them from dragging Keir away. As to where they'd taken him, no one could say.

"All right," Baldomar said. "And if the Rescuer chooses, can he not call you to the forge as he called me? Is that not the profession he himself chose when he came to walk among us?"

Kara had no desire to insult her teacher. Dag had told her the Baldomars of Huckleheim traced their heritage back to the smith who'd shared a forge with the Rescuer growing up in the Iron Mountains. That ancestor had then become the Rescuer's first disciple.

"That's not what I meant. I . . ." Her eyes fell to the master's bare, black arms—not big and brawny like Swordmaster Quinton's or Dag's, but knotted with muscles she could never hope to attain. Couldn't he see the obvious truth? "My body and mind are not made for this. The forge requires the strength of the Vanguard and the eye of a tinker. I have neither. My talents lie elsewhere."

"It's a shame." The comment came from the other side of the forge, where Tiran Yar sat at the grinding wheel–working on some project he'd been tinkering with for weeks. "The academy has no Sphere of Thieves, else your talents might have found their place the day you arrived." The thin smile he gave her told Kara he intended no malice with the slight.

She matched his grin. To be fair, she might have used those talents for one or two good jests since coming to the academy–perhaps more than two–so a jest in return held no offense. "My talents have a place among the rangers. See. I've already passed the Ranger's Quest–not that you came out to see it." She showed him the ringlet of green agate about her finger.

She hoped to stack two more ringlets there in the coming days, and two more on the other hand–the five symbols of progression toward the rank of cadet scout. The new Order's original cadets–Connor, Tiran, Teegan, Dag, and Lee–already wore them. For them, the hard part was over. They had only to wait for the Turning of the Spheres, when Master Jairun, listening to the whispers of the Helper, would assign them to one of the five Lightraider Spheres. Would Kara join them on that day?

Master Baldomar beckoned her back to the anvil. "Rangers. Tinkers. Comforters. Navigators. The Vanguard. You'll go where the Helper sends you at the Turning of the Spheres. But that day won't come unless you master the forge like the rest of your class."

Like the rest of your class.

Kara's steps grew heavy as she returned to take the hammer. They weren't her class–Connor and the others–not really. She'd joined them as a guide in Tanelethar, the Dragon Lands, ready to betray them, and found rescue instead.

Once she joined the Order as an initiate, Kara fought to catch up, closing a gap of months in training–or nearly so. The Turning of the Spheres came at the height of spring by lightraider tradition. She had less than two weeks to pass the other four quests. If not, she'd have to try again with the class that had arrived a year later, this last autumn.

A year's delay was too long. If she failed, she'd lose all hope that the Rescuer might allow her to save Keir.

Master Baldomar left her with her thoughts and her steel and walked out of the smithy, giving Tiran a look that Kara knew meant, *See that she doesn't hurt herself.*

He wasn't wrong to think it.

Kara set about her work again, fighting the steel with every swing–fighting her worries too. She couldn't enter Tanelethar on her own scout missions until she passed the Five Quests, so Connor and the others had promised to seek news of Keir for her. But the last two scout parties had been gone for days.

Where are you, Connor, she thought, raising the hammer for another futile strike. *When are you coming home?*

5

CONNOR
KELEDEV
MOUNT JUSTICE LAKE

CONNOR BLINKED AGAINST THE BRIGHTER SUNLIGHT of an upper vale in the Celestial Peaks, knee-deep in the frigid waters of Mount Justice Lake.

The colors always seemed sharper on this side of the barrier, as if none could know the truth of them until they passed through a hollow tree portal into Keledev. He imagined it might feel the same, only a thousand times so, when he finally stood upon the green hills of Elamhavar.

"Welcome, my new brehna," Teegan said, wrapping Elisai in a hug, "to Keledev. Welcome to the Liberated Land."

Before Connor could add a welcome of his own, he felt the cold air heating up. Master Belen had taught them some of the ways of portal travel in the Maker's creation. The impending arrival of any form, even one of the Elder Folk, disturbed the surrounding air, causing heat. The larger the creature, the greater the displacement and the more heat created.

The air now felt downright hot despite the cold of the lake.

Teegan widened her eyes at Connor. "Would the Rescuer allow a giant to pass through the barrier by swallowing a hollow tree?"

"I don't know. Move!"

They tried to drag Elisai out of the water, but the air burst behind them, knocking all three onto their faces in shallows.

Connor rolled over to see a large form arriving, but not nearly so huge as the giant.

"Dag," Teegan said with a wide grin.

The big miner touched two fingers to his deep brown forehead and then frowned. "Why must these lakes always be so cold?"

He was not alone. Lee also appeared, and between them a man, woman, and three children materialized. Five people, hence the heat from the portal.

Connor stood up to shake the water from his cloak and frowned at Lee. "This was supposed to be a scouting mission. Remember?"

"I could say the same to you, my friend." Lee lifted his chin toward Elisai. "Couldn't leave him?"

"No."

"Just as we couldn't leave these few once they'd opened their eyes."

The youngest of the children, a little girl, shivered, and Connor beckoned with his crook. "Come out of the water. All of you. We've still a long journey ahead before reaching the academy, and there's business to attend to first."

"Should we build a fire?" the little girl asked.

He smiled. "Oh yes."

Connor and the other cadets led their charges up a narrow path to a ridge above the Mount Justice pines. At the southern end stood a tower built from the white stone of its mountain host, topped with a faceted crystal half-globe and a shining copper-colored reflector.

"We'll build your fire there," Connor said, bending low to address the little girl and pointing with his crook to the tower's upper battlement. "But there isn't much room–just enough for Teegan and I and three others, as long as they're small. Would you and your brehnan like to come?"

The parents nodded their assent, and the children joined

Connor and Teegan in the climb to the tower's top. Together, they built a fire in the stone pit between the copper reflector and the crystal collector. Soon the fire raged. He bid the children stand well back.

Together, Connor and Teegan rotated the platform. The wheels beneath gave no hint of grinding, though the tower was ages old. Twice they directed the fireglass collector away from its mark and back again.

"Two flashes," Connor said. "One for the returning lightraiders . . ."

Teegan released her grip on the platform's arm and took in a breath. "And one for those they rescued."

After dousing the fire, they gathered the children at the front of the battlements and waited. Far below, where the low clouds resting on the chestnuts and pines began, they saw an answering flash, and then another.

Connor laughed. "Isn't that a wonderful sight."

THE SPRING HAD THAWED THE PASSAGE THROUGH Anvil Ridge, shortening the cadets' homeward journey by more than a day. Even so, twilight had come by the time they crossed the glade above the Forest of Believing. The giant colorful figures in the academy's gate towers shone bright, lit by the braziers inside.

Elisai caught up to Connor at the head of the company. "Who are they?"

"Elder Folk, the *Aropha* or First Ones. Those are great statues of semi-precious stone carved by the hands of a long-ago people. The winged figure with the downturned sword and the stern garnet countenance represents the *Lisropha*–the Aropha warrior class. The other, offering water made of pure blue opal, represents the Aropha servant class, called *Rapha*."

"The Elder Folk had an underclass of servants?"

"Not an underclass. A class who loved caring for others. The Rapha served all kinds, not just their own, in the same way that the Lisropha defended all the High One's children and the Dynapha sang his praises on behalf of all creation. They served, fought, and worshiped for the pleasure of the Maker."

Connor lifted his eyes above the fire collectors at the top of each tower to the many lantern-lit windows of Ras Telesar. When he'd first arrived here, the rising jumbled levels of the fortress had been cold and dark, a result of the Lightraider Order being disbanded for two generations. Now that the headmaster and the guardians had begun rebuilding the ranks, the passages were warm and welcoming–alive with new recruits. Connor looked forward to the hearth in the Salar Peroth, the Hall of Manna, and a cup of Glimwick's brambleberry cider. The old Black Feather innkeep's cider had become a frequent blessing now that he'd come north to work the academy's kitchens as his family had in generations past.

But such comforts had to wait. Tiran greeted Teegan, his twin, and Connor beneath the open gate with a clasp of Connor's arm and a grim look. "Welcome home, Brehna. You're wanted on the ninth level."

"I assume the cadet watch saw the two flashes."

"Yes, and the whole fortress is buzzing with the thrill of the first rescued Aladoth since the rekindling of the Order, but that's not why you've been summoned."

Connor gave Teegan a slight nod, and she took charge of their guests. She turned them toward the outfitter's chamber in the lower bulwarks. "Let's find you some clothes and gear before we take you up to your rooms, shall we?"

Heading the opposite direction, Tiran and Connor took a staircase cut from the second-level wall, the start of the long climb to the headmaster's chambers. "If Master Jairun's not angry with us for turning a scouting mission into a rescue," Connor said, "then what is this about?"

"Stradok. He's at it again."

Councilor Stradok–the Assembly representative to the Lightraider Order, a new and not entirely welcome permanent guest at Ras Telesar.

Tiran gave Connor no more details than that, reminding him that Master Jairun had warned the cadets to keep their opinions to themselves when it came to the Assembly or its leadership in the Prime Council, to which Stradok reported. But it was no secret that both had made interference in the headmaster's governance a habit. With or without details from Tiran, Connor knew he'd be walking into a battle nearly as perilous as the tussle with the giant.

He steered the conversation elsewhere. "You said the fortress is buzzing about the new Keledan, but they weren't the first to cross the barrier since we lit the braziers."

"True." Tiran paused on the ramparts of the fourth level to dab his forehead with a tattered kerchief–not to deal with the wound he'd sustained on his last visit to Tanelethar. It had never fully healed. "But Kara had a hand in the rekindling. She helped us close the dragon's portal. The new recruits and the townsfolk who've come to labor at the fortress–even Glimwick–see her as one of us."

"I wonder if Kara sees herself that way."

Tiran started up the next flight of stairs. "Perhaps you can ask her. She was summoned to the headmaster's chambers too."

What did Stradok want with Kara?

They found her crying when they reached the ninth level, seated on the stone pavers with her back against the ramparts, cloak wrapped around her knees, hood pulled down over her platinum hair. Whatever Stradok wanted to say to her, he'd already said it.

Kara looked up at Connor as if he was her only advocate in all Keledev. "It's about time you came home. I won't go. Do you hear? I won't. Don't let them make me."

6

TIRAN REMAINED OUTSIDE ON THE RAMPARTS TO keep Kara company, leaving Connor to enter the headmaster's chambers alone.

Ages ago, when the four concentric walls of Ras Telesar had crowned a green hill as an Aropha temple, these chambers were part of the outermost rampart, perhaps the lodgings of a Lisropha watchman, a member of the Elder Folk warrior class, much larger than men. Master Jairun had filled its two Lisropha-size rooms with human shelves and desks cluttered with parchments, candles, and old texts, giving it the look of a place caught between worlds.

"Councilor Stradok," Connor said with a deferential nod as he closed the door.

Stradok, dressed in his usual crimson robes, did not turn. He kept his balding head level, eyes focused on Master Jairun, only acknowledging Connor with a single word. "Cadet."

Master Jairun came out from behind a centuries-old canted desk. "My boy. It's good to have you home." He lifted a jar of balm from one of his many shelves and turned Connor's chin to expose his wounded cheek to the lantern light. "You saw battle. Ore creatures? Golmogs?"

"A forest giant."

"Then I assume this cut came from a rock fragment."

"Yes, Headmaster. The creature hurled stones pulled from its own body. One burst upon a boulder near me. Not long after, we tried to send the thing to its end in a river gorge, but it survived."

"Giants are notoriously resilient." Master Jairun pursed his lips. "And I'm sorry you had to face such danger on a mission I gave you. None of you are cadet scouts yet. Not officially. But you've passed the Five Quests, so I'll stand by the risk of sending you into Tanelethar. We must learn what trouble the dragons are brewing for us."

Always the renewer first and the head of the Order second—Master Jairun dipped his smallest finger in the balm and rubbed it into the cut, making Connor wince, then stepped back to assess the result. "Tell Mister Lee he did well in patching you up on the way home from the lakes. Check the wound hourly for the next two days. If the giant's infection sets in, you must deal with it quickly. I'll give you a passage from the Rescuer's words to meditate upon as a preventative measure."

"Ahem." A cough from Stradok drew their attention. "Headmaster, could we please return to the discussion at hand. Time is short. I must send my answer to the Assembly tonight, and the girl must pack. She has a long, twelve-day journey ahead of her."

"The answer," Master Jairun said, returning the balm to its place on the shelf, "is *no.* As such, Miss Orso has no journey for which to pack, long, short, or otherwise."

"Headmaster, please." Stradok's tone spoke of disdain rather than pleading. "We've waited a year and more. Rumors of an impending dragon invasion have spread throughout Keledev, thanks in no small part to your own unsanctioned letters to the five vales. The people are on the edge of panic."

Connor risked an interruption—not proper for a cadet stalwart, or even a cadet scout, but he needed to catch up to the conversation. "Pardon me, Councilor, but why do rumors and panic require Kara to make a journey?"

The assemblyman shot him a sidelong glance. "The girl was

Aladoth, rescued on the same mission that closed the portal. She represents hope amid the terror." He returned his gaze to Master Jairun. "She represents victory."

"For whom?" Master Jairun asked. "The Keledev or the Rescuer?"

"Both, from a practical point of view."

"A valid argument, sir. But I'm afraid my answer is unchanged. Miss Orso is quite busy preparing for the Turning of the Spheres. She has less than a month to complete the Five Quests if she wishes to advance with the cadets who brought her home."

"The spheres." Stradok gave him a wry chuckle. "The Lightraider Spheres belong to an age when the Order was full grown and hundreds strong. Right now, it's barely breathing–an infant reborn. Last I checked, you don't have enough guardians of the light to lead them all."

"I govern the Order. Leadership of the spheres is my concern."

"True. And the needs of the Keledan are mine. Right now, the Keledan need that girl to–"

"Kara." Connor did his best to keep his voice even. "Her name is Kara."

Stradok sighed. "Master Jairun, why is this *cadet* even here?"

"I'm here, sir, because the headmaster trusts my judgment."

Master Jairun raised a cautioning finger. "Careful, Mister Enarian. You're here because I want you to go in Kara's place."

In her place?

Before Connor could protest, Stradok did it for him. "That is not what the Assembly asked for." He stomped his foot. "Unacceptable."

"I . . . agree?" Connor cast a glance at the assemblyman. "I mean, I don't think either I or Kara should go. Master Jairun, the spheres. The cadets must prepare. All of us."

"Kara must prepare. The rest of you passed your quests. The remaining prayer and study may be accomplished on the road. You and Mister Lee will travel to Sky Harbor and recount the story of Kara's rescue and the closing of Vorax's portal to the Assembly." The headmaster turned to Stradok. "Both may give firsthand accounts. It is they or no one. Your choice."

Stradok would not give in so easily. "In the old days, the Order sent all new Keledan to walk before the Assembly. Will the new headmaster break with tradition?"

"You are young, Councilor–much younger than me, in any case. So I'll forgive you for misremembering. Those rescued from Tanelethar gave the High One their loyalty before men and dragons, at great risk and often great sacrifice. The Order asked nothing more of them. It was the Prime Council who summoned new Keledan to be paraded before the many seats of the Second Hall, as they summon Kara now. Back then, the Order relented. Not this time."

Stradok closed his eyes for a long moment, then opened them again. "You are putting my standing at risk, sir. What am I to write in my raven?"

"Tell them you compromised." Master Jairun sank into his simple wooden chair, as if to signal the meeting had ended. "Isn't that what you Assembly councilors do best?"

Connor swallowed a chuckle.

Stradok grumbled under his breath, then lifted his chin. "Fine. But before I go, I have one more bit of business."

"Which is?"

"My quarters. The air is thin on this mountainside, and I grow tired of climbing so many steps to bring you the Prime Council's petitions"–he frowned–"often only to be denied. The Order is still small in its new state, and this fortress has many rooms. I'm certain you can find lodgings on this level for the Assembly's representative."

"I'm sorry, Councilor. There's nothing I can do."

"Why not?"

"The Assembly advisor's quarters have always been on the second level of Ras Telesar." Master Jairun gave him a flat grin. "That *is* a tradition of the Order. And, as you noted before, who am I to break with tradition?"

7

"MISTER ENARIAN, PLEASE STAY," MASTER JAIRUN SAID when Connor tried to follow the councilor out. "And close the door." He waited for Connor to comply before continuing. "I sent you on a scouting mission, did I not? I must hear how it became a rescue."

Connor turned from the door, shrugging a shoulder. "Things got . . . out of hand."

"Out of hand? Do you realize how blessed you were to survive a giant? We've lost entire raid teams to such creatures."

Connor hung his head, and the headmaster softened his voice. "Don't hear this as a rebuke, child. Hear it as concerned advice. We've taken great risks with your class thus far. We must be cautious about taking more. Though I'm loath to admit it in his presence, Stradok is right. The rekindled Order is small and fragile."

"What of Elisai, the man we brought back? What of the family Lee and Dag rescued? Once their eyes were opened, should we have left them there?"

"Certainly not. But tell me, how did it come to such a choice? What did you find?" The headmaster offered him a chair next to his behind the canted desk, where they could speak in low tones, and Connor accepted.

"We learned of trouble in one of the Schisma Valley towns

not long after we arrived. People starving, vanishing. The giant had taken up residence there. The creature helped them build a wall and a tavern."

"Then he claimed the tavern for his own and never left, I presume?" The headmaster spoke as if such a result were inevitable–as if the townsfolk should have known better.

Perhaps that was true. "We learned from Elisai that the creature built itself a throne in the tavern's hearth room. One by one, it drew in the men of the town–some of the women too. Tending to it day and night took them out of the fields and shops, until no family could put any food but the giant's scraps on their tables."

"A common tale." Master Jairun lifted a text from a shelf behind him and thumbed through its time-stained pages. "A giant's infection is subtle. At first the creature seems like a boon, a useful compromise to suit an Aladoth's desires. Through its song sorcery, the creature casts itself as the perfect companion in labor or as a town defender. But in the end a giant is always destructive. Did this one begin eating those who tried to leave?"

"Not exactly. Townsfolk disappeared, but not down the giant's gullet. While grown men and women slept in the tavern like dogs at the giant's clay feet, their sons were taken, then their daughters."

"Orcs?"

Connor nodded. "And barkhides. Once they emptied the houses of the young and fit, they claimed the giant's captives, sending it into a rage. Teegan and I arrived in town not long after the orcs and barkhides had left. The creature burst upward through the tavern roof as we walked down the central lane. It swung at us with a timber. Elisai yanked us out of the way."

Master Jairun glanced up from the book. "Elisai saved you?"

"Pulled us into an alley and led us to a meat cellar where other townsfolk had taken refuge. It was only a matter of time before the creature brought the butcher shop down on their heads."

"Then you should have led the giant away–distracted him."

"We planned to, sir. But while I watched the street, waiting for our chance, Elisai peppered Teegan with questions. Who were we? Where had we come from? Why come to a dying town when word of the danger had traveled?" Connor leaned forward in the chair. "He was ready, Headmaster. Teegan felt that readiness and shared the Great Rescue just as you and the other guardians taught us."

Master Jairun made no effort to argue. He only scratched the back of his head. "Yes. We did. And I'm certain Mister Lee and Mister Kaivos will share a similar story. I won't fault any of you for stepping outside the bounds of your missions." He met Connor's eye and raised a brow. "This time. But let's come back to the orcs and barkhides taking able-bodied townsfolk. We've seen it before, haven't we?"

"Trader's Knoll," Connor said, "and the other towns in the Highland Forest. Last time, we saw the mocktree Krokwode recruiting locals for dozens of barkhide camps. But this is something new. The camps in the Highland Forest are gone."

"All of them?"

"Every one. Not a tent in sight. And in many of the places we traveled, we saw much the same. A town here. A village there. Emptied of the able-bodied, leaving old women and children to tell of the orcs and barkhides who came in the night to drag their sehnas and tehpas, even their behlnas and mehmas, away. Yet we saw no mocktrees and no barkhide camps. Lee and Dag shared the same report on our journey home from the lakes."

"No camps." The headmaster stood and walked to his shelves of scrolls and texts, mumbling as if asking the texts for answer instead of Connor. "No mocktrees. Yet many are missing. A purge?" He picked up a tome and thumbed through its pages. "I doubt it. Haven't had one of those in centuries. No need these days. Not even with Miss Orso drawing their attention."

At the mention of Kara's name, Connor looked up. "Headmaster, what's happening in Tanelethar? What's going on?"

Master Jairun slid the old book back into place. "I have no idea. But we'd better find out soon, or I fear our ignorance will bring dire consequences."

8

KARA HAD LEFT BY THE TIME CONNOR EMERGED from the headmaster's chambers, but he had a good idea as to where she'd gone.

Ever since her arrival at the academy, she'd favored a small chamber in the fourth wall where she could work out the usual cadet frustrations on an old Talanian conquest game called Vanquish. She'd found the slate table unused, gathering dust, and had restored its smoothness and repainted the two sets of wooden balls representing the game's warring armies. On occasion, she roped Connor into playing with her, but he'd never matched her skill.

He found her at the far end of the long table, sending the white command ball into one of the colorful soldier balls with a loud *crack*. The soldier ball flew to the table's corner and dropped into a leather basket known as a pot.

"I suppose that one represented Councilor Stradok," he said, picking up a stick to join her.

"As did the last five."

"The balls are old. Master Belen says we shouldn't hit them so hard."

"I find the sound soothing. Especially tonight." She had

vanquished a striped ball, but now set her aim on one painted with whirls–a ball from the other army.

Connor raised an eyebrow. "Not sure which side you're on?"

"Beginning to wonder. I suppose it depends on what you have to say."

"Fair enough."

Since Kara seemed content to play both armies, Connor returned the stick to its holder and took a seat by the windows to watch. The mists of the nine waterfalls cascading from the fountain chapel above hung heavy in the lantern light spilling past him. "You could've waited. Our meeting didn't take long."

She sent the whirled ball crashing into one of the stuffed leather rails lining the table. It bounced away and dropped into a side pot. "I couldn't face him–Stradok, I mean. I didn't want to be there when he came out."

"Doesn't sound like the brave girl I know. An unfriendly face never sends you running."

"It's not about friendly or unfriendly." Kara bent close to the slate, as if eyeing her next target. The rules required players to pot the low-ranking balls first, known as corporals, and then the higher-ranking captains. To follow this order, she'd have to sneak the command ball around a captain. With a sharp jab she sent the white ball spinning on a curving path, and another corporal fell. She let out a satisfied grunt and straightened. "It's the way Stradok looks at me. His cold gaze. He sees me as a token, not a person. I'm a novelty, a talisman."

"If it helps, he means well. He told us he thinks you can give our people hope."

Kara straightened and turned, scowling. "I came to Keledev to gain hope, not grant it."

"It works both ways. The Rescuer is the source of hope, but the Keledan must still encourage one another."

"So you think I should go?"

Connor held up his hands. "I didn't say that. Besides, Master

Jairun made it clear I have no say in the matter. He made the decision on his own."

She left the table and came closer, gripping her game stick the way she might grip a spear. The flourishes of blue-gray freckles on her arms and hands remained hidden under the sleeves and wristers Teegan had sown for her, but those on her cheeks and forehead darkened against a red flush. "And?"

"You're staying. Master Jairun wants you to focus on the quests."

A heavy breath escaped her. "Thank the High One. I'm struggling as it is to be ready for the worst of the Five Quests. A journey south would have done me in."

"The worst of them?" Connor tried not to smile. "You mean the Tinker's Quest?"

That earned him a short smile, and Kara pretended to swing at him with the game stick. "Go ahead. Laugh. Enjoy yourself." She raised her hands. "These are not the arms of a blacksmith, and they'll serve me no better for the Quest of the Vanguard. Two failures will set me back so far as to make passing before the Turning of the Spheres nigh impossible."

Connor's smile faded. "Oh yes. The Vanguard. Not to be discouraging, but that's the one that should worry you. Cadets who've passed must keep the secrets of the Five Quests, but I'll say this, the Quest of the Vanguard proved far harder than I'd imagined."

Her arms dropped. "Harder? Didn't you know beforehand that you'd be fighting our overlarge swordmaster and his twin axes?"

"I did. But there was more to it. I can say no more."

"No matter." Kara returned to the Vanquish table. "You needn't share any secrets. Just . . . be here." She lined up another shot at one of the striped balls. "Now that you're back to help me prepare, I know I can do this."

Be here.

Connor winced. "Kara, Lee and I are going to Sky Harbor in your place."

"What?" Her game stick clacked against the table, and the

command ball rolled lazily past its target and dropped into a corner pot. She faced him again. “Connor, you can’t leave me right now. Why can’t Tiran go?”

“Tiran wasn’t sent. We were. Besides, he and Teegan are riding for Thousand Falls soon. Their tehpa joined the watchmen there, and they want to escort him back here for the Turning of the Spheres. They’ll leave four days after I do.”

She planted the butt of the game stick on the pavers between her feet and rested her hands and chin on its hard leather tip. “So you’re all abandoning me.”

“Dag will be here.”

“Dag can’t help me with the smithing. He’s near as bad as I am. Don’t you remember?”

Connor did remember, with a mix of mirth and revulsion. For their Tinker’s Quest, the class had been tasked with building field forges and using them to make weapons. The moment they’d learned the details, Dag had ejected part of his breakfast over the barracks balcony rail. And then he’d sent the rest over the third-level battlements during the march to the quest. Despite his weakened state, he’d pounded out a serviceable axe head, beating the metal into submission with brute force. Kara could not depend on strength like that to save her.

She seemed to sense Connor’s mind and lifted her chin. “Passing through the Shar Razel depended on the Rescuer, not me. I had only to accept his will. But passing the Five Quests is all about skill, Connor, and smithing isn’t a skill I have. How can the Rescuer let me enter his service and then ask me to do something I can’t?”

His lips parted for a reply, but she hit him with a glare. “Do you really think I want an answer to that question right now–one that will surely become a lecture on the Rescuer’s will over ours?”

“Um. No?”

“Correct.”

Kara went back to her game for a while, until all the corporals and captains of both armies were vanquished and only the black ball remained–the dragon. She'd sunk the others with force, but she gave the dragon ball barely a nudge, as if all her anger was spent.

The ball teetered on the edge of a side pot, then dropped in.

Kara laid her game stick on the table and returned to the sill to sit with him. "The road to Sky Harbor is long. You'll be gone nigh on a month–barely home in time for the Turning of the Spheres. When do you leave?"

"Sunrise. A little before, if I know Lee." He watched the mists sparkling in the lantern light outside, the caldrons burning below in the tall barbican gates with their giant figures. "Kara, you can pass the quests without me. I know you can."

"Perhaps. But I do better when I'm at ease." She bumped his shoulder with hers. "And I'm far more at ease when you're near."

9

KARA
THE FORGES
RAS TELESAR

"NO, NO, NO. THAT'S NOT IT AT ALL."

Kara could feel Master Baldomar's frustration–almost as strong as the heat from the Aropha-built forges. Connor had only been gone a few hours, and already she missed the calm he'd brought her in his short time home between journeys. She supposed she ought to get used to it. Such was life in the Order, or so they'd been taught–gone, home, and gone again, sometimes without so much as a sunset in between. And every mission brought the chance that a friend or two would pass on to Elamhavar instead of returning to the academy.

If the past bore any resemblance to the future, Kara could expect half their class's small number of six to leave their world of Dastan in the grim valor of battle well before any reached the rank of Guardians of the Light.

"The hammer is an extension of your hand," Baldomar said, shaking her from her thoughts. "It is a tool of your will, not a mindless, clamorous chunk of steel."

"I know. I know."

"Do you?"

Kara shrugged. What other answer could she offer? Baldomar had spoken those same words a hundred times. Spoken them, whispered them, groaned them. Lately, more often than not, he'd shouted them. But hearing had not become understanding. How could Kara make a heavy hammer part of her hand? Such a thing sounded terribly uncomfortable.

To her relief, Baldomar took the tool away. "Rest your arm. Let me show you again."

Under his guidance, her misshapen stick of metal lengthened and broadened, approaching the shape of a hunting blade before the anvil sapped the orange glow of its heat away. It took him mere moments to do what she'd failed to accomplish in a full half-tick of pounding. He laid the metal in the fire once more. "Did you see?"

As always, Kara tried to temper her answer with tact. "I . . . saw the pattern of your strikes. I saw you change the angle of the hammer in the fullering of the steel as you drew it down."

"Yes. Good. But did you *see*?"

Tact failed her. "See what? The skill of a master with five times my strength?" She wanted to clap her hand over her mouth. And she would have done so had she been able to lift her arm after a full morning in the forge. Instead, Kara lowered her gaze. "Forgive me."

"Still using the same old excuse, are we?"

Kara, eyes still down, stiffened. "Same old excuse?"

Baldomar gave her no chance to say anything else, perhaps as a mercy. He set his hammer on the anvil and walked out.

Just as Kara began to think he'd given up on her for good, the master smith returned with Dame Silvana. "Since you view the Rangers' Sphere with admiration," Baldomar said, "and your own strength with acrimony, I thought a different guardian should demonstrate the technique."

"Quite." Dame Silvana tied her leather-wrapped braid into a bun and strapped on an apron and glove. With her short stature, even the smallest apron in the forge hung near to her toes. "Thank you, Master Baldomar." She drew a hot stick of metal from the fire and set to work.

In nearly as short a time as Baldomar, Silvana finished her strikes and showed Kara the taper, the point, and the edge. She'd fashioned the steel into the clear shape of a dagger.

Kara shook her head. "How?"

"Let go of the idea that smithing is about physical strength, child. There are some in this fortress who can force steel into submission. You and I are not among them. We must understand the steel and lead it where we want it to go."

The dame cast her handiwork into the scrap pile and laid another hot stick from the forge on the anvil. She gave the hammer to Kara. "Start again."

Understand the steel. Lead it. How could Kara do either with an inanimate hunk of metal?

After a quarter tick of pounding and sparks, she lost control and the hammer clattered onto the floor. She let out an audible moan of pain.

Master Baldomar knelt to pick the hammer up, staying low so that his eyes were on a level with hers. "I think you've had enough for today."

Kara heard resignation in his voice. "No, I haven't, Master Baldomar. Please. My days are running short." She tried to take the hammer back and winced, unable to reach it, let alone grasp it in her aching fingers. A tear fell, mingling with her sweat.

"Come," he said, and led her out to the coolness of the ramparts. "Rest for the remainder of the day. Breathe. Study." He pointed upward, toward the fourth level and Ras Telesar's grand oak library. "Have you read Master Gof's *The Sword Inside* as I suggested?"

"Twice."

"Then read it again. And this time, let chapters one through six sink in."

EVERY STEP IN THE FACE OF THE FOURTH-LEVEL WALL felt like a jab in Kara's sore arm. Her body wanted nothing else but her mattress.

In chapters one through six of Master Gof's century-old text, he pontificated on the relationship of the unseen sword within a bar of steel to the unseen soul within a Keledan. Not that Kara didn't appreciate Gof's references to the Rescuer and the profession he chose at the start of his walk among his creations, but she could hardly find a drier read, even among the *Nine Laments of Lakarius*. She'd be fortunate if one of the younger cadet stalwarts didn't find her later, passed out on the library floor.

Wise counsel or not, Kara wanted no more instruction from a master who, in his time, wielded a hammer as if it were as light as a quill like Baldomar. She'd seen something new today–a hint of knowledge she desperately needed. She trudged past the library door to yet another staircase and kept climbing to the seventh level of the fortress. There, she walked east along the rear battlements to a squat tower that seemed to merge with the sheer rock face of the mountainside.

Dame Silvana was waiting for her–door open.

"Ah. Kara." She stepped back and motioned for her visitor to enter. "I thought you might stop by."

The guardian walked her into the tower's lower study and hearth room, which extended well back into the mountain, making the space larger than appeared possible from the outside. Kara found it warm and sparing at the same time. The head ranger and her predecessors had kept the furnishings sparse enough to let the fluid style of the Aropha builders shine through.

Kara examined some of the old artwork. Flaming hands making a winged warrior were sculpted into the wall. "Is this an Elder Folk view of the Maker?"

"Yes. Good. And over here as well." On the opposite wall, Silvana showed her a depiction of a fountain. A pair of Rapha filled their bowls from its basin.

In both pieces, smaller flying creatures surrounded the larger Aropha figures like stars. From her studies, Kara knew them to be Dynapha, shining with light as they sang the High One's praises. But she had always struggled with the two opposites. "Why is there always a fountain and a flame? Aren't fire and water opposed to each other?"

Dame Silvana took a chair by the hearth and motioned for Kara to join her. "They can be, in our hands. But both are gifts from the same Maker, and the Aropha chose to see him that way. The fountain represents the truth flowing from him and the life with which he nurtures his creations. The fire represents both his justice and his artistry–molding and baking clay, shaping and tempering iron."

"Shaping and tempering iron." Kara took the offered chair and smiled. "I get it. The Maker was a blacksmith even before we knew him as the Blacksmith. But to me, he is one more smith who is stronger than I am. Infinitely so."

"But I am not," the guardian said. "And that is why you've come."

"Your work at the anvil today. I was–"

"Surprised? Shocked? Stunned to see a woman my size pound out a blade so fast? You shouldn't be. Have you read–"

"Please don't say Master Gof's *The Sword Inside.*"

Dame Silvana grinned. "His insights are illuminating."

"Exhausting is the better word." When the guardian's smile flattened, she coughed. "Sorry, ma'am. I . . . um . . . came because I wanted to know your secret."

"My secret?" Silvana rose from her chair and stepped up on a stool to lift an ornate wooden box from her mantel. "My only secret is that I've been waiting for you to come to me. I must say"– she returned to her seat–"I'm disappointed it took this long. Every lightraider must learn the art of the forge, even me. Yet you did not think to ask for my help until you saw me work a hammer with your own eyes. A ranger sees the whole forest, dear, not just the trees in front of her."

That was not the secret Kara had come for, nor a tone she wanted to hear from the leader of the sphere she wished to enter. She hung her head.

"Oh, stop that. Take wisdom however it comes, hard or easy. Hard-bought wisdom is often the best. And don't worry about my rebuke. I have no say as to whether or not you enter the Rangers' Sphere, remember?" Silvana set the box in Kara's lap. "Now. Open that up and see what I've been waiting so long to show you."

Kara felt the box's weight. "What's inside? A magic hammer?"

"You've been Keledan long enough to know better."

True. She had. And what she found after popping the latch might not have been magic, but it *was* a hammer–white steel with a wrapped leather handle and a head etched with weaving vines. She lifted it from the green velvet cloth inside. "It's lighter than the hammers in the forge."

"True, but not too light. The head must still carry weight. The real boon of this tool is its alloy–polar steel, known as the unshakeable steel. A smith's hammer usually has a wooden handle to shield the smith from the vibrations of each strike. But a shield is a barrier that works both ways. A wooden handle makes it harder for a smith to feel the metal move."

Feel the metal. Kara hefted the hammer. "You're saying that because this hammer is made from a single piece of polar steel, it will feel like an extension of my arm, like Master Baldomar says?"

The guardian nodded. "It will give you the chance to learn what that truly means. And with less vibration, your strikes will be more effective, and your arm will hold out longer. I'll talk to Master Baldomar as well, and see if we can't push your Tinker's Quest almost to the Turning, even if you pass your other quests earlier."

Kara set the hammer back in the box and closed the lid. "Thank you."

"Don't thank me yet. That hammer will help you in your

training as it helped me when I was your age, but it won't do the work for you. You must still learn the smithing skill well enough to pass a difficult quest."

There was an awkward moment in which Kara was not quite sure what else to say, and when she said nothing, Dame Silvana clasped her hands. "Well, I must prepare for a noon archery class with our newest initiates. I like to arrive on the lists first, lest one of them shoot another in my absence."

"Oh. Right." Kara took the not-so-subtle cue and started for the door. "Is there any other smithing advice you can give me?"

"First, get your metal in the fire more often," Silvana said, walking with her. "There's nothing more futile then pounding away at cold steel. Second, and more important, learn to lean on the master of the metal."

"When I play the part of a blacksmith, am I not the steel's master?"

"Clearly you've not absorbed the most important point of Gof's excellent text. Don't fight the steel for control. Instead, realize neither you nor the metal is the master. The real master is the one who made you both." With that, Silvana motioned Kara out onto the ramparts and shut the door.

THE PRISONER
TANELETHAR

FACES IN THE MISTS. DEAD FACES–DRAWN, TWISTED, rotting. I never ask if the others see them, and not because any word I speak may earn the sting of a barkhide's whip. I don't ask because I fear the answer too much.

If I see them, perhaps I'm already one of them.

Day is much like night around here. The roving fog bears lighter shades of gray and green. Fewer wanderers and no ghouls roam about. But we are no less guarded.

The wraith general and its iron orcs move among the barkhides, prodding them as they prod us, driving them.

"You never died." Shan grunts out the words as we grapple on the muddy training field. The creatures pit us against each other daily–sometimes in pairs, sometimes two or three against one. We take lashings for refusing to fight. We take lashings when we're cut or when a bone snaps. We take lashings for being human.

"I did die. I saw the wraith, I felt its sting, and then it was morning. Another day. Another life."

Shan sweeps my feet from under me. My back slams into the muck, but I feel the pain most in my shoulder, where the wraith's claws dug in. Shan knows it, sees it, and he punches that shoulder again and nods when I wince. "Your pain says otherwise. Another life would heal your wounds and take you far from here. But such ideas are the dreams of a fool, Hosal."

Hosal is what he calls me since I do not know my name. He told me when we first met that it means *captive* in an ancient tongue.

I catch the wraith watching us with its lidless eyes. I hold my tongue. Shan does the same, and we start again.

This time I resolve to gain the better grip at the start of our wrestling. When Shan advances, I slap both his arms outward and lace my fingers behind his neck. Once I force his chin to his chest, he has little control. With a twist and a throw, I send him sprawling into the impression my back left moments before.

Shan's eyes, his eyes alone, give me the barest hint of a smile. He's proud of me. Shan taught me much of what I know.

We train this way daily. Hundreds of us. Men and women. Some too young to be called either. How long we've been training, and for what purpose, I can't say. Who holds captives in torment, yet trains them to fight?

The orcs offer no instruction. What little we receive comes from our nearly human troop sergeants and their captains—barkhides, Shan calls them. He once told me they're cursed slaves of a mocktree that roams this forest on his roots, taller than the tallest of its shaggy black pines. General Moach. But I've never seen him. And the barkhides don't look like slaves to me. Since when do slaves carry whips?

One of Shan's tales about the barkhides holds disturbingly true. Under the spell of song sorcery, they mutilate themselves to look like their mocktree masters. I can see it in the spikes driven through the arms of our troop captain and the missing fingers on our two sergeants' hands, making them look like the ends of barren branches.

Striated burn scars on my own arms, reminiscent of bark, hint that I was a barkhide too in a previous life. Me. A barkhide. How did I wind up on the other end of the whip? How did I fall?

"Swords and shields! Now!"

Our self-mutilated troop sergeants shout at us to take up our rusty, battered arms. In the breather, shuffling with the crowd to the racks, I see her face again. If I was a barkhide at the time I last saw her, she could not have smiled at me so. That means we parted sooner. Did I leave her behind and choose to become a mocktree's lackey, perhaps enchanted by its song sorcery? Did I abandon the bond of blood? Perhaps I deserve this punishment.

My argument with Shan is not finished. But I wait to speak until his sword smashes into my shield. The clangs and crashes filling the muddy field hide our voices. We need only keep our teeth clenched to avoid being caught. "How can you be certain I did not die? What do you know of death?"

"I know that many deaths are a myth. A man dies only once, and then worms and darkness take him."

I deflect Shan's downward strike and slam his shield with mine to send him stumbling back. "What of the apparitions? What of the ghost who spoke to me last night?"

"Animations, Hosal. Dragon sorcery. They are grotesque memorials of the once-living, not the dead returned." Shan circles, sword pointed at me, daring me to advance.

I take his bait on purpose. There are far worse things here than being struck with a blunt blade. "You can't know that for sure." I slap his sword with mine and lunge in for a thrust.

Shan moves like one of the ghosts we're arguing about–one beat, he's in front of me, the next, he's at my side. He could easily stab me in the ribs, but he turns his sword tip down and punches me in the temple instead. "I know because I know," he says as I crumple. "My father–my whole family–held to a similar myth. They believed in two deaths and thought they could escape the second." He glares down at me. "There is no escape, Hosal. Not from death. Not from here. Best come to grips with that now."

A scream interrupts the argument, ringing clear over the tumult. "No!"

Two iron orcs drag a prisoner from the field. The orcs rarely touch us. They leave the daytime torment to the barkhides and their tittering goblin companions. This is new.

"What have I done! I did nothing. Please, I–" The black-bone fist of the wraith ends the outburst. The prisoner goes limp, and the orcs drag him up the steps of a darkened stone hut. The wraith floats up the steps after them, and the door slams shut.

In place of the wraith, an enormous creature lumbers in from the forest, taller and broader than the black pines, yet one of their number. Shaggy boughs hang from its broken peak, and in two of its four branch-like arms it carries an axe and the longest whip I've ever seen. Six blazing eyes burn like points within uneven holes above its crooked mouth. General Moach. So, he's real after all.

The creature lets out a thrumming moan and snaps its whip with a thunderous *crack*. The barkhides answer by shouting and cracking their own whips to stir us from our stupor.

We throw ourselves once again into our fighting, lest we feel their sting.

Shan waits until our swords meet, then grumbles through clenched teeth. "Whatever this is, Hosal, it isn't good. The one true death may find us both soon enough."

10

CONNOR
KELEDEV
PLEASANTON DOCKS

"TRUST US," CONNOR SAID TO THE PLEASANTON dockmaster. "We can handle it."

When the dockmaster still hesitated to rent them a river skiff, Connor folded his arms, doing his best to project the knightly confidence he'd seen his whole life in the painting of his patehpa hanging over his family hearth. "We're in haste and traveling at the invitation of the Prime Council."

Lee took a more diplomatic approach. "The river is wide in most places from here to the White Ridge Narrows. And I know my work at the helm. It's in my blood."

The dockmaster glanced at the hollow tree emblem on the brooch of Lee's cloak and gave them no more argument. "Only for the Order." He opened his ledger for Connor to sign. "I wouldn't trust the chief of the helmsman's guild in Harbor Joy to run one of my boats through the narrows in spring. Those waters are the fastest in all Talania. But if a lightraider says he can do it . . ." He snapped the book as soon as Connor finished. "Well, may the Rescuer be with you both."

"Always and forever," Connor said, handing him back his quill.

Another voice interrupted before the dockmaster could say anything more. "Oi! Do my ears deceive me, or is that a young

Enarian I hear?"

A portly figure climbed out of a boat on the horse canal–a channel of slow-moving water used for short journeys upstream, walled off from the main flow of the Anamturas River by stonework. The figure waved what looked to be a turkey leg. "Connor the shepherd boy, as I live and breathe. And Lee Trang, the scribe. Haven't see either of you in an age of days."

"Hello, Barnabas." Connor clasped the parcelman's arm. "What a blessing to cross journeys with you."

The cadets set about helping Barnabas move his burdens from the canal boat to a cart, and he seemed glad for the extra hands–glad enough to let the cadets take most of the work. "What brings you boys south?" he asked, taking a bite of his turkey leg. "Lightraider business? All secret and secure?"

"Not so secret as that." Connor hauled a wooden crate of applethorn berries out of the boat, a staple of the towns along the southern coasts. Barnabas never ventured that far, so he'd likely brought them up from a market in Val Pera. "The Assembly wants a word. We've been summoned to–"

"Sort of summoned," Lee said, correcting him. "The two of us are not exactly what they were hoping for. What about you? Headed to the vales?"

"I am, indeed, sir. Stonyvale included. With that in mind, Connor, have you any message for your mehma and tehpa you'd like me to pass?"

"Give them my love. Tell them I'm sorry I couldn't visit on my way down to Sky Harbor." Connor thought about it a little more as Lee helped him lift a pungent barrel of salted fish out of the boat. "And . . . if she doesn't mind, have Mehma wrap up one of her cinnamon lardy cakes for Kara."

This raised both Lee's and Barnabas's eyebrows. Even the horse harnessed to the parcelman's boat turned his way and snorted.

He frowned at them all. "She could use the encouragement, with us gone and the quests bearing down on her. I'm assuming you'll continue north to the academy, of course."

"I will. I'll pass the message and collect the cake if she'll bake it." Barnabas winked, most likely because he knew Connor's mehma would bake the cake and she would add an extra one for him. "I must head east to the other outposts before heading north to the academy, but I promise at least a morsel or two'll make it all the way up the mountain to your friend."

The horse let out a whinny, casting a long look at the parcelman's boat, which now sat empty.

"All right, Your Majesty. Hold your horses." Barnabas blocked the horse's view of his mouth with his hand and whispered to the cadets. "Clarence hates it when I say that. Finds it downright offensive, I think." He lowered the hand and raised his voice again. "Best get Clarence hitched to the cart and off to the stables for the night. Driving upriver takes it out of him these days. Not as young as he used to be."

Clarence huffed, as if to disagree about his age, but seemed relieved when Barnabas began fiddling with his tackle for the cart change.

Connor and Lee said their goodbyes and pushed their skiff out into the river. The rushing flow pointed the boat south as soon as it cleared the docks. In spring, the Anamturas, fed by runoff from the Rescuer's impossibly high peaks, ran twice as fast as any river on the whole of Dastan—or so Master Belen had told them. When Connor said he wanted to shorten the journey, the tinker had advised taking the river. As long as they managed to keep the boat upright, he and Lee could cut the time between Pleasanton and Sky Harbor in half or better.

Belen claimed the Anamturas in spring moved faster than any gelding at a lope and faster than a gallop in the White Ridge narrows. By the feel of it as the river took them, this was no exaggeration. Connor swallowed hard and gripped the rail. "Keep her centered and straight."

Lee lowered his chin to fix Connor with a googly glare

through the upper edge of his spectacles. "I think I know this business better than you, my friend." He sat quiet for a few seconds, as if concentrating on his course, then added, "Kara needs encouragement?"

"Does she not?"

"Certainly. But so have I on many occasions, and I don't ever recall meriting one of your mehma's cinnamon lardy cakes. Is Kara also the reason you've been moody and driving hard since our first steps through the academy gates?"

Connor turned to face the bow. "No. I'm driven by what we saw in Tanelethar. And I'm moody because I don't like this mission. You and I are meant for dangers north of the barrier, not Assembly politics. Now hush and watch the river. It'd be more than tragic for us to drown heading south, going entirely in the wrong direction from our true calling."

11

KARA
THE ARENA
RAS TELESAR

TO CALL THE ANCIENT LISROPHA BATTLE CHAMBER large—to call it a chamber at all—seemed an insult. And in the dark, with only sparse circles of lanternlight to break the deep black, it seemed infinite. Quinton had pulled her aside after supper. "The Vanguard is callin' ya out, Cadet. Meet me in the Arena at the start of the third watch."

The third watch. The dreaming watch, the Keledan called it, when sleep is deepest and those who stay awake can't trust their eyes.

How could she trust her eyes to see anything in the vast dark of the Arena?

"Swordmaster Quinton?" Kara left the light and safety of the threshold. Three paces later, she felt a pulse of air. The big silver doors slammed closed behind her. She turned, padded sword up and ready and then, realizing her mistake, turned back again. The threat would come from the darkness, not a closed entrance.

Why had Quinton called her out at night?

Her own voice in her head answered the question. *To make the quest all the harder, of course.* This was the quest of the Vanguard. And to hear Dame Silvana tell it, the Vanguard made everything unnecessarily severe.

"Hello?"

No answer.

For two days, they'd left her alone, and for two days she'd made good use of Silvana's hammer. The lighter polar steel, unshakeable, allowed her to feel the metal in the way Baldomar had always spoken about. And she'd had help in her practice from the least expected source–Tiran the Recluse.

The two had never bonded, not in the way she'd bonded with the others. But was that Kara's fault? Tiran had withdrawn from everyone after the battle with Vorax and his return to Keledev. He'd buried himself in the Scrolls and texts about the Scrolls, declaring that would be his place in the Order. And he'd taken up metalwork as a way to draw closer to the Blacksmith.

Metalwork had brought him to the forge while Kara worked–not because she'd asked for his help, which she hadn't, but because he was madly trying to finish some little ornament before heading southwest with Teegan to collect their tehpa. But help he did, more than Kara could have hoped.

Cant your hammer more. Inward, not outward. Push as much as you pound. Yes. Good.

Don't still the hammer while you turn your steel. Bounce it off the anvil to keep your rhythm, and your arm will tire less.

Tiran gave her new methods, and explained others in a way that helped her understand better than when Baldomar said almost the same thing. Kara should have sought him out months ago. Too late. Now Tiran had left with his twin to ride for Thousand Falls. And with her second quest upon her, she was running out of time.

She advanced into the Arena, painfully aware that the deeper in she walked, the more exposed she became. What a way to begin a test of her combat skills. Long after the doors vanished behind her, a shape took form ahead, near what she perceived to be the Arena's center. The shape was not large enough to be Quinton nor any human. Had they managed to bring a goblin in? Was this some illusion–another secret of the academy?

No. Nothing so impressive. Drawing closer, she found a simple wooden pupil's desk with the chair attached.

Kara paused in her approach. "What is this?"

She heard the clack and flare of flint and steel striking a flame to a lantern's wick. The new light revealed Quinton's square chin. "It's yer test," he said. "Now sit yerself down an' pick up that quill."

As soon as Kara had squeezed herself into the chair, Quinton laid a parchment before her. Five lines were drawn, labeled with Elder Tongue numbers–*arosh* through *tethro*–drawn using the ancient symbols.

A written exam? Kara had expected something like this as part of the Comforter's Quest–from the sphere of clerics and bards–but not from the Vanguard. She glanced up at Quinton, who stood in his martial fashion, hands clasped behind his back. He nodded at the parchment. "The Great Rescue. All five verses. Write 'em out. Go."

Every cadet knew the Great Rescue by heart. It was the ultimate expression of the Order's calling–its mission and the reason for its existence.

Not wishing to appear as if she couldn't remember them, Kara began writing out the verses with a quick hand. She started with the titles. Each verse had one. *Ke'Aroshkef,* The One and Only. *Se Arosh Nakav,* Not One is Perfect. *Zebath Nakav,* Perfect Sacrifice. *Liberend,* Liberation. *Keledan,* Twiceborn. Master Jairun had told her the first son of Shapec, one of the Rescuer's beloved companions, had chosen to name the verses because each was a work of beauty in both prose and purpose.

Once she'd named them, Kara wrote out the verses, taking care with the vowel marks in her Elder Tongue script, then laid down her quill and handed the parchment and lantern to the swordmaster.

"Why does the Vanguard choose a written exam for its quest?" she asked as Quinton studied her answers.

He seemed satisfied with her work, and set the light and the parchment aside. "'Tis not the whole o' the quest. We start here, lass, because if ya canna prove ya know the Great Rescue by heart, the next bit has no point."

Without the slightest pause, the swordmaster drew his arms from behind his back and swung both his battleaxes down at her desk.

Kara dove out of the seat and rolled away. The wood shattered into splinters. "What are you doing?"

"'Tis a combat quest. What'd ya expect?" The swordmaster came at her, and Kara backed away, reaching for her training sword. Her hand grazed an empty loop at her belt. She'd set the sword aside when she picked up the quill. Now it lay amid the scrap wood that had been her desk, on the other side of Quinton.

Combat quest. She could handle this. It's what she'd been expecting when she entered the chamber, right?

Well, not exactly.

The blades of Quinton's twin axes caught the lanternlight, sharp as ever.

Kara drew a pair of bulky padded daggers–the clunkers she'd chosen to represent her folding whirlknives–and circled her foe. "Is it a fair quest in which the master carries real weapons to counter his pupil's toys? Is a guardian so afraid of a lowly cadet stalwart?"

Quinton chuckled and circled as well, which was what she'd hoped for. "I'm not afraid of gettin' cut, lass. Ya have the priv'ledge o' wieldin' clunkers in this test so ya won' be tempted ta pull punches. Now quit stallin' an' fight!"

She hurled one of the daggers, only to see it knocked away by an axe handle. But hitting him had not been her main objective. To stand any chance against those axes, she'd need her sword, and the distraction gave her time to rush past the pile of wood and sweep it up.

"Nice move, lass. But take care. Look close at yer foe an' see who yer fightin'. These rags I'm wearin' don' resemble an orc or a granog, do they?"

Orcs. Granogs. Who was she fighting? A key question in every bout of a cadet's combat training. Different dark creatures required shifting tactics–different aspects of a lightraider's dependance on the Rescuer. Other foes were unique also. Animals required care. Humans required love in the midst of battle. Kara had almost forgotten.

Watching as Quinton moved closer to a hanging lantern, she appraised his clothing. He wore a simple tunic with an oak emblem crudely sown into the shoulder and a leather gauntlet with steel pieces made to look like they were passing through his arm.

"You've taken the aspect of a barkhide, a mocktree disciple who mutilates his own body." Kara caught herself lowering her sword and raised the tip again, not bothering to hide the anger and hurt in her voice. "You've taken the form of those who took my brehna."

12

BARKHIDES, HOWEVER DEFORMED, WERE HUMAN. Kara had thrown a dagger at her opponent's heart without a second thought. If she'd hit that mark–a killing blow by the rules of combat training–she'd have failed the quest.

After another half tick of sparring with a blunt and padded sword and dagger against razor-sharp twin axes, her vision blurred. A complaint she intended as a thought slipped out amid heaving breaths. "When . . . does this . . . end?"

"When ya stop tryin' ta kill me an start tryin' ta convince me."

Had she not tried? Between blows and dodges, Kara had recited each Great Rescue verse in the Elder Tongue. "Gibberish!" Quinton had shouted. "I'm a mocktree's minion. Do ya think I speak the celestial language? Am I some dust-ridden archivist?"

Now he retreated, as if to give her a breather. "The Great Rescue takes a combination o' prayin', teachin', an' doin', lass. We speak the sacred verses as hymns o' praise. That's between the lightraider an' the Maker. We add the Aladoth ta that circle by teachin' 'em through words an' actions." He lowered his axes. "Do ya know why the Vanguard rushes into battle?"

Kara lowered her weapons as well. Relief flowed through her arms. "Faith."

"Wrong. Faith allows us ta rush in. True. But 'tis love that drives us. The Maker's love for his creations. Now, start again."

Start again? She was failing this quest.

How could Kara act in love while fighting? And how could she love those who'd robbed her of her brehnan? Yes, the orc guards had killed her older brehna Liam, but if not for the barkhides taking Keir, he'd have never gone to that camp in the first place.

Kara kept her weapons low. She wasn't ready to start yet, in body or spirit. "Why a barkhide? Why test me against a man instead of a monster?"

Quinton snorted. "Any ranger or navigator can trade blows with an orc or cut through a line o' goblins. Killin' monsters is the simplest part o' the work. The harder quest is fightin' a man who's tryin' ta kill ya an' still rescue 'im in the end." He lifted his chin. "Sword up. Let's go."

He came at her with axes twirling. She parried the first blow, once more reciting the first verse of the Great Rescue. "*Mi Rumosh kesavol ne avahend, mod benod aroshkef gevend, lut vykef alermod credam sedrengiond dar beath elam cresiond.*"

For the High One loved us so much . . .

As she finished, she caught one blade with her cross guard and used a turning step Silvana had taught her to yank the axe free. It clattered to the floor out of Quinton's reach.

Love. Kara forced the word to the front of her mind.

"The High One loves you so much he sent his son, the Rescuer, to die for you."

"Yer Maker doesn' love me." Quinton committed both hands to his last axe and banged her next strike away. The blow sent pain through her arms. "Look at me. Look at this burned an' corrupted flesh. Am I not evil in his sight an' yours? Admit it. Ya see me as an abomination."

She did. He was. Was she supposed to lie?

No. Master Jairun had taught her never to lie if she wanted to lead an Aladoth to the truth.

"He's your Maker too, not just mine." Kara sliced Barkhide Quinton's arm with her padded dagger, making him drop one hand away. "And you're right. Twisting yourself away from what he made you to be is an abomination. The Scrolls say so. The Scrolls are truth. But you're not alone. None of us are good enough."

She stood back, circling into the arm she'd cut, and offered the No One is Perfect verse to the High One. Then she tried to explain it while parrying the one-armed swings of his axe. "We're all corrupted–have been ever since the traitor-kings betrayed the Maker in favor of the dragons' sorcery. Yet we're all precious. All loved. That's why the Rescuer came and died. To restore us."

Kara gained the advantage over his awkward rhythm and took the offensive. Eyes flaring, she rained down blow after blow as if to chop his axe handle away. "Love! Can't you see? That's . . . why . . . I'm . . . fighting you!" Her blade smacked Quinton's fingers.

Real pain contorted his face. He dropped the axe. "Enough! Stand down!"

Kara blinked. Her sword and dagger tips were inches from his neck. With a short thrust, she'd have delivered a killing blow–a dangerous strike even with the training weapons. But would she have finished the move if Quinton hadn't stopped her?

The swordmaster walked away to recover his axes, scratching his chin.

Propriety kept her from asking the question burning through her mind. Had she failed?

When Quinton picked up his second axe, a black-and-white marbled ring hung from the upturned point of the blade–telesite, a lightraider stone cut from the rocks around Ras Telesar in the early days of the academy. Kara lifted her gaze from the ring to her teacher.

Quinton sighed. "I must keep this fer now, lass. Yer knowledge o' the Scrolls an' yer skills in combat have come far. But you've a lot ta learn. Don' fret. You can fail this quest an' one other an' still have a chance ta try both again before the Turning of the Spheres."

Kara nodded, fighting back her tears, as Quinton put the ring away.

"If ya ever hope ta lead a real barkhide ta the High One's forgiveness, lass, you'll have ta learn to forgive him first."

THE PRISONER
TANELETHAR

THE COOL WATER AT THE SAFE HAVEN RESTORES ME during yet another escape attempt. The drink from the sculpture's flaming hand gives me hope. I delight in it, too long for sure, but why not? This is all I have.

A cloud passes over the two bright moons, dimming the fog around the platform, and I'm reminded this respite is fleeting. To tarry longer is futile. Death and horror surround this place, waiting for me. I may as well rush into their arms.

I take a different course from the haven. No sense in running into the wraith again. I know now that the ghoul steered me to it last time. Even though I tried to turn the thing away, it pushed me from behind, led me from the front. I resolved never to let that happen again, and I took steps to make certain it won't.

I set my course by the place I last saw the moons. Shan says they travel in the south, even if you watch them from the far south of the land. He told me he knows this because he trained on ships in a harbor town. A family of fisherman. It sounds nice. When I asked him if he remembers what dragged him away from such a paradise, he told me he does, but he said no more.

Moving east, I feel the terrain rising. The higher I climb, the drier the ground and the thinner the underbrush. This feels like progress, but is it? Am I moving closer to the wall that hems us in or farther from it?

A creeper crawls out on a branch before me. I pause only for a beat as its wings begin to vibrate. This is a good test. I hear nothing. No droning buzz. No voices. Success.

Before leaving the barracks, I tore small bits of wool from my moth-eaten blanket and dipped them in lantern oil. These I stuffed into my ears like corks in water jugs. They work, blocking the drone of the creepers–the song sorcery, as Shan calls it–and keeping their voices out of my head. I see no reason these wool corks won't work the same with the ghouls.

I needn't wait long to find out. The ground levels, and I see a wispy hand before my eyes. An old woman floats in front of me, disjointed jaw flapping. I hear nothing.

She's not alone. Another ghoul appears, a little boy, then a man and woman who hover about him like parents. And they keep coming, one after the other, until a small army floats at my front. But with the fog failing, they are harder to see than usual. I can't make out much more than their pale faces.

I cannot hear them, but I fear their icy hands. I slow my pace, and instantly they close in.

No.

I won't be stopped this way. I won't let them. Her face, her laugh appear in my mind, and draw both anger and hope from the vision. She is the good I failed to protect. But if I keep seeing her, she may yet live. I hold the vision fast as a shield against the ghouls.

"You have no power over me. Do you hear?" I spin in a circle, swinging my blunt sword, and feel a wind rising. "Your time is past. You cannot bar the living from their own!"

They're gone.

The fog has blown away and taken the ghouls with it. My path is open.

But what path? Evil ghouls. They turned me about. For a moment, I'm frantic, looking this way and that in the shadowed trees.

The shadows. The moons have gone behind the high clouds, but the trees still tell me their position. I read the long shadows of the pines and find east.

My steps grow harder. The terrain rises fast. I'm climbing now, clawing the mud and grabbing bent trunks until the trees part and I step out onto an open hill.

The weight of this place hits me like one of Shan's punches. A flat disc of black pyranium dominates the hilltop. Two pyranium columns crowned with upturned dragon's feet, talons curling inward, stand at the disc's northern extent. The height of them makes me feel no bigger than the creepers. An open diamond joins the two columns like an empty window.

That disc platform is clearly not meant for humans. I dare not stand on it or linger here.

As I back toward the trees, the moons emerge, illuminating the landscape all around this hill. Despite my fear, I pause to look.

The sight destroys me.

The camp lies below to the southwest. The barracks roofs peak above the drifting fog, tiny mountains drowned in a gray-green sea. The orange lanterns of the wanderers move within the haze on their forever patrols. This alone is not what slays my hope. If I only saw one camp, I think joy might fill my heart. But there are many camps. Dozens.

The camp scene repeats itself to the east and west, over and over in a broad ring. The stone wall I found does not lead to freedom. It leads to the circle's center—the heart of this dark forest. If I am to escape, I must find a new path south, in the opposite direction.

I must start the slow progression of death, night after night, all over.

Letting my gaze settle on the center of the forest longer than I should, I see towers jutting above the pines. No. Not towers. Spires—four black spires, beset with pulleys and chains, surrounding a great dome formed of many plated sections. I can make out the top of a black pyramid fortress beneath.

The dome and spires are a dragon gate. How do I know that term?

"A dragon gate." Saying it aloud sparks a memory. I hear a voice like my own, but not quite mine. Is it the voice of a brehna?

When you find what the goblins are building, look for the foundations of four pyranium spires. Look for cogs and chains.

Yes. Obviously, I hear myself reply. *I know the signs of a dragon gate.*

My soul tells me I'm remembering the night I began the course that led me here. So that was my sin for which I must suffer. Pride.

A groan and a clanking of metal breaks the night. The four spires quake. The two halves of the plated dome split and sink back upon themselves. On my hilltop, sparks burst from the upturned dragon talons. Red flames light the pyranium platform. I've stayed far too long. The ghouls would be a comfort compared to this. I flee into the trees.

VALSHADOX

LORD VALSHADOX STILLED HIS BLOOD-TIPPED WINGS and glided down to the window. He stilled his thoughts as well. Through the disc, Heleyor could see all–know all. In the past, those unable to control or conceal their own complaints and designs had suffered greatly.

The diamond-shaped conduit opened the moment Valshadox's talons touched the pyranium. Through it, he saw Ras Pyras. The unending flame blazed at the center of Heleyor's throne room, a pillar of living, flowing fire. Pyranium orcs stood guard around it, the only non-dragon creatures able to withstand its heat.

"Speak. I am listening." Heleyor's voice shook the firedrake's mind. Ruby scales and six red eyes appeared amid the flame.

"The culling has begun, sire. We are breaking predator from prey, and the numbers are as I predicted. Mankind has not changed in a thousand years."

"Mankind never changes, not since I changed them. That is our assurance of victory–that and the *shaadsuth*."

Using curled forks, the pyranium orcs drew a hexagonal chest from the fire, larger than the four of them together and glowing orange. The metal cooled to black as the four set it on a cart and rolled it away.

Heleyor's eyes flashed in the fire. "This is the first shaadsuth in more than two generations of men. I will not let it be wasted. Tell me the horde you've built for it will be ready."

What other answer could Valshadox give? "It will be ready, sire."

"I'll take you at your word. Make it so or suffer the consequences."

Valshadox bowed his head, then launched himself into the sky. The conduit dimmed to empty, and he no longer felt his master's presence.

Make it so or suffer the consequences.

He had witnessed the price of failure time and again. Such would not be his fate.

A scent reached his nostrils, interrupting the thought–a salty tang buried under the must and damp of the forest. Familiar. Distant.

With slow beats of his wings, the dragon hovered, eyes searching, unhindered by fog or shadow. Whatever had caused the scent had moved on.

13

KARA
KELEDEV
BELOW THE CLEFTS OF SEMAJIN

THE GENTLE SPRINGS OF THE CHAPEL NEVETHAV.

The scent of brambleberry cider simmering at the hearth.

The old straw mattress in the chambers she shared with Teegan and four other cadets and initiates.

Kara kept these things before her as she pushed through the driving snow, hoping they might add warmth to her cloak and boots. She wondered if she'd ever experience any of them ever again. Of all the quests she had to face before she could pass into the spheres, who knew she'd fail the Vanguard Quest. And who knew the Quest of the Comforter would be the one to kill her?

Headmaster Jairun himself had woken her that morning long before sunrise, giving her less than a watch of sleep after her failure with Quinton. "The work of the comforters often begins at the height of exhaustion," he'd told her over a quick breakfast of pork-oat pastries. "Our ministry follows close upon the hardest battles. But that is not the reason for my timing. I'm sending you into this quest now because, at this moment, someone needs your help."

He'd given her no more hints than that, other than to tell her to dress in her warmest kit and steel her mind and body for the coming pain. At this, she almost laughed. "What pain could there be in the Comforter's Quest, sir? Is yours not the sphere of renewers, clerics, and bards?"

The headmaster had answered her with a look of heartbreaking pity. "Time is short, child. Meet me in the lower ward in half a tick."

Horses had brought them north and east, higher—always higher—on the Celestial Peaks. In a full day's ride, they'd passed the Eastern Vale of the Passage Lakes and kept on climbing to within a league of the Clefts of Semajin. By then, ice had begun to cake on her wool mask and her gelding's flanks. Her fingers had stiffened to the point she couldn't hold the reins.

And then Master Jairun had left her.

In the pitch black and piercing gales, the headmaster had ordered her off her horse, turned both mounts around, and ridden away.

But Kara was not alone, or so he'd said. "Find your charge high in the clefts. Find the one who needs your help. Do what you can. Apply the proper herbs and care, and then you may return to the academy."

Beneath the glove on her right hand, Kara felt the rangers ringlet on a cold and shriveled finger. Would she stack another with it before tomorrow? Not if the whole finger fell off from frostbite. She put the image away, in her mind, wrapping her hand around a hot mug of brambleberry cider instead, then raised her cloak against the wind to carry on.

In a rare quiet between gales, the blowing snow settled, and the clefts appeared. The fissure in the mountainside looked narrow because of its great height, but Kara knew from the guardians' stories that its base was wider than the whole of the academy. Somewhere in the dark network of clefts and caves inside, the snowflowers grew, pale blue and delicate as snowflakes—a medicinal gift from the Rescuer as powerful as the citrus fruits in the western deserts of Tanelethar. But the snowflowers were not her quest. She was to find her patient and render aid. The headmaster had been clear on that one point and little else.

"Who in their right mind would be up here?" she asked the

rocks. “Who am I supposed to help?”

Even as she spoke, she saw a figure on an outcropping ahead.

“Hello? You there! Are you seeking aid?”

No answer. A snowy gust flashed across her vision, and the figure was gone.

“Perhaps the lack of air is making me see ghosts.”

Kara decided against this. If she still recognized the danger of the thin air, she must still have her faculties. And if the figure was no illusion, he or she must be her patient. She abandoned the trail and struck out across the icy rocks. “Can you hear me? Come back!”

The outcropping proved well out of reach atop a near vertical wall. Feeling her way along its base, Kara found a new trail—steep and slick but passable.

“I’m here to help!” Frozen lips muddled her words, and the wind, blowing harder at the top of the outcropping, muted the call. Still, she tried. “Please don’t flee. I can bind your wounds.” Kara opened her cloak for just a beat to show the pouches of the renewer’s manykit she wore, filled with all manner of bandages and balms. A mistake. The wind saw its chance and blew in, and she snapped the cloak closed again, shaking. “P-p-please show yourself.”

The snow lightened. She saw a miniature version of the huge cleft before her—a cave of sorts. From within, came a growling white wolf.

PART TWO

CASUALTIES

"Even when I go through the darkest valley, I fear no danger, for you are with me; your rod and your staff–they comfort me."

Psalm 23:4

14

TIRAN
KELEDEV
EAST OF THE WINDHOLD

TIRAN PULLED THE ORNAMENT HE'D MADE FOR HIS tehpa from his saddlebag for the twentieth time since they'd left Ras Telesar two days earlier. He ran his fingers over the seams where the brass inlays met the steel. Perfectly smooth. A good job by even Master Belen's standards. The woman he'd sculpted from the two metals looked down with unconditional love on swaddled twins in her arms. He hoped he'd gotten the details of her face right. That portion of memory had lost its sharpness long ago.

"Quit fretting," Teegan said, reining her horse back to ride beside him. "He's going to love it."

"Will he? Or will he wonder why I've turned to making trinkets?" Tiran put the gift away and out of habit dabbed at the cut on his forehead with a well-used rag. "What if he asks what happened to the brave sehna who left his house to join the Vanguard of the Lightraider Order?"

"You may yet join the Vanguard, Tiran. Or the rangers. You performed flawlessly in your quests." She bent her head toward him and smiled, lowering her voice as if someone might hear. "Better than Connor. Far better than Lee and Dag. In fact, dear Brehna, if I were choosing, I'd place you among the navigators—destined to lead raid teams one day."

"Then it's well you are not choosing, for the Helper who works within us knows better." He stuffed the rag away and fixed his eyes on the trail. "I'll never enter the Dragon Lands again. My place is at the academy, as a cleric in the Comforters' Sphere, praying with the injured who return from the north and teaching the Scrolls to initiates."

His shessa gave him a look that said, *We'll see*, mimicked by the falcon on her arm. "Put it out of your mind for now, and think of supper. I can smell the sweet tarts baking at the Apple Barrel from here. I hope we reach the Windhold Outpost in time for–"

Aethia shot away, interrupting her with a shrill cry.

Tiran gasped and clutched his head. His wound burned like fire, worse than the night he'd earned it. "Arms, Teegan," he said through gritted teeth. "Draw your trident!"

The memory of the terrible night when the goblins had attacked them at Red Willow Hill–what the cackling creatures had done to the horses–spurred him to drive his gelding into the cover of the brush.

Teegan followed, drawing her trident as he'd commanded–a white ironwood shaft wrapped in a double spiral of steel that ended in three barbed tines. "What did you see?"

"It's not what I saw, but what I felt." He searched the trees, but the darkness yielded little. "It's what I sensed. Something is here–something evil."

Their training took over. Tiran placed his hand upon his shessa's, and the two prayed as one. *"Qezid, kastregah vi Rumosh po ravstregmod."*

Be strengthened by his great might.

Teegan's armor glowed sea green, and Tiran noticed the matching tint of his own. He hadn't seen it in a long time–hadn't expected to need it ever again.

Aethia let out another cry to their east, away from the passage.

The brush and vines here were too thick for the horses. Tiran leapt down and pressed through, sword and dagger drawn.

"Tiran, wait!" His shessa dismounted and followed.

He cut his way through the brush until stopping at a clearing for a breather. "Where is it?"

"Where is what, Tiran? You don't know what you're looking for." Teegan put her back to his. "Or do you?"

"No. But I know it isn't good."

Above them, Aethia wheeled in slow, widening circles. Her cries had become short and soft.

"What does she say, Shessa?"

"She's confused. She's telling me a threat is out here, but whether a bear or a granog, I can't tell. And those chirps mean she's lost it."

Aethia's falcon eyes could pick a green lizard from an oak branch in the heart of spring. How had she lost this foe?

The pain in Tiran's head subsided, replaced by a soothing chill as distinct as a mint salve. He'd never felt anything like it. "Whatever she saw," he said, "it's gone."

"How can you be sure?"

"Trust me."

Teegan sheathed her trident, but she did not return to the horses. "We're missing something. There is more here to see."

"You're right." Tiran called to the Rescuer for aid in finding some hint of what had caused his pain to flare. "*Mo pednesh Logosovu pyrlas, po mo vynesh e'las.*"

Your word is a lamp. For my way, the light.

A twig snapped. The Rescuer's illumination didn't always take the form of a light. Hurrying toward the sound, Tiran saw a possum race away into the shadows, and then he saw what had drawn the little vermin there in the first place. He groaned, and hearing Teegan behind him, pressed out a palm to stop her. "Come no closer, Shessa. I don't want you to see this."

15

KARA
NEAR THE CLEFTS OF SEMAJIN

KARA'S HAND MOVED TO HER DAGGER, AND THE wolf bared its teeth. "Sorry," she said. "So sorry to disturb you. I thought you were someone else. You know how it is. Hard to see up here. Blowing snow and all."

The wolf advanced a step, and Kara retreated in kind. "You weren't fleeing, I see. You were watching. Hunting? I don't suppose you get a whole lot of warm meat up here. I stopped being warm meat a while ago–probably not worth your time." She retreated another step. The dagger came another inch out of its sheath. The wolf snarled and advanced again.

Did she stand a chance against this animal in her current state, wielding that small blade? Or should she seek a different path?

"Right." Kara pushed the dagger into place and moved her hand away. "Tell you what, if you'll allow me to leave, I promise not to disturb you again."

The wolf studied her, and in the relative quiet, Kara heard a soft yelping. Pups?

"Are you a mehma?" Perhaps she'd been wrong. The wolf was, indeed, afraid rather than hunting. The fear of a threat against her pups had drawn her from her den.

Kara widened her vision beyond the immediate danger. She

saw pawprints in the snow, little pawprints and pink flecks of frozen blood.

"One of your pups is hurt."

The wolf stared back at her, as if close to understanding. Close. But would the guardians send a cadet up this mountainside to face a wolf pack alone? Kara risked a glance at the larger cleft, her original goal. It loomed much nearer now than before. If this wolf let her go, she might continue on to finish the quest before she froze to death.

The yelping came again from within the smaller cleft. Mehma Wolf glanced over her shoulder.

Kara could not leave the wounded pup to die. She'd treat the animal as fast as possible, then move on and hope she survived long enough to reach her real patient.

"I can't believe I'm doing this."

She removed a glove, exposing her skin to the cold, and held out a hand. "Easy, Mehma Wolf. Easy now. I only want to help."

The wolf allowed her to approach, backing away one slow step at a time, until Kara found herself within the cleft. The change surprised her. Without the wind, the cold lost its bite, and she had no trouble striking a flame to her small traveler's lantern.

Yellow light fell on a brood of pups, huddled together in a bed made of pine needles and the dried stalks of some plant Kara did not recognize. She bent near them with the lantern.

Mehma Wolf barked.

"Sorry. I meant no offense. I promise I won't hurt them."

Her next moves were slower—painfully so. The light revealed her patient. A strange chill, so different from the wind outside, passed through her. "Oh, no."

A cut ran from the pup's shoulder to his hip, red and black and festering with pus. His little body heaved with rapid, shallow breaths. Had she promised his mehma more than she could deliver?

She had to try.

"Clean, soothe, bind," Kara said aloud, remembering Master

Jairun's training. Lee, too, had taught her much between classes. For instance, he'd taught her to add butter balm to her vinegar before cleaning a wound to ease the sting. This, she did, but the pup still yelped. An instant later she felt hot breath at her cheek.

"It's all right," she said without daring to turn. "I know you don't understand me, but I really am helping."

I hope.

Once she'd wiped away the dried blood and the pus, Kara saw the true extent of her task. Infection had set in deep. But what kind?

Lacy patches of white appeared in several places along the cut. "Lace means lichen," Kara said, reciting another phrase Master Jairun had taught the cadets. "And the remedy for most lichens in the cold places of Talania is . . ." She knew the answer, not that knowing it helped much. She dropped her head, then looked toward the howling cold outside the cleft. "I need snowflower petals."

Kara turned to Mehma Wolf, uttering a silent prayer for help in making herself understood. "I have to leave. I'm not abandoning him, or you. But I must go find the right medicine."

Whether through the softness of her voice or the intervention of the High One, Mehma Wolf seemed to take her meaning. The wolf lowered her muzzle and made room for Kara to stand. But when Kara started to walk toward the moonlight and the gales of snow outside, she leapt ahead to bar her path.

"I thought you understood. I have to go. It's the only way I can help him." Kara tried walking around her, but Mehma Wolf blocked the way again. She barked, ears forward, looking past Kara to the unseen depths of the den.

"That way? You want me to go deeper in?"

Mehma Wolf licked her lips. Kara wasn't quite sure how to interpret that but decided to trust the instincts the Helper had given her. "All right. But I don't know the way. You'll have to lead."

The wolf obliged, leading her away from the pups, which Kara thought must run against all the power of her nature. She thanked the Rescuer for his help and followed.

At first, Kara's lantern offered the only light as they climbed and crawled through the tunnels and cracks. But, after a long while, hints of glowing silver colored the rocks ahead. When the passage widened, those hints formed into rays of moonlight falling through openings above. The ground leveled, dusted with snow, and the wolf jogged ahead into a grand cavern.

Snowflakes wafted down through the moonlight shafts until they touched the frozen rock, only to be swept up into eddies and swirls by a wind blowing through a natural portico at the cavern's front. The wolf had brought Kara to a high, open cathedral in the Clefts of Semajin—a cathedral of the Rescuer's making, carpeted with frost-blue snowflowers.

"You found what your pup needs. Well done!"

Mehma Wolf set her nose to the ground and pressed forward to the field of flowers. *No time for praise,* she seemed to say. *Help my sehna. Save him.*

Kara needed no other prompting. She hurried to the flowers, but the petals of the first she touched disintegrated. "Right. Delicate as snowflakes. How am I to carry them down through the cave?"

Mehma Wolf seemed to answer with an insistent whine. *Find a way.*

What way? She stretched out a hand toward several flowers growing in a bunch, hoping a few might survive, but her fingers never reached their stalks. A creature of the same pale blue as the flower petals swept down from cavern wall and forced her back with a blast of cold. A line of icicles sprung from the floor between her and the little bunch.

Mehma Wolf barked, but not at the intruder. She barked at Kara. The wolf lowered her muzzle and lifted her gaze toward the creature, now circling on wings tipped with white fur so fine it might be feathers. A long tail with the same fur flowed behind it. From her ranger training, Kara knew the wolf's posture to be deference. The wolf saw this creature as her superior, but not as a threat.

One aspect of the creature seemed familiar. The eyes. Kara saw Crumpet in them—her mischievous friend from the Forest of Believing. Could this be a cousin? "I am a friend to your kin, who I'm sure pictures your wings when he tries to fly. He is not as graceful as you, but he is a help to me, or tries to be. Will you help me as well?"

The creature landed on a ledge and cocked its head, regarding her with a keen, admonishing stare.

Kara bowed her shoulders. "I'm sorry I destroyed one of your flowers. I didn't mean to. I need them to bring healing to this wolf's cub. Won't you give us your aid?"

She doubted the creature understood, until it launched itself once more from the ledge. It flew to another bunch of flowers a few paces away—larger, with thicker stalks. A blast of its cold breath froze the snow at their bases, and then it spread its wings wide and soared out through the portico to ride the high gales.

Kara hurried to the bunch, taking care not to disturb any other flowers. Using her dagger, she pried up the ice block. It came free with ease, a crystalline base for a bouquet of ten. She nodded to the wolf. "I'm ready. Lead on."

They made good time on the return, downhill all the way, slowing only for the cramped and narrow bits, where Kara lost only one of the flowers. She spoke the first of the renewer's prayers as they neared the pups. "*Kefilom bi amun kefalavor dervi, po ke'Rumosh mod eleviond.*"

The prayer of faith will deliver the sick.

Hear my prayer, dear Rescuer. Make me your hands of healing.

She pressed the petals one by one into the full length of the pup's wound and let the heat of his body dissolve them. After that, she applied a balm of beeswax, honey, cinnamon, and clove.

"I can't wrap the cut with cloth," Kara said to Mehma Wolf. "I won't be back to remove it." She pulled a bound stack of parchment dressings from her manykit and let the mehma sniff them before pressing them to the cut. "I'll use these instead, and seal them in place with oak sap. The sap will guard him from infections, then harden and fall on its own as his hair grows and sheds. The parchment will keep it from opening the wound when he moves."

Once Kara finished spreading the sap, she took a breath to speak the second of the renewer's prayers, but as she did, a different verse came to mind. *"Mi koth qevola kesil aparateni, kemoqeva ala rasa aroshias."*

Every beast of the forest is yours. And on a thousand hills.

"And on the mountainside," Kara said, lifting her eyes. "Though this pup cannot speak like the Havarra, you know his name. You know the number of his days. If it is your will, take this offering of service and heal him."

The pup's mehma licked Kara's cheek, then whined and bowed her head.

"What is it? What's wrong?"

Another voice joined them, as rough as the mountain trail. "She is not distressed, daughter of winter. She is showing respect–to me." A second adult wolf, much larger than the other, stepped into the circle of light. His eyes shone golden under the lantern's flame. Kara let out a quiet laugh. "Pedrig. You're back."

"At the headmaster's call. Yes. I was your keeper for this quest. None of the guardians could have stayed with you this long."

His phrasing gave her pause, but Kara let it go for the moment and began packing her gear. "Have you come to guide me to the other patient? Or are you here to tell me I've delayed so long the patient has died and I've failed the quest?"

Mirthful rumbles shook the wolf's silver chest. "Daughter of winter, can't you see? There is no other patient." He pawed at the pine needles where the pups slept, then pulled a length of gray ribbon free with his teeth. A blue talanium ringlet hung from its end. He laid it at her feet. "The quest is over. You passed. I'm here to guide you home."

Shaking, Kara removed the ribbon and slipped the blue ringlet on her finger to stack it with the green one. Two quests completed. Three remained, assuming she could recover on her second attempt with Quinton and overcome her troubles in the smithy. Then, perhaps, Master Jairun would let her scout in Tanelethar with the others, and she'd learn more about Keir's fate.

Kara and Pedrig said their goodbyes to Mehma Wolf, each in their own way, and started down the mountain. Pedrig watched her walk, ears up, as if listening to her labored breathing. "The headmaster waits with horses a league above the Eastern Vale. Until then, you may ride on my back."

Kara could not deny the ache in her limbs. But she also remembered the portal battle in Tanelethar—how Pedrig, who had felt the jaws of a poacher's trap only days before, had leapt into the black storm with Faelin to fight the dragon. His honored, battle-worn legs did not deserve to carry her as a burden. "Thank you for your kindness, but I'll be fine."

"Mmm. I thought as much."

She sensed more behind his answer than an acknowledgement of her respect, and this brought her back to what he'd said about the guardians earlier. "Pedrig?" She had to raise her voice above the whistling gale to be heard.

"Speak your question, daughter of winter."

"You said the guardians could not have stayed with me this long. If this quest posed such a danger to the highest echelon of lightraider knights, why would they place it upon the shoulders of a mere cadet?"

"They did so at my request."

Kara stopped to look at him. "Yours?"

The wolf padded on, ears back against the wind. "I heard the howl of the pup's mother from the woods above Ravencrest, where I've been lodging these past months. And on my way to investigate, I stopped at Ras Telesar and asked the guardians to make this your quest. You are one of the few left among men who can survive this cold and thin air long enough to apply a healer's touch."

One of the few. Kara caught up to him. Before she could ask, he answered.

"I sensed it in you when we first met, smelled it in your blood and breath. Do you not remember who you are?"

"I do." She'd thought of it, only for an instant, in the high cathedral. The swirls and eddies of snow looked so much like the flourishes of blue-gray freckles on her skin. The hint of blue in the snowflower petals, a near match to the hint of blue in her platinum hair—a blue she'd worked hard to keep hidden most of her life. Keledev. Tanelethar. In either land, the snow and frost were part of her. "I am queensblood."

"You are suited to the cold, daughter of winter, as suited to it as your royal ancestors, whose lineage traces back to the tundra of Arkelia at the top of the world. I have also noticed you have a connection to the High One's animal creations. That was how I knew you'd choose charity over violence when faced with a snarling wolf mother."

Kara took this in. Charity over violence. The line between the two choices had been thin. "And the pup. What caused the cut? I thought perhaps he'd taken a fall against a sharp rock, because of the lichen in the wound. Or did his tehpa reject him?"

The wind died for a beat, and Kara heard another rumble from Pedrig's chest. This time, there was no mirth. "The pup's sire is dead. I heard it in the mother's howl. And the lichen in the wound is not of this mountain."

"Then where did it come from?"

"That is a question we must answer as soon as we can."

16

CONNOR
SOUL'S JOURNEY CANYON

CONNOR WOKE TO THE FEELING OF LEE SHAKING HIS arm. He rubbed his eyes, then pushed up on an elbow, throwing his cloak, which he'd used as a blanket, aside. "Is it my turn at the tiller?"

"No." Lee returned to the rear of the skiff. "I'll guide us into the city. Stay at the bow. I want you to see this."

"The city?"

Gray light dawned at the eastern rim of the river canyon. They had traveled day and night for four days, despite the dangers of navigating the Anamturas in the dark. If by *the city,* Lee meant Sky Harbor, that effort, combined with the hard ride from Ras Telesar to Pleasanton, had cut a twelve-day journey down to six.

Connor leaned out to snuff the bow lantern with a breath, but his lips never made it that far. His eyes drifted upward, jaw hanging open. A fireglass tower guarded the river, supported by a high wall built into the stepped eastern side of the canyon. This was no small post like the towers at Watchman's Gate. Banded with gleaming steel, it rose twenty stories at least above the white applethorn scrub lining the canyon top. Connor was tempted to see it as the handiwork of the Aropha, like much of Ras Telesar, but the stone blocks met the landscape in harder fashion–less fluid. This tower bore the mark of men.

"Steel bands or not," he said, "how does it not collapse under its own weight? Especially with that giant fireglass at its crown?"

Lee worked the tiller to ease them toward the gap between the manmade wall and the sheer natural cliff on the west side of the river canyon. "The stone masons, the glass blowers, the wrights and finishers–all the guilds and their best craftsman live in Sky Harbor. This is the work of their forbearers. We call it the Sentinel, and it is only the beginning. Wait until you see the Second Hall."

The Sentinel was, as Lee said, the beginning–the northern gateway to Keledev's capital. The early Twiceborn Assembly had chosen to build their mightiest city here, on the southern shore of the great peninsula, as far from the mountain barrier and Tanelethar as possible, rather than the center of the land. Connor had occasionally heard the clergymen in Stonyvale debating the wisdom of this choice when they thought younger ears weren't listening. Did it show shrewdness or a lack of faith?

Not far beyond the gateway, houses and shops lined the arched roads carved into the canyon walls. And when the canyon broke and the river widened, the houses continued, stacked one upon the other on stilted platforms and on stepped terraces stretching back into Sky Harbor's steep mountain foothills. Ahead, far downriver, the huge blue dome of the Second Hall shone in the new sun above the harbor's many-colored rooftops.

Lee nodded toward the morning traffic of merchants and laborers heading into the city. "See the high and low roads? The stone walkways atop the arches carry foot traffic, making room for wagons and beasts of burden on the wider gravel below. Nearly all roads in the city are built this way. Some see them as the symbols of our capital."

"So many people," Connor said, listening to the murmur overpowering the river's rush–a thousand voices and a hundred wagon wheels all groaning together. Groaning, at least, to his ear. "I could never live here. Mehma either. And I think such a crowd would render Barnabas speechless."

"Barnabas is a parcelman. He travels."

"Within the vales and the Central Plain. Val Pera is the largest and southernmost town on his route. Here, he'd be speechless, I tell you. And dizzy from all the noise and people."

Connor felt a little dizzy himself. He scanned the endless rows of arched walkways and houses. "Where, in this roiling sea of timber, wattle, and painted tile, is our inn?"

"We've been assigned a house, actually. The Assembly keeps several for its guests." Lee pointed east and almost skyward toward the outer rim of foothills. "Ours is there, with the red roof, on that hill face." He lowered a lens of his new spectacles—a less bulky version of the original set Master Belen had made him—making one eye larger than the other. "Lovely. I'd say it has a commanding view of the city."

"I'd say it sits as far from the Second Hall as possible, exactly where the councilors want us."

Far as the house was from the river, Connor had no trouble distinguishing the crimson roof from those around it, most painted in blues and greens. Perhaps all the Assembly's properties were colored red, like Stradok's robes, to make them easy for visitors to identify. Or to stake the Assembly's claim.

A bright flash from an upper window made Connor blink. He glanced at Lee. "Did you see that?"

"See what?"

"A signal from the guest house. A flash."

"It's morning, Connor. In a city with ten thousand windows, dawn flashes are common." He laughed and turned the boat toward an approaching dock. "Set your lightraider senses aside for a time and enjoy the day."

Connor did not know if such a thing were even possible for him. He pointed downriver. "Keep us straight. Take us farther on toward the lower docks."

"You don't want to go to the house? Clean the dust from our

clothes before we present ourselves to the host of delegates in the Second Hall?"

"We were summoned"–he shrugged a shoulder–"in a manner of speaking. But we are certainly not petitioners. The delegates can take us as we are, and if our conversation is quick, we can be back on the river by nightfall."

Lee frowned. "You know the road north is harder and longer, right? We'll have to ride the passes to Val Pera and take the horse canals from there. Don't you want a night in a nice warm bed? Perhaps a hot meal or, dare I say, two?"

"I'll get you a bowl of soup. Two, if you wish. And I'll lead your horse while you eat them. I don't want to be away from Ras Telesar any more than necessary."

"Away from Ras Telesar, or Kara?"

This again. Hadn't Connor already explained? "I won't deny I wish to give her all the support I can for her quests. But I told you in Pleasanton, I want to get back because I don't like what we saw in Tanelethar. You should feel the same."

The words came out harsher than he'd intended, but Connor made no apology.

Lee steered the boat back to the center of the river, grumbling about the fleeting nature of goose-down mattresses and casting a longing look at a rotisseur turning a spindle of hot meats near the docks. He sniffed the air and sighed before settling back against the stern. "I'm as concerned as you about events north of the barrier. Every tick and watch of every day and night on this river I've wondered what they mean. But I also have faith in Master Jairun's ability to discern the Rescuer's will."

"And you believe the Rescuer wills that we should indulge in hot meals and goose down?"

"I believe the Rescuer wants us here, in Sky Harbor. His reason shall be revealed at precisely the time he wishes. Not before."

"I hope that time is soon," Connor said, setting his gaze on the Second Hall's dome. "Very soon."

17

HOT MEALS AND GOOSE DOWN SEEMED A LIKELY future by midday–much more likely than the road Connor had hoped for.

He paced up and down the passage leading to the Petitioner's Door of the Second Hall's main chamber, known as the Sky Chamber. The wooden door, with its iron bolts and unadorned arch, looked like a child's entrance in comparison to the grand entrance he'd expected to use.

He and Lee had gone to the grand entrance first, with Lee boasting as they climbed the steps that the doors of the Sky Chamber were three stories tall and solid bronze. Lee had also told Connor they'd find the doors open, as they always were, even when the delegates were in session. This had not been the case. They'd found the doors closed and guarded.

Connor had demanded the guards let them in, to no avail.

"All petitioners must wait at the Petitioner's Door."

He'd matched the guard's stern look. "We're not petitioners."

Lee had tried to turn Connor around with a tug and a whispered warning, but Connor had held his ground. "The Prime Council requested a firsthand account of the troubles north of the barrier. So here we are. We were summoned. I may have been raised in the vales, but I know the traditions of propriety. In Keledev, *in all of Keledev,* one who is invited is given the honor of entering by the front gate."

Not one muscle in the guards' stolid faces had moved. "Petitioner's Door," the older of the two said. "No exceptions."

Other words were spoken—or grumbled—on both sides, but Lee had succeeded in steering Connor away. So here they were, at the Petitioner's Door. Still waiting.

Lee stopped Connor's pacing with an outstretched arm. "You're making me ill."

"Lack of breakfast is making you ill."

"That too, along with the anticipation of missing the midday meal. Face it. Master Jairun refused to send Kara, and now you and I must suffer retaliation for the slight. The headmaster holds power at the academy, but Stradok and his masters hold it here. At some point, we must give in."

"And do what? Come back tomorrow? What if they refuse us?"

"Then we keep coming back until they've made their point. In the meantime, we enjoy the comforts of the city. When, if ever, will we have this chance again?"

Connor backed up to lean against the other side of the passage. "You wanted this."

"Yes, I did. Was I unclear before? You act as if every moment we spend here is torture. How do you think that makes me feel? Have you forgotten this was my home for more than four years?"

How could he forget? Lee hadn't stopped reminding him, offering snippets of the city's history at every turn. *This foundation stone was laid by So-and-So the Humble, a lesser-known companion of the Rescuer* or *Did you know the Sky Chamber and the base of its central dome are perfectly round? Perfectly! To the breadth of a snow fox's hair.*

Connor had stopped him before he'd explained why, specifically, the builders had used the hair of a snow fox to check their work. But had he been right to stop his friend in that moment? Why shouldn't Lee be excited to show him a place that had been such a big part of his life, not to mention part of a great achievement? To earn a place as a scribe of the Assembly was no small feat.

"All right."

Lee raised the lens through which he'd been inspecting the masonwork. "All right, what?"

"All right. I give in. They're not letting us in today. Show me your city."

Lee took him to the harbor, where seawater lapped at the steps of the Crescent Plaza in front of the Second Hall. "We're starting here instead of the high road," he said as they left the building, "because, of course, the Crescent Plaza offers the best view of the Assembly's home."

Connor nodded and smiled, but he suspected Lee's choice had more to do with the plaza's many food stalls.

Lee proved him right. "We might as well stop for a bite while we're here, yes?"

"You're becoming like Dag."

"Dag was never starved for this long. I know this because he's never had to make a six-day journey south with you."

The two solved Lee's hunger with redfish from an open grill, followed by bread pudding filled with roasted applethorn berries and wrapped in a stiff crust, and watched the tall ships idling out in the harbor.

"Why don't they bring their cargo in one after the other throughout the day?" Connor asked between forkfuls of fish. "Wouldn't it be easier than trying to come in all at once?"

Lee directed his friend's gaze to the stone docks, four on each side of the harbor, curving inward. "See how the water sits low? The ships must wait for the evening's high slack tide, or their cargo planks won't sit true on the docks, not to mention the risk to the hulls of the larger vessels."

The scribe had not overstated things when he'd told the

Pleasanton dockmaster he knew his business on the water. He still spiked his hair with the red paste worn by most of the fishing families in Lin Kelan, the port to the northwest where he was born. He'd once explained to Connor that it kept the water from soaking their heads when diving for an anchor or a net.

Lee's eyes lingered on one of the larger ships, and he twisted a blue talanium ring about his finger, as he often did. They both still wore the five ringlets they'd earned during the quests and would continue to wear them until their sphere was chosen. But Lee had worn the thicker talanium ring as long as Connor had known him. Connor had asked about it once and learned from the sharp response that he should never do so again.

The scribe set his fork down beside his half-finished fish. "You know, I'm not as hungry as I thought. We should go. There's much to see, and I'd like to reach the house before dark."

They took the puddings with them, and Lee ate his quickly, despite his claim of not being hungry. Normally the more observant of the two, his focus on the pudding prevented him from catching a shadow that Connor insisted had followed them out of the plaza.

"You're making a paradragon into a dragon," the scribe said. "Like the flash you saw this morning." He nudged Connor toward a stair that would take them up to one of the city's high roads. "This is Keledev, not Tanelethar. There are no threats here. And there were hundreds of people in the plaza. Even if someone had followed us, how could you tell?"

"Call it a feeling." Connor glanced over his shoulder but did not see the drab green shirt of the person he'd spotted before. "She was watching us."

"She?"

"I think so. And now she's working hard to remain hidden."

"Or she's gone on her way like everyone else." Lee finished his pudding and licked his thumb. "Worry less about phantoms in the crowd and more that the Sky Chamber's grand entrance is closed. Rarely in our history has that happened."

"Rarely. But sometimes?" Connor followed him upslope on the raised path of cobblestones. Lee was not leading him north toward the house where they were to stay, but eastward, toward cliffs that hooked out into the Great Sea–one half of the harbor's crescent. "When in the past have they done so?"

"Early in our history. And near the days when the Order was disbanded. The Prime Council closes the bronze doors in days of fear."

After a time, the low road beneath them–the wide gravel path for horses and wagons–turned north, and the high road joined the rising terrain, becoming gravel itself. Strangely, the number of people sharing the road with Lee and Connor did not thin much. What special attraction on these cliffs should draw such a crowd?

Try as he might, Connor couldn't spot the woman he'd seen before. Or perhaps Lee was right, and she wasn't there at all. His time in Tanelethar had made him paranoid.

They reached the cliffs overlooking the harbor, and as they walked on with the masses, Lee took to staring at Connor, as if waiting for him to speak.

Connor squinted at him. "What?"

The scribe squinted back, then lifted his eyes.

Most of those around them stared upward as well. When Connor followed their gazes, he caught his breath. Tiny ships floated on the air high above him, tethered by ropes and held aloft by long, bulbous bags of glittering silk.

"What are they?"

"They call themselves the Airguard. Folks in the city are calling them stormwatchers. Zel Boreas, a friend from my scribe days–my first friend in Sky Harbor–sent a raven to tell me about them. She says the airships are actually quite large, but"–Lee dropped two of his lenses into place–"even with my sight, from down here they look like Celestus toys. They must be sailing as high as the clouds."

"Higher," Connor said, and then uttered the only other word he could manage. "How?"

"Young crafters from the silk spinners and the shipwrights joined together in the best work the guilds have seen in years–perhaps since the Sentinel. The materials are light but frail, and the risk of fire is great. One ship has crashed and burned already, killing two watchers."

"Yet the guilds let them continue."

"Thanks to a unity of purpose under the charisma of one man–an older apothecarist."

All the people looking upward kept bumping into each other. One jostled Lee. "Come on," he said. "Let's get away from the road and all these gawkers."

Connor chose not to bring up the fact that they, too, were gawkers and followed his friend into the applethorn scrub, where they found a clear patch to lie back and watch the skyborne curiosities. He didn't need to ask what necessity had driven the apothecarist and his guild followers to invent these *airships*, as Lee called them. "The same terror that closed the bronze doors of the Assembly drove the guilds to put watchers in the sky, didn't it? My goblin."

Lee flopped a thumbs-up into the blue sky filling Connor's vision. "Correct. The creature that attacked your parents' farm brought this fear, as did all the other dark creatures that appeared in Keledev before we closed the portal. Many think they came over or under the Celestial Peaks. The apothecarist claimed they might come through the Storm Mists, and he stoked enough dread and alarm among the guilds to bring the Airguard to life. He's been making small paper flying ships to entertain children at the Forge and Celestus fairs for years, powered by candles and his special vapors."

"And now," Connor held a hand above his head, encircling one of the ships with an open fist, "with guild support, he's made them large enough to carry and kill his acolytes. But why take to the sky? Why not build great towers like the Sentinel?"

"Towers are more costly. And the Mists lie twenty leagues

offshore. Even a tower as tall as the Sentinel, manned by watchmen with Master Belen's spyglasses, could not command a view that far out to sea. The horizon is too near."

This had not occurred to Connor. And he didn't quite understand the reason, but he trusted his friend on such things. "So what does your friend Zel think of them? Could you tell from her raven whether she views these airships as a matter of fear or good caution?"

Lee sat up and leaned into Connor's view. "I think her opinion on the matter is clear. She was among the first captains of the Airguard. The apothecarist is her father."

"Her tehpa? You mean this man lets his own–" Connor didn't finish the question. He had turned toward Lee, bringing the crowd at the road into his sight. "There she is!"

Before Lee could ask what he meant, Connor was up and running. He'd spotted the girl who followed them before. But when he reached the place where he'd seen her, she was gone.

Lee caught up to him, puffing. "Seeing shadows again? Now who's acting on fear?"

"I saw her. No doubt in my mind. Green shirt, drab, like the leaves on this applethorn scrub. With gray trousers. Does that describe the colors of any Sky Harbor guild?"

"No," Lee said, slowing the word. "But I'd say your shadow is a scribe, like I was."

"Why is that?"

He bent to pull an object from the grass by the road–a feather quill with a parchment impaled on its shaft. He showed it to Connor. "The script is written in the shorthand of my former profession."

"What does it say?"

"Not a lot. The first three lines are an archival address–a way of finding a text or scroll in the Assembly Archive below the Second Hall. But the last line is a message. 'Come at slack tide,' it says. 'Tell no one.'"

18

AARON
THOUSAND FALLS OUTPOST

BUILDING A BARRICADE IS NOT ENOUGH.

Defenses need maintaining. Ropes must be checked for wear, and nails for rust. Logs must be replaced when rot sets in or when the beavers and pine badgers get at them.

The watchmaster had shared this wisdom, as he'd called it, and much, much more when Aaron had asked why Thousand Falls had called for more recruits. He'd reminded the watchmaster that the barracks were already filled to bursting and the food stores were getting short.

We'll build more barracks, and those, too, will need maintaining, which will require even more men, the watchmaster had said, laying out what Aaron saw as a never-ending cycle of more structures and more defenders. And then, for the offense of his question, he and Sireth had been assigned to check the eastern run of the company's defenses–what the first recruits called the marsh run.

"Next time a wondering strikes you," Sireth said, trudging beside him up the valley wall east of the outpost, "ask me your question first. You'll get an answer without paying for it with a half-day's slog to the coldest and wettest half-league of the barricade." He shot him a sidelong glance. "And me with you."

Aaron lowered his head. "I'm sorry. Something about the

watchmaster makes me want to question his every decision."

"We can't all be Talin the Third or Avner Jairun, lad. The watchmaster is a good man, well-chosen for his post." Sireth slapped him lightly on the back. "Now raise that chin. I'm not mad–glad to be off the logging crew for a day, actually." He gestured uphill with his axe. "How about taking point?"

Aaron eyed the ridgetop where the morning crew worked at extending the western barricade. A full league of thick forest separated their end from the eastern works and the sopping cold marsh where he and Sireth were headed. No trails. Just trees and brush. He shook his head. "I'd probably lead us in circles. I'd rather follow you."

After a long and thorny march, the *squish, squish* of Aaron's steps and the cold seeping into his boots told him they were finally close, and when they cleared the trees, he saw the crisscrossed logs and mossy stone of the early barricade not far ahead.

Labor on the Thousand Falls leg had started in the deepest vale between their outpost and the Windhold–a flat expanse of reeds, willows, and biting flies. The watchmaster had wanted to build the farthest extent of his outpost's portion first so Windhold Company would have a place to connect their own barricade, even if Thousand Falls fell behind. And they *had* fallen behind, because building the first part of the barricade in a marsh took two full months.

"I can't fault the watchmaster for his choice." Sireth pushed against the first heavy log to check the fastness of its ropes. "Our company's hardest labor is done, thanks to him. The Windhold will likely have to build their half of the marsh run in winter."

Aaron tugged at his own leg, trying to pull his foot out of a deep hole filled with muck. "In winter, the ground will be frozen, so Windhold Company will walk here without fear of losing their boots." He waved a hand to fend off the flies around his face. "And they won't be eaten alive like us."

Sireth lent him an arm to help him find a firm footing, then gestured to one of the sharpened pairs of crossed logs spaced every ten paces along the run. “See how deeply these are buried? That is the proper way, especially in a marsh like this one. Windhold Company will have to fight frozen mud to set their cross posts. I do not envy them that battle.”

The two slogged along from post to post for some time, pressing their shoulders to the logs and stones to see if they might budge, checking ropes and nails. When Sireth found a rope that had come loose, he cut a new length and handed it to Aaron. “Time to do some real work, lad.”

The repair called for lying on the ground. Otherwise, Aaron could not work the rope into place as tightly as needed. He grumbled as he wiggled his way under the cross posts on his back, feeling the muck soak through his cloak. “Who ever heard of a marsh on a mountain any–”

A flash of white and gray whipped past the edge of his sight. A sharp pain pricked his arm. He tried to sit up and smashed his head on a log. “Sireth, help! Something’s here!”

In an instant, he was out from under the barrier, yanked free by his ankle. “What did you see?”

“Not much,” Aaron said, regaining his feet. “A bit of gray and white. I heard a snarling rasp.” He clutched his upper arm. “And it stabbed me.”

This earned him a worried look. The older watchman turned him by the shoulders and pushed Aaron’s muddy cloak aside to examine the spot. He frowned. “I see no wound or puncture mark. Are you certain?”

“I know what I felt.”

“Either way, you’re well enough to fight. Which direction did it go?”

“West. Toward the outpost.”

Running beside the barricade was no option. The marsh made sure of that. Instead, Aaron and Sireth tramped through the reeds, making what haste they could. “Shh,” Sireth said, holding up a fist. “Do you hear that?”

Something rustled and huffed under the barricade. Aaron had imagined a lot more fighters and weapons surrounding him when he met his first dark creature, not to mention firmer ground. “This is less than ideal.”

“Shh,” Sireth said again. “Right there.” The reeds on their side of the barricade quivered. “Get it!”

Sireth lunged, and Aaron followed, drawing his hunting knife, but the older man blocked his view. He heard a hiss and snarl, then a yelp from his friend.

“Back!” Sireth yelled, waving an arm covered in long white barbs. “Get back!”

Once his friend had moved out of the way, Aaron saw their quarry–a pine badger baring its fangs, with a wide ridge of white quills raised upon its back.

Sireth let out a pained laugh, picking barbs out of his arm. “There’s your dark creature, lad, and likely the reason for our loose rope. He’s been gnawing on it. Be grateful he only poked you. They can cover a man in a foul scent when they wish, one no amount of bathing can remove.”

The badger ceased its snarling and huffing and looked toward the edge of the marsh. For a moment, Aaron thought he might be about to experience the scent Sireth had spoken of, but the little saboteur scurried south through the reeds instead.

A rider emerged from the trees and waved. “Sireth Yar?”

“Yes!”

“Come quickly. A raven has come for you from your behlna, and I’m afraid the news is not good.”

THE PRISONER
TANELETHAR

SHAN IS GONE. THEY TOOK HIM, DRAGGED HIM INTO the stone hut.

I'm next.

We are lost.

Last night we ran a new course together. Shan said my discovery from the hilltop was a boon. Now we know which way to run.

I showed him each trick I'd learned–how to count the paces, how to watch for wanderers. I turned him away from a ghoul that rose from a broken well to claim him. I denied him her icy touch, her scream. We made it past a second fence south of the camps unscathed. Almost free.

Almost.

Barely ten paces into the pines beyond the outer fence, Shan tripped and fell. The forest saw its chance. Vines broke from the soil and wrapped his limbs. Spiders buried their pink fangs in his neck. Perhaps I should have left him. I couldn't.

I have died many deaths. In this one, I suffered the most. I watched terror widen those eyes I believed could never know fear. I heard a voice that always spoke with confidence pleading for mercy.

Apparitions know no mercy. The ghouls dove upon us both like starving dogs.

I woke in our old camp, watching iron orcs drag Shan's limp body into the stone hut. He's been in there a long time. I expect the orcs will emerge soon, without Shan, and haul me in there to share his fate. As Shan himself predicted, the one true death has finally come for us.

Orcs have been dragging prisoners into the hut one by one—ten or more in a day. Some return, often trembling and mumbling. None can speak of what they saw inside, even when they try. More than half are never seen again. Whatever this place is, whatever our purpose, they are culling the weak from the herd.

I am weak.

Shan was strong, but last night's death drained him. I don't think he can return from another. We are lost. Both of us.

As the truth of it burns through me, the door to the stone hut opens. The orcs emerge, and Shan is with them, walking on his own. They shove him down the steps, and he manages to keep his feet. I was wrong. Shan *is* strong, the strongest of us all. He will survive long after I'm gone.

He reaches me before the orcs do. I grasp his shoulders. "What happened in there? What did you see?"

Shan smiles—a weak smile, but confident, with no sign of the pleading terror that twisted his face last night. "I saw myself, Hosal. He showed me."

"Who showed you?"

"You'll meet him soon enough. He looked into my mind, opened shadowed reaches I didn't know existed. He saw my secret, and cared not—judged not. Instead, he reveled in it with me."

The orcs pull me away. I strain to look over my shoulder, toes dragging in the muck. "Shan! How did you survive?"

He gives me a reassuring nod. "Don't fight him, Hosal. You'll return. You'll see. And we'll survive together."

My mind is spinning. Death is coming. I am not strong like Shan. A hundred questions bounce around my head as the first of the stone steps hits my feet. I grasp the only question I can. "What was your secret, Shan? What did you tell him?"

"A secret I've tried to show you, my friend." Shan cocks his head and offers me a look of pity. "That I am not from this land."

The door slams closed behind me. Shan is gone. Darkness has me.

I am lost.

19

CONNOR
KELEDEV
SKY HARBOR

LEE SAID THE LATE SLACK TIDE WOULD COME DURING the first watch of evening, four ticks after they'd received the mystery woman's message. They spent the time getting settled in the house the Assembly had arranged for them.

Settled.

Connor disliked the word. He'd never intended to spend more than a few ticks in Sky Harbor. With the provisions in the house–cured ham in the cupboard, linens for bath and bed stacked in his wardrobes–the Prime Council seemed intent on keeping him and Lee for a month.

Clothes hung in the wardrobe as well. Connor felt the sleeve of a yellow silk tunic, then frowned and drew out a shirt of blue-dyed wool instead. He laid it out on the bed with a set of leather trousers before taking his turn at the bath. When they'd arrived, Lee had walked straight to the hearth to claim the first pail of hot water. Connor doubted he would have prevailed had he tried to intervene.

When the two passed each other in the passage outside their rooms, Connor saw Lee had chosen silk. The smoother fabric suited him, but he found the color scheme bracing. "Stripes?"

"Lines," Lee said, "on the uniform of my former life. It seems our hosts remembered. Two vertical lines on the upper portion, one blue and one amber, on a crimson field to represent the two texts of the Sacred Scrolls." He waved his hand over the lower half, a dizzying blend of silver, green, brown, and every other color Connor might think of. "The waving horizontal lines of the lower half represent the thousands of other texts the scribes have preserved."

"You thought this was the perfect mode of dress for this evening's encounter?"

"Of course." Lee looked Connor over with a frown, blinking because he had not yet donned his spectacles after his bath. "This is a secret meeting, Connor. At least one of us should blend in."

By the time the two began their walk to the harbor, the sun had sunk behind a southward branch of the White Ridge Mountains. The lamplighters moved through the lower city, dotting the roads and houses with lights. Looking east, Connor saw matching lights in the sky. They looked smaller than the lamp flames, yet he knew from what Lee had told him about the airships that they were much larger—an ever-present danger to the passengers. "What do they hope to see at night?" he asked, still gazing upward.

"They hope to see nothing. Zel says they pray through every tick and watch that they'll see nothing at all."

A good answer.

The failing daylight did not dim the traffic on the high roads where they walked. But fewer wagons and horses passed beneath them. Connor tapped Lee's arm and pointed at a stairway leading down. "We should walk the gravel below. There's more room."

"We cannot. To walk there without packs or horses is an impropriety. The locals have a word for it, a sort of insult. Lewaker, meaning low walker—one who walks the low road unburdened. It also means one who carries an imaginary burden."

Lewaker. Connor narrowed his eyes. "The Assembly guard used that term with me earlier."

"Yes he did. And I said nothing about it. If I'd let your delicate sensibilities become offended, you'd have only prolonged the argument."

"Delicate what? That's absurd. I never–"

Lee raised an eyebrow.

Connor frowned. "Yes. I see what you did there. Well done. Two points for the fisher-scribe. But what did the guard mean by such an insult?"

"To many in Sky Harbor, all lightraiders are lewakers. They believe the Order shows a lack of faith in the Rescuer's ability to save those whom he desires to save by trying to do the work for him. I'd guess such folk also accuse the stormwatchers of lacking faith in the protection of his barriers."

A similar thought about the stormwatchers' faith had crossed Connor's mind earlier, and he did not want to be on the side of those who scorned the Order. He slowed. "The two are not the same."

"Perhaps not." Lee sharply tilted his head, signaling him to keep up. "Or perhaps it's a question worth pondering."

A long walk still awaited them once they'd descended into the harbor plaza. According to Lee, the high roads that formed a semicircle around the Second Hall were built at the exact distance necessary to keep their shadows from ever darkening the high stained glass windows beneath its dome. Those windows glowed with light from inside, bringing life to scenes from the Rescuer's time on Dastan and others from the early days of creation.

"Are they in there?" Connor asked. "The councilors, I mean."

"Not all at this hour, but a dozen or more at least. Always talking. Ever debating. The Assembly never sleeps."

Connor made for the main steps of the Second Hall, but Lee steered him toward a smaller door in the low outer circle of the building. "The Archive has its own entrance from the plaza. Besides, the guard who insulted you earlier won't be in there. His shift ended hours ago."

"I never said I was eager to confront that guard."

"You didn't have to."

They passed through an outer door into a small chamber where another door waited. Lee held a finger to his lips. The second door opened upon a scriptorium. Scribes wearing the same colorful tunics as Lee sat on high stools at rows of canted desks, scratching away on parchments with feather quills. Inkwells hung from posts spaced evenly among the rows.

Connor watched a worker climb down from her stool and walk twenty paces to recharge her pen. "Is this some kind of discipline or sacrifice," he whispered, "to make the scribes slog all that way for ink?"

Lee did not answer until they'd entered a small antechamber, where other scribes chatted and flexed their fingers. "That is often suggested. Yes. Especially by new recruits. But there is a practical purpose. The long walk allows the ink to settle on the quill so that the lines of script are perfect. No splatters or spills."

Connor imagined his friend, day in and day out for four years, marching back and forth from desk to inkwell, slowly losing his sight to preserve the knowledge of the Keledan. "I have known you more than a year, fought with you and fought beside you, yet now I see you anew."

They passed through two more scriptoria before coming to a narrow staircase leading down. There, the yellow-orange of lanterns gave way to white luminescence tinted with purple. This came from pale plants growing in water-filled sconces.

"Sea candles," Connor said.

Lee flicked one of the sconces, causing a quiet ring. The plant inside glowed brighter. "From the Gulf of Stars, near my birthplace in Lin Kelan. Stewards charge them with saltwater each afternoon."

Not long after, one wall of the staircase ended, and the two emerged into a vast open sea cavern. Waves tipped with foam lapped at a black shore beneath story after story of carved shelves, nooks, alcoves, and passages, all filled with scrolls and texts.

Lee lifted a water-lantern and set off along an upper walkway. "Welcome to the Archive of the Scribes."

Connor spent the next half tick worrying over Lee, who went from nook to nook, checking the chiseled symbols below each shelf, never once checking how close his heels came to the edges of the open walkways. This process led them to the lowest level and down a short passage away from the lapping waves to a steel door and a seated woman wearing an Assembly-crimson tunic and cloak.

A flush of anxiety twisted Connor's chest. The scene looked familiar. Another metal door, shut and guarded. Had the Prime Council lured them all the way down here only to be turned away? Was this more repayment for the Order refusing to send Kara?

The guard rose from her stool, looking as stern as the one who'd called Connor a lewaker.

Lee caught the hood of Connor's cloak and pulled him back before he could speak, then nodded to the guard. "He's with me."

She made no reply, but opened the door and motioned for them both to carry on.

"Told you," Lee whispered, once they were inside. "One of us needed to blend in."

The chamber proved another natural cave, a chaos of turns and branches. Lee found the archival address from the mystery woman's note chiseled into a rock shelf in a deep alcove near the center of the maze.

The shelf was empty.

The scribe held the light up to his face. "I don't understand."

Before the soft echo of his words faded, Connor felt a presence enter the alcove behind them. Slowly he turned, and saw three men. One stood taller than the others, dressed in a councilor's robes–like Stradok, but far more imposing. A thin smile spread across his gaunt face, and he shook his head. "You truly are a disappointment."

20

CONNOR HELD UP HIS HANDS. "IF YOU'RE THE ONE who sent the note, then we came at your invitation. We want no trouble."

"Too bad," the tall man said. "Because trouble has come for you. Trouble has come for us all." He strode past his two friends, right up to Connor, glaring down at him. "Move. You're in my way."

It took Lee's hand to move his friend aside. "Connor, this is the apothecarist I was telling you about. This is Councilor Boreas, Zel's father, the founder of the Airguard."

The assemblyman seemed little interested in introductions. Once the two cadets were out of his way, he reached back into the empty shelf. Connor heard stone sliding against stone, and a beat later, Boreas pulled a leatherbound codex into the light.

Lee held the sea candle lantern closer, illuminating the silver script embossed upon the cover. "You hid it behind a secret panel?"

"The Prime Council hid this codex. Not me. Its contents were once an obsession for their body"–Boreas lifted an eye toward Connor–"and for the lightraiders, at a great and terrible cost. That is why I'd hoped to have this conversation with someone without such familial ties to the Order and its leadership."

Lee caught Connor's eye. "Look at the shield on the cover–

emblazoned with a hollow tree, fruit laden branches spreading almost to the edges, tangled roots extending down. Our symbol."

The title above the tree was written in the Elder Tongue. Connor didn't recognize all the words, but he sounded it out. "*Sofar ke'Samanis.*"

"Literally the Book of the Heaven Ore," Boreas said. "But we translate it as the Celestium Codex." He spoke as if the revelation should spark some memory in the cadets.

It didn't. At least, not for Connor. "Celestium?"

"The fact that you do not know is a credit to your father and the Order's guardians, all of whom were commanded never to speak of it. I was given the same command. But Keledev is threatened. Now is the time for secrets to find the light, and this secret is the key to destroying all dragon-kind before they can invade our land."

"THE MINERS OF HUCKLEHEIM FOUND CELESTIUM first." Boreas had led the group to the center of the passage complex, where they charged more sea candle lanterns from pitchers of salt water and gathered around an oak table. The codex lay at its center, open to pages filled with sketches of weaponry.

"Celestium was a gift from the Rescuer, encased in his impossible peaks. The miners say Kerias Baldomar discovered it. They say the Helper led him to a spring where he thought he saw the sparkle of shairosite."

"Banishing powder," Connor said. "The substance we used to close the dragon portal."

"The same. But Kerias was wrong. When the miners dug into the slope above the spring, they found veins of an unknown black ore, speckled with shimmering constellations like a night sky. The Baldomars are known for their smithing, in part because their ancestor shared a forge with the Rescuer. Kerias formed a new steel alloy from this ore and fashioned a fine sword for the head of the Order, Talin the First. I'm sure you are familiar with his life's tale."

Lee raised a finger. "Talin the First. The lightraider who was taken up. When a firedrake ambushed his party, Talin rushed ahead to defend them. The dragon's flames split around him, leaving him unburnt, and he ran the creature through. Both vanished in a great white flash. But I don't remember anything about a special sword."

Boreas let out a huff. "The sword is the reason he vanished, Cadet. And it's also what split the dragon's fire. Like shairosite, celestium exists on the border between the realms of flesh and spirit. A weapon fashioned from its ore can utterly destroy a dragon."

"Dragons can't be killed," Connor said. "Not entirely. We can vanquish their bodies, but their spirits flee to Ras Pyras. And from there, the Great Red Dragon pushes them into the next egg fitting their kind."

"Do you really think the High One so feeble?" Boreas turned back a few pages in the codex and showed them a drawing of a lifeless dragon with a celestium dagger lodged in its neck. Beside it, a creature resembling a twisted Lisropha warrior hung in the air, shattering like glass. "He gave us a tool to end the dragon's cycle of regeneration into corrupted bodies. He gave us the means to finish this war."

"So what happened?" Lee asked.

"We squandered the ore. Every last ounce." Boreas turned to a chart of the Celestial Peaks marked with pickaxe symbols, some black and some red. "These are shafts where the miners searched for celestium. Those colored red proved fruitful. See how few there are? Once the Order and the Assembly understood the power of the Rescuer's gift, the smiths fashioned every bit the miners found into weapons." He returned to the sketches of weaponry, then flipped through page after page of the same. "Spears, swords, daggers, arrowheads. They amassed enough to the lightraider armory. And over the decades, the Order made good use of them. They sent a hundred or more dragons to the eternal abyss."

Lee lifted his eyes from the book and raised a lens. "But the hordes of the Great Red Dragon number in the thousands."

"Exactly." Boreas paced away from the table. "Your Order spent the weapons as if there would always be more celestium."

"But there wasn't," Connor said.

"No. The mines ran dry." Boreas turned past the sketches of weaponry to another chart of the peaks. This time, there were far more black pickaxe symbols but no new red ones. "The Assembly has always governed the mining of the Peaks with care. It doesn't serve to dig too many holes into a barrier the Rescuer raised to defend us. But when the celestium mines ran dry, they suspended all restrictions. They set Huckleheim loose and brought tragedy down upon their heads."

Huckleheim. Tragedy. When Connor first crossed the bridge at Mer Nimbar, staring down into the mists of the empty chasm, his tehpa had told him how the lake was emptied.

It was not our Blacksmith who drained the lake, boy. That achievement belongs to the miners of Huckleheim.

"The miners dug too close to Mer Nimbar." Connor looked from Boreas to Lee and back. "Their digging breached the lake wall beneath the waters and ruined the city."

"And destroyed several mining families." Boreas sat heavily on a reading stool near one of the water lanterns. "Whole lines were ended when the mine flooded. Half the Baldomars were wiped out. And your friend Dagram Kaivos will never know the cousins he might have had. All because our people spent the celestium without plan or thought and could not come to grips with that failure."

Connor had heard more secrets than he'd expected when he and Lee came looking for the mystery woman. Too many secrets. How much of this did Dag know? He remembered the way the miner had lowered his gaze after Tehpa's revelation at Mer

Nimbar—the way he'd ridden off into the fog. Dag might not know everything, but he knew parts of the story for sure. And he hadn't shared any of it with the rest of them.

And then there was Tehpa. And Master Jairun. And the other guardians. With dark creatures entering the land and a dragon opening a portal, wasn't the tale of such weaponry an important story to tell?

Perhaps not. Not anymore.

Connor closed the codex and brought it to Boreas. "If the celestium weapons are gone—if the gift is already squandered—why bother sharing this with us now?"

"Ah. Now we see an inkling of that supposed lightraider intelligence. The celestium isn't all gone. Once they saw their error, your Order held one weapon back, a dagger called Lef Amunrel."

"Amunrel," Lee said. "The leopard constellation. He who walks the night with confidence in his Maker."

Boreas nodded. "The Faith Walker. That constellation appears in the stars of the celestium blade. However, some in the Order called it the Red Dagger because of the ruby enamel in the hilt and the red starlot in the pommel."

Connor was unimpressed by the assemblyman's answer. "What good will one dagger do against the dragon horde?"

"A good question. But before we come to that part, you'll need to find the weapon. The Order lost Lef Amunrel years ago."

"Lost it? How?"

"On their last mission into Tanelethar. It was your grandfather's mission, and the one upon which the lightraiders pinned all our hopes. Faelin's party failed, routed and destroyed, all but him sent onward to Elamhavar." Boreas shrugged. "That is the real reason he never came home."

21

CONNOR COULD NOT HIDE HIS SIMMERING ANGER. Who was this blood-robed assemblyman, playing at intrigues deep in the safety of the Liberated Land, to speak so unkindly of Faelin Enarian, who slayed the dragon and closed the portal? "What do you know of my patehpa's mission?"

A hollowness bored through Connor's gut the moment he gave voice to the question. Perhaps the councilor knew plenty–much more than him. Connor's argument with Faelin in the dragon's stronghold filled his thoughts. In that moment he'd learned Tehpa knew Faelin still lived.

But he told me he thought you were dead.

For a time, he did. Until Avner settled an arrangement with a few key leaders in the Assembly.

A few key leaders in the Assembly. The Prime Council, or perhaps an even smaller, more exclusive group. Had a young Boreas held that much sway all those years ago? Or had these secrets been handed down to him–little gems of power passed from the older councilors to their favorite disciples.

"Easy, Cadet." Boreas held out a steadying hand. "I meant no offense."

Connor did not believe that for an instant, and he felt compelled to say so.

Lee intervened before he could. "How much do you know of the dagger's fate?" the scribe asked.

"Too much. Not near enough. Faelin's raid party set out to find an ancient Rapha key that would enable them to enter Ras Pyras unnoticed. The key to the bread gate. They were to start at the ruins of Ras Heval, the Hill of Grace, an Aropha temple much like Ras Pyras and Ras Telesar in that age." Boreas signaled one of his companions, and the young man drew a rolled map from a leather cylinder slung over his shoulder. He unrolled it on the table.

The assemblyman placed a finger near a mountain range at the eastern extent of Tanelethar. "The mission started here at Graywater Bay, named for its perpetual fog. The whole region is steeped in a thick haze flowing up from a canyon bog. They had almost reached a nearby temple ruin when the party stumbled into a dragon flanked by granogs and ore creatures of all kinds. A hard battle separated Faelin and the wolf from the other three. Lef Amunrel was lost with his companions."

"And Faelin searched for them, I presume," Lee said.

Boreas nodded. "For nigh on a full year, Faelin scoured the battleground and the whole region. He found his friends, or what was left of them, but no sign of the Red Dagger."

A year. But Faelin had remained in Tanelethar for decades, letting most of the Keledan believe he'd died. "If he'd given up finding the dagger, why did he stay?" Connor asked. "Why not come home?"

"He and the wolf spent the following decades traveling the land, building what the Order calls sanctuaries, until he took an interest in the girl, Kara Orso, and settled next to Trader's Knoll."

Faelin had said little of Kara when Connor questioned him about his choice to stay. Then again, Connor's greater interest had been in why no one had told him that his patehpa still lived. Faelin offered barely half an answer before their mission ended the conversation.

You are young, and my work here must remain secret. There are still some from Keledev who enter Tanelethar and might betray me to the dragons. Not all who are born there choose the gift. You know this.

Connor had understood the reference. *The ships,* he'd answered–meaning the faithless few who choose to take the ships from Sky Harbor and sail into the Storm Mists. It was the darkest day of each cycle in Keledev. But Faelin had said nothing about Kara. "Why did my patehpa take an interest in one young woman over all the Aladoth in Tanelethar?"

"An excellent question, Cadet. I'd hoped to get the answer when I pushed my friends in the Prime Council to request a visit from her."

"*You* pushed for Kara to come." Connor had suspected as much in the way the councilor had called him and Lee a disappointment. "So the raven sent to Stradok was a lie?"

Boreas shrugged one of his broad shoulders. "Not a lie. All the Prime Council said in their letter was true. But I personally had other reasons for pushing the request. We need to know more–where she comes from, Faelin's interest, and the like." He gestured at the codex. "I'd also intended this celestium discussion for her. No offense, but I'd hoped to avoid trusting the search for Lef Amunrel to another Enarian."

Connor's fists tightened at his sides. "Speak that way once more about my family, and I'll–"

"Father!" A young woman entered the chamber, green shirt and gray trousers half hidden by her cloak.

Lee slapped the table. "Zel?"

Connor forgot his anger and stared at him. "That's Zel? She's the one who followed us."

Zel ignored them, walking straight to Boreas. "Father, an Assembly raven arrived at the guest house with a message for the lightraiders."

"They are cadets, Zel." Boreas turned away from Connor to face his behlna. "Lightraider *cadets,* and barely so. They've not even entered the spheres."

Lee coughed. "Yet we've faced one more dragon than you, I'll wager."

This earned no response from the councilor. He kept his

attention on Zel. "A raven is no reason for you to interrupt. I'd say you were looking for an excuse to involve yourself in this meeting."

"I was looking to do your bidding, Father. If you insist on using me for your intrigues and politicking, you must allow me the freedom to do it right."

Connor raised a hand. "I hate to interrupt these proceedings, but I've two questions. First, did you truly send your behlna to spy on us?"

"I've been reporting, not spying," Zel said, leaning to look past her tehpa and meet his eye. "And steering. I got you and Lee down here for his little ambush, didn't I?" She shifted her gaze to Lee. "I see you found the tunic I left for you. Good work. Too bad your friend missed the clue. He would have blended better in the yellow silk of a city-dweller. I thought you said in your letters that he was clever."

Connor matched her flat look and continued. "And second, Councilor Boreas, do you think the guardians will take the news lightly when I tell them you had your *spy*"–he narrowed his eyes at Zel–"intercept a raven meant for us?"

Again, it was Zel, not Boreas, who answered. "I didn't intercept anything. I received the raven as a help to the housekeep. And when I removed the message from the bird's leg, I saw the last two words by accident." She handed him the little roll of parchment. "Those words alone told me you should see this immediately."

"Two words, huh?" Connor passed the message to Lee, whose spectacles allowed him to read the tiny script of a raven's parchment better.

The scribe unfurled the parchment and dropped a lens in front of his eye, then blinked and dropped a second lens into place. His hands trembled.

"Lee," Connor said. "What's wrong? What does it say?"

The scribe's voice caught in his throat. "Teegan writes to us from the Apple Barrel at the Windhold. 'Found Barnabas dead in the highlands. Tortured and murdered.'" He looked up from the parchment and swallowed hard. "Her last two words are 'They're back.'"

22

BOREAS RESIDENCE
SKY HARBOR

COUNCILOR BOREAS REACTED TO THE NEWS FROM Teegan with speed and purpose. His two men returned the codex to its hidden shelf while he, Zel, and the cadets left the Archive. He insisted that they continue this discussion at the Boreas family home.

The smallness of the wattle house, with its ground-floor apothecary, surprised Connor. The councilor's rich robes and all his maneuvering had reminded him of the counts and magistrates he'd witnessed in Tanelethar—dragon lackeys and sorcerers. He'd expected Boreas to live in some grand house overlooking the harbor, not an old shop home tucked behind a high-road arch.

The councilor had an abrasive manner, but he was not the enemy. Far from it. Boreas was Keledan, driven by service to the Rescuer and his people, even if Connor didn't agree with all his methods.

"Go on upstairs," Boreas said, leading them through his shop of herbs and salts. He stopped at the bottom step and motioned them onward. "Our common room is comfortable enough. Light a fire. Rest. Zel and I will be up in a moment." As Connor walked past, the councilor caught his sleeve. "Cadet, I *am* sorry about your friend."

Connor waited for the *but* or the *I told you so*—some proclamation that Barnabas's death justified the Airguard's fears. Boreas offered none. Connor gave him a thankful nod and continued up the steps with Lee.

"I can't believe he's gone," Lee said moments later, standing over Connor, who was building a fire in the hearth. "I have no heart to speak with the Assembly now. And if I did, what would we say?"

Connor said nothing, glaring at the growing flames.

"I know you don't want to discuss our duties, but we must."

"He died because of me."

"What?" Lee turned Connor from the fire by the shoulder and took the poker from his hand. "How can you say that? Barnabas died at the hands of evil—an evil you did not bring into our land."

"He died at the hands of an evil he'd never have faced had I not interfered. I asked him to delay at our farm, to collect a silly cake for Kara. If I hadn't, he'd have passed through the highlands several ticks earlier, probably made it safely to the Windhold outpost."

Lee led him to a cushioned bench and sat him down. "I don't believe that. Whatever he encountered may have been waiting there for a long time. You asked for a friend's help in a kindness, and out of kindness, he obliged. Do not shame yourself for that or any of the Nine Core Strengths of the Keledan. That is a tactic of a dragon, a liar and an accuser, not a lightraider."

Connor nodded, though he could not stop the tears.

Lee shed tears with him. "We may mourn him, you especially, who knew and loved him most, but we may also take heart because Barnabas now walks untiring along the rivers of Elamhavar."

The effort to compose himself took Connor quite a while. Councilor Boreas and Zel did not appear from the staircase until his eyes were dry and his voice under control. But once they entered the common room, with Zel carrying a tray of cider and biscuits, the assemblyman wasted no time. "We must determine the best message for the Assembly—decide our strategy."

Connor accepted one of the mugs from Zel with a nod of

thanks, then turned a hard look on her tehpa. He pointed to Lee and himself. "Our strategy is to return to Ras Telesar at once. What you say to the Assembly after we're gone is none of our concern."

Lee lifted a finger in protest, but Connor stopped him before he could speak. "Don't. The Assembly had their chance to hear from us, and they turned us away. Our duty is to Rescuer and the Order. We belong at Ras Telesar. We never should have left in the first place."

Boreas took a sip of his cider and set the mug on the mantle above the fire. "I agree."

This turned Connor's and Lee's heads. Zel's too. "You do?" she asked.

"Are you so shocked? My purposes for voting to summon Miss Orso have been served"–Boreas glanced at Connor–"as much as possible, given the circumstances. As for the Prime Council and the rest of the Assembly, they expected the Order's representatives to bring words of reassurance. What word will you bring now?"

"I asked the same question," Lee said in a dry tone. "And all I can think is, 'Oops. The portal must not be as closed as we thought.'"

"Or the dark creatures have found another way in," Connor added. "Neither is reassuring, and both demand our presence at the academy." He set his mug aside. "Thank you for your hospitality, but we must go. We have an eight-day journey ahead at the fastest, even if we ride through the nights between stables."

"Ride?" Zel stood at the same time Connor did. "What if you could–"

"Zelacia." Her tehpa shot her a warning frown. "Not now."

Zel marched up to Boreas. "If not now, then when, Father? Did you and the guilds not build the Airguard for such a moment as this? It doesn't matter whether the threat comes from the mountains or the mists. We can help."

Connor stepped closer to the two of them. "How can you help, exactly? Are you saying you have a way to get us home to Ras

Telesar that's faster than a horse?"

Boreas tried to speak, but his behlna spoke over him. "Father's airships have far more potential than serving as floating watchtowers. We've been . . . testing other capabilities."

"Zel!" The councilor's expression would have hushed even Connor. But not Zel, perhaps the only person in all Keledev immune to his charisma.

"There's no need for you to ride hard all the way to Ras Telesar," she said, "not if you can fly."

THE PRISONER
TANELETHAR

UPSTAIRS. DOWNSTAIRS. MY STUMBLING DOES nothing to impede the sureness of the orcs' gargoyle feet.

They dragged me up a set of steps to enter this place. Now they drag me down. Down, down, we descend, tick after tick, on a forever staircase with no walls and no end in sight.

No. I see the bottom. Red fire. Iron torch stands burn with it like the dragon-talon pillars on that hill. And like those pillars, these torches fill me with dread.

The orcs reach the bottom and stand me up. For the first time in what seems an age, I have control of my legs.

"Walk, human. Move."

I walk ahead of their poking halberds down a road formed by more iron stands. More red fire. I walk for another two ticks, at least, until the path opens into a giant circle of torches. At the center of the circle–on a throne of pyranium and black silk, suspended by chains from the emptiness above–rests fear.

"Come closer, child."

I am no child. Yet to him I am an infant. Less than an infant. I feel the echoes of antiquity in his voice. His name reverberates in my head, and it slips from my lips as I approach. "Lord Valshadox the Devastation."

"Good. Your mind is open." His tail uncurls from around his talons, and with one beat of his mighty wings, he leaves the throne. He lands with a stone-quaking *crunch* before me. His long neck bends and curves to the side until the tendrils of flesh hanging from his chin brush the floor. Boiling breath that reeks of sulfur and rot threatens to set my whole body ablaze. "Kneel!"

The torches flare in concert with the command.

Trembling, I obey. I'm not sure my legs could hold me much longer anyway, not in the presence of a dragon lord.

The air cools as the dragon suddenly sniffs my form. Then his great head retreats into the dark heights. Laughter reverberates within my skull. "Can it be? Have you been taking walks in my woods, child?"

I cannot lie. I see all my lives at once, all the failed paths through the fog. He sees them too.

"Yes. You are the one who came to my hill. Interesting. You have courage. But are you teachable? Are you trainable?" The voice turns away from my thoughts, addressing the orcs at my back. I hear it only in my head.

Begin.

One orc hauls me up and steadies me, while another presses a knife hilt into my hand, forcing me to grip it. This is no blunted training blade. It is sharp. Deadly. What do they want of me?

I hear a terrible squeaking–iron wheels with no grease.

At the edge of my vision, two more orcs enter the circle of torches, dragging an iron rack. Another prisoner hangs from its shackles, toes scraping the floor.

Though I do not turn my gaze, I remember this was a man the orcs dragged into the hut days ago. What have they done to him? The remains of his clothes hang from an emaciated body. Cuts and charred flesh speak of unimaginable pain. Why bring him near me? My downcast eyes settle on the knife in my hand.

"Go to him."

I cannot resist. I walk to my fellow prisoner–my brehna.

"See him."

The dragon wants me to look this man in the eyes. I do, and behind them I see a despair like none I've ever known. Dead faces formed from green mist. Ghouls in the night. Creepers. All are trifles compared to this.

"He is your enemy. One of you must die."

An orc halberd presses against my spine. The message is clear. Either I kill my fellow prisoner, or the orcs will kill me, all for the dragon's sport. Is this the whole purpose of the camps?

The mind inside my mind answers the question. *No, child. That is not the purpose. And do not kill him yet. Start with a cut. Just a nick. He must suffer first.*

Hasn't he suffered enough?

By the resignation in this brehna's eyes, I know he hears the dragon too. He blinks. A slow blink that says, *Go ahead. What difference will it make?*

"I can't."

The halberd point digs in, making me wince. The dragon's voice crushes all other thoughts. "Cut him!"

I do. A slash across the arm, drawing fresh blood. I match the drops with tears.

"Good. Now end him. Slash his throat."

My brehna's gaze pleads with me to obey. *End it. End my suffering before he changes his mind.* But a cut was one thing, prolonging both our lives. To kill him?

"Please don't make me do this."

"Kill him, I said. Now!"

I am numb, so numb I'm not sure the weapon still sits in my hand, and I must check. The blade reflects the torches. Red flames mingle with the blood on its edge. I raise the knife to my brehna's neck–and stop.

Motion in the dark. The dragon's neck snakes down again. His breath is beside me, red eyes burning through me. "Free yourself. A sacrifice is required to buy your salvation. Kill him that you might live!"

Like a shield against his fury, I see her face–our mother's face. With it comes a melody I can't quite grasp. The knife drops from my fingers. The dragon rears up, ejected from my mind. The halberd at my back presses in. Pierces me.

"Wait!" Lord Valshadox's voice is a cackling roar. "I know you. I *know* you! The tang in my woods. Your blood. Guards, hold him back!"

They pull me away, and fire streams down until the stone floor and the rack glow red. When it subsides, my brehna is gone, naught but lingering ash, and the orcs shackle me into the smoldering irons in his place.

23

CONNOR
NEAR VAL PERA

ZEL RETURNED THE AIRSHIP TO THE GROUND IN A wheat field east of Val Pera, the first farming town north of the White Ridge Mountains on the Central Plain. She called this haphazard descent *landing.*

Connor called it terrifying.

The ground rushed up at the airship, and Zel hurried them all to the back of its wicker boat so that the rear curves of its steel runners would dig into the dirt first. This worked for only an instant before the bow slammed down and threw them all to the floor.

"Are you trying to kill us?" Connor asked, pulling himself up by the rail.

Zel straightened her fur-lined cloak–a provision the cadets wore as well, keeping them warm in the cold air where the clouds hung. "Are you still alive?" When Connor flattened his lips, she cocked her head. "Then there's your answer. Besides. I'm not the one who insisted we stop."

Lee raised a hand. "No. That was me. A matter of necessity made more urgent by the force of your docking."

"Landing," Zel said.

"Whatever." Lee vaulted the rail and ran toward a grove of oak and tall sycamore, calling over his shoulder, "See you in a beat or two."

The eastern Storm Mists glowed with a rose hue. They'd flown all night. The Common Tongue translation of a verse from the Scrolls would not leave Connor's mind. *They will soar on wings like eagles.* "We flew *over* the White Ridge Mountains," he said. "Over them."

"I'm surprised you noticed, cowering on the floor like that."

"I was seated—not cowering—in what seemed the safest position in this glorified orchard basket."

He knew Zel wanted him to call it a ship. Or *The Starling,* as her tehpa had named it. But *ship* seemed too strong a word, no matter how the wrights had shaped the wicker. *The Starling* had a pointed bow, a tall hull, and a giant silk rudder at the stern. But with its small size and flat keel, it felt more like a rowboat—or one of his mehma's fruit baskets.

On the other hand, the upper structure rivaled the largest of the harbor galleys for size. What Connor had seen as one giant silk bag from the ground was actually three long pouches, supported inside by lightweight alderwood ribs and girders and fixed to the hull by long trusses. Contraptions that looked to Connor like big glass oil lamps supplied each pouch with heated vapors. With those lamps in a ship of notoriously flammable alderwood and lacquered wicker, he could see why the risk of fire was so great.

Risk or not, he couldn't complain about the result. "We crossed the mountains in three watches—less than nine ticks. It took us thrice that on the Anamturas, even heading downstream on her spring rush."

"The air is fast above the clouds, and *The Starling* moves with it in straight lines, as the bird flies, cutting the distance." Zel patted one of the ship's trusses. "The wind carries her inland at one height, holds her still at another, and sends her out to sea higher up. Think of it like a great invisible globe, rolling forever against the Rescuer's Celestial Peaks. By choosing our place in it and using the rudder to steer east or west, we can travel anywhere in Keledev." She gestured toward the center of Val Pera. "One day, all Keledan will travel and carry goods this way."

The Starling's giant pouches cast their morning shadow over half the farmer's field, making all of Val Pera, the Sea of Grain, feel smaller. Connor compared the pouches' size to the tiny wicker boat beneath, then tried to imagine the number and size of airships required to equal the carrying abilities of horses and wagons. "Yeah. I'm not so sure."

That response brought him a downcast look. He'd meant no insult, so he tried to recover by changing the subject. He tapped the toe of his boot against a big iron block on the floor. Handles jutted out from both sides. "I still don't understand the purpose of this thing. Why must we carry such a weight when our goal is to be light?"

"We call that a bar," Zel said. "The galleys use them for ballast. Airguard ships can only carry one, but if we ever need a quick rise, you'll be glad we brought it along. On that day, I'll have the option of throwing the bar overboard instead of you."

"And this?" Connor bent to push open a hinged hatch in the lower stern, exposing the underside of the hull. A stiff linen string and a wicker cylinder poked out between the runners.

"That"–Zel swatted his hand away from the hatch–"is for a very bad day."

Her response sparked more questions, but Lee returned before Connor could ask them. Zel donned a pair of gloves, preparing to add her tehpa's ingredients to the vapor lamps–caustic vitriol and alum grit. "Are we ready to launch?"

"Yes," Connor said, as Lee climbed in. Then he gritted his teeth and shook his head. "I mean no. I'm sorry. I think I need to visit the grove as well."

They launched a quarter tick later. Zel dumped her tehpa's concoction into the lamps, and blue-gray smoke poured upward into the pouches. Connor returned to his place on the stern floor, hugging his crook against his knees. He didn't like the going up part. He didn't like the going down much either, or anything in between.

He frowned at Lee, who leaned over the bow like a lion figurehead. "How can you take to this . . . this *flying* so easily?"

"How can you not, my friend? Is it any more frightening than a ship in a storm or that giant you and Teegan faced in Schisma Valley? One death is as good as another, I suppose."

Lee's own words seemed to wound him, and Zel took his arm to help him sit on the bow bench. "I haven't heard that saying since the day we met. The day your brother . . ."

When she didn't finish, Connor narrowed his eyes at both of them and matched the formal speak of the two city dwellers. "The day his brother what?" He focused in on Lee. "I didn't even know you had a brehna."

Lee took his arm away from Zel. "I don't. Not anymore."

The Starling went quiet for several ticks. Zel occupied herself with finding the best height and steering the ship. To do this, she moved the rudder by degrees and used ropes and pulleys to open and close small ports in the pouches. She had told them earlier they needn't worry about flying to Pleasanton or Ravencrest. They'd take a direct route almost due north to the academy, passing over the inlet at Harbor Joy.

Lee stayed at the bow. And Connor kept out of his way, seated in the stern, occasionally getting up to watch for landmarks from the rail. The last time he tried to check their progress, he had the brilliant idea that instead of standing, he might open the stern hatch that gave access to Zel's very-bad-day device. Through it, he saw Keledev drifting past, like the floor of a crystal-clear sea a thousand leagues below a rowboat. He slammed the hatch closed.

"He took one of the ships," Lee said, looking out from the bow, as if stirred by the sound.

A moment passed before Connor understood his friend had returned to the question from so many ticks earlier. Again, Faelin's words returned to him.

Not all who are born there choose the gift. You know this.

"You mean a ship from Sky Harbor. On the Day of Reckoning."

Lee kept his gaze forward, toying with the thicker talanium ring on his finger. "It is a matter of shame to my family–my father, especially. His greatest failing. He couldn't watch my brother sail into the Storm Mists. He turned his back, and the whole time kept his eyes on the Second Hall. It was then that he decided his second son would be an Assembly scribe, as if proximity to the Scrolls might have saved the first."

What was Connor to say? He'd never met anyone with a family member who'd taken one of the ships. He knew only that two sailed each year on the same day, built by the wrights for that one purpose. None were forced to board. But those who'd become discontented with Keledev–those who hadn't accepted the Helper's gift and those seeking something other than the Rescuer's provision–always took their chance to leave. Always.

"One death is as good as another," Lee said. "Those were the last words my brother spoke to us. He gave me this." He held up a hand and turned the blue ring about his finger with his thumb. "It belonged to my great-grandfather, a lightraider renewer. Even my brother, who hurt us so deeply, understood it was wrong for him to keep it."

Connor approached his friend, doing his best not to take in the view of the long fall waiting beyond the rail. "He may yet live, you know. Master Jairun told me he believes the ships end up in Tanelethar."

"Believes," Zel said. "As most do. But does he know this for sure? Did you ask if any lightraiders ever encountered one of our lost sheep north of the barrier?"

"I did." Connor swallowed, hating the answer for his friend's sake. But he wouldn't lie. "And Master Jairun didn't know of a single one."

Lee nodded. "Yet that is the prayer of my mother. Every morning and every evening. She prays her son will be like the boy in the pigsty who saw the error of his malcontent spoken of in the Scrolls. She waits for the day when we will celebrate his return with a feast. My father is not so hopeful."

"And what do you think about it?" Connor asked.

"I don't. I told you. I don't have a brother. So I don't think of it at all."

That wasn't true. Connor knew it. Too often he'd seen Lee turning that ring about his finger as he'd done a moment ago. And now he understood what was going through his friend's mind when he did. But he wouldn't dare point that out.

He tried something else. "You have a brehna now, you know–in me. Don't you remember what you said to me when we first met? 'We're going to be lightraiders, you and I–brothers of the Order.'"

This earned him a thin smile. Connor moved to put his arm around his friend, but a gust of wind shook *The Starling*, and he fell into the rail instead.

The ship blew sideways. The rudder creaked against its hinges, threatening to rip and break.

Lee pulled Connor away from the rail. "What's happening?"

"I don't know!" Zel hurried from lamp to lamp, turning dials, then pushed the rudder hard over. "Nothing's working!"

Connor didn't like the sound of that. "What's not working?"

"The steering. I need to turn her against the wind to gain control and keep us on course, but the rudder's not big enough. I can't get control." She went to her ropes and opened several ports. "We must go lower. The wind may slow, and perhaps drive us north again. If not, we may capsize."

Her efforts at changing height proved more effective than her steering. *The Starling* descended, but flying lower did nothing to change their speed or direction. And the lower they flew, the louder the wind whistled in their ears. Zel threw her hands in the air. "What's happening?"

"I just asked you that!" Lee shouted over the noise. "Shouldn't you know? Aren't you the mighty stormwatcher?"

Connor hardly heard them. The world off the port rail had drawn his eye. He saw the coastline and a growing gap of blue water between it and them. He turned to the others and saw gray, flashing clouds off the bow. The blood drained from his face. "Zel! You must get control! We're being pulled into the Storm Mists!"

24

CONNOR CLUNG TO THE WICKER AS *THE STARLING* leaned farther starboard, threatening to dump her passengers into the sea. "Zel, do something!"

The look she gave him could have burned the eyes out of his skull. "Do you not see me running about, pulling ropes and turning dials like a madwoman? Nothing works."

"What of the device underneath–your very-bad-day device. Isn't this day bad enough?"

"Father calls it the blaze, with good reason, and it won't work if I can't turn the ship against the wind." The statement seemed to spark an idea. She ran to the rudder and threw its lever to the opposite stop.

The Starling groaned, but she righted herself. This was a poor relief for Connor. Zel had given up on turning them into the wind, and had turned *The Starling* to fly with it instead. The ship accelerated toward the roiling gray wall of the Storm Mists.

"Put her down!" Lee shouted. "We can't go into the Mists!"

"If I do, we'll sink. She's an airship, remember?"

"I have no fear of the sea. I'll keep us alive."

The scribe looked to Connor, who nodded his agreement. "He can do as he claims. Put her down!"

Zel tried. At least, she gave every appearance of trying. Connor had no real understanding of the controls. *The Starling* descended until its runners skimmed the waves and sea spray burst over the bow, but it sank no lower. Soon the Storm Mists filled all of Connor's vision. Those born in Keledev who'd seen this sight had not returned to tell their stories.

The looming mists had far more depth and substance than Connor had ever imagined over a lifetime of watching them from afar. Ripples of lightning illuminated a chaos of billowing clouds flying against one another like warring creatures. Waves as tall as mountains crashed within.

"Zel!"

"I see it. But there's naught we can do!"

For an instant, Connor considered telling his friends to jump, and then the maelstrom took them.

An electric streak split the air among them, missing the vapor lamps by inches. *The Starling* bucked against a wave. Seawater drenched them all. Yet onward, she flew.

More purple flashes lit the spray. Beneath the roar of a powerful wind, Connor heard a voice, low and smooth, but he couldn't hold on to its calm long enough to understand. His ears focused on a whistling screech, then on snaps and scratching.

A pine bough slapped him in the face, and before Connor could consider the implications, *The Starling* jolted to a stop, knocking them all off their feet. The flashes had ended. There were no rocking waves or wind noises—no seawater seeping up through the wicker floor.

"Ow," Lee moaned, then drew a bristlecone pine out from under his rear. He fixed his crooked spectacles and held it close to the lenses. "I don't remember seeing pines at sea. Where are we?"

Connor pulled himself up by the rail. Instantly he recognized a nearby hovel, with its grassy roof and large shed. "How is this possible?" The answer came as a soft voice in his head. *For you, it is not. But with the High One, all things are possible.* "I know this place. This is my patehpa's sanctuary."

25

CONNOR
TANELETHAR
HIGHLAND FOREST

AFTER TAKING A FEW BEATS TO RECOVER, CONNOR rolled out of *The Starling,* dropped to his knees, and blessed the wet, mossy earth of his patehpa's old Tanelətharian homestead. "No offense, Zel, but I don't think I'll be flying in your airship again anytime soon."

The stormwatcher failed to notice his jibe. "Faelin's sanctuary." She clung to her ship. "Are you saying we're in Tanelethar? Are you sure?"

"The Dragon Lands," Lee said, peeling a pine bough out of *The Starling*'s port truss. "And if he's not sure, I am. Connor and I stood on this very spot, not much more than a year ago."

Connor gazed up at the airship's pouches, higher than the bristlecone pines around Faelin's clearing. "The Storm Mists acted as a portal. I imagine the pouches look much like a strange blue hill showing above the trees. We'll have to trust the Rescuer to shield us from discovery."

The scribe patted his shoulder. "He has us well in hand. The forest is thick and hilly here, hiding *The Starling* from eyes on the ground—even those at Trader's Knoll. We know from our last visit that the local granog hates to fly like most of his kind. And Pedrig and Faelin destroyed the dragon lord of this region."

"Granogs? Dragons?" Zel dropped onto the bow bench inside the ship, shaking her head. "I'm not prepared for this. I never wanted to cross the barrier. I'm not meant to."

"I might agree with you," Connor said, helping Lee out onto the grass. "But it seems the Rescuer does not." He caught Lee's eye and thrust a chin toward the hovel. "Looks like goblins came through here."

Faelin's home had been ransacked. The door hung on one hinge. Goblins had stolen charwood from the shed and scrawled their nonsensical script on the mud walls both outside and in. The open shed concerned Connor most. "We've a lot to do."

"Agreed." Lee turned and offered Zel a hand, but she didn't move.

"Now who's cowering?" Connor said. "You're in the Dragon Lands, whether you set foot on its soil or not."

"What if it corrupts me?"

He tried not to laugh. "There are evils here that will try. But the Rescuer is your protector. And this land belongs to him, no matter what. The earth and grass, the pines, and especially the people are the Maker's creations. In sanctuaries like this one, the Rescuer restores that creation." He looked around, and his smile faded. "But if we don't defend them . . ."

Zel remained stubbornly put. "Even so. I don't need to climb out of *The Starling* because she's still in good shape. She can fly."

"Fly where?" Lee asked.

"Wherever you lightraiders go to cross the barrier. We need to go home."

"No, we don't. Not yet." Connor walked back to the other two. "The Rescuer brought us here for a reason. We need to determine what it is. And then we need to get to work."

Connor and Lee spoke a sacred verse together.

"Oveh luminati'ana poveh vy yeluth howdi'ana. Bi kazelnesh ala'ov, logoalas geviana."

I will show you the way. I will give counsel.

When they finished, Connor quieted his heart and listened. Instead of a direction or a location, another verse came to his mind. *Kavah po mashteliov.*

Seek, and you will find.

He opened one eye and glanced at Lee, who seemed to have finished listening before him.

"Find the Red Dagger," Connor said.

"Find the Rapha Key," Lee said at the same time, then scrunched his brow. "Wait. What?"

Zel looked unimpressed. "So much for lightraider discernment. The two of you received different answers, and you're both probably wrong." She lifted her chin at Connor. "Your grandfather searched for Lef Amunrel for a year, and he was there when it was lost. As far as we know, he gave up all hope of finding the Rapha Key, without which the dagger is useless. How do either of you expect to do better, especially when you can't agree which to seek first?"

Lee shrugged and pointed upward. "His timing. Not ours. Do you think it a coincidence that your father chose this moment to reveal Lef Amunrel's existence, after all these years? *This*–a mission to Tanelethar–this is why the Rescuer, through Master Jairun, sent us to Sky Harbor. This is our mission."

Connor could not argue with that part. Everything Lee had said as they rode the river into the city had proved true. Knowing the dragons were up to something, Connor had not wanted to travel south, farther from the barrier. But the Rescuer had laid that path for them in advance.

The peace Connor had felt when last he visited this homestead had dimmed. It was not vanquished entirely, but frail. "Whichever of these two items we seek," he said, "we must first shore up Faelin's work, or this place may soon be overrun." He looked to Zel and made a quick tilt of his head. "Come on. Hop out of there. We need your help."

At his behest, the three knelt in the clearing together, hands joined in the center.

"Ke'Rumosh kamelnesh. Tav sho'emana cresana . . ."

He is my shepherd. What I need, I have . . .

Connor and Lee taught Zel the Prayer of Sanctuaries, as the guardians had taught them. And all three prayed together, ending with its last line of ultimate hope. *"Po haviana elamid aler hav Rumosh."*

And I will dwell in his house forever.

When they finished, Connor breathed deep. The air tasted sweeter. The pines looked greener. But Faelin's house and shed were still a wreck, marred by goblin script. "Come on. We've much to do before going after the dagger."

While Zel took care of *The Starling*, removing pines and checking the wicker and the lamps, Connor and Lee cleaned up. The char marks proved hard to remove, but they managed. More concerning were the thefts. The goblins had cleaned the house out, even taking most of the pictures from the walls in Faelin's work room—the charcoal drawings Kara had made for him in the years before the dragon Vorax came to the highlands.

"Look, Connor. One picture remains. An important one." Lee lifted a drawing of Kara herself from the wall. Behind it, in a small niche dug out of the mud brick, lay a key and a knife. "They didn't find these."

"Only by the High One's sovereignty and grace." Connor crossed the room and took the drawing, framed in driftwood. He wondered how she was fairing. With news of dark creatures once again breaching the barrier, plans at the academy might change. *I know you've laid a path for her as well,* he said in his heart, and carefully set the picture on Faelin's old worktable. "If the goblins never discovered the key, then how'd they open the shed?"

They went out to look and found Zel inside, restacking the charwood the goblins had strewn about. When Connor pulled an armload of logs out again, she frowned. "What are you doing?"

"This is more than a woodshed. Help me move these aside."

While they worked, Lee examined the mangled padlock.

"They broke the first lock. Spent a good deal of time on it too—unusual for goblin mischief. They don't have that kind of patience."

"I don't understand." Zel set a stack of wood next to Connor's and dusted herself off. "The first lock? What are you two talking about?"

"We'll show you." Connor twisted the dagger's pommel. The cross guard slid apart. He removed the blade and showed her the key hidden beneath. "Faelin built a secret door."

All of his patehpa's stores were still inside the armory—weapons, coins, clothing, manykits, and maps. Connor and Lee struck one of the lanterns and immediately began picking out gear.

Zel accepted a manykit from Connor and slipped off her fur-lined cloak to try it on, eying the confusion of leather straps as if they were a puzzle bought at a fair. "Are there other sanctuaries like this in Tanelethar?"

"Several," Connor said, helping her interpret the clusters of pouches and fasteners, showing her how to buckle the straps. "Assuming your tehpa is correct. I'm hoping one of these maps will tell us."

"This one, I think." Lee took a large map of all Tanelethar down from its hook. The scribe had dropped a red lens in front of his eye. He scanned Faelin's inkwork and nodded. "Oh, yes. Definitely this one. I'll show you in the house."

Before they left the shed, the three gathered the rest of their supplies. Zel had no skill with a sword or bow, but she told them she could wield an axe well enough. Connor gave her a small one and added a double-stacked crossbow. "Use this with caution."

She loaded two bolts and raised the bow to her eye. "I think I can handle it."

"Can you? Wait for your enemy to draw near. It takes training to hit a distant mark, but at close range"—Connor pushed the tips down to point at the floor instead of his neck—"you can't miss."

In Faelin's hearth room, the three righted his table and laid out the map. "I brought a special map glass from the stores," Lee said, showing them a brass triangle with a red lens and wolf's paws for feet, "much like the one we found here before. Master Belen says the Order used them often for passing secrets in the old days." He leaned over the table with his lantern to slide the triangle across the map. "If you look here, you can–"

Connor snatched the lantern away. "I'll hang on to this if you don't mind."

The scribe pressed his lips together. "That's not funny."

"I'm not laughing. Remember what happened last time we were here? There's no sense in sending another map up in flames."

Lee held his gaze for another beat, then continued his work. "Fair enough."

The scribe's red lens revealed marks and sketches in a secret ink they'd seen before on another of Faelin's maps. These hidden drawings made secret paths and places hover above the parchment. "Whether we look for the dagger or the key, we should start here, where Faelin's party was routed." Lee held the lens over an inlet on Tanelethar's northeastern coast labeled Graywater Bay and panned it around the nearby foothills. A drawing of a glade appeared, surrounded by ridges. "This must be a sanctuary, perhaps the first Faelin built. We can base there, and hopefully we may find some notes or records to steer our course."

"But how will we get there?" Connor measured the distance with portions of his crook. "Look at the size of Tanelethar compared to Keledev. Even in *The Starling*–and even if we could fly during the day without being seen–the journey would take a week or more."

"Ah." Lee rubbed his hands together. "That's why this map is such an exciting find. Faelin did his work well, and I have a plan."

26

AARON
KELEDEV
THOUSAND FALLS OUTPOST

THE TIMBER DINING HALL AT THOUSAND FALLS buzzed with the news of Teegan Yar's raven. She'd sent it to Sireth, her tehpa, rather than the watchmaster, but none among the company blamed her for blood loyalty. Some did, however, blame her and the other lightraider cadets for this new threat. Dark creatures had entered the land once again.

Their grumblings made little sense to Aaron. Was that not why they'd come to Thousand Falls? Did they not expect, after Avner Jairun's warning, to one day fight evil in these foothills? Perhaps they'd only come to play at soldiering and eat the pork and bread granted by the Assembly.

Sireth left the meal line and set his plate down across the table from Aaron's. The two had stuck close since their arrival with the newest cohort. Aaron could not speak to Sireth's motives for the partnership, but for his part, the young man stayed by Sireth because he recognized wisdom and skill. When swinging axes and hammers, whether in labor or battle, Aaron preferred the company of a man of experience over those his own age.

"It seems some of the others have heard," Sireth said, stabbing a square of cheese with his fork.

"Every soul in the outpost has heard. I saw it in the pale faces of the logging crew when they left this morning, as if they all expect to take a dagger in the chest or a black arrow in the throat as they strip the branches from the felled pines."

"I think a portion of such awareness is wisdom. But fear is folly. What do you say?"

Aaron had to chase a mouthful of bread with water from the falls before he could reply. "I say I'd rather find the creatures that killed the parcelman before they find me, though I hope we don't find them riding pine badgers on the unstable ground of the marsh run."

"Now that shows awareness *and* wisdom."

The way Sireth waved his apple slice before tossing it into his mouth told Aaron he'd been thinking the same thing. More than thinking, probably. Sireth was never idle. "You've already spoken to the watchmaster," Aaron said. "You already have a plan, right? Are you putting together a crew to search the woods?"

Sireth raised his graying eyebrows. "Crews are for work. This is a scouting party. And Thousand Oaks will send three. We'll cover the forest between here and the Windhold, while the Windhold's parties search to the east. I expect Ravencrest and the other companies to complete the line. Something dark walks these foothills, lad. And we must find it." Sireth stretched an open hand across the table. "We are the watchmen."

Aaron let out a quiet laugh, realizing that like the others, part of him had only come north to play at soldiering. That part was now gone. He gripped his friend's hand and gave him a grim nod. "We are the wall."

TIRAN
APPROACHING RAS TELESAR

AFTER THE FRIGHT AND SORROW OF FINDING BARNABAS slain by some unknown dark creature, Teegan and Tiran had cried and prayed, commending him to the Rescuer. A mournful whinny had led them to his horse, Clarence, head hung low, still harnessed to a cart and stuck in the trees, but otherwise unhurt. Barnabas had likely died defending him, leading the creature away. The horse's last service to his master was to carry his remains to the inn.

The twins had sent ravens north, south, east, and west from the Apple Barrel, spent a sleepless night in borrowed beds, and then set out for Ras Telesar. Tiran's gift for their tehpa would have to wait.

Now, arriving at the academy, they found the younger cadet stalwarts and initiates guarding the lower ramparts. Master Quinton walked among them, checking the sharpness of their blades and the resin on their bowstrings.

"Barnabas was never meant to cross the barrier," Teegan said as the two walked through the gatekeeper's door into the lower courtyards. "He never should have had to fight whatever evil he encountered in that forest."

"Such is the age we live in." Tiran lifted a hand to greet the cadet who closed and locked the door behind them. "Our parents let evil fester north of the barrier. Now that evil has found inroads into Keledev, and we must deal with the consequences."

When they reached the lower ward, Tiran looked up toward the fifth rampart and saw Master Belen waiting there. "No time for rest or grief, I see. Looks like we're getting straight to work."

Belen ushered them into the Hall of Manna, where Master Jairun and several other guardians waited. Pedrig stood with them, and Teegan ran ahead to hug the wolf the moment she saw him. To Tiran's knowledge, she remained the only human for whom Pedrig allowed this indulgence.

"Hello, daughter of autumn," the wolf said in a constricted grunt. "I missed you too. It pains me to meet you again under such circumstances."

"It pains you because of her fierce squeezing." Tiran lightly kicked at his shessa's foot with his own. "Let the wolf be, Teegs. He's Havarra, a shepherd of the beasts, not a fleece toy."

"Let her be." Headmaster Jairun closed the doors behind them. "Such moments will become fleeting now that the war has begun." He sighed. "I'd hoped we'd be given more time."

"The enemy knows nothing of hope," Dame Silvana said, "nor of giving. I'm surprised we made it this far before another breach, especially since we never learned how Vorax opened his portal in the first place."

Master Jairun shot her a glance, and she gave a slight bow of her head. "Forgive me. I meant no criticism. I only meant it's clear the Rescuer held the monsters at bay. To my reckoning, nothing else explains the time we've had."

Several in the hall voiced their agreement, and with that prompting, Master Jairun opened their discussion with a prayer. "*Vynovu, Rumosh,*" he said as he finished. "*Se vy'enu.*"

They all answered in the Common Tongue. "Your ways, High One. Not ours."

Dame Silvana leaned against the hall's great hearth and bent her head to one side. "So, Headmaster. As you said, war is upon us. What now? Go north again? Look for a second portal?"

Master Jairun shook his head. "A single portal proved a poor tactic for the enemy. Vorax ruled the southernmost cantons, ignored by the greater dragon lords for generations. He may have leapt ahead of his master's wishes by sending goblins into that unstable hollow hill."

"If a portal could still be opened, ya think Heleyor would've waited this long?" Quinton asked.

"He is waiting. Plotting. Building. Always. But he may not have known the full story or power of that portal. Heleyor is not omniscient. He only pretends to be. And true to his own dragon nature, Vorax acted in pride. And that may have prevented him from reporting his efforts to Ras Pyras. We know for certain that growing and directing the portal took all his abilities–so much that a handful of fledgling cadets were able to stop him."

Pedrig flattened his ears. "A handful of cadets aided by a

Havarra wolf and a battle-hardened guardian of the light, I'll remind you."

"Yes. Of course. My point is, Vorax's plan was rushed and ill-conceived. Heleyor is equally prideful, but he won't be so rash. The hollow hills are few. I doubt he'll risk losing them on a tactic that already failed."

Tiran worked to understand the guardians' exchange. The dragon Vorax had used his mind to steer an unstable hollow hill–a portal formed by a fold in the fabric of creation–to send dark creatures into Keledev. The cadets had collapsed the portal, and it had reappeared in a new location as one of the Rescuer's hollow trees, out of the dragons' reach. This was a victory, but troubling questions remained. "If this new incursion is not the result of a hollow hill, then how did the creature enter our land?"

"How indeed, Mister Yar." Master Jairun nodded toward the wolf. "I think Pedrig may shed some light on the question."

In answer, Pedrig asked Tiran a question of his own–a hard one. "Tell me, son of autumn, when you saw the parcelman's wounds. Did you see any sign of infection?"

Tiran shuddered to picture Barnabas lying there in the brush, red wounds tinted black in the dark. The old cut on his forehead flashed with pain, and he touched his rag to the spot. "He'd been there a while. I saw insects and . . ."

"Lace," Teegan said, coming to his aid. "A growth with the look of gray lace surrounded the cuts."

"Mmm." Pedrig padded in a slow circle. "The daughter of winter and I saw the same. On a wolf pup high on the peaks."

Belen, who'd remained silent and watchful up to that moment, stood from the bench where he'd been sitting. "Lichen. And lichen means frost goblins. They alone infect their victims with such fungus."

The wolf's ears came forward, and he lowered his muzzle, which Tiran had learned was his way of nodding. "Agreed. Both the parcelman and the pup suffered wounds from a frost goblin's soiled ice blade. The attack on the parcelman makes some sense. These corruptions are drawn to humans. But why should one appear so near the Clefts of Semajin, where no humans live, and few may tread?"

Dame Silvana left her place by the hearth. "What are you saying, Master Wolf?"

"I'm saying it is possible our enemies have found a way to harden the frost goblins even more. I'm saying these creatures may need no portal. They may have climbed over the Celestial Peaks."

As Tiran tried to take this all in, his shessa glanced around the room. "Daughter of winter," she said. "You mean Kara. So, she saw evidence of a frost goblin as well. But where is she now?"

It was the headmaster who answered. "I have not disturbed her with this news of Barnabas. Not yet. I sent her out on her fourth quest before dawn–into Argallan's Maze."

27

KARA
ARGALLAN'S MAZE

"ADMIT IT. YOU'RE LOST."

Kara glanced back from the bow of the rowboat and pursed her lips at the young cadet manning the oars. "I'm not lost, Paskin. I chose the right stream." But the instant she looked forward again, the confidence in her expression waned. *I hope.*

The steep, gravelly walls of the ravines all looked the same. And to get lost during the Navigator's Quest was to fail, and another failure would kill her chances of entering the spheres with Connor and the others. By the time she tried again, Keir might be dead.

Her small party of three had been rowing upstream for more than an hour since she'd called for the turn off the main flow of the Gathering. They had to find the Sleeping Unicorn promised by her cryptic map before midday. So far–nothing. And now the featureless scree slopes were closing in on them.

Dag, resting from his last turn at rowing on the bench between her and Paskin, massaged his arms and looked up at the slopes as if they were the most interesting landmarks in all Keledev. "Have either of you read *Argallan's Woes*?"

Paskin snorted. "Who wants to read tales of another's sorrows? No living soul in all Talania has read that text–apart from you, I guess."

"Then I *guess* all Talania is missing out," Dag said. "Sometimes we must read another's sorrows to better understand ourselves."

A rebuke from an older cadet–especially of Dag's size–should have shut Paskin's mouth for at least another league. And by the faint upward turn of his lips, Kara gathered that this was Dag's intent.

"The writer," the miner said, "who remains unknown, says this maze was the last of Argallan's woes. Argallan left Ras Telesar to explore it not long after the rising of the Celestial Peaks and never returned. Hence the name."

Kara cast a hard look his way.

"What? I'm not saying we'll be lost forever. The maze has been mapped a dozen times or more since then."

She nodded, but as she turned her eyes to the map Master Jairun had given her–purposefully incomplete–a thought struck her. "But did the others who mapped the ravine ever find Argallan's body?"

"Now that you mention it, I don't think so."

Paskin stopped rowing. "Well, that's not disconcerting at all." Apparently not even Dag could shut him up–a good thing, because he clapped and pointed off the starboard bow. "Look there!"

It took Kara's eyes a little longer to break the formation out from among the gray rocks, but when she did, she smiled. She saw the bent knees and hooves, the head bowed in slumber with a long horn. The empty spaces and shadows between the rocks formed a Havarra horse king–a unicorn. Now she understood why Master Jairun had told her to find it before midday. Once the sun passed to the west, the shadows would turn, and the picture would vanish.

The changing position of the boat began to obscure the shape. Kara locked her gaze on the spot and ordered Paskin to put in. "Good work," she told him. "Sharp eyes."

He seemed surprised by her praise. "Um. Thank you."

Kara hurried her companions out of the boat and walked up the steep gravel straight to the unicorn, where she turned to face the direction its horn had pointed and checked the map. "The way I read this, we should find what the map calls the Narrow Way a half league from here—perhaps a crevice passing through one of the ravine walls. Then there's an empty space on the map. Once we cross it, we're done."

"Easy as brambleberry pie," Paskin said.

The task proved him wrong. When they came through the Narrow Way to the empty space on the map, they found it quite full.

Since the party had first rowed into the ravines, they'd been surrounded by scree—steep slopes of gravel formed by ice breaking bits of rock from the ridgelines. But here, the ice had broken off huge chunks and dropped them into a wide field. Hundreds of blocks and pillars created alleys and thoroughfares, like a city of stone without doors or windows.

Paskin walked out in front of the other two and turned, spreading his hands. "It's a boulder field."

"No," Dag said. "It's a maze—one within another. And Kara must lead us through to win her third ringlet."

She eyed him, feeling the two stacked ringlets already on her finger. "You've been here before."

"On my own Navigator's Quest. Yes. And I'm here to make sure you come through yours alive. Make no mistake, this is a perilous place. Only one path will lead you to the other side. Others may leave you trapped here until you die of exposure and lack of water."

Paskin sidled up to the big cadet and cocked his head. "Are you sure you can get us out of here—you know, if she flubs it?"

Kara hit him with a frown.

Dag shrugged. "Pretty sure."

Within half a tick, Kara was hopelessly lost, so that even backtracking did her no good. Dag remained inscrutable, and knowing he knew the solution made her agonize over his every sniff, cough, and grunt. Exasperated, she paused for a breather at a rough circle of standing pillars—one they'd seen before. When she sat on a round stone, the look in Paskin's eyes posed the same challenge he'd voiced in the rowboat. *Admit it. You're lost.*

Another failure. Oh, how she'd underestimated these quests.

Her hope of passing them before the Turning of the Spheres—of heading into Tanelethar to seek Keir—were over.

Letting her head fall back in defeat, Kara noticed one of the blocks in the circle stood taller than the rest. Much taller. "Huh," she said out loud.

Dag leaned against the boulder closest to the tall one. There were three in all, like stair steps. He raised an eyebrow. "What are you thinking, Raidleader?"

"I'm thinking that if you climbed up to that middle boulder, you might lift Paskin high enough to climb onto the tallest. He could see our way out."

The miner grinned. "He's kind of short. I can't lift him high enough for his hands to reach, but I could probably throw him."

Paskin jumped up from his resting spot. "Hey! That's not—"

Kara screamed. Pain shot through her body. She clutched her midsection and doubled over, falling from her seat, and her shoulder slammed into the gravel. But that was nothing compared to the searing burn at her belly—like a hot blade tracing a line from hip to hip. "Dag . . . Help!"

The miner held her still and moved her hands away from her stomach. "What is it? What's wrong?"

"I don't know."

Kara's eyes popped wide. She arched as another invisible blade sliced into her back. It drew an *s*-curve down her spine. She rolled over and tried to knock it away, but her fist swiped through empty air.

Her head swam, and in the strange waves of light and dark, she saw black scales and wings tipped with red. She heard a terrible laugh. Beneath it, a familiar voice cried, "No more!"

"No more what?" Paskin yelled.

Had Kara's own voice joined the one in her head? "Dag, get us out of here."

"Are you sure? To pass, you have to lead us."

"Now, Dag!" Kara barely got the words out, and then the knife hit her again, and all went dark and silent.

28

THE PRISONER
TANELETHAR

ALL THINGS ARE PAIN. ALL IS SORROW.

I cannot lift my head, so that I cannot look away from the blood at my belly, the cuts on my legs. My brehnan visit me, apply the knife at the dragon's behest, while his thoughts mingle with mine. He revels in my pain, my fear.

He sees her.

With each cut, her face flashes before me. I tried to hide her from him. I was supposed to protect her. Liam told me to protect her—a name, a brehna, that I remember now. I failed them both.

Lord Valshadox calls to her, and I cannot stop him.

Another prisoner comes. He is weak, as I was. He applies the knife. I scream.

KARA
KELEDEV
RAS TELESAR

"KEIR!"

Kara bolted upright on the straw mattress.

Calming hands caught her and eased her back again.

"Shh," Dame Silvana said. "Breathe, girl."

Teegan was there too, adjusting the pillow as Kara's head came back. "You're safe, Shessa. You're in the barracks at Ras Telesar."

"My stomach. My arms and legs. My back. The blood. The cuts."

"There are no cuts, dear. You're under attack–a special kind." Dame Silvana laid a hand on Kara's forehead and prayed. *"Alosov adverenu rethro delanu. Alos numovu adverenu malpedanu.* Do you recognize this verse?"

Through you, we drive back our foes. Through you, we trample them.

"Yes, Dame Silvana."

"Take hold of the words. Understand them and know the Rescuer is greater than any enemy. Let his peace fill your mind and heart."

Kara breathed deep. *You are mighty. You are sovereign.* The rapid beating of her heart slowed, and once she felt steady, she sat up and swung her legs out of the bed. Teegan tried to stop her from standing, but Kara pushed her hands away. "I'm fine–well enough, anyway. I need to see the headmaster."

She expected an argument, but Silvana offered none. The guardian stepped back, giving Kara room to walk on her own. "If you feel you're ready, dear."

Dag waited in the passage outside the women's barracks, hands red from wringing. "Thank the Maker, you're all right."

"I am." She waved off his offered arm. "And getting better by the moment." She let him walk beside her on the way to the ninth level. "The maze. You carried me out, didn't you?"

"Paskin helped, or tried to. Turns out the best way to shut him up is a crisis. He stayed quiet when it mattered and kept his head about him. You'd have been proud."

She answered only with a fleeting smile, unable to get past his choice of words. *A crisis.* Her crisis. Keir was suffering now, and Kara knew for certain she was on the edge of losing him. At the same time, she'd failed a second quest. Her hopes of finding him were almost gone.

Rescuer, I know I gave this hope to you when I walked through the door. But I always believed you would grant it to me in your time. Help me understand why you've taken it away. Why must I let my brehna die without knowing you?

"Thank you," she said to Dag, swallowing a sob. "Pardon my tears. I'm not ungrateful. But since I failed another quest, my hopes of joining you and the others at the Turning of the Spheres are over."

"You mean your hopes of finding Keir?"

She glanced up at him, and he gave her an embarrassed shrug. "You spoke his name a dozen times or more on the journey home. I put two and two together. And, if he hadn't yet, the headmaster has now. I had to give a full account."

"That's it then."

"Don't think about the quests. They'll keep. And you'll enter the spheres in the Rescuer's time, this year or next. Right now, we've much larger concerns."

The graveness of Dag's tone told Kara all she needed to know. She'd guessed much from her talk with Pedrig on the way home from the Clefts of Semajin. "Dark creatures have entered Keledev."

He nodded. "And taken a life. Keledan blood was spilt on Keledan land. As Luthelan the Herald wrote in his unfinished epic, 'The first sorrows of war have come. Many more will follow.'"

Master Jairun came out from behind his desk as Kara entered his chambers. He leaned upon his staff, looking her over. "Feeling better, are we?"

"Well enough to make the climb to the ninth level." She gave him a wry smile. "A test, I assume."

"We often claim we're all right when we aren't. Usually, a physical test is only half the measurement. A renewer must also consider the patient's spirit. But in this case"–he bent to examine her face and tilted his head at an odd angle, as if to look past her eyes–"the two are linked. Are you aware of what happened?"

Painfully aware. "My brehna Keir is being tortured. I felt every stab and cut as if the knife were in my own flesh."

The headmaster returned to his desk. "A dragon attacked you through him–pushed its way into your thoughts."

"I didn't know that was possible."

"It is if you do not choose to push the creature out. You know how."

"The song. The Scrolls."

"Yes. Yet you applied neither until Dame Silvana helped you. And that tells me you chose to endure the pain. Why do you think that is, my girl?"

Kara knew why. "I wanted to see Keir, feel his presence and the life still in him. I wanted to learn what I could about where he'd gone."

Master Jairun nodded. "What you suffered is an old and well-used tactic—meant to tempt a Keledan into danger through a family member. Each generation believes they are seeing something new, but the gambits of the enemy rarely change." He narrowed his eyes—not at Kara, but at something beyond her, in a place only the headmaster could see. "To be honest, I expected to see such an attack on another cadet first, much sooner."

She didn't ask which cadet. That was not her place. "So, in the future, I am to flee from the dragon's attack. I'm to put Keir out of my mind and give him up for lost."

"Oh, no." Master Jairun used his staff to lower himself into his chair and pushed his long legs out in front of him. "You see, Miss Orso, we flee from some attacks. For others, we hold our ground, shield ready. And some attacks, like this one, we rush to meet head-on with spear and sword."

Rush to meet. Spear and sword. Kara tightened her fist to keep control of her hands and heart. "Sir, what is it you want of me?"

"By calling you out through your brother, this dragon has overstepped—exposed its scaly flank, so to speak. Your connection to Keir—not the creature—may allow you to find him, and perhaps solve the mystery of where *all* the disappearing Aladoth have gone." Master Jairun bent forward in his chair. "I'm sending you into Tanelethar. Go find your brother and save him if you can."

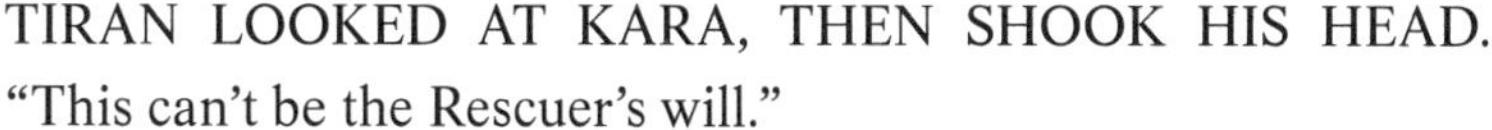

TIRAN LOOKED AT KARA, THEN SHOOK HIS HEAD. "This can't be the Rescuer's will."

Master Jairun had brought her down to Nevethav, the chapel on the outcropping at the academy's center. The other guardians waited there with Tiran, Teegan, and Dag, seated around the steaming hot spring fountain. Pedrig had also come. He stayed aloof, walking the stone paths through the nine sections of the chapel's fruit garden, thinking whatever thoughts wolves think when war comes to them.

The headmaster had ordered Tiran to join Kara on her mission to find Keir. "I can't go into Tanelethar. I'm not meant to enter the Dragon Lands anymore–not after what happened."

"Are you questioning my discernment as the head of the Order, Mister Yar?"

"Well . . . Yes."

Belen coughed. Quinton dropped his forehead into a hand and muttered, "Help us."

The headmaster leaned upon his staff and offered a patient smile. "I appreciate your candor, Cadet. But you're still going."

Tiran. He, out of all of them, was the one Master Jairun had paired with Kara for her first expedition across the barrier since joining the Keledan. She took up his cause, not for the same reason. "Shouldn't we wait for Connor and Lee to return from Sky Harbor? They've been on more missions. Surely, a larger raid party would be best."

"Mr. Enarian has sent no reports from the road, so I do not know how soon they may arrive." Master Jairun lowered his chin and lifted his pupils to look at both of them. "Will the two of you make Keir wait for rescue to suit your own comfort?"

Neither answered.

"Good. Then it's settled. Mister Yar will accompany Miss Orso in the raid to seek her brother and the missing Aladoth.

Mister Kaivos and Miss Yar will search the slopes between the clefts and Thousand Falls for signs of frost goblins."

"What about us?" Quinton said. "Will the guardians always leave the fightin' ta the cadets?"

"I'm sorry, my friend. Our time to fight is coming soon. But for now, the academy's work is doubled. We must speed the training of the new recruits."

"And defend them," Belen added. "If goblins roam the slopes, it won't be long before they try to breach our gate."

The mention of goblins at the gate ended all discussion. Master Jairun wasted no more time and set them all to praying in preparation for their missions. They began together, and then the cadets and Pedrig broke into their separate parties, each joined by two or three guardians.

Kara and Tiran prayed with Silvana and Baldomar around a small pool among the brambleberry shrubs. Silvana prayed first, reciting the High One's words back to him. "*Kesehcer ala'ov lut perah fi shalom nakav sestenoliov, mi alerov credol.* The mind dependent on you. Perfect peace. In the face of fear and doubt, bless these two with trust in your goodness and might."

Baldomar stood over them, gripping Kara's shoulder and Tiran's with powerful blacksmith's hands. "*Okethi, anu mi ke'Liberavor logopedorah, okeb Rumosh filelod aloslanu krafah, ma ke'Liberavor shegamanu yi Rumosh kaforov.* As ambassadors for him, we seek reconciliation. There are many to be rescued. Though they fight against us, let your servants show them your love."

After these prayers, Silvana brought Kara to the side, under the pink blossoms of a cherry tree. She lowered Kara's sapphire pendant into her palm by the chain. "This jewel is a token of your family, correct?"

Without taking her eyes off the pendant, Kara nodded.

"I thought so. You've never said as much, but there was no need. And I understood when you stopped wearing it. But now, a dragon has your brother and troubles his mind." The guardian closed Kara's fist around the necklace. "When you find him, this may help him to see you for who you are."

Master Jairun spoke one more prayer over the whole group before sending them off to the armory and the outfitter. "Leave tonight," he said once he'd finished. "And make haste. Every tick we lose in discovering the enemy's plans may cost a hundred lives or more in the end. Never forget, the Rescuer is with us."

In unison, they all answered, "Always and forever."

29

CONNOR
TANELETHAR
HIGHLAND FOREST

ZEL HOVERED *THE STARLING* AT TREETOP LEVEL–NO easy feat. Connor watched with growing respect as she worked the lamp dials and the vents to hold their position.

"You won't have to do this long," Lee said, tossing a rope over the side. "Once we're down, return to Faelin's homestead and wait for us. Try to land there before sunrise."

"Alone?" The airship started to sink, and Zel increased the vapors pouring up into the center pouch to raise her again. "You want me to wait alone in the Dragon Lands?"

Connor shook his head. "Not alone. The Rescuer is with you. And as you said before, you're not trained for the dangers of Tanelethar. My patehpa's homestead is the safest place for you–a sanctuary. Wait there for our return."

"And if you don't return, what then? Am I to move in? Settle down as a charwood merchant in this land of monsters?"

"Some make that choice. They were once called salt warriors. But we're not asking that of you. In the armory, you'll find a map of the area around Trader's Knoll. The red glass Lee found will show you the location of a hollow tree portal. If we don't return in a week, go there. By the Rescuer's will, he'll send you home. But first, scuttle *The Starling*."

Zel let go of her dials. "Do what?"

"You heard me. We can't leave your tehpa's design for the enemy to find. The enemy steals and corrupts–uses what is good for ill. Flying dragons and granogs are bad enough. The last thing the Order needs in this fight are goblins and golmogs taking to the Taneletharian skies. Or worse–giant cave spiders falling on our raid parties from above."

"Thank you." Lee slapped him in the arm. "Thank you very much. Now I'll have nightmares for a month." He climbed over the side and started down the rope.

Connor followed, pausing at the rail. "If anything foul approaches while we're on the rope–anything that looks neither human nor animal–shoot it." He started down, then paused again and looked up. "Shoot it twice just to be sure."

Once they'd dropped onto an overgrown trail, Lee tugged on the rope, and *The Starling* rose, fading into a low cloud. He watched until the last trace of the airship vanished. "I could get used to that."

"I'd rather not," Connor said. "The Maker gave us no wings of our own. We should take that as a sign." He started down the trail. "Come on. Show me where you found the entrance."

In the year since their last visit, Connor, Lee, and Kara had taken to calling this place the Meadow Beneath, the same name Faelin had given it on his map. Lee often said the mineral formations–a perfect model of a green meadow and a golden path under deep blue sky–gave evidence of the Maker's whimsy.

Whatever the Maker's purpose in the crystal cave's design, they'd found that such formations were signs of shairosite. Banishing powder. The key ingredient of the hollow hill portals once used by the Elder Folk and the kings and queens of men.

"Are you sure about this?" Connor asked as the two entered the cave. He stared at the pools among the sharp green crystals that formed the meadow's grass. "Last time, this cave and its portal gave us no end of trouble."

"The rattlefish is gone. You killed it. And once we settled down and leaned on the Rescuer, the portal brought us to the place we were supposed to be–to the valley of the dragon's stronghold."

Sometimes Connor wondered if Lee actually heard the things he said. "Let's pray the portal doesn't send us to the doorsteps of any more dragons. We're here for the Red Dagger, not a rescue."

"You mean the Rapha Key," Lee countered.

"I don't think so. But we'll have to decide one way or another soon. By the Rescuer's will, the powder and this portal will get us to the sanctuary at Graywater Bay within the hour."

They had learned on their last visit, thanks to one of Faelin's maps, that the waterfall pouring into the cave's largest pool brought shairosite with it, leaving a rich deposit of the silver powder at the bottom. Lee stood guard while Connor dove to collect some.

Filling the leather pouches while floating with his back to the dark water brought terrible memories. Red eyes. Flashing scales. A hard battle for survival. But Connor put his faith in his friend and the Rescuer and kept working. He surfaced moments later with his prize.

Lee knelt at the water's edge beside their lantern and took both pouches, then handed Connor two more. "We should take as much as we can carry. Wouldn't want to run out if things go awry."

"You know the longer we stay here, the greater the chance of attack, right?"

"Then you should hurry."

Connor kicked away from the crystal-lined shore. "Remind me why you, the better diver, aren't doing this?"

"I'm also the better shot." Lee clipped the pouches to the belt of his manykit and took up his bow again. "Tell me you can shoot a fish in a pool, accounting for the trickeries of water, and we'll switch places."

Connor gave him a frown, then dove under.

Every beat he was down there, he imagined red eyes coming at him, the sharp tailfins of a river troll ready to slice into his legs.

None appeared, and before he knew it, Lee was pulling him out onto a smooth piece of shore. "See," the scribe said, handing him his manykit vest. "No river trolls. No golmogs."

Lee waited until Connor had secured his straps and clipped the second pair of pouches to his belt, then clapped him on the shoulder. "We cleared this place of its foul inhabitants last time, my friend. There are likely no other dark creatures that know this place exists."

"Dark creatures know and remember little, Lee. It's the dragons who steer them that we must worry about, and dragons know and remember much."

Before the echo of Connor's words returned from the crystal walls, a black arrow whistled past his ear.

30

NOT AGAIN.

Connor heard the twang of Lee's bow beside him, followed by his cry. "You were right! Grab your arms!"

Once more, Connor found himself in a field of sharp crystals, sword and crook out of reach and facing a dark foe. Existing in the present and a memory at the same time made his movements feel slow and languid, like swimming through the cave pools around him.

"Connor, hurry!"

Two more creatures fell from the scribe's arrows before Connor finally swept up his weapons and cloak. Once he had them, he urged Lee toward their only path out of there–the same one they'd used before. "We should retreat into the falls."

"You first. I'll hold them off."

Goblins kept pouring through the entrance–twelve, perhaps fifteen–growing in number. Connor didn't stop to count before backing through the sheets of frigid water.

Lee backed through after him, exchanging his bow for one of his double-bladed sikaria throwing knives in preparation for a close fight. "Gird your weapons and take the lantern. I'll keep them at bay until the shairosite takes effect."

The waterfall would give them only a short reprieve. As soon as Connor had his sword and crook in their sheaths, he ran over the slippery wet stone to the back, where they'd last seen the cave's unstable portal. What he found there made his heart sink.

"Lee!"

The scribe, with ghostly red Keledan armor glowing all about him, slashed open a goblin's neck as it pushed through the falls, swiped a curved pyranium sword from its hand, and kicked it out again. "Are you ready?"

"No. I think we're in trouble."

The remains of the river troll Connor had killed before lay right where he'd left them–fleshless legs of woven fish bone cut off at the hip where the portal had closed on the creature. But the portal was not where Connor had left it. The black void had solidified into a wall of rose-colored crystals. "The portal's gone!"

"Try the shairosite."

"Working on it." Connor drew a handful of silver powder from one of the pouches. "Please, let this work." He threw it against the wall.

The shairosite fell into a glittering heap on the floor. Did the Rescuer want them to battle this whole horde on their own?

Goblins, due to their number and the pleasure they took in torturing Aladoth, ranked high among the targets of the Order. The guardians had taught Connor and the other cadets never to leave these fungal creatures alive unless engaging them might hinder the mission. Of course, it seemed to Connor that getting killed here in this cave might hinder their quest quite a bit. He glanced upward and whispered, "Really?"

Lee backed toward him, swinging against a surge of foes with both knife and sword. "I can't hold them alone!"

"You don't have to." Connor drew his crook from the sheath at his back and stabbed into a goblin's chest with its spiked foot. "There's nothing else for me to try. The portal's gone. We'll have to fight our way to the cave entrance."

Together, aided by the narrow passage, they pressed their enemies back. Connor's sword, the dragonslayer Revornosh, passed through the cave goblins' fungal flesh without the slightest resistance. The ram's horn of his crook crunched their brittleknit skulls. Only by sheer numbers could this enemy give the cadets a challenge. But their numbers were great.

Smashed by a goblin knife, the lantern at Connor's hip went out. He needed the Rescuer's light to keep fighting. "*Se lashov fi kebreesel mahesoth amord, dar letu dorlasov*!"

Take no part in the deeds of darkness, but expose them!

Brilliant white flame shone from Revornosh. Black irises at the centers of the goblins' yellow eyes narrowed in unison, and they shielded their faces.

"Forward!" Lee shouted.

They sped their advance, bashing the creatures with their Keledan shields and trampling them under glowing boots until they reached the falls. The two paused at the sheet of water long enough to share an *Are we ready?* glance, then let out a mighty cry and leapt through.

The crystal meadow was empty, except for the lifeless bodies of a few creatures and a single living goblin who hadn't joined his comrades in the charge. That last standing goblin stared at them with blank eyes, then fell dead as a fresh crossbow bolt lodged itself in its skull.

A voice called down from above. "Connor? Lee?"

"Zel?" Connor rushed to the edge of the big pool, where he could see up through the hole in the cave ceiling. *The Starling* hovered above, silk pouches brushing the pines.

A rope fell down. "Quickly. More are coming!" As if to emphasize her point, Zel looked away into the distance, and loosed a bolt at an enemy outside the cave, beyond Connor's sight.

Connor jumped across the water and grabbed the rope, feeling *The Starling* dip with his weight. He scrambled up several feet to make room for his friend and swung for the shore. "Lee, time to go!"

The moment Lee caught the rope, Connor heard a powerful rush of flame and vapor from the airship's lamps, and *The Starling* shot upward. More goblins ran into the cave. Arrows plinked off the ceiling's blue crystals as the cadets rose through the hole. Other goblins waited in the forest above, but Zel kept their heads down with her crossbow, firing blind in the end, until she'd carried the full length of the rope and its passengers into the cloud cover.

Connor kept his eyes skyward in his climb. "Rescuer help me. *Podovu motah se natholiond. Shalorovu se sumiond.*"

He will not allow your foot to slip.

Connor had always been a skilled climber, but something about flying and climbing at the same time made the task seem formidable indeed, like swimming against a current. Once he clambered over the rail, he turned to haul Lee in behind him. They both dropped to the wicker floor. "How?" Connor asked between heavy breaths. "Why?"

Zel seemed to take his meaning. "The creatures entered from the bare hills to the west–dozens of them. I expect one of them noticed our arrival and went to get his friends. I saw them only by the grace of the High One. If not for a break in the clouds, I'd have flown back to Faelin's sanctuary none the wiser."

"His grace, to be sure. And we needed you for more than a rescue." Connor frowned and shook his head. "The portal we were counting on has sealed itself. As dangerous as it may be, *The Starling* is our only way north. The journey on the ground could take a month or more–far too long."

Lee pulled himself up and gave her a hug. "What my good friend means to say is, 'Thank you.' Coming back for us, knowing those goblins might pierce your silk with an arrow and bring you down, showed real courage."

Zel shrugged. "What good is a ship captain if she leaves her passengers behind?"

The scribe grinned, but his smile froze when his eyes turned to Connor. He pointed. "Connor, your hand. Does it hurt?"

Connor felt no pain—perhaps some tingling, but that was expected after climbing a rope. He squinted at his friend, then glanced down and gasped. Dark gray mist lit by purple flashes swirled like a storm in his palm, gathering strength from the cloud that hid the airship. He jumped to his feet, palm out at arm's length. "What is this?"

"The shairosite," Lee said. "Your hand was covered with it after your efforts in the cave."

Shaking his hand did little to remove the powder, and Connor dared not wipe such a volatile substance on his cloak. He'd seen firsthand what might happen if part of a creature entered a portal—the rest might be left behind. He tried blowing the miniature storm away and achieved minor success. Sparkling shairosite flew from his hand and carried wisps of cloud with it.

Lee let out a short laugh. "Oh, I have a lovely idea. Lovely! And you're both going to hate it."

PART THREE

STORMRIDER

"For I know the plans I have for you–this is the Lord's declaration–plans for your well-being, not for disaster, to give you a future and a hope."

Jeremiah 29:11

31

CONNOR
TANELETHAR
ABOVE THE HIGHLAND FOREST

"NOT ON YOUR LIFE, LEE TRANG." ZEL STOOD BETWEEN the scribe and *The Starling*'s three vapor lamps, arms spread wide. "You'll not get anywhere near them with that powder. Are you intent on bringing us all to a fiery end?"

"Quite the opposite." Lee made no effort to get around her. He rested his back against the rail, shaking a pouch of the volatile shairosite as if it were a bag of figs or coins. "This is the fastest way to reach the place where Lef Amunrel disappeared and where the search for the Rapha Key ended. The Storm Mists didn't destroy *The Starling* when the Rescuer brought us through. This active shairosite has done no harm to Connor's hand. How many hints must our master give us before we take his meaning?"

As Connor listened to his friend, the voice from the Storm Mists returned to him, and in the calm of the moment, he remembered the words clearly—a verse from the Scrolls. He spoke it out loud. "*Howda'anu koth kolama vadsepah mi kerator ma aneth avah'od, ma aneth vi zamethod hal serend.*"

Zel turned to look at him. "What was that?"

"A sacred verse. Do you know it?"

She shook her head, so Connor translated as best he could. "It means the High One works all things together for the good of those who love him and who are called for his purpose. And the verses that precede it tell us he intervenes to help us, even when we don't know what to ask for."

"You're taking Lee's side, aren't you? You're willing to risk the ship. Our lives."

"Risk," Connor said, repeating a saying of the Vanguard that Swordmaster Quinton had taught them, "is both the consequence and the reward of faith."

Zel studied him for several beats, then nodded to Lee. "Go ahead, then. Either we leap through creation to Graywater Bay, or we go this hour to Elamhavar."

"We'll go where he sends us," Connor said. "That's all we can ask."

Before letting Lee put his plan into action, Connor took both their hands and led them in the verse he'd quoted one more time, taking its assurance and making it a prayer. When he finished, he opened his eyes. "*Vynovu, Rumosh.* Your way, High One."

"*Se vy'enu,*" Lee answered. "Not ours. Zel, guide us into the heart of this cloud."

Zel sailed *The Starling* deeper in, until the air itself soaked the fur collars of their cloaks. Once she matched the ship with the cloud's movement, Lee lifted the bag of shairosite up to the vapor lamps and spread the powder into their rising heat.

A smoky dark blue vortex formed above each lamp, glittering with silver flashes. The apothecarist's concoction had mixed with the banishing powder to create a new substance. Connor's instincts commanded him to sweep the vortexes away from the lamps before they grew, but he resisted. He fought for trust in the High One.

Soon, the vortexes joined together and spread outside the wicker ship to encircle it and the pouches. Blue smoke spiraled around them, then enveloped the entire craft in a thick curtain, inside and out.

"Lee?"

"Still here!"

Connor felt a hand on his, and then another on his arm. His

friends were with him. As for *The Starling,* he couldn't tell. He no longer felt the floor beneath his feet.

The smoke evaporated.

Clear night air. Wicker. Silk. The sound of a tremendous rip.

Falling.

"Zel!" Connor shouted, hanging on to a truss as his feet rose above his head.

"I'm on it!"

The Starling plunged toward jagged peaks. Zel clawed her way along its alderwood structure to the lamps and turned the dials to their maximum. One by one, she drew three vials from her belt and dumped them in. Vapors, with no sign of the shairosite glitter, billowed upward into the pouches.

Their fall slowed. Connor's feet returned to an appropriate position relative to his head, and he alighted on the bow bench. But they were still descending. In the distance, he saw moonlight snaking across black water. The light seemed alive. How was that possible? Waves?

No. Fog.

The mission started here at Graywater Bay, named for its perpetual fog. The whole region is steeped in it.

Moving his gaze northwest from the shore, he spied a hilltop ruin. Three ring-walls surrounded its chapel, much like the four walls of Ras Telesar had been before the rising of the peaks.

"*Ras Heval,*" Lee said. "The temple ruin where Faelin was attacked. The Rescuer brought us to the place we hoped."

The mountains below drew closer still. Connor lifted a hand to get Zel's attention. "Hold us here if you can. We must find the sanctuary."

"Would that I could! The main pouch is damaged. I can't stop our descent!"

Looking up, Connor saw vapors trailing *The Starling.* The silk had torn in the trip through the portal. But why? Hadn't they done what the Rescuer wanted?

He'd have to worry about that later. "Lee, is my patehpa's map still sharp in your mind?"

"Yes. And with Ras Heval and Graywater Bay in sight, I can fix the position of the sanctuary glade despite all this fog. It's close." He dropped a green lens over his right eye and leaned out from the bow, then snapped his fingers and pointed with his whole hand. "Got it. Port, Zel. Thirty degrees. That's our fastest line."

"Wait!" Connor called. "Not yet." He'd watched Zel enough to learn that a turn meant more than a rudder movement. She also had to vent vapors from the opposite side, and venting meant a faster fall. "There's a high ridge to port. If we turn now, we'll drop too fast and hit it for sure."

Zel turned the ship anyway.

Connor whipped around, eyes wide. "Didn't you hear me?"

"I know what I'm doing. Grab the bar and stand at the bow."

"The bar?"

She jogged his memory with a nod toward the iron ballast block—the one she'd shown him way back in the field outside Kamel Rov.

"Right. Lee, help me."

The two cadets lifted the bar by its two handles, all the way to their shoulders. "On your call," Connor said, gritting his teeth under the bar's weight.

The Starling raced toward the mountain ridge.

"Hold . . . Hold . . ."

The ridge rose to hide the horizon from Connor's sight. *The Starling* looked sure to crash into the gray mist clinging to its rocky flank. "Zel!"

"Now!"

Connor and Lee heaved the ballast weight over the bow, and *The Starling* lurched, both slowing down and shooting upward. The horizon reappeared. But no sooner had hope bloomed in Connor's chest, than he felt the ship begin to sink again. "Was it enough?"

Zel kept her hand on the rudder and made no other move to work her dials or vents. "It'll have to be. There's nothing more we can do."

Lee had a better eye for targets and trajectories. Connor could see him trying to work it all out. "Well?"

"Too close." The scribe's features twisted in an expectant cringe. "Much too close to tell."

The ridge did not wait for him to decide. It rose to meet *The Starling.* An instant before they hit, Connor cried out, "Hold on!" and gripped the wicker rail.

The runners sparked off uneven stone, jolting the three passengers right and left. *The Starling* bounced and was airborne once more, then hit and bounced again. But there was no third impact.

Lee slapped the bow, laughing. "We're over!"

"Nothing's over yet." Zel returned to her place at the rudder. "We crossed that ridge, but we're still going down."

"Yes," Lee said, "but we're almost over the glade. Just keep the runners level and let her fall as gently as you can for your docking."

"Landing."

"Whichever."

Neither would be as easy as Lee made it sound. Looking below, Connor saw the same fog that had clung to the southwest side of the ridgeline filling the glade. He could only take it on faith in the Rescuer and the occasional treetop poking through that the glade truly existed. The map had called this range *Rimoth Shumordi,* the Fading or Muddled Mountains. Now Connor understood why–the mountains perpetually seemed to fade as if being devoured by the fog.

That fog devoured *The Starling* soon enough, and still they fell–much longer than Connor expected. Waiting for the impact was excruciating.

"Oof!" He let out a grunting shout when the runners hit. She jerked left and right, then skidded long and straight through tall, wet grass.

When they finally came to rest, Lee flopped down on the bow bench and looked up at the other two. "Well. We're on the ground. And the oddest part is, we're back in the clouds too."

All three burst into laughter.

32

KARA
KELEDEV
WESTERN VALE OF THE PASSAGE LAKES

KARA HADN'T VISITED EITHER VALE OF THE PASSAGE Lakes before, eastern or western. When the Rescuer brought her and Connor to Keledev after the destruction of the dragon's portal, he'd chosen to send them to a pool in the Forest of Believing, almost on the doorstep of the academy. Kara had found that a mercy at a time when Connor had lost his patehpa and they both thought all their friends had perished, but she'd also felt pangs of jealousy each time the others had set off for these lakes on their scouting missions.

She marveled at cascades higher up the Western Vale, catching the moonlight as they carried cold waters down from one lake to the next. She and Tiran had arrived in late evening at Lake Humility, the lowest of the western lakes. She knelt at the shore to lift a handful of black sand and let it sift through her fingers. "Do they all have black shores? Is that some special quality of a lake portal?"

"Only this one," Master Belen replied, lowering himself from his saddle. He'd ridden with them as a guide and to bring their horses back to the academy. "Each of the Passage Lakes is unique, much like we are–one more way the Maker reveals his glory."

The guardian dug in his saddlebags, and after a moment drew

out a circular brass box. He opened the lid and called Tiran closer, placing the object in his hands. "No matter where you are in the Dragon Lands, my boy. This will guide you south to the Rescuer's mighty peaks."

Kara stood at Tiran's shoulder and watched as he turned the box slowly back and forth. Beneath a glass plate, a needle quivered and spun.

"So the needle is core stone," Tiran said, "and always points to the Celestial Peaks, like the water compasses on the ships that run from Sky Harbor to the northern gulfs of Keledev?"

"Correct. Except this contraption holds no water, so you can carry it in your pocket and use it in the worst storm. Look closer." Belen pointed to the center. "Can you see it? I used a firestone starlot as a fulcrum to balance the needle's disc. Crystalized and purified dragon fire. It will never rust or wear."

The two went on for a while, with Tiran asking more questions and Belen giving the longwinded answers typical of a Tinkers' Sphere master, until Kara put a fist to her mouth and coughed.

"Yes," Belen said. "Sorry. Must get on with the mission and all that." He raised a hand to stop Kara from turning away. "I have something for you as well, my girl. A trade of sorts."

The tinker lifted a cloth behind his saddle to show her a pair of jeweled silver whirlknives–each with a short central handle and two blades that folded forward to become a deadly piercing weapon or spread for slashing and throwing.

"The sheath is gray goatskin," Belen said, "and rests comfortably at the small of a lightraider's back. Dame Silvana found them for you from the rangers' vault of the armory."

Kara removed the leg sheaths holding the two unadorned whirlknives she'd picked months ago from the cadet stores and traded them for the others. Before adding the gray sheath to the manykit at the small of her back, she took a moment to admire the jewels. Each whirlknife boasted two starlots at the hinge points of the blades, one sapphire blue and one emerald green. "They're beautiful."

"Truly. Which reminds me. Silvana asked me to tell you she'll want them back once you return."

"Of course. I am not yet part of the Rangers' Sphere, and may never be, especially at this rate."

The tinker gave her a smile. "We shall see. Now, off with you both to save a life and solve a mystery. The Rescuer is with you."

"Always and forever," the cadets answered and waded into the lake.

The sharpness of the water's cold struck Kara–the way she could almost see the rippling surface rising up her calves purely by feel. Yet this cold did not carry the harshness of the gales higher up at the Clefts of Semajin. In a way, she found it soothing. Tiran did not seem to agree. As they neared the center, treading water, she saw him shivering. "Are you all right?"

"I will be, I think. The waters of Sil Tymest where Teegs and I grew up are warm in every season. Nothing like this." He lifted a hand from the water and looked at his own trembling fingers. "But these may be tremors of mood. The last time I dove into one of these lakes, I did so in disobedience, and let the others carry me through the portal."

"And this time?"

"This time the disobedient part of me wants to swim back to shore and go home."

Despite expressing this desire, Tiran showed no sign of giving up their assignment. When they reached the deeps of the lake, he took Kara's hand. "You'll pass through unharmed, not even wet. I promise. *Kesehcer ala'ov lut perah fi shalom nakav sestenoliov. . .*"

You will keep the mind dependent on you in perfect peace . . .

Kara took his prompt and finished the sacred verse in the Common Tongue. "For that mind is trusting in you." She nodded. "I trust the Rescuer."

"We go on the count of three, then. One . . . Two . . ." Tiran took a deep breath. "Three!"

Together, they stopped treading water and dropped.

The quivering moons above the lake surface faded to dim gray, then vanished in an all-encompassing dark. Sooner than she expected, Kara's feet sank into silt. A small hazy light appeared ahead. She and Tiran walked toward it in the languid movements forced upon them by the water's resistance. With each step, the silt firmed, until Kara felt rocks and clumps of weeds under her boots. The light did not wait for them to reach it. Instead, it rushed and burst over them in a blast of cool, dank air.

Both cadets drew in a gasping breath. Kara released Tiran's hand and turned to see an elegant maidenhair tree with a twisted hollow in its trunk. Before her eyes, the green leaves yellowed and blew away into nothingness. The hollow closed. The tree, now bare, shrank and shriveled to match the other skeletal trees in the forest.

Mist hung around their ankles, as gray-green as Tiran's cloak. He knelt to touch the soil beneath it, then rose again, wiping his hand on his trousers. "Wild grass and stony earth, shriveled maidenhair trees. This could be the remains of Sil Belomar, the Forest of Tranquility. I read that the Aladoth now call it Gloamwood."

"What do you mean *could be*?" Kara asked.

He shrugged. "We'll find out soon enough. We need to look for a town. Have you any clues from the visions of your brehna?"

"You'll know the moment I do. Either I'll speak up, or I'll fall to the ground writhing in pain." Kara glanced around. Other than the shadows of outcroppings in the distance, hinting at rising terrain, the whole wood looked the same. "Which way shall we go, oh master of the compass?"

Tiran consulted the tinker's contraption, turning his body slightly, as if lining himself up with the needle. "The Peaks lie directly in front of me. If this is Sil Belomar, then I'm facing west by southwest toward the great expanse of the Tarlan Plains. To the east are the Fading Mountains."

"And north?"

Tiran didn't answer. He put a hand to his head.

"Tiran? What's wrong?"

"Draw your weapons," he said through clenched teeth. "Something's coming." He tucked the compass away and pulled his sword from its sheath. "Something evil."

Kara saw movement not far away. A dark shape glided through the withered trees. "There," she said, pointing with a closed whirlknife. "We should follow. If the creature saw us step from the tree, it might give us away."

They gave chase, but no matter how fast they ran, they could never close the distance. The creature always remained exactly as far away as when Kara first spotted it, until she began to think the shadow they chased was their own.

"Stop," she said to Tiran, catching his sleeve to slow him.

As she'd predicted, the shadow stopped as well–but not entirely. It glided in a slow circle.

"Am I going mad, or is that thing waiting for us?"

"Or leading us into a–"

Instead of finishing, Tiran let out a cry and clutched at the wound on his head. A faint orange glow colored the fog at their feet. Lantern light? The glow didn't come from their front, from the direction of the shadow they'd been chasing. It came from behind.

Kara spun and found herself staring into a gaunt white face and deep, hollow eyes. In the orange lanternlight, she could see all the way to the back of the empty sockets.

She screamed.

Tiran's sword pierced the creature, and it recoiled–a dead thing draped in a ragged, hooded cloak and carrying the lantern that had revealed its decrepit visage.

Kara regained control of her limbs and flicked both wrists to open her whirl knives. She gave the dead thing a menacing glare. As if mimicking her, it flicked its free hand, and yellowed claws appeared, each two or three inches long.

She let out a dry laugh. "Nice."

The creature slashed at her, and Kara's training kicked in. She raised an arm, and for the first time, her Keledan armor came to life. A shield on the blue side of indigo flashed as it deflected the creature's claws. Though she felt no weight, the shield stretched from her chin to her knees.

From her right, Tiran lunged in for another stab. The thing saw him coming and countered with a swinging lantern. The blow knocked his sword aside in a burst of sparks. Neither the lantern nor the strange, candle-shaped light inside seemed harmed in the least.

The creature took the opening and pressed Tiran, swiping at him with its claws and forcing him into retreat. But in doing so, it ignored Kara. She ran in close. Tiran's sword had done no damage to the lantern, so she slashed with both knives at the arm holding it. She felt the blades sink deep into decayed flesh. The creature shrieked.

The lantern fell from its grasp, and it turned on her with a wild swipe. Kara sliced the two longest claws away.

They grew back.

"Tiran!"

Tiran had left the creature to her and turned his attention to the lantern.

"What are you doing?"

"One moment!" He stabbed directly into the orange light and snuffed it out.

The dead thing shrieked again and threw its hands in the air, one forearm hanging lopsided where Kara had slashed it. Red fire glowed beneath the creature's rags and spread to its limbs and head. She reeled backward, but not fast enough. The blaze inside intensified until the creature shook and finally burst into ash and dust. Its remains washed over her.

Kara spat. "Oh, disgusting. Some of it got into my mouth." She brushed the dust off her clothing and shuddered. "Bleh! What was that thing?"

"A wanderer." An old man limped out of the gloom, supporting himself with a knobby tree-limb crutch. "And by destroying him, you two meddlers ruined everything."

33

TEEGAN
KELEDEV
PELLION'S FLOW

THE ORDER CALLED THEM ICE RIVERS. BUT TEEGAN had never seen rivers so steep that were not called cataracts or falls. "Are these metal spikes truly necessary, Pedrig? I fear my feet may never recover from the bite of their iron braces."

The wolf neither turned nor slowed his march across the flow of snow and ice they had entered. "Have you claws like mine, daughter of autumn? Or talons to match those of the falcon who wheels above us?"

"Sometimes they come out," Dag said, crunching along behind her. "Mostly when she fights with her brehna."

Teegan reached back to smack his arm, a broad enough target that she could hit it without looking. "I have neither claws nor talons, Pedrig."

"Then you must wear the iron spikes the outfitter gave you, whether they bite or not. The Rescuer's ice rivers are too slippery for men."

Despite his joke, Dag seemed to like the spikes as little as Teegan. "In a fight, iron shoes will slow us down."

The wolf glanced back. "You cannot fight if you cannot stand. You must make do with the encumbrance. Yes, the spikes will make any battle more arduous, but your training will help you overcome the difficulty."

The ice rivers, known collectively as Pellion's Flow, lay on a direct line between the Clefts of Semajin and the place in Dayspring where Teegan and her brehna had found Barnabas. The three had searched a full day, starting at the Forest of Believing, but found nothing. And now, as the night grew long and their limbs grew weary, they searched some of the most dangerous terrain in all Keledev.

According to Master Jairun, the ice rivers never ceased to move and change. A lightraider whose leg became trapped between the flow and the ridges jutting up through it could expect that limb to be crushed and severed in the most slow and agonizing way imaginable. At the same time, crevices and sinkholes might open at any instant and swallow a lightraider whole.

"How about we call it a night?" Dag said, as if reading Teegan's mind. "We'll camp on an outcropping. Tomorrow we can head south toward Thousand Falls, into the forests where your nose is less hindered by ice and wind."

"And lose three days in the journey? No, son of summer. We're hunting frost goblins. They love the cold. Whatever reason the creature that killed Barnabas had for moving south, I doubt it stayed in–" Pedrig halted his march, ears up and twitching. He scanned the ice rivers. "Come forward," he said in a low voice. "Come see."

As the cadets knelt beside him, Pedrig pawed the ice and grit, drawing a short line. "Look there, in the snow at the edge of my mark two paces away. Do you see them?"

With this help from the wolf, Teegan saw the nearer footprint– three impressions made by long-clawed toes, and a fourth angled to the side. A goblin foot. The impression was faint. Fungal goblin flesh and hollow brittleknit bones weighed little. "Can you smell anything?"

"Not much. But my nose is not our only resource. Were you not a huntress before you came to Ras Telesar?"

Aethia. Teegan looked up and saw her wheeling, searching. So far, the falcon had given no sign that she saw their quarry. Then she heard Silvana in her head, reminding her that she also had eyes. The guardian had warned her Aethia would not always be there for her to lean on, and she'd given Teegan a sacred verse to consider.

"*Mi amun shuranu, po se ma kazon,*" Teegan whispered. "By faith, not sight. With your help, we can find and overcome this threat."

Aethia let out an echoing cry. An answered prayer, perhaps, in a way different from what Teegan had expected.

"I see them! Up the flow!" Pedrig set off at a run.

Teegan and Dag had no hope of keeping up in their iron spikes. By the time they reached the wolf, his pine-green armor had come to life and shone with dark intensity. He faced down three frost goblins, standing between them and a crevasse in the ice river.

Perhaps thanks to the combined weight of the combatants, the ice let out a terrible *crack*, and the crevasse opened wider. Even with the moonlight, Teegan couldn't see its floor. "Pedrig, watch your footing! That chasm is deep."

"I'm fine. Take them! Leave one alive for questioning."

"Aye." Teegan drew the trident from her back and used it to motion Dag to her left, a signal for him to flank the enemy.

He acknowledged with a dual flourish of his battle axes, and his bronze-colored Keledan armor glowed.

The wolf sensed Teegan's approach and shifted right to give her the center. As he moved, a goblin flung a dagger made of grimy ice. The wolf obliterated the weapon with a bark.

The goblin seemed unimpressed. It scraped up a handful of snow and packed it together. When it drew its hands apart again, an ice scimitar formed.

Dag came in hard from the side with an awkward gait. As predicted, the iron spikes on his boots slowed him down. But they did nothing to hinder the swing of his axes. The goblin made a futile stab with an ice knife. Dag shattered the blade with one axe, and with the other, he split the creature down the middle.

Pedrig growled. "Take one alive, I said!"

"I heard you. There's still two more."

Those two took one look at their cloven comrade and fled.

Pedrig ran one down and caught it by the leg.

One throw of Dag's axe would surely end the remaining creature. Stopping it was up to Teegan. She hurled her trident at its thigh and scored a hit.

The goblin let out a squeal and fell, landing on its back. Teegan cast her chain mail net. Its weights, all in the shape of spikes, dug into the ice flow and held the creature fast.

"Got him!"

The trapped goblin let out a cackle. "Enjoy your death, deary. Enjoy it. Enjoy it well." It dug a hand into the ice flow, and a line of icicles sprang forth from the hardened snow. When Teegan tried to jump out of the way, her metal boot spikes hampered the escape, and an icicle tore her trouser leg and scratched her calf. Returning her gaze to her goblin prisoner, she saw only a shriveled mass of lichen clinging to its netlike brittleknit bones. The creature had drained itself just for the chance to scratch her.

She lifted her chin and snorted. "Mindless dragon corruption."

The ice and snow gave way beneath her.

Teegan fell into a narrow stream of meltwater and sailed down a watery ice slide toward the crevasse she'd warned Pedrig about. An instant later, she flew over the edge.

34

LITEH PLUMOND, OND SE MORADIEND, OKEB KE'RUMOSH mod eledol bi yadod.

When I fall, I will not be overwhelmed. He holds me up.

Sea-green light shone all around Teegan an instant before her body slammed into the wet ice. Pain rushed through her, yet she felt no muscles splitting, no bones breaking. A good thing, but she was still sliding. The water carried her down the sloping crevice into the dark, and clawing at the walls did nothing.

Claws. Iron claws. Teegan rolled over and kicked the spikes at her toes into the ice. It worked. She slowed, then stopped. With effort, she found her feet, and the spikes gave her the grip she needed to stay upright.

Again, she checked her body for wounds. She found none beyond the scratch in her calf and a lingering ache.

Onoriov, Rumosh. "Pedrig? Dag!"

"They're not here, little firecap. Not here. Not here. Only the dark, the cold, and us."

More voices answered. "Us. Yes. We. Only us, pretty firecap. Us. Us."

The small chasm dampened and channeled the sounds so that Teegan could tell without question that not all the voices came from in front of her.

Her eyes adjusted, and the goblins took shape—three in front and four behind. All carried knives or scimitars of ice and bore long dirty claws. Teegan reached for her trident, but realized she'd left it pinned to the dead goblin above. She had no weapons beyond her hunting knife and the small ice axe the outfitter had given her. She drew both. "You will not prevail."

The guardians had taught her a sacred verse for moments like this—a declaration of the Maker's sovereignty over his creation. The truth of his words and power alone would disrupt the dragon corruption of fungus and unravel their flesh. But when she tried to bring the verse to mind, a cold burning flared in the scratch on her leg. She let out an involuntary cry.

The goblins cackled and advanced.

A screech broke their laughter. Aethia soared down through the crevasse and shot past Teegan's shoulder to harry the creatures at her back. Teegan smashed her shield into the goblin at her front, then swung her ice axe and buried its pick in the staggering creature's skull.

The next goblin in line paid no mind to its fallen comrade and stabbed at her with its scimitar. Her shield held, but the goblin dodged her axe. It ran up the wall of ice and attacked from her side, landing a blow that rang against her glowing helmet. Though it did not penetrate, the force of it put all her weight on her wounded leg. She crumpled.

The goblin fell upon her, sword descending. Teegan rolled her shield into place in time to defend, but how long could she hold? Sea-green sparks sizzled and popped where the creature stood atop her shield, wounding it terribly. Yet it did not stop, and despite her falcon's efforts, the others closed in.

Doused in meltwater, Teegan shivered with cold and fear, but she fought through it to grasp one of her favorite verses from the Scrolls. "*Men kemaqoth Rumosh serana'yov! Rumosh, kowlesh thimah. Pav thoma'ovu yi shegam mi zower hal kashav.*"

Out of the depths I call to you. Hear my cry for help.

His answer came in the form of a great shadow breaking the strip of starlit sky above the crevasse. Teegan's own trident pierced the goblin riding her shield. From above, a battle cry outmatched the creature's screech.

Dag.

Teegan looked left to see her friend sliding down the ice walls with his back against one side and his spiked boots scraping down the other. He chopped a goblin in half before he landed. To her right, she heard growling wolf-speak and a deep, reverberating bark. A man-sized orb of green light rolled through the crevasse, bounced over Teegan, and burst into fading stars on Dag's bronze armor. In its wake, it left piles of boiling lichen.

All the goblin laughter had ended.

Teegan let her head fall back into the flowing meltwater and resisted the urge to sob. Exhaustion took her, until Dag declared he'd found a tunnel.

"Looks like the ice river split right on top of it."

Tunnels. That's how the creatures moved about unseen–how the one that attacked Barnabas had disappeared. Fungal goblin corruptions were digging beneath the free soil of Keledev.

AARON
ON THE RIM OF THE WINDHOLD

SIRETH PULLED DYING CHESTNUT BRANCHES AWAY from the hole they'd found and held his lantern inside the opening. "It's a tunnel all right. Not some wolf den or bear cave. Those animals don't break branches from trees to hide their work." He shook his head. "I can't believe goblins are digging under Keledev. How has this come to be?"

"Neglect," Aaron said, "as you suggested before. Or perhaps some new device of the dragons."

The older watchman straightened and held the lantern close to his face. "There is nothing the dragons can invent that the Rescuer hasn't anticipated, and these are his mountains. He has a plan. I just wish I knew the details." He shifted his gaze to the tunnel entrance again. "We should go in."

"I'm sorry. I could swear I heard you say we should go in. But surely not."

"Is hunting these creatures not our duty?"

"Our duty is to be the wall of the foothills. And that requires more than two men." Aaron looked downhill toward the Windhold outpost, a natural formation that snatched water from the wind to feed a crystal-clear lake. Wind blew down the sheer northern wall, depositing its dew. Over time, the dryer air cutting upward across the southern wall had hewn a honeycomb of caves from the rock. These were the home of the Windhold Company.

Aaron saw no lanterns among the trees between himself and the outpost. The rest of the party from Thousand Falls might already have reached it–the end of what had seemed a fruitless search–until Sireth's discovery. "We should mark this spot and get more men."

"A good plan," Sireth said, but then he drew his sword and ducked inside. "And we'll execute it once we make sure the tunnel has not collapsed. I'd hate to bring them up here for nothing."

"Sireth!"

He was gone. Aaron hurried in after him, grumbling to himself. "Since when am I the wiser one?"

Sireth gave him no answer.

"Sireth?"

"Shh!" The lantern appeared from around a bend, shielded by Sireth's hand. His head followed, eyes flaring. "Do you want to bring the goblins all running to us? Hush, lad."

The older watchman carried a war hammer, half the length of the watchmaster's, which he'd told Aaron was the proper size. Aaron carried an axe not much different from those he used when chopping trees for the barricade, except it had a curved and bearded blade and a spike. When told to pick a weapon from the outpost armory, he'd figured it best to choose a tool he'd already learned how to use.

"All right," Aaron said. "The tunnel's not blocked, and it's not an animal den. Let's go back."

"A little farther. We need some proof the creatures used this passage if we're to rally the companies–a forgotten weapon or a fragment of clothing."

Sireth didn't wait for Aaron to respond but wandered deeper in, holding the lantern to the walls and floor. Both had to crouch as they walked, one behind the other. These creatures were shorter and thinner than men.

Not long after, Sireth paused and dropped to a knee. "What's this?" He scraped the dirt floor with the spike of his war hammer. "A broken claw, perhaps."

Aaron leaned over his shoulder, trying to see. "Take care. I hear these creatures carry poisons in their bodies. We should leave it, show the company when we bring them back."

"I'll be fine, lad. If it does carry some poison or infection, it won't penetrate the leather of my gloves. Besides, we need–"

With a horrible shriek, a goblin caked with mud came out of the wall and swung a dirty ice blade at Sireth. Aaron didn't think, didn't even cry out. He only reacted. He swung his axe at the arm wielding the blade and removed it from the creature's body.

By then, Sireth had rolled out of the way, and before the goblin could fall upon him, he spun on his knees and smashed its skull with the hammer. The creature gurgled, then fell lifeless to the floor beside its own severed arm.

Sireth looked up at Aaron with thankful eyes and let out a quivering chuckle. "I always thought I'd be the one to save you from a dark creature's blade."

"Me too." Aaron stared at the goblin. "Is that enough proof for us to share with the company?"

"Indeed. And there's more to tell." Sireth lifted the hand still attached to the creature and showed Aaron the fingers. "The second claw is missing. This goblin heard me say I wanted proof, then broke off one of its own claws to distract us and hid itself for an ambush. Cunning." He passed the lantern to Aaron and motioned for him to reverse course. "My behlna tells me dark creatures of the same type share the same tactics–ingrained in them by their dragon puppet masters. Hurry. We must spread word to all the companies of this danger before any other tunnels are found."

35

TEEGAN
UNDER PELLION'S FLOW

THE FROST GOBLINS MIGHT HAVE BEEN ABLE TO WALK abreast in the tunnel, but not humans–especially not Dag. He'd taken the head of their small column with a lantern in one hand and his axe in the other, big shoulders almost brushing the swirled blue-white walls. "How far can this tunnel go?"

"Frost goblins move quickly through ice," Pedrig said, bringing up the rear behind Teegan. Glowing blue pawprints appeared in his wake, marking their path. He'd assured the cadets no dark creature could see them. "The ice is part of them, and they can claw at it day and night without feeling the cold."

"I feel the cold." Teegan pulled her cloak tighter about her shoulders. "I feel it to my bones."

She felt the wolf's keen eyes on her. "Mmm," he said. "Do you, now?"

"Of course, I do." She didn't mean to snap at him, but what a silly question. "I fell in that runoff when I dropped into the crevice. I'm soaked." Teegan softened her voice. "I . . . I'm grateful for the way you eliminated the goblins coming after me. I don't suppose you could teach me the prayer you used to ask the Rescuer for that rolling sphere of light."

"That was a declaration of the Maker's sovereignty over all

creation, similar to a sacred verse you should already know. The words I used were given to the Havarra, and they are not part of your story."

His refusal grated at her, especially in that gravelly wolf voice. Why should there be secrets between the High One and the Havarra that the Keledan couldn't know? "Fine. If you won't equip me to do the job, then don't expect my help the next time goblins are bearing down on you."

Dag stopped and turned, raising an eyebrow.

The wolf looked up at her with his head cocked, ears turned outward. "Daughter of autumn, I don't think you mean that."

"No. You're right. I'm sorry." Teegan shivered. "I don't know why I said it."

Dag lifted his chin, giving a look as wary as the wolf's. "I think I do. Are you wounded?"

"A scratch. That's all. I can deal with it later."

Pedrig growled. "One so near the rank of cadet scout, waiting only for the Turning of the Spheres, should know better. Let me see."

Teegan gave him a frustrated sigh, but she pulled up her trouser leg to expose the scratch. She was not prepared for what she saw.

Gray-white lichen spread from the wound, turning the flesh around it blue. Goblin poison.

"You see," the wolf said. "We can never leave even the smallest wound from a dark creature to fester, not when we have the chance to heal it."

Dag opened a satchel hanging from one of the two raised posts at the shoulders of his manykit–what he called his mule posts. "A good thing we knew what we were hunting. Master Jairun sent me with the right medications." He gave her a small vial. "Drink this while I put a salve on it."

She did and felt the warmth of the serum spreading through her. It tasted of mint.

Master Jairun had also sent them out with a sacred verse that served as a reminder to counter the influence of a frost goblin infection. Pedrig spoke it for her, then asked her to repeat it back to him.

"Hal shesav po zowelim yi okuran," she said, dwelling as best she could on each word, *"okuran soldi, ka Rumosh fi Liberavor solendov.* This sacred verse reminds us to be kind with each other and forgive each other, just as the High One forgave us through the Rescuer."

Glancing down at her leg, Teegan saw the wound responding to Dag's salve and the Rescuer's words. The lichen flaked off and fell away. The flesh turned pink again. She breathed a sigh of relief. "Thank you for your patience, Pedrig."

"You are welcome, daughter of autumn. The sooner we deal with such infections, the easier they are to heal. Now, let us keep moving."

For all their efficiency in ice-tunneling, the frost goblins seemed to have little sense of direction. Or perhaps it was a strategy to confuse their enemies. The tunnel split in several places, and on more than one occasion, the party ran into a dead end. Pedrig's glowing footprints kept them from losing their way, leaving a double set wherever they had to backtrack.

And backtrack, they did. After an hour or more of searching, Dag wondered aloud if the creatures might have come from higher up the mountain. The party returned to the crevasse where they'd started, then tried the route northward, and they were soon rewarded. The ice tunnel widened into a passage of gray rock.

"We're inside the Celestial Peaks," Teegan said, coming up beside Dag in the wider space.

He patted the wall. "The territory of my family. But never this high. Are you short of breath?"

As she nodded, Teegan heard Pedrig behind her. "You'll both find it hard to breathe here, and harder still, the higher we go. If we don't find the den soon, we'll need to turn back. Master Belen has devices that will help. We can return with those, and with a larger force."

But as he made this pronouncement, the passage opened into a squarish cave with a passage entrance at the opposite end and another in the wall to their left. Teegan held her trident at the ready and advanced, side by side with Dag. When they reached the far tunnel, too small for them to enter together, he nodded for her to go first.

Her heart dropped into her stomach at what she saw at the other end.

Beyond and beneath the short passage stretched a goblin den, easily larger than the academy's library and lit with torches burning with frost-green fire. She bit her lip and retreated into the square cave, cringing at the sound of each step. She motioned the others closer. "We've found the den. There must be a hundred, if not more–far too many for the three of us."

"Agreed," Pedrig said.

"Watch out!" Dag shoved the wolf aside and raised his shield in time to absorb the blow of a charging ice creature. The impact sent him sliding to the cave wall.

The creature had come from the side passage–a two-legged monster with an aspect between a man and a long-toothed cat, formed entirely of edged ice spikes. It glared at Dag, eyes and joints burning with same frost-green fire Teegan had seen in the goblin den. A low, watery hum began within it, growing in intensity, and she heard words in the song.

Lightraiders. Never enough. Never strong enough to contend with us.

"North troll," Pedrig growled. "Iceblade. Don't let it sing."

Teegan lunged with her trident, whispering a prayer to the Rescuer as she struck. "*Hevalesh miyov da'es, ma prematesh aler moremat nakaveth.*" *My grace is sufficient. My power is perfected in weakness.*

The trident's tines glowed red as it stabbed into the creature's midsection and bored into the ice. The creature lifted its head as if to roar, but Dag was already up and swinging. His blade shattered its head, so that Teegan had to lift her shield to deflect a shower of ice shards. The glow in its joints evaporated. The troll toppled over and broke into a thousand pieces when it hit the ground.

All three backed away from the den's entrance, weapons ready, but no goblins came.

"Retreat," Pedrig growled, "for now."

The party followed the wolf's blue tracks out of the tunnels. "We must return to the academy and report what we found," Pedrig said as they ran, "and hope these creatures do not flee to a new den once they find their troll guard destroyed." He shot a glance at Teegan. "Do you see now the value of treating your wound as soon as we could? Had you still been under the influence of the poison, you could not have struck so quickly. The iceblade's song might have brought the whole horde out of their den."

She nodded, struggling to keep pace with the wolf. "I get it. Don't leave a dark wound to fester."

"Just so, daughter of autumn. The results may be disastrous."

36

KARA
TANELETHAR
GRENTON VILLAGE

AFTER A GREAT DEAL OF COMPLAINING, THE OLD MAN who'd accosted Kara and Tiran brought them to his village on the edge of the dead forest. Kara, supporting him with an arm under his, had calmed him some, but not enough to keep him from reminding them every few moments that their meddling had ruined his plans—his eternal plans.

"I could have joined that wanderer," the old man said, referring to the creature. "Here I am, traipsing along with you sword-swishing imbeciles, when I could be happily beginning an eternal death. Where did you come from, anyway?"

Tiran told him the truth, and together, the two tried to convince him that perhaps becoming a mouth-gaping dead thing wandering forever in the fog was not the best of plans. "You would not have joined his kind," Kara said. "Those creatures are dragon deceptions, corrupted matter like all the others. But there is another way to face your eternity."

She tried to share the good news of the Rescuer, but the old man, Nole, wanted none of it. He declared Kara and Tiran to be young, upstart know-nothings, who should've stayed behind the Southern Overlord's ludicrous barrier where they belonged.

He repeated a slightly jumbled version of the same sentiment as they reached his village. The state of the main thoroughfare sent a rush of cold through Kara. "It's so much like Trader's Knoll before I lost my brehnan. So much like the day the dragon passed over."

"A dragon?" Nole said. "We should be so lucky. There are things worse than dragons here, girl. Better to be roasted alive than dragged into the depths of the Ghost Moor."

According to Nole, Grenton had been a bustling spice town only months before, an important stop on the Westward Road between the coastal ranges and the Tarlan Plains. Those days were gone. Hardly a soul moved between the houses and shops, mostly cobbled together from green rocks and dead wood. An old woman hurried across the street, pulling a small child. Another elderly Grenton citizen appeared at a window for a beat, then threw his moth-eaten curtains closed.

"How quickly we've come to ruin without the strength of young backs." Nole leaned upon Kara's arm and gestured toward a shop with his crutch. Just enough paint remained on the sign over the door for Kara to make out the word *Baker.* "My sons were the first to go. They used to stoke the fires for our bread each morning before dawn. But I awoke one morning to a cold and empty house. Our friends said the boys had finally left me, but I knew better, and soon they did too."

"Others began to disappear?" Tiran asked.

"Yes. At first, the wraiths took a few young harvesters who worked the forest herb rows. They vanished from the company longhouse. But a few dead were left behind, throats slashed. Then the wraiths came for the foreman's daughter, then the foreman himself."

"Wraiths?" The word gave Kara a shiver. A flash of the wanderer's long claws appeared before her. "Is that another word for the wanderers?"

"Not the wanderers. They keep to the forest and have long been seen there at night. The harvesters believe their lanterns bless our root spices with flavor. No. Not the wanderers." Nole turned his gaze to the far end of the town, where the fog thickened to muddle the houses. "I'm speaking of the moor wraiths. In life, House Suvor ruled with unnatural power, gifted by the dragons for being the first to swear allegiance. In death, that power persists, but they've long kept to their ancient capital, Tagamar, down in the canyon moor. No longer."

Kara felt her mind stretching to believe his story, wanting to share his dread, even though she knew some other dragon mischief had robbed this town of its strong. She fought back the fear. "Have you seen these wraiths?"

"I've seen shadows in the mist at the edge of the moor now and again since childhood. And I saw them the same night the butcher was taken. Lived here our whole lives, him and I. So did our fathers and their fathers. Generations of our families yielded profit mere yards from an age-old evil. Should've known it'd come for us one day."

"Nole," Tiran said. "Your sehnan are gone–taken, as you say. But what of your wife?"

"Long departed. The madness took her years ago, growing worse until I couldn't put a spoon in her mouth." He drew his arm from Kara's and hobbled backward, shaking his head. "I'll not go like that. And I shan't let those Suvoroth wraiths take me down into their putrid mud either." He turned about and set off toward the forest, calling over his shoulder. "Take the Westward Road while you still can. Up ahead, at the crossroads. Center of town. The wraiths took the last of our young three nights ago. I'll wager they're thirsty for blood by now–your blood."

"Nole!" Kara shouted.

Tiran touched her shoulder. "Let him go. We did all we could. We must shake this dust from our boots and carry on."

"Do you think a wanderer will get him?"

"I doubt it. The dragons are crueler than that. They'll let him chase his illusions in vain until he starves to death."

They started once again down the main thoroughfare of Grenton. Kara could not say for sure why it frightened her so. "There are no wraiths, right?"

"Not as Nole described–at least, not that I know of. Our scouting missions revealed disappearances in towns all over Tanelethar. One village left alone, the next emptied of its young and strong. None of those affected were anywhere near this moor." He let out a mirthless laugh. "These Grenton folks built a story around their own legends. But the truth is, orcs probably took them in the dark–same way they took your brehna and all the rest. Sounds like they killed some of the herb harvesters in the longhouse to stop them from crying out."

"And if that's true," Kara said, "the orcs took them to the same place as Keir."

"Which means we can track them through the moor to find him."

The moor–the Ghost Moor, Nole had called it. Kara fixed her gaze on the greenish fog beyond the town center. Shifting figures within spread their arms to claim her. She closed her eyes tight, and when she opened them again, the figures were gone. She had faced orcs, goblins, a dragon, and now the wanderer. Why did a little mist frighten her so?

She had to save Keir. Hiding the fear from Tiran, she squared her shoulders. "Yeah, all right. Into the moor we go."

THE PRISONER
TANELETHAR

THE CUTS ENDED HOURS AGO, BUT THE PAIN LINGERS. The dragon can see every fiber of my flesh. He knows how much my body can endure before giving in to the final death, and he takes me to the brink every time.

With heat, he seals my wounds, then leaves me until the time comes to start again. *Rest,* he says to my mind. There is sleep in those times, but no rest, only nightmares.

Footsteps. I hope for water and bread, but barkhides usually bring such things, and these are not human footsteps.

Stuttered. Quick. Claws scratching the floor. Goblins. Two of them.

The way I hang from these shackles, the goblins cannot reach high enough to feed me. They must be here for some other reason.

A shaft of light, quickly lost in a moving shadow, tells me the dragon has returned. He lands before his throne, and the goblins bow.

Report.

I hear the command in my head, and I see what he sees–a confusion of jerky scenes through yellowed and narrow vision. The dragon searches the fungal brains of both goblins at once. I work to separate them. The effort strains me, but it's a good distraction from my wounds. What else have I to do with my last hours?

Yes. Two visions. Two reports. I see a dark mass emerging from a storm cloud. A ship of the air, held aloft by bulging silk. An item falls from it, and it soon disappears over a ridgetop.

From behind the corner of a house built of rocks and dead wood, I watch three figures enter an abandoned town—a young man and a young woman with an old grumbling patehpa on her arm. The vision shrinks back behind the corner as they approach, but through one goblin eye, I see their faces.

I see her.

My heart screams. I try to contain it, suppress it, but the dragon hears. He sees. He knows. This is why he let me watch!

The chaos of the two goblin brains returns. Clawed feet racing through trees and tunnels. Tittering, repetitive voices. Thoughts passing from creature to creature. None of it matters. She's here, and his eye is upon her.

His thoughts question the goblins. *Where is the ship?*

The two have been carrying an iron block by its handles. They drop it on the floor with a heavy *clank,* and one replies aloud with a whiny, scratching voice. "The flying thing. The thing that flew. The storm flyer. It threw this device. Tossed it. Dropped it. And then we lost it in the Muddled Mountains. Lost it, we did. Not far from the bay. Lost it near the bay."

That flying thing is a tool of the enemy, a ship to carry his forces. Find it.

"Hemlock Clan is searching now, m'lord. Searching. Searching. Watching the sky."

Good. And the others?

The second creature answers. "Grenton, m'lord. The spice town. Spice town. They're moving north toward the Ghost Moor, that wretched, cursed moor."

Stay with them, but keep out of sight. Don't touch them.

"But we can take them, m'lord. We can take them. Two, there are. Only two."

I said, leave them be!

The red torches around us flare. The goblins cringe under the weight of the command.

Control is needed here, and your kind has none.

The dragon's thoughts shift to fill my mind instead of the creatures', and he speaks. "There is no need for my goblins to capture this pair. They are coming to me."

The creatures hobble away, and orcs pass them on the torchlit path, bringing another prisoner. The dragon speaks to my captured brehna as he spoke to me.

"Go to him. See him."

An orc presses a blade into my brehna's hand.

We begin again.

37

KARA
NORTH OF GRENTON VILLAGE

STARING DOWN AT HIS COMPASS, TIRAN ALMOST tumbled headlong over the cliff at the edge of the moor. The fog had enveloped them well before they reached the edge, and only by the Rescuer's grace did Kara spot it soon enough to cry out and catch hold of his cloak.

He hung there, balanced on his heels for a long moment before she pulled him back. Tiran clutched his chest. "Thank you. The moor west of Sil Tymest was a patch of hills, and hills have no cliffs."

"This one may yet be hilly too, but don't forget, Nole mentioned that it lies within a canyon. We must get down there, but it could take hours to find the trail."

"Roads shift over time, but not much–not the important ones. I'll wager the Grenton crossroads marks the place where a path from the Suvor kingdom once met the Westward Road. In that case, the way down should be close."

They picked their way along the cliff, unable to see more than ten paces through the fog. Kara had never found heights a bother before, but after Tiran's near fall, she hated being close to the edge. She walked on the other side of him and looped two fingers through the belt of his manykit.

"What are you doing?" he asked.

"I don't want you to fall."

"I won't."

"Strange that you should make such a claim, given recent events."

"Yes, but I know where the cliff is now." Tiran sighed and pushed her hand away. "You're acting strange—ever since the wanderer attacked."

"I'm fine. Keep looking."

He said no more about it, and neither did Kara. But she didn't feel fine. Everything—the fog, the cliff, the very idea of the wraiths—everything filled her with dread. Was this part of the dragon's attack on her mind? Was it a share of her brehna's suffering under its evil talons?

"There," Tiran said. "I see the road."

Road was too strong a word. A narrow path led down along the cliff face, protected from the sheer drop by a rocky lip just high enough to trip the unwary and send them flying into a gray-green oblivion. Kara hugged the wall. "The air tastes of metal."

"Yes," Tiran said, a shadow ahead of her. "I thought the same." He ran a finger across the rock face and turned it over to reveal a film of faint glittering green. "This is no ordinary fog, not like the low clouds of my home or Mer Nimbar. Hilly or not, I suspect what lies below is a bog. Tehpa used to say every bog has a smell of its own, and their mists hold all manner of strange vapors. He warned us never to enter a bog with no birds."

"Why not?"

"Because a lack of birds means the vapors may be poison."

Kara listened for a few heartbeats. She heard nothing but the scuffing of their boots on the rocks and mud. "Tiran, there are no birds here."

"I know."

She waited for what might follow—a reassurance that there was no poison here, a caution to cover her mouth and nose with a rag—

almost anything would have served, but Tiran said nothing else.

If Kara's hands had not been trembling with the dread that plagued her, she might have flicked him in the back of the head. "Didn't you say you wanted to join the Comforters' Sphere?"

"Very much so. Why?"

"No reason."

The path widened into the road they'd hoped for, allowing them to walk side by side. It slanted down, straight north into the moor, supported by manmade arches. And as they left the cliff wall behind, the mists lightened. This was poor consolation for Kara. The deeper she looked into the swirling vapors, the more she imagined–or saw–creatures waiting there. One of these shapes kept pace with them, the way the shape had followed them in the forest before the wanderer struck. This time, Tiran didn't see it.

"You're imagining things," he said. "It's only fog and fear."

"I never said I was afraid."

"You didn't have to."

The shapes multiplied, until Kara counted eight in total, gliding in and out of her gaze's reach. What did they want?

The elevated road leveled, exchanging gravel for flagstone, and an instant later, a breath of wind stirred the fog. A pair of gargoyle faces emerged, larger than any orc she'd seen, with teeth bared.

"Tiran, look out!" Kara drew both whirlknives, snapped them open, and flung them with all her might. Both hit their marks in a dual flash of sparks, then clattered onto the road.

At the same time, Tiran drew his sword and advanced on one of the creatures, but pulled his swing short. "Kara, stop!"

He fell into laughter.

Kara thought, perhaps, the unknown poison in the vapors had taken hold of him, but when she arrived at his side, she saw the reason for his hysterics. She lowered the sword she'd drawn. "Statues."

"A gate. I'd say these two were meant to welcome travelers to the home city of the Suvoroth–Tagamar, Nole called it. You had me going. You pulled me into your trepidation, and I almost chopped this fellow's head off."

"I am not afraid, Tiran."

"You are." He bent to the flagstones, smile turning sour. "And you've paid a price for it. Whatever gives the stone here its green color gives it strength too." He showed her a whirlknife, broken. One of the weapon's two blades had shattered, the pieces lost to the fog beyond the road's gutter. A moment later, he found the other whirlknife. "This one looks the same. Two broken weapons, Kara. Quite a mishap."

He didn't have to tell her. Kara felt the loss in her gut as he placed them in her hands. "These knives are a loan of sorts, from the Rangers' Sphere. What will I tell Silvana?"

"The truth. But I'll stand with you as you do. I've never been among her favorites, anyway."

"Thanks. But there's no need if–"

Pain stabbed at her chest. Black scales. A blade wet with blood. A scream.

Kara dropped to a knee. "Keir."

"Kara? What's happening?"

"My brehna. Another vision. Strong. We're getting closer."

"Can you continue?"

"I think so."

"You're shaking," Tiran said, helping her up.

She was. And no matter how hard she concentrated, she couldn't stop it.

"Are you certain you can go on?"

"I must."

"Then let's make what haste we can."

The gargoyle gate served as the entrance to a rod-straight road, raised high above the moor on supports made of the same gray-green stone as the statues. As they hurried along its expanse, the fog continued to lighten, until Kara could see buildings and more. Towers rose from the thick cloud covering the bottom–

natural towers of rock and sod with low, twisted trees growing on their ledges and recesses. The bridge passed close to one, and Kara noticed stairwells and columned porticos. “Those rock formations are hollow. It looks as if the Suvoroth lived inside them. How strange.”

“Why is it strange?” Tiran asked. “Many in Keledan use caves for their cottages, even chapels.”

“Yes, but these caves are high above the ground, and aside from this one, I see no bridges. Life here must have been exhausting. Up and down stairways day and night.” She fixed her gaze on another close tower and slowed, tilting her head to try and make sense of what she saw. The Suvoroth had crested it with a statue—a beast of some kind, larger than the gargoyles at the gate of the land.

As Kara stared, the statue turned its head to look at her and leaped from its perch. The creature crossed an impossible distance to land on the bridge in front of them. She drew her sword and charged.

Pain. A slice across her arm. Black scales. A red eye, huge. A scream rocked her mind.

“Keir!”

“Kara, stop!”

She couldn’t. She wouldn’t. No creature, no matter how huge, would bar her from saving her brehna.

Fangs. Fear.

A voice, deep and filled with wicked delight. *He’s mine. And so are you, Queensblood.*

Another scream.

“No!” Kara slashed at the creature before her.

Long claws countered the blow, sending up blue-green sparks.

“Don’t, Kara! The fear is taking over!”

“No! The creature is real. Can’t you see it?”

More shapes landed on the bridge behind it. She didn’t care. She’d fight them all. The narrow bridge would even the odds.

Kara struck, and again the beast countered. Those claws—

long like the wanderer's—sent cold fear straight to her heart, until the beast became the wanderer. The gaping mouth. The hollow eyes. "You can't have him! I won't let you. Take me to Keir, or I'll end you!"

Tiran grabbed her arms. Her sword fell.

She fought him. "Don't! The wanderer will kill me!"

More pain. A slash from her neck to her navel. This time the scream was hers.

Kara writhed against Tiran's hold. He took her to the ground. A great weight stopped her kicking legs. A second voice, coarse but feminine, joined his. "Hold her still, lightraider. Speak the Cry of the Fearless if you know it."

In unison, Tiran and the coarse voice spoke over her. "*Ke'Rumosh lasesh po dervimesh—vym strakanad? Ke'Rumosh mi beathnesh kestregar—vym morkanad?*"

He is my light and salvation. Whom shall I fear? He is my stronghold. Whom shall I dread?

The truth of the sacred verse passed over her like a warm breeze, and Kara's shivering stopped. The Rescuer was her salvation. He had made her Twiceborn. He was in control, no matter what terrors the Ghost Moor held. She quit struggling.

The terrible visage of the wanderer evaporated into the mist, leaving behind a broad face with a gray nose and a snout covered in blue-gray fur. Kara blinked. "You're . . . a bear."

The bear let out a huff and lifted her great weight from Kara's legs. She sat back on her haunches, regarding Kara with eyes of midnight blue. "Given your bloodline, I was hoping for something more profound."

Kara tried not to look surprised but doubted that she had any success in the endeavor. She hadn't yet grown accustomed to Pedrig, and now this? "You're Havarra."

"Well, of course, dear. Only the shepherds of the beasts are permitted to speak. Our charges are not. That is the Maker's plan."

With Tiran's help, Kara collected her sword and regained

her feet. She gave the bear an apologetic shrug as she sheathed her weapon. "I'm sorry I attacked you. I was not myself."

"That's in the past. We'll hear no more about it. Now you need rest."

"I can't. I mean"–Kara glanced at Tiran–"we can't. My brehna is in danger, held and tortured by a dragon. I saw and felt his pain just now. We must find him before it's too late."

The bear stood to all four legs, bringing her nose even with Kara's, and grunted. "It was not a suggestion. You need herbs and prayer to purge this poison. And I know all about your brother. To save him, you'll need your full strength."

38

"HOW DO YOU KNOW ABOUT KEIR?"

"Is that his name?" A thoughtful growl pulsed in the bear's throat. "Kara and Keir. So, some traditions of House Arkelon still hold. Interesting. But we can talk more later. We must leave this bridge."

She moved aside, nodding her muzzle at the bear behind her. "This is my daughter, Ioanu. You may ride on her back. I am Ingaru. I'll take the wartroot."

Knowing nothing about the facial expressions of bears, Kara could not be sure, but she thought Ioanu bristled at her mehma's declaration that Kara should ride her. Even so, the younger bear made no delay in lowering her belly to the flagstones. "Right, then. Climb on, Queensblood."

Ingaru lowered herself as well, but Tiran hesitated. "Wartroot? Did you mean me?"

The bear huffed. "On or off, Wartroot. Either way, we're leaving. This bridge is not safe."

Once Kara was on her back, Ioanu raised herself then crouched as if to leap.

"Wait!" Kara wrapped her arms around the bear's great neck. "Shouldn't you get a running start or something?"

Ioanu laughed. Kara felt it in the bear's throat and chest as much as she heard it. "You know nothing, Queensblood. Hold on tight."

Ingaru leapt first, and Tiran gave a shout of surprise. Kara couldn't blame him. The same shock hit her as Ioanu followed. The closest tall rock formation sailed beneath them. Kara had pegged it as their target, but the bears had grander plans. Another tower materialized out of the fog, its top already rising above Ingaru's level.

"We won't make it!" Kara said.

"That is the fear infection speaking," Ioanu countered. "Don't listen. Trust."

Even as the bear spoke, Kara saw a portico midway up the formation. Ahead of them, Ingaru and Tiran landed, and Ingaru jogged to a stop between the portico's rear columns. She moved out of the way just in time for Ioanu to land in the same place.

Kara, wishing to be respectful, dismounted the moment she was able. "Forgive my fear, but we humans couldn't see this place from the bridge."

Ioanu walked ahead of her into an open vestibule. "Nor could we bears, but we know the scent of our own, and that gives us direction."

"May I?" Kara lifted the lantern from her manykit and showed her. "Our sense of smell is not so keen."

The bear looked to her mehma, who nodded, and Kara struck her light. Once the flame had steadied, she held the lantern high.

This was no cave. Light swirls of mist hung high in green alloy rafters. Wisps drifted in the colonnades along the walls. This was a human dwelling, the kind reserved for the wealthy. "Made by the Suvoroth, I presume," Kara said. "Do any still live on the moor?"

Ingaru walked past her, heading deeper in. "Not for ages."

The bears brought them to a salon with stone couches. The cushions had rotted away, but Kara was grateful for the opportunity to sit.

Tiran sank down beside her. "Wartroot. Why call me Wartroot?"

"It is a swamp plant," Ingaru said, turning to face him.

"Yes, I know. We have it in my home forest of Sil Tymest. Ugly, knobby little plant. Smells like onions."

"As do you."

A pair of *thumps* from the portico interrupted them, and two more bears lumbered in. One larger than Ingaru and one smaller—much smaller.

"Goblins on the bridge," the larger bear said. "Four of them. Baghu clan will keep watch until they pass." He eyed Kara. "They were tracking your humans."

"If so, the trail has now grown cold." Ingaru leaned her shoulder into his side—a sort of hug if Kara read it rightly. "Queensblood, Wartroot, this my husband Boianu and our son, Bordu."

Bordu, the cub, sat on his haunches directly in front of his mehma. "I ran with Baghu clan, Mama. I kept pace."

"I'm sure you did." Ingaru bent her neck and nudged him aside, so that he no longer sat between her and her guests. "Your leaps grow longer by the day."

Tiran lifted his nose from his tunic, which Kara noticed he'd been sniffing in various places. "About that. Are great leaps a skill of Havarra bears?"

"More and more," Boianu said. "But only among the clans who made the Tagamoor their den—those who've drunk from the moor pools and breathed its thick air since birth."

Kara set her lantern down on a pedestal and pushed back to sit with legs crossed on the couch. "Thick air. You mean the vapors? The same vapors that poisoned me with fear?"

Ingaru had been grumbling in her son's ear, but at this, she lifted her muzzle and laughed. "It was not the fog, dear. The Tagamoor's vapors are a gift of the Maker, always have been, and though they were used for ill purpose by House Suvor and the dragons, they remain uncorrupted."

"But I thought—"

"It was the wanderer who poisoned you." Ioanu, the younger she-bear, stepped forward and bowed her head, but only a little. "Forgive me, Queensblood, but I was following you when the wanderer attacked. I had caught your scent in Gloamwood while on patrol."

"Patrolling beyond your range," a growl rumbled under Ingaru's words. "Where you've been forbidden to roam."

"That is beside the point, Mother." Ioanu kept her gaze on Kara. "I followed but held my distance, and before I was sure of you, the wanderer struck. It is the wanderer's poison that plagues you. You learned how to destroy one quickly enough—to separate it from its lantern and pierce the flame. And for that I commend you both. But there is another lesson. You must flee before a wounded wanderer bursts, or its ashes will corrupt you. A parting blow."

Kara recalled the horrible taste of the wanderer's remains in her mouth. "Oh. Right."

"Fear not. Wanderers are part of our range, and we know well how to deal with their infections. Wherever the dragons spread their corruption, the Maker provides an escape."

Her brehna returned with a mouthful of leafy stems and laid them out on the couch beside Kara. "*Jiborrel*. Bog heather. It fights the wanderer's poison." He gave her a bearish grin. "I chewed it a bit for you already, to make it go down easier."

Kara lifted the soggy stems and cleared her throat. "Uh. Thank you. Thank you so much."

Tiran waved a hand. "I'm still not clear on how we made it from the bridge to this house. We covered half the length of my home village in a single bound. How is that possible?"

Without any sense of effort, the husband, Boianu, jumped from Ingaru's side to a ledge above them—what looked to be the entrance to another level of the tower—and for the first time, Kara realized she'd seen no stairs inside the structure. "The minerals of the moor become part of those who live here," the he-bear said, "and they mingle with the vapors to carry us, even in here, where they are thin. In the thickest clouds, we can almost fly."

"I did see you, then," Kara said. "When we first left the cliff. Many of you. Just out of sight."

"We thought you were Keledan, but we had to be sure. And once we were, we moved quickly to get you off the bridge. Orcs and goblins cross it from time to time, more often of late."

Tiran snorted. "We can handle orcs and goblins."

"She couldn't." Ingaru turned her snout toward Kara. "You saw how the poison affected her mind when she saw me, combined with the dragon's torture of her brother. Imagine if she'd faced a sulfur orc or a quicksilver, or something more ancient. Neither of you would have survived."

Something more ancient. Kara had the sense from the protective glance Ingaru gave her cub that this ancient something roamed nearby. She let it go for the moment. "Tracking orcs was our purpose, whether we were prepared to face them or not. We'd hoped those who'd looted Grenton of its young Aladoth might lead us to Keir. And that is still our goal. My brehna is in pain, so much pain." She rose from the couch. "Please forgive my ungratefulness, but we are in haste. If you'll just tell us what you know, we'll be on our way."

Ingaru pressed her great head into Kara, sitting her down. "Haste and recklessness are close companions, dear. Your brother's circumstance is dire. His rescue will be perilous when you are well rested. In your current state, it is nigh impossible."

With a look, she sent Ioanu and Bordu up to the ledge where Boianu had gone. "My young will bring you fruit to eat and dried heather for under your heads. You will sleep here, and in the morning, we'll discuss Keir."

"But, what if–"

A deep grunt cut Kara's protest short. "No more discussion. If it eases your conscience, you have no choice but to stay. You can't reach the bridge without us, and the moor is impassible for humans. In short, consider yourselves our prisoners."

39

CONNOR
FADING MOUNTAINS

THE FOG CLINGING TO THE GLADE AND ITS MANY rock formations traveled in slow-moving clouds, revealing tall green grass and drooping hemlock in an ever-shifting landscape. It had diminished after sunrise but had yet to fully disappear.

Lee shook the dew from his cloak, which he'd used as a blanket. "Not the best night of sleep I've spent. Couldn't see a thing on my watch."

"Nor could I—on either of them." Connor had taken the last tick of the first watch after their landing as well as the full fourth watch, leaving the middle two for Lee and Zel. In the growing light, once all had awoken, he'd turned to inspecting the damage to *The Starling.*

The ship's alderwood trusses and wicker hull looked sound, as did the steel runners, apart from a few nicks and scratches. But the center pouch had suffered a dire wound.

Connor stared up at the long tear in the silk and sighed. "Can you mend it, Zel?"

"Not properly." She sat in the ship, where she'd slept after refusing to lie on Taneletharian grass, lest some tiny goblin-ant or orc-beetle crawl into her ear. Connor's efforts to convince her no such insects existed had been futile.

"Are not wood sprites and cave sprites the corrupted forms of insects?" she'd asked, looking down at him over the rail the night before.

"As far as we know, yes."

"And have you catalogued every type of dark creature in this land?"

"Likely not."

With a curt nod, she'd disappeared from the rail, leaving only her voice. "Then I shall sleep in here, thank you."

She crawled out from this hiding place now to stand with him in the grass and stare up at her wounded ship. "I have neither the skill nor enough silk to make a good patch."

"What about a stitch. If we find a needle and thread and stitch the tear, will it hold for a flight or two?"

Zel shrugged. "Never been tried. Flying about Keledev, let alone the Dragon Lands, is a new frontier. Mostly the stormwatchers go up and come down again. Our collective experience has little else to offer."

Lee slung his bow over his shoulder and joined them. "I think *stormwatcher* is an outdated term, Zel, at least for you. After yesterday, you should be called a storm*rider.*"

"Stormrider." The frustration in her features softened. "Yes, that'll do. It'll do nicely. But if the Rescuer wanted us to ride that storm, as you put it, why did he let his portal damage *The Starling?*"

"Perhaps we made an error," Lee said. "Now that we know what the Rescuer can do with your father's design, some changes may be in order."

Zel hit him with a hard look. "Are you saying my father's design is imperfect?"

"It is a first design, is it not? Or perhaps a second?" The scribe pointed to his spectacles. "This is a third design, much lighter and nimbler than the first, and Master Belen says there'll be many more. That is the nature of inventions. Also, the alternative solution is that the Rescuer's design is imperfect. Which do you think is more likely?"

She frowned but gave no argument.

They broke their fast with the way rations Zel had packed for the journey from Sky Harbor to Ras Telesar and back–wheat cakes filled with applethorn berries, oats, and dried meat. Lee included a prayer for aid and guidance with the blessing.

"These will not last long," he said after they all had finished their ration. "We'll need to find a town if we can and buy provisions."

Faelin's markings in his secret ink had identified this place as a sanctuary, but Connor saw no obvious hovel or shed. The ground fog did not help. Despite the morning getting on, it still had not cleared.

"No wonder your grandfather couldn't find the dagger in these mountains," Lee said as they explored the glade. "Were I to drop a coin, I doubt I'd ever find it again."

"And yet we must." Connor walked around a lone hemlock–the largest he'd seen. "Find the dagger, I mean."

"Or the Rapha Key. We haven't decided which the Rescuer wants us to seek yet."

Connor gave him a flat look. "We'll see. Either way, that lost coin is your affair." He stopped halfway around the hemlock. "Hello. What's this?"

A rock poked out of the fog, so close to the hemlock that the tree's sagging evergreen boughs covered its top. A spring flowed from under the boughs and down a natural furrow in the rock to fill a dark pool not much broader than a village fountain. Connor's *hello* was prompted by a doe watering at the pool. She bolted the moment he spoke.

Nothing about this seemed out of place–a rock, a tree, a spring, and a deer–except that Connor caught a hint of lighter green under the branches. As the others hurried over, he pressed the boughs aside. And the more he uncovered, the odder the rock became.

The spring bubbled up through a small well within the rock's flat peak before flowing down the furrow. A highly translucent crystal surrounded the well. Connor might have thought it was a deposit caused by the water, except that suspended within the crystal were green emblems. "Those symbols look like malachite," he said to Lee, "and they're definitely manmade. But I don't recognize them."

Lee bent closer. "They're liege runes, still used in many Taneletharian cantons. The one that looks similar to an *A* is House Advor."

"Advor." Connor recognized the name. Kara had once told him her brehnan both wore the brand of Advor. She too might have worn it if Liam hadn't borne her and Keir away while she was still young enough for a crib, after the orcs killed their parents. What were the odds that out here, looking for one of Faelin's sanctuaries, he'd find a rune tied to the very girl Faelin had helped him rescue? "What about the symbol that looks like a bird?"

"Fulcor. Wealthy house that spread from the hills known as Miner's Glory to the fishing towns of Winter's Bight." Lee shrugged. "Advor owned the Frost Isles, farther north. I don't know how the two are related."

"Oh! I do!" Zel slapped Lee's arm. "I know a bit of Talanian history that you don't. Splendid. Fulcor and Advor are at the heart of a story–one my father tells by the hearth every winter. It is the *Lay of Luco and Kaia,* two of the Blacksmith's first followers." She cleared her throat and took up the posture of a festival storyteller, shoulders straight and hands lightly spread. "To ease their flight to Ras Telesar, the nobleborn Luco gave Kaia his family's liege rune–the falcon of House Fulcor. Following the custom for thralls traded from one house to another, he drew it over Kaia's House Advor brand."

"This doesn't sound like a very pleasant tale for Kaia," Lee said.

Zel frowned at him. "She bore the pain and indignity to keep Luco and his sister safe–not to mention herself. And in doing so, she became the first besides the Blacksmith to bear his sign. For when Luco had finished combining the brands, they were both astonished to see that together, the symbols formed a star. Later they would learn that this was the Blacksmith's birthmark, and Luco resolved to carve a matching star into his own arm to honor his new liege and Kaia's humility."

From the way Zel spoke her last sentence, Connor sensed she had more to say about it. "And did he brand himself in this way?"

Zel shook her head, grinning as if Connor had walked right into some snare she'd set. "He did not. The Blacksmith stopped him, and told him that no more liege runes were needed. Luco's love for Kaia, and for the other Keledan, would be the symbol marking him as a follower of the High One's son."

Throughout Zel's tale, Lee had kept his nose close to the rock and its spring, examining the crystal top and the runes from all angles. "Together, the symbols form a star," he said quietly. "Together. But here, they remain apart, separated by the fountain."

This sounded odd to Connor's ear, and instantly he knew why. Many Keledan weddings took place at village fountains because Keledan fountains represented the Rescuer's sacrifice. The clergy never said anything about a couple being separated by the fountain. Just the opposite. He spoke the common liturgy out loud. "The two of you were once souls apart. Now you are together, joined by the fountain."

Lee glanced up from the bubbling well. "Right. Not separated. Joined." The scribe dropped a lens in front of his eye, let out a laugh, and then grasped the edges of the crystal around the well. He slid two pieces together, so that one slid under the other. They locked into place over the hole, with the symbols overlapping to form a star. He stood back. "Joined by the fountain."

The water stopped flowing, and the little pool drained, exposing stone steps leading down.

40

"THIS IS NO LIGHTRAIDER CONSTRUCTION." CONNOR led his party down the steps, holding his travel lantern before them, illuminating sculpted murals on both sides. He lowered the light to show them a chain running through a descending trough. "I might attribute this and the symbol lock above to my patehpa's genius, but the murals are Elder Folk work."

"Truly." Zel touched a flowing vine formed from the same malachite as the symbols in the lock, and laughed. "Growing up among the guilds, I've seen our most skilled artists work their craft, and they are incredible. Yet none could match this."

The steps brought them to a bridge over an underground river. A solid gate, held up by the chain and a set of gears, had risen to let the water flow out. Connor lifted his chin as they crossed, pointing it out to Lee. "The symbol lock opened the gate. That's how we drained the water, I think."

"Agreed. That little spring above could not have filled this stairwell. It simply covered the upper edges after the river filled the rest." Lee nodded to a black slate door ahead of them, taller than the height of two grown men. "Now, how do we open that?"

The door had no lock and no mechanism Connor could see, nothing but an etched forest scene. His patehpa's symbol lock mimicked the engineering of the Aropha–the Elder Folk–but this was the real thing, with mechanisms inscrutable to humankind. "I don't know."

"Well," Zel said, "clearly other lightraiders opened this door. And one was your grandfather."

"That doesn't mean I can. Knowledge doesn't pass through blood."

"Did I say that?"

"In a way. Sorry. I didn't mean to bite at you." Connor stood at the end of the bridge, surveying the door and the wall around it. Nothing about them looked useful, only a continuation of the sculpted mural from the stairwell. "Faelin's candle burned brighter and shone much farther than I ever knew. It's a lot to live up to."

Zel gave him a strange grin. "Faelin's *candle.* Interesting choice of word. You might also have said he cast a long shadow."

"Don't start."

"I'm not being mean. A candle. A flame. I have an idea. May I?" She took his lantern and held it closer to the mural near the door. "If there's one thing I've learned about the Aropha from their influence on guild artistry, it's that they often represent the High One as both water and flame."

"We have the water," Lee said, joining her.

Zel nodded. "But not the flame." She traced a finger along a vine with sculpted flowers until she came to one near the door with its petals upturned, forming a half bowl. "Here. Yes. This must be a sconce." Taking the candle from the lantern, she stood on tiptoe and dipped its flame into the flower.

With a hiss, the candle went out, leaving them in darkness.

"Oh, well done," Connor said.

He heard her snap her fingers. "Wait. The sconce is full of water because the river had filled the well. But your grandfather added that feature to hide this place. In the Elder Folk days, the water would have stayed in the underground river where it belongs."

"She's right." Lee said in the dark, and followed those words with shuffling and grunting. "Yes. The sconce is filled with water, but there's oil beneath. I can feel it. Give me a moment."

More grunting. Splashing. Then Lee struck a flame to a candle and held it close to his face. "Let's give it another go, shall we?" Just as Zel had done, he pushed up on his toes and dipped the candle toward the sconce.

This time fire leapt from the wick to the flower. With a great *foomp*, the oil in the sconce took the flame. The black door slid silently open. Beyond it, with a ripple of matching sounds stretching into an echoing distance, more sconces lit up, nearly blinding them with yellow-white light.

Shielding their eyes, the three entered an underground chamber far larger than Connor could have imagined–so large that if there'd been an opening in its vaulted ceiling, Zel might have dropped *The Starling* inside and still had room to maneuver. *Not a bad idea*, he thought.

"Huh," Lee said. "The sconces are joined in sequence. It's like the water device Master Belen made to strike flames to all the lanterns in his tower. Surprising."

Connor, unable to look away from the white-marble room taking shape before him, gave a tiny shake of his head. "No. It really isn't. This place was likely his inspiration."

The flame had traveled to more than just flower sconces. A thousand small lights shown down from the ceiling like stars, illuminating a haven with its own well, beds, forge, and a dormant garden overgrown with yellowed vines.

No columns supported the roof. There was no need. The builders had sculpted tall trees from the walls with branches that stretched out toward the middle to hold it aloft. Jeweled creatures populated this stone forest. Garnet squirrels were frozen in mid-scurry on the trunks, and faceted amber birds perched in the branches alongside reptilian creatures of several colors. The reptilian creatures reminded Connor of Crumpet, except they were larger and still had their tails, forever curled. Some bore wings tucked close to their backs. The largest bore coats of fine crystals that might have represented fur or feathers.

"*Lashoroth*," Lee said. "The paradragons of old. My father says they were the only animals to exist simultaneously in the spiritual and physical realms. That's why the dragons chose to steal and twist their forms before purging them from Tanelethar."

Zel frowned at him. "That's a myth."

"Is it?" Lee gestured up at the jeweled creatures. "The Aropha didn't think so." He looked from one end of the chamber to the other and shook his head. "Faelin might have chosen to stay here, a palace by any account, and still do the Rescuer's work. Yet he abandoned it for a hovel near Trader's Knoll and the grubby life of a collier. All for one girl."

"So it seems." Connor took the lead and walked a path down the middle of the chamber. "All I can say for sure is that he tried to do the Rescuer's will."

Faelin had added shelves, racks, chests of drawers, and the like and filled them with cloaks, weapons, and other items of kit. In that way, this place was similar to the hidden outpost near Trader's Knoll. Except, where one was an armory crammed into a woodshed on the enemy's border, this chamber felt like a secret garrison deep in his territory.

"This may seem a palace to us," Zel said, "but what was it to the Elder Folk?"

"A hideout." Lee sat on one of several benches, part of a long, sectioned wardrobe filled with eberlast cloaks and manykits of all sizes. "When the dragon scourge began, the Aropha left, but not all at once. I'm guessing they transferred what they could from the sanctuary at Ras Heval before the dragons moved in to destroy it."

Connor gave Zel a nod. "You find a needle and thread, and perhaps cut the eberlast lining from one of those cloaks over there–whatever you can scrounge up to patch *The Starling*. Lee and I will search for anything that tells us how close Faelin came to finding the dagger."

"Or how close his raid party came to finding the key before they were routed," Lee added.

The scribe did not waste time in their search. He and Connor had walked only a few paces down the path before he suddenly ran ahead. "Connor, look! Come on!"

He ran straight to the far end of the chamber and up a set of steps to a raised platform. When Connor caught up, he understood why. "Is this a map table?"

To Connor's eye, the table–glistening stone like the table at Ras Telesar, but white instead of green–had blended with the marble wall. But Lee, with one of his colored lenses in place, had spotted it quickly.

"The table at home is shaped like the continent of Talania," Connor said. "This one is round."

"It may cover a larger area, perhaps the whole of Dastan."

"Or it may not be a map at all. It's not even the same color."

Lee examined the table's surface, flipping his lenses. "The stone is similar–with infinite depth under the surface. Let's give it a try. Through the table at the academy, the Rescuer allows us to see what others have discovered."

"But only when we have a letter from another lightraider." Connor turned his gaze to the rest of the oversize outpost. "We need to find a parchment with Faelin's handwriting."

It sounded easy–find some record left by Faelin in his former hideout. It wasn't.

Pouring over shelves and digging through drawers and crates, they found maps, journey writs, and passages from the Sacred Scrolls. Lee found an accounting of every item stored in the outpost and a ledger of the coins in the money chest, but they found no account of the lost dagger or the failed mission to claim the Rapha Key.

Once Zel had gathered all she needed to patch *The Starling*, she joined the search, and still they came up empty-handed. No parchment for the map table. No clues of any kind to point them toward the Rapha Key or the dagger, which Connor had hoped might be a sign of the Rescuer's reason for bringing them here. After hours of searching, they had nothing to guide them forward in their quest.

Connor plodded up the steps at the rear of the chamber and stood alone at the round table. He stared up between two of the sculpted, white-marble trees supporting the roof. "What do you want from me? I can't finish Faelin's mission without his guidance. I'm not him. I'll never be him!"

The empty stone reflected his voice back to him—the harshness and defiance in it.

The foolishness.

Another voice followed in the echo, quiet and firm. *When did I ask you to be Faelin, child? When have I asked you to be anything but my servant?*

The question struck at his heart. Where had the burden he carried come from—the idea that he must redeem Faelin's memory and find the dagger to save all Keledev? Not from the Rescuer. Not even from Councilor Boreas. But looking back, Connor realized he'd fashioned that burden for himself, out of wisps of cloud and the assemblyman's unkind words, the moment the Rescuer pulled *The Starling* through the Storm Mists. Had he become the *lewaker* the Assembly guard accused him of being—carrying a foolish and unnecessary burden?

Connor laid that burden down at the Rescuer's feet. He bowed his head, resting his hands on the table's cool stone. "Forgive me. I know you brought us here for your purpose and not ours. Help us to understand your will and serve you now."

A sacred verse came to him, one he'd studied during his preparation for the Trial of the Navigators. "*Howda'ana ke'sabetoth miyov cresana—Ker decla'im ke'Rumosh—sabetoth mayovu thamim, se mo morgom, yi e helam po e tiqam gevana'ov.*"

I know my plans for you. To give you hope. A future.

The table grew warm against his hands. Motion drew his attention to the great marble trees. A garnet squirrel moved–slow at first, then scurried up and around the tree trunk, out of sight. An amber bird fluttered its faceted wings. A mischievous sapphire paradragon launched from its branch, tumbled backward in an aerial flip, tail whipping into a perfect circle, then tucked its wings and dove straight into the table. The creature exploded into blue and gold sparkling dust. And when the dust cleared, the table was a sea of moonlit waves.

Across the table, where there had been nothing but a wall before, Avner Jairun stood with his bushy eyebrows pressed together in a deep frown. He looked Connor straight in the eye. "Mister Enarian. I should have known. What have you and Mister Lee done, now?"

41

"MASTER JAIRUN?"

The headmaster looked to be in a tower room at Ras Telesar, such was the shade of the stone floor and the curved wall behind him. But higher up, the wall wavered like heat above a flame and disappeared into a night forest. The giant trees on either side of the table, once marble, now breathed with rich bark and living creatures under a starry night sky.

Connor reached out a hand. "Are you here or there?"

Master Jairun waved him off. "Don't. To reach through this portal is to abuse its purpose. And to answer your question, I am neither here nor there." He shrugged. "Or perhaps it's the other way around. I am here. But I am also there. And so are you. These windows are a gift of the Maker, wrought by Aropha hands. Their workings are a mystery not fathomable to us."

"I take it, then, that you have a white table like this one, somewhere at Ras Telesar."

"In the second tower on the eighth level. I felt the Helper pushing me to climb the stairs an hour ago. I must say, I thought I had come for a very different reason."

"And are there other secrets of the academy you haven't shown us?"

The question seemed to surprise Master Jairun. "Which of us is the headmaster, and which is the cadet? Are you implying you've a right to know all the secrets of the Order?"

"No, sir. I suppose not. But I've learned too many secrets in recent days. Secrets like that of Lef Amunrel and Faelin's mission to find the Rapha Key."

"So, the Rescuer has brought you to the sanctuary in the Fading Mountains, near Ras Heval."

"He has. I believed we were to recover the dagger so the Lightraider Order may end the war. But now I'm uncertain."

"As you should be. Your belief was dead wrong."

The headmaster may as well have struck Connor in the chest with his staff. Connor opened his mouth to reply but found he didn't have the breath to make a sound.

"We'll discuss that in a moment," Master Jairun said, "along with the details of who told you about Lef Amunrel and why. But first, tell me how you came to be a thousand leagues north of the city to which I sent you."

Zel and Lee appeared at Connor's shoulder. He hadn't heard them come up the steps. "In my airship, *The Starling,*" Zel said, "on the wings of the Rescuer's storm."

Lee stretched out a hand, just as Connor had done, and Connor gently pulled it back by Lee's sleeve. The scribe took the hint and lowered his arm to his side. "We came through the Storm Mists, sir. We flew as the ravens do, in a ship of the air invented by Councilor Boreas of Sky Harbor, intending to arrive more quickly at the academy."

Together, the three gave an account of all they'd experienced in their travels, from the first meeting with Boreas in the Archive of the Scribes to their near calamity and rough landing in the meadow above.

The headmaster took a long time to consider what they'd told him, leaning on his staff with both hands resting on its knot. Finally, he lifted his gaze from the waves on the table. "I am sorry to say it, Miss Boreas, but your father was wrong to share his knowledge of the dagger in this way."

"But that knowledge brought us here," Lee said. "Surely, the Rescuer–"

"The Rescuer would have taken you through the barrier with or without that knowledge. Tell me, what drove your haste in flying north? What drove you to cast aside the Assembly's request for an audience and risk taking to the sky in the councilor's invention?"

Connor thought back to that evening in Sky Harbor. It was not Boreas nor the story of Faelin's failed mission that sent him rushing back to Ras Telesar. He'd wanted to head back long before then. A single catalyst had changed his desire into action. "Barnabas. The news that dark creatures once again roamed Keledev and that this evil had murdered our friend."

Master Jairun nodded. "Mankind will always muddle the High One's plans with our own. He will use all to our good and his glory, but you must discern between his will and man's interference."

"Interference?" Zel's expression had grown dark at the first mention of her tehpa's actions being wrong. She clearly had something else to say on the matter but seemed to think better of it before continuing. "If not for the dagger, then why did the Rescuer bring us to the exact place it was lost?"

"Any number of reasons, child. Perhaps to restore that sanctuary and the one at Trader's Knoll. I suspect we'll need both in the coming war. Or perhaps you're there to complete the first part of the last lightraider mission of that age."

"You mean the Rapha Key?" Lee cast an *I told you so* glance at Connor.

"The same. Faelin's raid party carried the celestium dagger on that final mission, yes. But they went to those Fading Mountains to find the key. If the dagger is meant to separate Heleyor from his dragon form once and for all, then it is of little use without a way into Ras Pyras."

Connor shifted his gaze past the headmaster to the night

forest behind him, knowing full well that it was daytime in the Fading Mountains and at Ras Telesar. The forest seemed a place apart from either Keledev or Tanelethar. A lashor–a paradragon–in one of the large trees, tail curled in a spiral around the branch, gazed back at him with a sleepy look of perfect peace. How could the Keledan find such peace while the enemy still roamed free?

"The Rapha Key it is, then, Headmaster."

"That is what my heart tells me, what I feel the Helper saying. But there's something else." Master Jairun uttered a prayer, and the waves on the table drained away, soaking into the land to reveal a gloomy forest of dead trees. One tree near the northern edge took life and blossomed with deep-green leaves. A hollow opened within its trunk, and two travelers stepped out, hooded and cloaked–a young man and woman.

The guardian watched the pair, brow creased with concern. "You're not the only raid party in Tanelethar. Last night, I came up here to pray, and the Rescuer saw fit to show me where he'd sent them. You're looking at old Sil Belomar, near Grenton and the ancient Tagamoor canyon." He lifted his hand, and the map expanded, shrinking the forest to reveal the province around it.

To the east, Connor recognized the portion of the Fading Mountains where his party had landed, fog clinging to the ridges and gathering in the valleys, and Graywater Bay, which he'd seen from *The Starling*. With the table's broad view, he saw gray-green mists and low fogs plaguing the whole region, all coming from a single source–a moor at the bottom of a canyon. "We're close to them," he said. "At least, we're close enough to reach them with the aid of Zel's airship."

"Those two have their own mission. And you have yours. But keep them in your prayers and listen to the Helper. The Rescuer may yet want you to join them."

"Was that the twins?" Lee asked. "I couldn't tell with their hoods up."

The forest and mountains sank once again beneath the waves.

"You saw Mister Yar," the headmaster said. "That's correct. But his sister is not with him."

Connor blinked. There were few women at the academy at present–a growing number with the new initiates, but not among the older cadets. "If not Teegan, then the woman we saw could only have been–"

"Kara Orso." Master Jairun gave him a hard look that said, *Try to keep calm*. "I sent her north across the barrier to rescue her brother Keir. A dragon has taken him."

42

TEEGAN
KELEDEV
RAS TELESAR

TEEGAN PLACED AN EAR TO THE UPPER-ROOM DOOR IN one of the eighth-level towers. Looking up from the barracks balcony far below, she thought she'd seen Master Jairun enter. Stradok, in his unmistakable crimson assemblyman's robes, had gone with him.

"Well, that's a development," she heard Stradok say. "Or two or three developments. Zayn Boreas has been keeping secrets and having clandestine meetings in the Archive. We'll see what his admirers on the Prime Council have to say about that."

"Is that all you took from what you saw here?"

Yes. It was Master Jairun's voice in there with the assemblyman. And apparently Teegan had missed much. She'd taken too long to work her way up to this tower through Ras Telesar's maze of passages and stairwells.

"Certainly not," Stradok replied. "But you must agree it is poor behavior for an assemblyman."

"There is much assemblyman behavior that I consider poor. Thus, I must confess that Zayn's actions are difficult for me to judge. In any case, the Rescuer has seen fit to use him to send my cadets on a mission–however misguided at the start."

"Your cadets"–Stradok let out a derisive grunt–"and that

troublemaker Zayn's daughter. Do we now have two orders of self-proclaimed knights heading into Tanelethar to stir up the enemy? The Lightraider Order and this Stormguard or whatever they're called?"

"Careful, Councilor. You know as well as I that the Rescuer himself commissioned the Lightraider Order. In person. So say the Scrolls."

"So say the Scrolls. Yes. Of course. But Zayn and his airship captains may make a similar claim–a commission by epiphany, like Luthelan the Herald."

"We don't have time for this argument."

With that last declaration from Master Jairun, Teegan heard the two men coming toward the door. She rushed down the stairs and did her best to pretend she was idling at the eighth-level ramparts for no other reason than to observe Aethia's flight over the Forest of Believing.

"Did I not command you and the rest of the hunting party to rest?" the headmaster asked, clearly not falling for her ruse. "You especially, to let your wound heal."

She put aside any pretense. "I am healed, sir. Thanks to you and Pedrig. And we are rested. We are ready. I came up here to tell you so and urge you to action." As if to add to her argument, Aethia cried out from below. "See? Even Aethia is wondering what you've been doing since we brought our report of the goblin den. She wants to know when we'll attack."

Stradok cut Master Jairun's reply off before it began. "If you *must* know, Cadet, we were communicating with your classmates, Mister Enarian and Mister Lee, who found an Aropha window device in northeastern Tanelethar."

"Connor and Lee are in Tanelethar?" How had she not heard of this?

The councilor waved the concern in her voice away as the two men resumed walking. "Long story. Famous weapon. Rapha Key. Flying airship from Sky Harbor, flown by an assemblyman's daughter. We can discuss it later."

Teegan stopped, staring after the two men. A scout mission kept secret was one thing. But that last revelation from Stradok was something she most certainly hadn't expected to hear. "Exactly *which* assemblyman's daughter?"

A hard glance from Master Jairun over his shoulder made her regret her tone. She and Lee had grown close over the last year—a closeness the guardians had noticed. She suspected that was why they never sent the two on the same scouting mission. And Teegan didn't mind, at least not when they partnered Lee with Connor, Dag, or her brehna.

Stradok looked over his shoulder as well. "I thought a Sil Tymest falconer like you would be more interested in the news of a flying ship. Gives the name of our capital a whole new meaning, doesn't it? Now quit dawdling, girl. There's a goblin den in the Rescuer's Celestial Peaks. We've much to do."

She rolled her eyes at the assemblyman's back. "Yes, I know, Councilor." Teegan felt her tone growing harsh again and did her best to rein it in. "I saw the den with my own eyes. The question is, what are we going to do about it and when?"

Master Jairun held up a hand to stop Stradok from answering and motioned for Teegan to join them. "We're going to do what we must always do when such soulless corruptions show their ugly faces," he said as she caught up to them. "We're going to root the creatures out and annihilate them—every single one."

CONNOR
TANELETHAR
FADING MOUNTAINS

KNOCK, AND THE DOOR WILL OPEN.

Those were the words Master Jairun spoke when Connor asked where to find his patehpa's quest journal. *That is the only clue Faelin gave us as to where he hid it,* he'd said, *and all the knowledge either I or Pedrig wanted as to the location of such volatile information. I'm afraid it's up to you and your companions.* And then he'd vanished, along with the night sky, and the creatures in the trees had once again frozen into their crystalline forms.

Lee had immediately begun knocking on every marble panel in the sanctuary walls. The others followed behind him.

"How do we know that's what Faelin meant?" Zel asked.

They passed near the dormant garden, and Connor sat down on the edge of its well. "We don't. This is how Lee thinks—by doing. Watch, in a moment he'll come up with a completely different solution to the riddle."

"Or I will." Zel left Lee and hurried over to the shelves and racks Faelin had added to the sanctuary. "Well, not a *completely* different solution." She parted a pair of eberlast cloaks hanging in the sectioned wardrobe and knocked on the wood behind them, then she knocked on the seat. After two more sections, the sound of her knocking changed. "See? I've got something."

As the others joined her, Zel felt around the edges of a wardrobe bench, until Connor heard a pronounced *click*.

"I'd have figured it out eventually," Lee said.

"I guess we'll never know, will we?" The stormrider lifted the bench seat and rummaged around the hidden compartment. "Oh. Here we go." She pulled out a thick leather book, hesitated a moment, then handed it to Connor. "This was your grandfather's. You should be the one to read it."

Connor held the book between his palms, feeling the leather of its cover. The last person to open it had been his patehpa, perhaps decades before Connor had found him and lost him again—all in the space of a few hours.

"I can read it for you, if you like," Lee said.

It was a gentle push. Lee was ready to burst with curiosity, Connor could feel it. But he appreciated the kindness of his phrasing. "No. I'll do it. Let's take a look." He opened the book and found a loose page tucked inside the front cover.

Resteram, 26th of Perabeyth
Year 571 of the Third Era
Faelin Enarian, Lightraider Knight

An unfinished quest gnaws at the soul of any lightraider. And I have two–a dagger and a key. I learned the fate of Lef Amunrel months ago, but my captain, Avner Jairun, has forbidden us–Pedrig and me–from trying to reclaim it. I will respect his command. More than that, I agree with him. The dagger is safe. In a way. And the risk in retrieving it is far too great.

"He knew." Zel had been reading over Connor's shoulder. "Faelin knew where to find the Red Dagger years ago."

Lee leaned in to take a look with one of his lenses lowered. "As did Master Jairun, I see."

"Then why didn't they tell us?" Zel asked. "Why didn't your headmaster tell us moments ago, when we spoke to him?"

"Because he doesn't want us to go after it." Connor stepped away from them both to avoid another interruption. "The key is our assignment now, remember?"

"If you're not going to let us read over your shoulder," Lee said, "then read it aloud."

"Must I?"

The scribe and Zel both answered at once. "Yes."

"Fine. But don't interrupt." He started with the next line, the one after the bit about Master Jairun and the dagger.

Since Avner's decision to leave Lef Amunrel be, I have thrown myself into the pursuit of the Rapha Key. The rout we suffered seemed too great a victory for Valshadox, the local dragon lord, to be the result of some chance meeting. A goblin I captured when I searched for my companions confirmed this. His tribe had been watching the Ras Heval ruin near Graywater Bay for centuries. The dragons are a patient bunch. Thus, I suspected Valshadox had taken the key.

I was wrong. He's been searching. But so far, the key has eluded his grasp.

The Havarra have long memories, passed down from mehma and tehpa to cub and pup. Thus, I sent Pedrig in search of his own. Another wolf led him to isolated clans of bears hiding in a place I will not mention here. He learned from them the story of a thief in the early days of the traitor-kings. Dacon of Suvor and a thief he hired used the key to enter Ras Pyras, and Dacon died for the offense. But the thief escaped, or so the bears told Pedrig. Together, my wolf-friend and I have tracked this thief ever since. We were close, but now I feel the Rescuer pulling us toward a new mission. Who am I to argue with his sovereignty?

I recorded every step and misstep of our search in this journal–every clue and false lead–for the day when either I or another knight might once again take up this quest. I suppose that's you, the one reading this note. Guard these pages well, Lightraider. If you lose them to the enemy, one door to Heleyor's final destruction may be closed to the Order forever.

Connor folded the page and tucked it into the journal. "So, this is it. This book holds all the clues we were looking for, clues that let the Lightraider Order storm the stronghold of Heleyor."

"Sneak in is more like it," Lee said. "But whatever works."

Connor took the book to a wooden table where they could study it together. Zel followed, but Lee hung back, looking longingly toward the window device where they'd spoken to Master Jairun.

Connor gave a short whistle to capture his attention. "Something wrong?"

"Is it worth placing the journal on the window, just to see if a living map appears?"

"I don't think that's how this particular table works, Lee."

The scribe kicked a toe into the pathway for a moment longer, then jogged over to join them. "You're probably right. But I should have liked it to work that way. Ras Telesar's living map is my favorite among all the blessings of the High One that the Aropha left to us."

43

KARA
THE TAGAMOOR

FOR BREAKFAST, THE BEARS OFFERED BERRIES AND trout, served on centuries-old porcelain decorated with winged men. Ingaru's husband had brought the fish from the River Phantom, which he said ran east to west through the moor, before heading out again to check with the bear clans watching the bridge.

Kara and Tiran had managed the dishes, which they'd found in what had been the home's dining room. But they ate on the portico to take advantage of what daylight the moor allowed. Ingaru let Tiran build a fire there.

The mehma-bear understood that humans needed to cook their fish before eating it.

Her cub did not. Bordu scrunched his nose as Kara raised a portion to her lips. "Your fish smells of burnt tree and ash. It will make you sick, Queensblood."

Ingaru bent to bump his flank with her head. "The Maker created humans to be different than the Havarra. Do not pester her, son. Be gracious. Feel blessed. In the days of your foremothers, a cub of five winters would never have dined with a noblewoman."

"Noblewoman?" Tiran's fist, filled with berries, hovered near his mouth. He grinned and set them down again. "I'm afraid you're mistaken. No offense to Kara"–he shot her an apologetic look that said as much–"but before she came to Keledev, she was a charwood-seller and a furrier."

"And what does that matter, Wartroot?" The growl in Ingaru's response was sharp enough to wipe the smirk from Tiran's face. "Her profession cannot change her heritage."

"Please stop calling me Wartroot. I bathed last night. There was a basin upstairs."

"Yet your scent remains."

"I know of my heritage," Kara said, "But our family's blood has not been noble for centuries. Far from it. We are to be purged. Exterminated. The dragons made our very existence a crime."

Ingaru replied with as much harshness as she'd used with Tiran. "The dragons have no right to make laws. Their claim to wield that authority is among their greatest deceptions." She looked around at her family. "Our clan still remembers the honor of walking with yours, the last human kingdom to hold out against the scourge."

"Your clan . . . and mine?"

"Yes, dear." The bear cocked her head, ears forward. "I see that you know little of your past–that which transpired before your eyes first opened. We bears take care to pass such memories down mother-to-cub, but I suppose that is a blessing of remaining hidden on the Tagamoor all these years. Your line found no such safety. And without it, your shared memories were lost."

Kara pushed her plate aside, the grumbling of her stomach forgotten. "Restore my memories, Ingaru." She had only one–her mehma, smiling through tears and singing the lullaby known to the Keledan as *The Sleeper's Hope*, while an orc tore her away forever. "Tell me–" The plea caught in her throat, and she paused to collect herself before starting again. "Tell me of my foremothers. Please."

"May I?" Ioanu sat with her mehma, so that her paws and Kara's knees nearly touched.

Ingaru nodded, and Ioanu gave Kara a bearish smile. "You

are born of House Arkelon, the queendom that once shared the Frost Isles with the Leander Kings and the Aropha of Ras Pyras." Ioanu stretched out a paw, and with a deftness only a Havarra bear could manage, she touched a blue-green claw to the sapphire pendant at Kara's neck. "And this is your family sigil."

Kara lifted the pendant in her palm, the polar sapphire, as dark blue as the deepest, coldest sea, hugged by a silver bear. She remembered the terrible night on which it had come to her. Liam, her eldest brehna, died in her arms as Faelin Enarian defended them from an attacking horde of iron orcs. In his last moments, he had drawn it from under his blood-soaked shirt.

This was Mehma's. She'd want you to have it.

Ioanu lowered her paw. "I am the bear in your hand, Queensblood, as is my mother and her mother's mother. Your clan and mine are joined by the ages, and only the Maker could have brought us together this way. Hunted and hidden, we walk side by side once more."

Your clan and mine. Family. Keir.

Ingaru seemed quick to correct her behlna. "Ioanu means to say we will walk together across the moor. Our clan and the others have remained here in safety for a long time. We will not put that safety at risk."

Kara gave the younger she-bear a sad but grateful smile, then shifted her gaze to Ingaru. "Even so. If our families are joined by shared history, then show me the courtesy of trust. Share what you know of my brehna."

44

"THE CAMP IS DEEP IN *SIL SHADATH,* QUEENSBLOOD–the Black Forest, which the Aladoth now call the Forest of Horrors."

Ioanu fell through the mist, with Kara on her back and Ingaru and Tiran falling ahead of them. The bears had invited them on a ride to some special place in the ancient Suvoroth capital. Though in their usual roundabout way with important information, they had not yet given a reason.

The bears had, at least, shared how Ioanu found Keir. Patrolling beyond the borders of the Tagamoor to the north, well beyond the bounds her mehma set for her, she'd caught Keir's scent the same way she'd caught Kara's. She'd never known the smell of a queensblood, but the clan had passed the description down across the generations–ice and lux flowers, iron, and cinnamon. Using her ability to almost float on Gloamwood's ground fog, Ioanu had crept past ghouls and wanderers deep into the forest, near to a high fence, in time to see Keir's companion fall. Dark creatures rushed in, too many for her to fight alone. And she was forced to let them carry both men off.

"He has spirit, your brother, but spirit alone will not get him out of the camps."

"And your love alone," Ingaru said, looking back at Kara, "will not be enough to save him. You must be fully ready for this fight."

The speed of the fall slowed as the mist thickened, until Ioanu and Ingaru alighted on a road of bricks so dark green they were almost black. Kara heard the moor river close by—very close—but could not see it. Perhaps that was the reason for its name. She slipped from Ioanu's back. "Thank you for carrying me. I sense that was never part of the life our families shared together."

She heard a low rumble in the bear's throat. "No. It was not." But then Ioanu brightened. "Of course, neither were the Lightraider Order or the mists on the Tagamoor. A new history together is being wrought. And we shall take it as it comes."

Kara smiled, and without thinking, rested her hand in the deep blue-gray fur between Ioanu's shoulder blades. The bear didn't seem to mind.

"Come along, Ioanu," Ingaru said. "Do not delay our guests. They've much to do."

The vapors on the moor road, with their metallic taste, threatened to choke Kara. But the bears believed she could safely walk there. She had asked them to trust her, and now she would trust them—an effort made all the more difficult by the poor visibility. "How far to the—"

Before she finished the question, great shadows materialized ahead—giant horns forming an archway over the road.

"Sel Suvor's Passage," Ingaru said, looking up. "Welcome to Tagamar, the Green City."

The horns spread to the east and west, becoming a great circular wall. The moor hills ended, giving way to a monstrous plaza of the same dark brick as the road. With the fog around them, the plaza seemed endless, until the four passed between the first columned buildings of the city. Open doorways high up and rooftop gates suggested the long-ago residents stepped out into the air and floated down to the streets the way the bears had floated down to the road earlier. The idea would have painted a lovely image in Kara's mind had it not been for the rubble on the street corners and the scorch marks and deep gouges on every building.

"Where are we going?" Tiran asked after they had passed several blocks.

"There." Ingaru thrust her snout toward a smaller version of the outer horn wall. "The citadel. That's where we'll find the forge and the metals you'll need."

"A forge?" Kara slowed. "What for?"

The bears and Tiran slowed with her, until they all came to a stop. Ingaru turned her ears outward and furrowed her brow. "For your weapons, dear–those you broke in your fits when you first entered the bridge. The task ahead will be hard enough. The creatures in the forest to our north are unlike any you'll find in Tanelethar. Many fly, thanks to the Tagamoor vapors leaking into their domain. Some can pass through barriers like ghosts. And their corrupted bodies emulate death. All of which makes them hard to kill. Don't rush in to such a fight with broken blades."

Ioanu matched her mehma's confused expression. "Surely, you can use a forge and a hammer, Queensblood. You have the human blessing of dexterous hands, do you not?"

"I have hands." Kara cast a glance at Tiran and caught him fighting a grin. "But as *Wartroot* will gladly tell you, they are not as dexterous as I'd wish."

The city blocks of the citadel inside the second horn ring were smaller and shaped like slices of Glimwick's pies, all pointing toward a round edifice, perhaps the ruin of the Suvoroth seat of government. Dark gray clouds poured forth from that central building's collapsed dome.

"The Tagamoor was not so lost in its own vapors in the ancient days," Ingaru said, stopping beside an unadorned structure with no windows a half-block from the geyser. "It is true, they seep up all over the moor, but the Suvoroth nobles controlled the primary source–a well within the high family's palace. They loosed enough to give them flight without hiding the city in a shroud." She inclined her head toward the windowless building where they'd stopped. "The forge is in here, but the entrance is on the roof. We'll carry you up."

After so many months working–or fighting–with the huge anvils at Ras Telesar, Kara found the Suvoroth smithy unexpectedly ordinary. She appreciated the human-size shop and wondered if the intimidation of the academy's Aropha forges might be part of her problem.

Tiran seemed more impressed. The bears had brought them to the top floor of the building and led them down through an open stairwell. Once they'd descended into the forge, on the top floor, he'd run straight to a pile of discarded armor pieces. "Look at this!"

"That's scrap," Kara said.

"Yes, but some of the best scrap I've ever seen." Tiran picked up the lower quarter of a breastplate and carried it to an open window where he turned its edge to the light. "The grain of this steel is so fine, I can barely see it. And then there's this." He raised the piece as high as he could reach and let it go. Instead of falling like a rock, it drifted down to the windowsill slower than a feather. "I have so many ideas."

Ingaru used her head to steer him back to the forge. "You've no time to play, Wartroot. I forced you both to rest, but Queensblood was right to hurry us. The longer we wait, the more her brother may suffer."

"I'm well aware, but you may be forgetting, to use a forge, we humans need more than our dexterous hands. We need fuel."

"Do you mean coal?" Ioanu hooked a claw into the floral pattern of an iron grate in one wall. She swung it open, and a black chunk tumbled out. "Like this?"

"Yes. Yes, I supposed that'll do."

Kara took a set of tongs and stirred the contents of the quenching trough. Beneath a layer of glittering green scum, the oil looked clear. "This quenching oil is still good–or good enough."

Scrap in the corner. Coal in the locker. Oil in the trough. If not for the film on the tools and counters and the scum on the oil left by the moor vapors, Kara might expect the owners had simply left for the evening. It had been the same with the dishes and such at the home where they'd slept–nothing missing, except for the people. She gazed out the window at the geyser billowing forth from the broken dome. "What happened here?"

"Dragons," Ingaru said.

Tiran had set to work with a shovel, filling the forge. "The dragons destroyed Tagamar? But the old man we met in Grenton told us the Suvoroth were the first to swear allegiance."

"True. But as the dragons themselves know, creatures with easily shifted allegiance put no value on loyalty."

"You mean House Suvor turned against them?"

Ingaru nodded. "Just as the dragons had turned against their Maker. And, as might be expected, nothing angers one traitor more than a betrayal by another. When Dacon Suvor tried to sever his sorcery from dragon control, they destroyed his kingdom."

Tiran called Kara to the forge. "The fire's ready. It's time." But when she tried to hand him the broken whirlknives, he pushed them away. "You must repair your blades. Not me."

A hollow opened in her gut. "I can't, Tiran. You know I can't."

"What I know is the forge frightens you–not in the way the wanderer's infection terrified you last night, but still"–he glanced down at her weapons–"this is a fear you must face."

Before she could argue, Ioanu stepped in to support him. "Listen to Wartroot, Queensblood. I can smell the fear on you. How can you defeat the terrors of Sil Shadath if you cannot first defeat this one?"

Kara looked to Tiran for aid, pleading with her eyes for him to change his mind. "Even if I could do this, your skill is far better. Shouldn't the better smith work the forge when time is short?"

"Like I said, you broke the knives. You fix them. I have work of my own that needs doing." He set off toward the pile of scrap. "If the dark creatures of Sil Shadath are as dangerous as Ingaru claims, we'll need every advantage, and I've thought of a way to gain one."

45

KARA TIGHTENED AND LOOSENED HER GRIP ON THE hammer, preparing the muscles of her hand as Baldomar had taught her, while she watched her bar of Suvoroth steel gather heat. The local ore gave the alloy a light indigo hue, instead of yellow, as it neared the working stage. "Is mine ready?" she asked Tiran.

"Sorry." He lifted a glowing piece of scrap from the fire. "Busy. Can't afford to watch your metal while I'm watching mine."

It seemed a poor excuse. Why wouldn't he help her the way he'd helped at Ras Telesar?

Still, Kara caught him stealing a glance at her bar, and she gauged by his expression that it was, indeed, time to pull it from the fire–if not past time. With her tongs, she laid it on the anvil and made her first strike.

The Suvoroth steel gave, but not in the direction she'd intended. She let out a sigh. "Tiran, I–"

"No questions, please." He pounded his metal on another anvil a few paces away, keeping his back to her. "I need to focus."

She gritted her teeth and kept trying. Again, the metal moved opposite the flow she'd intended. Making this blade might be a battle she couldn't win.

A battle. Fighting the steel.

What had Silvana told her? *Realize neither you nor the metal is the master. The real master is the one who made you both.*

"Right." Kara closed her eyes and prayed. "*Aler lavech aduth hal sabetoth rabeh, dar driumi decret ke'Rumosh.*"

Whatever my plans, it is your plans that prevail.

"*Rumosh,* Exalted One, I can no more fashion these blades on my own than I can rescue Keir without your aid. Help me. You placed me here in this moment for your purpose, so I give you control. You are the Blacksmith, the master of this steel and the master of us all. Guide my arms to shape these weapons so that we may both be tools for your service."

Kara opened her eyes, expecting to see cold steel needing a return to the fire. Yet, the bar blazed indigo-white, waiting for her strike. She let the hammer fall. The steel moved–not in exactly the way she'd intended, but on a path she could envision. She followed this path and struck again.

With each strike and bend, the blade took shape, a different shape than she'd seen in her mind when she began–a better shape. At times, Kara's will intruded, and her muscles tensed. She finally understood what Baldomar meant in the many times he'd told her to stop overthinking. To combat this, she asked Ingaru to occupy her mind with the full story of House Suvor's fall. The she-bear's rumbling tale blended with the rhythm of her hammer.

House Suvor reigned over the Tagamoor from the early days of man. House Leander, who walked with the white lions of the far north, would become the first kingdom to capitulate under the dragon scourge, but House Suvor turned traitor before the scourge began.

Able to leap great distances within their domain thanks to the moor minerals in their blood and bones, Suvoroth warriors repelled every invader until no kingdom dared. Nearing the end of the first age, in the days following Heleyor's betrayal of our Maker, the Suvor lords fell into brooding discontent. They wanted the lands outside the moor. But, in those days, the canyon remained whole, and kept the mist and the source of their advantage from drifting outside its walls.

Zalcon Suvor, their king, grew jealous of House Leander and House Arkelon's influence–the expanse of their lands, spreading south from the Frost Islands and King's Cradle. Nothing, neither the reason of Zalcon's queen, Kezia, herself an Arkelon queensblood, nor the soothing songs of his youngest son could cool his burning envy. His elder son, Prince Dacon, and the other lords were much the same.

Heleyor, the cunning Great Red Dragon, had placed spies in every kingdom. Word of House Suvor's discontent reached him, and he sent emissaries into the Tagamoor under the cover of night–winged corruptions with the aspect of both man and dragon, the first of the granogs.

These creatures lured Zalcon into his throne room, near the well of vapors, and presented him with a chest full of black sorcerer's gems. Any who wore just one could carry the mists of the Tagamoor far beyond its cliff walls, wearing the vapors like a shroud. The granogs offered as many gems as Zalcon desired. But it was not a true gift. To claim it, House Suvor had to bow to Heleyor and reject the Maker.

Queen Kezia entered the throne room as Zalcon's knee began to fall. With sword in hand, aided by the thick vapors near the well, she fought the granogs until they fled. Some say that this humiliation–outflown by a wingless human in the infancy of their kind–is the reason all granogs hate to fly. As they fled, a single black gem fell unseen from their chest and lodged itself between the throne-room tiles.

Kezia had stopped her husband from bowing, but the first dark creature infection had been cast, and soon it spread to Prince Dacon through his father's tales. One evening, alone in the throne room, Dacon found the black gem. In secret, he journeyed beyond the Tagamoor canyon. The granogs had spoken true–as far as he could tell. For a shroud of vapors followed him, enabling him to leap with unnatural strength deep into Sil Belomar, what is now Gloamwood. He rushed home to tell the king.

A year of intrigues followed, enough to fill a book, but by the end, Queen Kezia and her youngest son lay dead, and Zalcon, with his new queen and Dacon beside him, bowed before a crude granog-made effigy of Heleyor. The first betrayal was complete.

Wearing a sorcerer's amulet and a cloak of Tagamoor vapors, Zalcon led an army west toward the Tarlan Plains. Dacon led the rest of their warriors north into Sil Shadath. And both took whatever lands they wished. For a time.

Heleyor had lied. The dragons, even their leader, are not all powerful. They corrupt and manipulate the Maker's creation, but they are still bound by his sovereignty. The black jewels could only carry the Tagamoor mists so far. Though the Suvoroth lords studded their armor with more and more gems, they could not carry their power beyond the Green Mountains at the western edge of the plains or beyond the northern extent of Sil Shadath.

Zalcon believed this was a dragon limit on House Suvor's influence, and submitted. But Dacon railed against it. When his father died, he sought to throw off the dragon yoke by his own might and cunning. He searched every dark street and dingy port in Talania until he found a magician-thief who'd stolen a key from the Aropha temple at Ras Heval, one that opened the lost bread gate of Ras Pyras. The fool claimed that by sneaking into Heleyor's stronghold and reciting a few incantations, they could wrest the sorcery of the jewels from the dragons and grant it to House Suvor forever.

They tried. Heleyor caught them at the center of his den. Dacon died instantly. The thief escaped, or perhaps the dragons let him flee because their anger burned hotter against the traitor Suvoroth. From all sides, the dragon lords and their orc armies drove the Suvoroth warriors back into the Tagamoor. There, in their homeland, the Suvoroth fought their hardest and most futile battle.

It was not the dragons, but House Suvor that destroyed the dome above the well and unleashed the vapors that still pour forth today. They filled the moor to the tops of the cliffs and fought the dragons in the sky. But the dragons were ready. Their goblins had dug a great tunnel deep into the northwestern rim beneath the Phantom's waterfall. On Heleyor's command, they collapsed the cliff. Vapors flowed like water into the hills and, from there, north into Sil Shadath and east into the eastern range, known ever since to common folk as the Muddled Mountains.

Brought down to their own streets, the Suvoroth fell victim to the raging orcs. The creatures dragged every man, woman, and child from their homes and shops and left none alive. Such was the rise and fall of the Suvoroth and Talania's first traitor-king.

As Ingaru finished her the story, Kara completed her last pass at the grinding wheel. She'd welded the old steel with the new so that the blue-white lightraider steel merged with the Suvoroth steel in a rolling eddy of sea green–blue paired with green, like the starlots at their hinges. The deeper bend of the repaired blades no longer matched the crescent bend of their partners on each whirlknife, but the completed weapons closed and opened well and fit into their sheaths. Perfect or not, the sharpness of the double edges would kill when needed.

Kara wiped her new blades with oil. "I did it."

"Don't sound so surprised," Tiran said, then smirked. "It took you long enough."

In the time Kara had repaired her two knives, he'd forged ten armor pieces, making her stop her work more than once to take her measurements.

He gave her a wide belt of curving green steel plates joined with leather straps. "Put this on under your manykit. Make sure it's tight. And then put those on." He pointed to a set of greaves and matching bracers lying on his anvil.

Tiran had already donned his own set. They were not what Kara would call fashionable–hammered metal, shaped to fit. No decorations. She fastened the belt around her waist. "You know as well as I that lightraiders have no need of traditional armor. What's it all for?"

"This," he said, and leapt out the window.

46

KARA RUSHED TO THE WINDOW WITH IOANU AND watched Tiran fall. He didn't fall fast, but he lacked a certain grace. His body rolled, and his feet slipped out in front of him, rising above his waist despite a flailing effort to stay upright. He landed on a shoulder with a light, "Oof."

"Well done!" she called, implying the opposite with her tone.

Tiran pushed himself up to a hip and thrust his chin at her. "Yeah, yeah. Not a success by any means, but you won't do any better on your first try."

Kara accepted the challenge and jumped.

Instantly she regretted it. She felt her feet kicking out as Tiran's had. Were the greaves on her shins too thick? She needed something more than the bracers on her arms to counter the motion. *Her new blades.* Kara whipped the knives from their sheaths, flicked them open, and pressed them against the vapors at her back.

It worked. Her feet rotated beneath her in time to make an unsteady but vertical landing.

Tiran frowned. "Beginner's luck."

"You wish. I compensated for your error, so perhaps it was an easier test for me. The greaves on our legs are thicker with

Suvoroth alloy than the bracers on our arms. They react more with the vapors."

He opened his mouth as if to argue but closed it again and nodded. "You're right. I'll have to make adjustments."

"We can't delay any longer. Keir needs us."

"If we can't fight the creatures of Sil Shadath, we can't help him."

Ioanu landed between them and with her mouth, laid a pair of daggers in black leather sheaths at Tiran's feet. "Try these, Wartroot."

He drew one of the weapons–nothing ornate, a simple curved blade with a guarded hilt, but the whole thing was made of the same Suvoroth alloy.

"I found them among the arms on the smithy wall," the bear said. "I expect you may use them to balance your lanky human form the way Queensblood used hers."

Tiran strapped the sheaths to his legs, then drew both blades and jumped straight into the air. He teetered in the descent, arms swinging back and forth, but managed to land on his feet. The moment he touched down, he locked eyes with Kara and grinned. "Race you."

Never had Kara beat Tiran in a footrace. And even now, though she saw him struggling with the balance of bounding through Tagamar, she lost ground. The moor vapors flowing skyward from the dome loomed ahead. Tiran veered in his long, flying strides to go around the structure, and Kara saw her chance. She jumped straight into the geyser and shot high above the streets.

Ingaru roared behind her. "Queensblood, no!"

What a feeling. The power of flight, as sure as the wings of Teegan's falcon. Kara emerged from the geyser still rising, leaning into the vapors with her whirlknives outstretched, cloak flapping behind her.

Below, Tiran rejoined the street, heading for the far city limit. With the challenge of his changing course and the extra speed she'd leveraged from the geyser, she passed him. "Ha! Tiran!"

He looked up, jaw dropping. Distracted, he careened off a statue at the center of the lane. The fall looked bad, but Kara could not keep her eyes on him while maintaining control. How was she to stop?

There was no stopping, beyond what the strange nature of the Tagamoor alloys and vapors allowed. And when the black street finally came at her, it came fast. Kara fought to get her boots under her again, punching the air with her knives. She touched down in a clumsy run that soon became a somersault, and she rolled to a stop against the broad paw of a bear.

Ingaru stood over her. "*That*, young Queensblood, was foolish."

Ioanu walked up a moment later with Tiran leaning on her for support. "Did she live?"

"She did. Thanks to the Maker. And I hope she's learned her lesson."

Tiran let go of the bear and rubbed the back of his neck. "I dare say, we both have. Leaping through this mist with my inventions is nothing like running or swimming. And though the vapors may soften a fall, they do little to slow us down." He gave Ioanu a sheepish grin. "You make it look so effortless."

"We were born here, after generations before us. The moor is part of our bones, blood, and fur." Ioanu touched one of his bracers with a claw. "This metal skin is no substitute."

"It may soften your falls here," Ingaru added, "in the heavy air of this canyon moor. But in Sil Shadath, the vapors are much lower. They'll give you speed and distance, enough to fight your enemies, but if you jump above treetop level, you risk great harm. The fall will come fast, and the gray cushion hovering over the ground will not be sufficient to break it."

Kara collected her knives, having dropped them in her tumble, grateful she'd broken neither of her new blades nor any bones. "I'm sorry. The power of it carried me away."

The older bear nodded her great head. "Now you see the start of the first traitor-king's failure. It is easy to look back on him with derision, but humans still carry his nature. What drove you to leap into the vapor well?"

"I . . ." She sighed and cast a sidelong glance at Tiran. "I was afraid I might lose the race."

"Mmm," growled the bear. "Fear and power. A terrible combination. House Suvor reveled in its power yet suffered from the fear of being *lesser* than the Leander-Arkelon alliance. This made the Great Red Dragon's temptation all the harder to resist. Your flight into the geyser put your body at risk, but it put your heart in even greater danger."

Tiran reached for the buckle of a bracer. "Should we leave these behind, then?"

"No, Wartroot. You have done well in their crafting. They will still broaden your leaps in Sil Shadath. The elements of this region are the Maker's gift. Like all his gifts, like the promise of Elamhavar and your Keledan armor, take care to use them for his service and not your own glory."

Bruised but not injured, the cadets and their Havarra escort left the citadel and strode past the city's outer horn wall, onward toward the far side of the canyon. When they felt ready, Kara and Tiran tried maneuvering in the vapors again, practicing the use of their weapons for balance and strikes. Kara also tested the flight of her whirlknives with their new blades. They spun far and high, and returned to her as they should.

As the cadets grew in their confidence, Ingaru gave them leave to move faster, and they bounded alongside the bears. Moving so, the party passed the final leg to the canyon's collapsed northern wall at a good pace.

"Incredible," Kara said as the breach came within sight. The bridge above them had survived, with its northern supports set into the high terrain farther east. But the low road led straight through the age-old gap next to the fallen river. "I thought there'd be more boulders and such left over from the destruction of the cliff. But I suppose time grinds such clutter to dust."

"Time and dragons," Ingaru said. "Valshadox, dragon lord of this canton, took a wound from a Suvoroth spear in the battle and vowed such would never happen again. He fashioned an army of ore creatures from the Tagamoor rubble, capable of the same flight as the vanquished house, and set them to guard his stronghold. A thousand years later, they still haunt Sil Shadath–the worst of its many terrors."

A memory flashed in Kara's mind–one not her own. A black skull under a ragged hood. Gargoyle fangs. Green flames in empty eye sockets. "Wraiths," she said. "Real wraiths, not the fancies of Grenton townsfolk." She looked to Ingaru. "Keir has seen them, black orc skeletons floating over the underbrush in tattered cloaks."

The bear let out a sour grunt. "Correct. Their orc flesh has long since rotted away. To hide the shame of it, they shroud themselves in rags. But the dragon's fire still burns in their bones–in their eyes and rib cages–and their Suvoroth halberds do not rust. Keep clear of them if you can."

When they reached the northern edge of the gap, the party halted. Ingaru plodded a few paces ahead and turned to face them. "This is as far as my daughter and I may travel. You are as rested and ready as you may be. Go now and fight, and rescue your brother, and feel the blessing of our clan fighting at your side."

Kara had to admit, she'd rather have the bears fighting at her side than their blessings. She rubbed Ioanu's back between her shoulder blades. "I will miss you, friend."

Ioanu's thick muscles tensed under hand. "No, Queensblood, you will not. For I am going with you."

The fur on Ingaru's back rose into a spiked ridge. "Daughter! What did you say?"

"I'm going with them, Mother. I will defend this queensblood as our clan defended them in the early days of the scourge."

"You will do no such thing. If you are taken, or if you are seen with these two and they are taken, then our long safety in the moor is over." The growl behind Ingaru's words reverberated through Kara's body. She felt the threat of it in her chest. "Valshadox is older than this gap, and he remembers much. If he senses Havarra near, he will lash out. We'll be driven from our home. Many may die."

"We will not let it happen, Mother." Ioanu looked to Kara, bear eyes pleading for her support. "We will give our lives before we give up the clans."

"Valshadox will not give you the choice. The queensblood knows how well he deals pain while sparing life, don't you, dear."

What was Kara to say? Ioanu's mehma spoke true. She swallowed. "Yes, but you see–"

"What of our heritage?" Ioanu asked, interrupting to push her argument. "Am I to set all honor and courage aside to remain in hiding?"

"Your head is too filled with old tales, Daughter."

"If it is, then they are your tales, Mother."

"My error, and one I will now correct. Those were stories from another age. They all have endings. They are all complete."

Ioanu lowered her head and shoulders, softening her voice. "Then let me build a new story. Queensblood"–she glanced at Kara–"*Kara* needs me. I know where to find her brother."

"She can find him on her own. The dragon has seen to it with the very torture I speak of. He has sent this torment to her mind."

Kara coughed, striving to get a word in. "Not anymore, Ingaru."

Both bears shifted their gazes to look at her. "What do you mean?" Ingaru asked.

"You're right. The dragon caused Keir suffering to draw me here." Kara shut her eyes, searching for something she did not wish to find, yet despairing when she didn't find it. "But when you first spoke of that connection, I realized I haven't felt it for some time–not since my fit when you approached me." She met Ingaru's gaze. "The connection brought us this far, but now it's gone. Without Ioanu to track his scent, I'll never find Keir."

Tiran gently turned her to face him, concern creasing his brow. "Are you certain?"

She nodded. "Yes. Quite certain. I can't feel him. Something has changed. And I'm terrified at what it may be."

PART FOUR

THE COURAGE OF BEARS

"Be strong and courageous; don't be terrified or afraid of them. For the Lord your God is the one who will go with you; he will not leave you or abandon you."

Deuteronomy 31:6

THE PRISONER
TANELETHAR

I SLEPT. I DON'T KNOW HOW LONG. A DEEP SLEEP. A blessed sleep of pure black.

How is that possible?

The dragon has gone, leaving me alone in his dungeon with no orcs to watch me and no goblins or barkhides to torment me. Strange, but strangest of all are the torches.

Their flames are dim, more orange than red. They, like the dark creatures, are connected to the dragon's thoughts when he chooses. Even when he's gone, they've never lost their strength or color. Until now. Some distraction draws the dragon's will away from his throne room.

All is quiet. There's no sound–not even the scratching of rats.

My arm moves, instinct rather than choice. My body seeks relief from the pain. And when my wrist turns, I hear a quiet *crick*. Looking up is too hard. Instead, I turn my wrist the other way. Another *crick*. Louder. A lump of burnt iron falls to the floor.

"Huh."

The sound I make in my surprise is hardly audible. A rasp. I try licking my lips and swallowing, but a dry tongue does parched flesh no good, and the swallow is a dagger to my throat.

Is there any other conclusion besides the obvious? The

shackle that holds my right arm has cracked. All the fire this rack has suffered before my time and since has made it frail.

I consider going further, trying to break it. What have I to lose?

Nothing. Everything.

Shan calls out from what remains of my memory. *There is no escape, Hosal. Not from death. Not from here. Best come to grips with that now.*

All right.

Gathering all the strength I can, I jerk my arms. The right shackle breaks. The left does not, and I hang awkwardly with one blistered foot flat on the floor. The leg, which has not been asked to support me for days, is not up to the challenge. About the time I resolve to jerk my left arm again, the leg gives. I drop. With a sharp *snap*, my shoulder takes the weight, and now I am turning, spinning, aching as I hang from one chain.

So . . . that went well.

When the dragon returns, will he laugh? Will he fry me to cinders? Most likely both.

I resolve to look up, despite the overpowering stiffness of my neck, and take stock of my chance for escape. I groan with the effort, and about the time my eyes first behold the shackle, the chain breaks. The floor rushes up and smacks me in the face.

The sting wears off before the full understanding sinks in.

I push my next thought through my dry throat and around my swollen tongue because I need to hear it out loud. “I’m free.”

The stubborn shackle that failed to break clanks on the stones, chain trailing behind as I drag myself down the dim path of yellow-orange torches. The sound hurts my ears, makes me cringe. But what can I do? I do not have the strength for stealth.

Stairs. Beautiful gray-black steps. Smooth. Cool.

Steep.

One at a time, I take them. Each one lifts me farther from the dragon’s dungeon, and each brings more vigor, not less. After a dozen steps, I find the strength to stand. After three dozen, I no longer need the rail. I'm walking on my own. Up. Up. Legs screaming, until I see an outline of daylight.

Forgetting my exhaustion and all thoughts of danger, I throw open the door. Instantly, I'm blind. Light and ringing dominate my senses. I stagger forward and tumble down steps into mud.

But sight returns. And sound. Voices. Many shouting voices. The *clink* and *clang* of steel on steel. Men and monsters flow around me. A battle?

A revolt.

Prisoners fight the barkhides and orcs. They fight each other. They stab and slash at harrying goblins. I see a man close to the fence take his chance and flee. The wraith appears out of the fog and cuts him down with a single stroke.

"Hosal!" Hands lift me from the mud until my feet take the weight. "You're alive!"

Shan's face resolves before me. His grip is strong. His gaze is healthy.

"How?"

"A prisoner being dragged away took hold of an orc guard's halberd and fought. His spirit was as a spark to tinder. Now the whole camp is ablaze." He supports me with an arm and pushes a bloodied barkhide axe into my hand. "Come with me. I know a way out."

"The wraith."

"I see him, Hosal. He's nowhere near my secret exit. And in the daylight, we can survive the forest."

"I thought you'd grown to love the dragon. You said–"

"I said"–Shan shuts his eyes as if blocking out a memory–"and did only what was required to live another day. Nothing more. Now, move your feet, prisoner. Let's go."

Shan leads me away from the wraith and through the battle, knocking prisoners and barkhides out of the way with a black orc scimitar that dwarfs his hand. An iron orc challenges us, joints and eyes flaring with fire. I swing with all I have and cut into its arm.

Shan jabs the scimitar deep into its shoulder. The creature howls and recoils and fixes its rage on an easier target.

That man is doomed. But we turn our eyes from his fate and carry on.

The battle lightens near the fence, mostly prisoners fighting prisoners with useless blunt weapons. Is this a fight between those who've killed fellow prisoners and those who might have been victims? Or in their terrified delirium, do they all think this is some new training?

We fight our way through to the fence. I see no hole, but when we reach it, Shan stabs his scimitar into the earth long enough to rip two planks down. They come free without trouble. He prepared this spot beforehand. A heartbeat later, we're through, and Shan makes no effort to replace the wood or cover the gap. "Can you run?"

"I think so."

"Know so, my friend. Believe it. For now is the time."

With that, he lets go of me and races for the trees.

I run too, but I'm falling behind. His legs are powerful, his stride long. "Shan!"

Can he hear my rasping cry?

"Hurry, Hosal. Find the strength. You can do it!"

He's in the trees. I've lost him.

No. The moment the light changes in the pines, I find him again–not much more than a disturbance in the fog. It is Shan, not a ghost. I know this because the apparitions move with the fog more than through it.

"Keep going!" he calls. "I counted the paces and set the courses as you showed me. Follow my steps, and you'll make it. We'll make it together!"

He reaches the outer fence, and more planks must fall. These, he did not prepare, and tearing them down slows him. I close the distance, but soon we're through, and I'm falling behind again. My legs are giving way. I wore them out on the steps from the dragon's throne room.

"What if I lose you?"

"Find the shrine and head east–always east, until you come to a low stone wall. Follow the wall south to the ruins of a twisted tower. I saw it on my last run. You can't miss it."

The shrine. East to the wall. South to the tower.

"Keep running! I'll meet you there!"

Within moments, Shan is far out of reach, at the ragged edge of my vision.

I remember no shrine in our previous excursion. But if I ask now, he'll never hear me. My lungs haven't the strength to shout. My voice is worthless.

The disturbance in the fog turns sharply, toward a creature looming out of the gray.

Not a creature. A statue–a dragon half the full size, backed by a triangle arch and surrounded by torches. It is the image of Lord Valshadox himself. I know this by the fear welling up inside. A shrine to the master of this forest? I fixate on the torches as I draw closer. Dim and yellow orange. Weak flame. I suppose that's why I didn't see them sooner. But even as the thought occurs to me, the torches spark and flare ruby red.

He's coming.

I look to the sky in time to see a black shadow soaring on broad wings. Diving for the trees.

The voice bellows in my mind. *Fools. Ingrates. You will pay.*

I try to warn my friend. "Dragon!"

My cry is too frail and far too late. Fire splits the forest at the place I last saw my friend.

47

TEEGAN
KELEDEV
PELLION'S FLOW

TEEGAN SPOTTED PEDRIG ON HIS RETURN FROM scouting the flow–a blur of shifting silver among the rocks skirting the edge of the ice. She walked in a crouch past Dag and Quinton to Master Jairun. "Here he comes. I'm afraid the news is not good."

The headmaster followed her gaze and grunted. "Pedrig always looks grim."

"He does, but I think I've learned to read him. Let's hope this time I'm wrong."

She wasn't.

"Our dark creature invaders have taken to the open ice south of the den," the wolf said when he reached them. "They are forming ranks. Goblins, golmogs, and iceblades–a hundred or more so far and growing in number. They know we're coming, and they're ready."

Baldomar planted the tip of his two-handed greatsword in the ice. "So much for surprise. Now what?"

Teegan surveyed their group. From the cadet ranks, they'd brought Dag and Paskin plus four younger cadets Master Jairun had selected. From the guardians of the light, Silvana, Quinton, Baldomar, and the headmaster himself. She shook her head. "We're too few."

Quinton snorted. "Not for a pack of goblins."

That earned him a dour look from Silvana. "This is no time for the Vanguard's bravado. These are not cave goblins on sunlit snow. We're facing frost goblins on their favorite terrain with dark approaching fast. Razor sharp north trolls and golmogs too. The danger is great. And if we're defeated, will they not march to Ras Telesar and find it poorly defended?"

Dag frowned and adjusted one of the big satchels hanging from the shoulder posts of his manykit–playing the party mule as always. "What of the watchmen?"

Master Jairun turned his gaze to the south. "I sent ravens. The company at Ravencrest is nearest. If we wait for them, we'll have a little less than the numbers we need."

"If we wait," Quinton said, "the dark creature numbers may double. Or worse." He cast a fleeting glance at the young cadets at the end of their column. "I wouldn't choose this battle for any new recruits to cut their teeth on, not ours and especially not watchmen who've never trained with the Order."

Silvana drew a frustrated breath, as if about to offer argument, but Master Jairun cut her off. "He's right, Silvana. And so are you. We cannot wait. But neither can we face them on the ice with such a small number."

"So, what do you propose?"

"We must flank them. Find a way to get behind the creatures and drive them south into the rocky terrain. This will spread them out, which is a risk but also makes them easier for the watchmen to sweep up. It's the only way to avoid a bloody ending."

Pedrig padded his way down from the rock where he'd been perched, looking north, since his return. "I may have a way. In my scouting, I found an entrance to another ice passage. The flow shifts fast in spring. This one may lead to a dead end, but if it's still good–"

"We could use their own tunnels against them," Quinton said.

"Just so. We might destroy their den, cutting off escape, and then attack from upslope. The mountain is steep"–the wolf traded a glance with Master Jairun–"and the shadow of the ox lies upon their rearguard."

The shadow of the ox. Teegan could not imagine any ox this high on the peaks. But neither Pedrig nor Master Jairun said more about it. The headmaster gave him a single nod. "As good a plan as any. And better than most. Show us this passage."

The party stayed low and moved at a careful pace, keeping watch for the enemy's scouts and preserving their strength. To aid them, Master Belen had given all the raiders one of his recent inventions. He called it an *air bladder* and told them it provided nothing more than air as warm and thick as they might find on the islands known as the Many Blessings in the far south of Keledev, but such air would be vital on the mountainside. They each wore an eberlast bladder between their tunics and manykit vests with intestine piping running up to their noses. Inside the bladder, a lump of diver's folly–a false gold that grew violent when removed from seawater–boiled in a renewer's wound-wash called bluebitter. The smell bordered on torture, but Teegan could not argue with the extra strength the thicker air gave her. Plus, the reaction spread heat under her cloak to stave off the cold.

"This is a risk," Silvana said, cautioning Master Jairun at the entrance to the ice passage. "If we're seen–if a runner escapes a confrontation and warns the others–they might bring the ice flow down on top of us."

Quinton patted a large pitch torch slung at his side. Every party member had brought one at Master Jairun's command. "These might do the same. The fire will crack the ice. We hadn't planned on entering the tunnels so soon. Torches will do us no good until we reach solid rock."

"Then we'll look to a better source of light." Master Jairun closed his eyes and uttered a prayer. A blue orb appeared ahead of him in the passage. He set off with Pedrig at his side. "We must trust the Maker. Whatever happens tonight, the victory is his." He pointed at the light with his staff. "The Rescuer is with us."

The others followed him in, two by two, responding in quiet unison. "Always and forever."

Pedrig left the same glowing tracks as before. Teegan, marching with Dag at the column rear, watched them fall behind her into the dark. On her last visit to these goblin ice tunnels, she'd been drenched in runoff without the benefit of Belen's apparatus to warm her. Yet now, watching Pedrig's tracks disappear into the long dark, she felt a deeper chill. These creatures might be soulless dragon corruptions, but their masters were cunning.

The dragons had a plan to take Keledev, and it likely began with the slaughter of the Lightraider Order.

48

TEEGAN TRUSTED MASTER JAIRUN AND PEDRIG TO find the way. The wolf had been to the den with her, and the headmaster, though a guardian of the Comforters' Sphere, was known to have discernment to match the best of the navigators. They'd find the den, assuming the dark creatures let them get that far. Every cross tunnel heightened her concern. An attack from both sides in the narrow passage would force all the fighting upon the front and rear guards.

"We must reach the den soon," she muttered to Dag, growing impatient, "where we can remove our ice spikes and fight on wider terrain. And we must reach it undiscovered."

It proved a vain hope.

"Look out!" The shout came from the column's front–the headmaster's voice.

Then Silvana's. "They're bolting! Pedrig, clear the way!"

With the big forms of Dag, Quinton, and Baldomar all between her and the fighting–along with Paskin and the four younger cadets–Teegan could make out little. She pressed a cheek against the ice wall and saw Silvana unleash two arrows at the same time.

"They're down," the headmaster said. "Quickly, Pedrig. Make sure there were no others."

Teegan laid a hand on Dag's back as he advanced, to let him know she was with him. "What's happening up there?"

"Three goblins entered from a side tunnel. They're dead. Pedrig is looking for others. We're forming up."

"Hold here." Master Jairun gathered his force where the side tunnel intersected theirs. "There may be more."

The party formed a knot beneath the Rescuer's orb of blue light. Paskin held close to Teegan's shoulder. "Are they coming?"

"I don't know."

"Quiet," Silvana said. "All of you. Listen."

Not an easy command, given the pounding of Teegan's heart. She begged it to be still. A verse from her studies came to her, a reminder for Keledan to open their ears to what the Rescuer might show them. *Nim ewanond oku nelam. Thomesh ewanond yi thimah ka oltum lemoth luminatem. He awakens me each morning–to listen as one being instructed.*

Her heartbeat stilled. She listened to the silence of the tunnels and heard the echoing *drip, drip* of water and the near-imperceptible *crack* and *ping* of the flow in its eternal movement. Then she heard the heavy breath and scraping claws of a wolf racing back to them on the ice.

"Arms!" Pedrig barked from the other tunnel. "Arms! Here they come!"

Through the knot of raiders, Teegan watched him skid to a turning stop beside Quinton. He faced the way he'd come and let out a deep howl. Green flashed around them. The ice flow shook, and chunks of it rained down. Creatures shrieked in the dark.

"Careful, Master Wolf," Silvana said.

"I am always careful. But I will do what I must."

Those were the last words spoken before the goblins struck.

They attacked from two angles, from the side tunnel and from the main passage at the column's front, putting the brunt of the fighting on Baldomar and Master Jairun at one part and Quinton and Pedrig at the other. Silvana stood between them and loosed arrows in both directions, shooting between their shoulders and over the wolf when she could.

"Agh!" Dag shouted, shaking his axes. "We're out of it."

He started to push his way through the four other cadets, but Teegan grabbed his cloak. "Our place is here. The goblins know these tunnels. They must connect somewhere behind us."

Dag relented, and both of them stood at the ready in this strange waiting, listening to the guardians fight the creatures while they stood idle, watching the passage behind.

"Come on," Teegan said under her breath. "Where are you?"

But the passage remained dark and empty–nothing but Pedrig's glowing footprints.

Paskin stuck his head between their elbows, as if peeking out from a bush. "Huh. Perhaps they haven't the numbers to spare."

She glanced down, ready to push him back by the forehead, but paused.

Paskin's eyes had gone wide. "What is that?"

Teegan followed his gaze. Living black threads writhed through the ice ceiling. They were in the walls, too, and the floor.

"Rime runners!" Dag said. "Ice leeches. Frost goblin pets. I read about them in *The Battle of Agam Glas*." He pressed the newer cadets back. "Don't let them latch on to open skin. They burrow under."

Teegan groaned. "Of course they do."

The first wave burst from the roof, boring white holes and wriggling out. The knot formation behind the guardians instantly broke as the cadets ducked and dodged. Teegan caught several leeches with her tines and flicked them away. Paskin sliced one in half with his sword, and the moment the two pieces landed, they launched themselves at his boots. Dag chopped into the ice walls on both sides, but the gouges he made only released more attackers.

One of the cadets called out to warn the fighting guardians. "Headmaster! The worms!"

Without turning from his fight, Master Jairun shouted in the Elder Tongue. The Rescuer's blue orb burst into a broad dome that shone over him and the others. The falling rime runners burned to dust upon it. "We are harried at the front, Cadets. Deal with these parasites as you can!"

The writhing creatures now covered the floor. Dag stomped, grinding some into slop, but others swarmed up his legs. He let out a cry like none Teegan had ever heard from him and swatted them down–a losing effort.

"Too many!" she yelled, fighting them back in the same way. "What do we do?"

Dag continued swatting at his own boots. "At Agam Glas, Lady Olaya used fire."

The torches. But could she spare the time to pull out a flint and steel and strike one? Would lighting fires bring the whole ice flow down?

Before she could try, Teegan saw Paskin draw his dagger and stab into his own side. She feared the leeches had bored into him and driven him mad, until she saw him reach in and pull out a dull gold rock. He'd cut the diver's folly from his air bladder. Exposed, the rock began to burn. Paskin yelped and tossed it down, where it exploded into a shower of debris and purple sparks. The leeches hissed and shriveled around it. And wherever the remaining pieces of the diver's folly dropped, they also exploded, killing more.

Taking her chance, Teegan drew her torch and lit it on a sizzling fragment. The pitch flared to life. She waved the flame at her feet and cooked the vile worms. "Your torches! All of you!"

Dag matched her actions, and the others quickly followed. Soon, they were all waving their torches about. The leeches hissed and shriveled. Teegan found one in her hair, pulled it free and held it to the fire. It shrank to half its original length and shattered with a quiet *pop*.

Ridding the tunnel of the leeches didn't take long after that. And what was more, the guardians finished their work. With a final arrow from Silvana, the last attacking goblin died. In the calm that followed, one of the cadets passed her torch along the walls and ceiling, illuminating a thousand tiny boreholes. "Look at them all."

Quinton snatched her torch away. "They've weakened the ice," he said. "And so have you. Douse yer flames."

Too late.

With a tremendous *crack,* the roof gave. Teegan felt herself yanked backward by her cloak. Dag knocked two others out of the way. Great blocks of ice fell into the passage, frozen dust choking the air.

When the quaking settled and the air cleared, they found a new passage had opened opposite the side tunnel where the first three goblins had appeared. And it was not empty. Light flickered at a bend not far away. Deep voices droned.

Paskin grit his teeth. "What now?"

"Cadets," Master Jairun said, pushing his way to this new front of their battle. "Get behind us."

But Teegan held her place. "Wait, sir. Let me listen. Give me quiet, please."

To her surprise, the guardians obeyed, and from the new tunnel, she heard a voice she'd known her whole life. "These are not enemies."

A troop of watchmen came marching around the bend, with a single torchbearer in the lead. Teegan ran to him, hardly able to believe her eyes. "Tehpa?"

Sireth Yar halted and smiled at his behlna before shifting his gaze to Master Jairun. "The watchmen companies are reporting for duty, Headmaster." Then his smile faded. "What's left of us, anyway."

49

CONNOR
TANELETHAR
BEZIK HILLS

THE MAPS IN FAELIN'S JOURNAL MAY NOT HAVE BEEN the living, Aropha variety Lee favored, but they proved valuable. He'd inked them in great detail. Connor had learned of his patehpa's mapmaking skills when the cadets first entered Tanelethar the year before and found the sanctuary near Trader's Knoll. Faelin's work had guided their party to the shairosite needed to destroy the dragon's portal and then to the portal itself.

Now Connor hoped his patehpa's work might guide them to the Rapha Key. But evening had come, and as the light faded in the rolling terrain known as the Bezik Hills, so did their chances of finding the last location Faelin had marked in his quest.

"Is that it?" Lee pointed a sikari knife at the remnants of an ancient village. Nothing remained but odd-shaped mounds and crumbling rock walls among the drifting wisps. "Is that old Barihav?"

Connor held up the journal to compare the map to the landscape. "Possibly."

"That must be the ruin," Lee said, sheathing his knife. "Or this quest is over. If that isn't old Barihav, then King Dacon's magician-thief and his final resting place are lost for good."

"Yes." Connor turned the map sideways, then back again,

cocking his head. "The more I look at it, the more I think you're right."

Zel used one finger to ease the journal back from the rail, as if Connor might drop it. "I told you we'd find the village, even from this height."

He'd asked her to fly higher to let them see more of the land before they lost the light. Zel had refused, arguing the view from a lower height would serve them better and her repair of *The Starling*'s silk might fail higher up.

"Aren't you glad we didn't have to destroy my good work to find this? Besides"–Zel hefted the leather bag filled with her tehpa's caustic vitriol and alum grit–"we're getting low on fuel for the lamps. I'd say we only have two flights left. Three at best. If we fail to ride a storm home on the last of our vapors, we'll have to scuttle her with fire and walk."

Above them, *The Starling*'s gorgeous blue silk captured the last of the sunset, taking on a deep purple hue. Burning such beauty to keep it out of the dragons' talons seemed a great shame. "We'll be careful. Set her down in that low point between the hills southwest of the village. The higher terrain around it should shield her from prying eyes."

After a landing much improved over the last, Lee and Connor disembarked and left Zel with the ship. "Are you sure you'll be all right guarding *The Starling* alone?" the scribe asked.

Zel lifted a war whip with metal spikes sown into the last third of its length, which she'd found in the Aropha sanctuary. She cracked it within an inch of his boot, tearing up the spongy turf, and laughed when he jumped back. "I'll be fine. Go find the key so we can get out of here."

Ancient Barihav had taken up seven hilltops in the shape of a simple cross, with buildings on the hills and roads in the valleys between. Connor knew this from a copy Faelin had made of an ancient map. But the boys crossed the last high hill before the town to find a different reality. Earth, scrub, and time had all but consumed the town. What was left could barely be called a ruin.

"No markers," Lee said, flicking his various lenses up and down. "No memorials or headstones. How are we to find the thief's grave? For all we know, these mounds were mostly houses and barns. By now, the tombs may be all but flat."

"We'll find it because we must."

"So you say. If only we had more light and less fog." Lee made a futile kick at the gray-green mists drifting past his boots. "Barihav. Bright Home in the Common Tongue. Ha. Far from it. I'm so tired of this fog. In the mountains. In the forests. Clinging to the hills and drowning the vales. How can we hope to find anything?"

Connor could sense his friend's growing despair. He felt it too. The longer they stayed in Tanelethar, especially this place so close to the deep dark of Sil Shadath, the greater the threat became. "We'll find the grave by putting our hope in one far stronger than we. The High One helped us get here and find this village. He won't let his own work go to waste." Connor closed his eyes. "Speak the verse of hope with me."

They both said it together. "*Kowuthana mi ke'Rumosh. Kowuthana po fi logosyod tiqana. Mi ke'Rumosh kowuthana someh ka pazratha mi kenelam kowuthah.*"

I wait for him. I put my hope in his word. I wait for him more than watchmen wait for the morning.

Lee took a deep breath and gave Connor a nod. "All right. Let's get to work."

They started with the journal, which noted Barihav as the birthplace and final resting place of Alavro Kaliphan, the magician-thief who'd stolen the Rapha Key. The town pre-dated the fall of Heleyor and had survived the dragon scourge.

Lee found this fact important. "If the town was built before the fall, it would have had a temple to the Creator—even a small one—near the town center. The temple might have been destroyed during the scourge, but villagers are creatures of habit and tradition. Graves or tombs would still be placed close to the spot the temple once stood." He started toward the intersection of the cross. "I say we start there."

Connor followed after him, grateful to see his friend's determination restored, and in a short time, Lee found the first marker. A mossy stone obelisk jutted out from a hillside near the intersection of the cross. Only two or three fingers' worth of stone showed above the turf, but that was enough for the scribe's sharp vision. He tore the grass and soil away and dropped a blue lens down over his eye.

"Can you see anything?" Connor asked. "Any writing?"

"Yes."

Lee said nothing else for a long time.

"Well, what does it say?"

"Give me a beat or two, please. This script is a poor derivative of the Elder Tongue, perhaps a thousand years old. I might not be able to read it at all."

He could. Connor heard it in his protest. Free of despair, the scribe's quick mind was working at its full potential. But as always, he hated to speak anything out loud that might be wrong.

Finally, after far longer than two beats, he lifted his eyes from the marker. "The name is worn beyond reading, but I can tell you this man was a farmer and a father and grandfather to those who buried him. He's not our thief. Besides, the date is too early–by about two hundred years."

According to the journal, the thief Kaliphan had died five hundred twenty-one years before the Blacksmith revealed himself. Barihav had been founded more than three hundred years before that. Connor looked downhill, trying to gage the distance by time. "If this graveyard grew down the hill over time, we need to move to the base. Do you agree?"

Lee nodded. "Let's start again in the valley between this hill and the next."

"And what are we to do when we find the grave? Dig him up?"

"If we must, but I'm expecting a full burial chamber, with

a door and everything. Kaliphan remained free his whole life and managed to escape the ire of the dragons after invading their stronghold. That would make him quite good at his chosen profession."

"You mean he died rich."

"By the standards of Tanelethar, yes. Very rich."

Their search proved him right. Walking the valley around the hill, Connor and Lee found a misshapen mound, tall and thin but covered in turf and surrounded by thick scrub. The scrub was shallow, and in a short time, they'd cleared it all away. Connor dug into the front of the mound and tore off strips of turf until the shovel clinked against something hard. He cast a glance at Lee. "That doesn't sound like stone."

"I told you our thief was rich." Together they pulled away grass and soil to expose an ornate door of drab gray steel. "Some local alloy, I expect. Resistant to rust." The scribe took the shovel from Connor and pounded on the metal. His effort left not even the slightest scratch. "Strong and incorruptible. There's a good chance whatever's in here withstood the centuries."

"If only we knew how to get in."

The door had no visible lock or bar—only a single large pull ring. Lee tilted his head for Connor to move aside. "Let us see, my friend. Let us see. Remember the answering verse to the hint Master Jairun gave us." He lifted his closed eyes toward Elamhavar and whispered the words. "*She'am po naboliov, kavah po mashteliov, doq po keshar felasiov.*"

Who asks, receives. Who seeks, finds. To the one who knocks, the door will open.

"*Onoriov, Rumosh,*" Lee said, thanking the High One in advance, and then rubbed his hands together and grasped the ring. He put all his weight into a pull.

The door didn't move.

He tried a push.

Nothing.

After staring at the ring for a long moment, Lee frowned and gave it a sharp twist.

The ring and its mount turned, letting off a terrible, grinding *squeak*. But the door still didn't move. Lee let go. "Strange. I could swear I'd unlocked it."

The broken turf at his feet gave way. Metal hinges squealed, and Lee fell through an ancient trap door.

50

"LEE!" CONNOR DROPPED TO HIS CHEST AND SHOVED his crook down into the dark after his friend. He felt Lee grab hold. "I've got you!"

"Don't let go," came the breathless reply. "There are spikes!"

Connor fought his way to his knees, pulling the crook up until the scribe's face came into the gray light.

"Wait," Lee said, still holding tight to the crook. "Stop! There's a chain–placed high as if one might reach it from above by opening the trap door." The crook wiggled in Connor's hands as Lee let go to loop one arm through the chain. "All right. Pull me up."

Once Connor had him high enough, Lee scrambled onto the muddied grass, keeping hold of the chain. He tried to pass it to Connor. "Perhaps you should do the honors."

"And set off the next trap? No, thank you. You started this. You finish it."

"Fair point."

Neither of them did much beyond lying there and breathing for several minutes, until both got up and moved away from the gray door as far as the chain would allow. Lee held it at arm's length, ready to give it a tug.

"One moment," Connor said and took a wide step backward.

"All right. Go ahead."

"I know you jest, my friend. But somehow, I'm not laughing." Lee winced and pulled the chain. They heard a solid *click*.

The door cracked inward.

Connor laughed. "Well, the Rescuer opened the door as you asked, though not as you expected."

"He did more than I expected. He opened two."

Connor lit a lantern and went first, pushing open the door. A path of cobblestones led inward from the threshold. "Watch for loose pavers or low ropes. The thief may yet have a surprise for us."

They found none. Kaliphan, or whomever had commissioned the tomb, had depended on only the one pitfall to secure his rest.

Or perhaps the pitfall was designed to secure something else. Lee whistled as Connor's light glinted off gold coins and bars. Jewelry of all kinds sparkled from disintegrating chests. There were other riches—or what had once been riches. Rusted weapons and armor. Fine clothes, eaten to nothing more than dust and faded threads. But among the piles, whether fine or decomposing, one thing was missing.

Connor glanced at his friend. "Where's the sarcophagus?"

They searched the full chamber and found no sign of a body or any vessel large enough to hold one. Nor did they find any urn filled with ashes.

After a while, Lee sat on a curved jade bench that looked like it might have been taken from a queen's bedroom. "This isn't a tomb at all."

"No," Connor said, leaning on his crook. "It was Kaliphan's treasure hold. He's buried someplace else."

When he'd thought about it long enough, Connor realized that to imagine this was the last step in Faelin's search for the Rapha Key had been foolish. His patehpa had searched for a solid year. He'd made much progress, but why should the cadets think he'd all but finished the quest for them?

"All Kaliphan's stolen gains are here," Lee said after a time. "The key might be here too."

"That key opens a hidden gate into Ras Pyras, the stronghold of the Great Red Dragon himself. Kaliphan would have kept it close his whole life. If the dragons ever came looking, the only thing worse than getting caught with the key would be getting caught without it."

"He might have sold it to rid himself of the danger."

"My patehpa thought of that, according to his journal notes. If Kaliphan sold the key, there'd have been other evidence for it in history–another attempt to breach the stronghold, or some prince or magistrate bragging of his purchase." He bobbled his head. "And to sell the key was to admit possession. After his scare with King Dacon, he'd have kept it. We should search the treasure anyway, just in case Kaliphan was not as clever as my patehpa thought."

"Show me the drawing of the key again," Lee said.

Connor turned to the page where Faelin had drawn what he expected the key to look like, based upon a sculpture he'd found of a Rapha wearing a similar device. "We're looking for a stone disc, about the size of my palm, hanging from a chain made from one of the Aropha's inscrutable alloys. There may be a figure carved upon it–the bread symbol, I'd guess, since the key was meant for the bread gate at one of the two greatest Aropha temples in Talania."

"A disc doesn't seem a likely key–with no mechanism to work the lock."

Connor frowned at him. "That's because it doesn't open any lock we humans understand. The Rapha walked the length and breadth of the Talania when serving the Maker's creations. The journal says the disc opens a portal of sorts–a lost portal accessed from one or more places that might be leagues away from Ras Pyras itself."

"The lost gate." A smirk spread across Lee's face. "The GRD has lost a door in his own stronghold." He'd told Connor early in their training that he preferred to use those letters rather than say *Great Red Dragon* out loud. "With all his false bragging of omnipotence and omnipresence, this must be quite an embarrassment."

They both chuckled and returned to their work, and Lee sighed as he set his lantern down to dip hands into a pile of gold. He raised them up and let coins sift through his fingers, filling the chamber with the music of their clinking. "Think of all the good this could do. Not to mention the price of the gems."

"Stolen goods," Connor replied. "But then again, they're goods stolen from families whose lines perished a thousand years ago." He frowned at a stack of silver bars. "We'll lock the place up when we leave. Cover it as best we can. Then we can seek the wisdom and prayer of the guardians. For now, don't take a single peta."

"Right." The scribe dropped the rest of his gold onto the pile all at once, causing a shift. Coins and bars slid down, and the lantern light fell on parchment. It yellowed before their eyes. Lee shot Connor a wary glance. "The gold protected it all these years, but it won't last now." He stretched out his fingers to within an inch of the scroll. "Do I dare?"

"You must. We need all the clues we can get."

With a ginger hand, Lee drew the scroll from the pile and unfurled it.

Connor could see the paper cracking from across the chamber. "Read it quickly."

"There is no *quickly* with script like this."

If Lee had translated the worn carvings of the gravestone up the hill, he could read a scroll from the same period. Connor had faith in him, and his faith proved well-founded.

Much sooner than before, the scribe spoke up. "It's a letter from our thief. Written to anyone who should overcome his trap and enter his treasure room. Listen to this."

My eyes grow dim, and my days short. I find that after a life collecting others' treasures, my pains have bought me nothing but a rich tomb. Piling it here, I feel this gold weighing heavy upon my inevitable death. Surely none of this may pass beyond the grave's black barrier.

My heart returns, then, to the one treasure that haunts my mind at my first waking until my eyes close each day. My blessing. My curse. Though it brings me danger to go near to those places connected to the disc, I've found I cannot resist. I must know more about these creatures who walked with us for so long, then left when the dragons came. Who were they?

Dynapha, Lisropha, and Rapha. Worshipers, warriors, and servants. All dedicated to one Maker, one King. And was the world not better in their time than it is today?

The Lisropha fought for this King and carried his messages to the far ends of Talania and to the uncharted lands on this sphere of Dastan. The Dynapha sang his praises day and night. And then there were the Rapha who served him and served us. They cared for us, though we did not deserve it even then, out of love that flowed both upward and outward. What treasures such love must have gained them–treasures gathered into storehouses on the other side of the black door.

Dearest thief, or whomever you are, take this gold and do with it what you will. I no longer need it. I no longer want it. After all these years of selfishness, this one treasure opened my ears to the Maker's call. I return to that fading faith now, no matter what it may cost. And in the time he grants me, I'll study in the presence of his servants, that I might learn to serve him too.

The scroll turned gray, and a breath of wind from the open door carried it from Lee's hands as dust. He stared after it, then shifted his gaze to Connor. "Our thief is not here. That much is certain. Nor is the key. So now where will we continue our quest?"

Connor had opened the journal to flip through its pages and stopped on one near the end. "I think I know."

He and Lee began the walk back to the airship, but before they left the bounds of old Barihav, they heard a scream.

Lee met Connor's eye. "Zel."

Connor tucked away the journal, and the two raced over the hilltops to see a swarm of goblins closing in–cave goblins by the gray hue of their fungal flesh. "Must've followed *The Starling* from the Fading Mountains," Connor said, panting as they ran.

Lee dropped to a knee and drew his bow, falling behind, and

a beat later, an arrow sailed past Connor's ear. The goblin closest to *The Starling* crumpled. Then the next closest.

Another made it to the wicker rail, but Zel shot it in the face with her crossbow. With her right hand, she snapped her war whip and wrapped a goblin's neck. She jerked her arm, and the creature's head came free.

Her efforts, combined with Lee's, gave Connor time to join the battle. He stabbed one with the spike of his crook and slashed another in half with Revornosh, then planted both weapons in the soil and prayed. "*Ker sporo po koth alerol, Dastan po sibothol, yi ke'Rumosh aparah.*"

The world and everything in it are his.

Three goblins that had turned from *The Starling* to attack him crumbled into black dust. Brown and gray spotted mushrooms sprang up where they fell.

With the goblins pressed back, Zel vaulted out of her ship and charged. Lee ran down the hill from his archer's perch with his sikari knives flashing. Soon, the goblins lay dead. All but one.

A gurgle and cough drew Connor to the one creature that still lived–if their existence could be called living. He planted the spike of his crook in the goblin's one remaining arm to make sure it did not try to kill him before it passed. "How did you find us?" he asked, lowering himself to a knee. "Did you spot us from the mountains?"

The creature gave him a nod. "Waited . . . we did. Watched and waited. He said you'd . . . fly. Fly . . . you would."

"Who said?"

"Val . . . Valshadox."

Lee stood over them. "The dragon knows we're here."

The creature let out a gurgle–probably a laugh, but Connor couldn't be sure. "The dragon knows all. Knows all . . . he does. Knows about you. Knows . . . about your friends. The other lightraiders."

Connor glanced up at Lee. "Tiran and Kara. If the dragon knows they're here . . ."

"Isn't that the point, though? Master Jairun said they're using the dragon's lure to find Keir. They knew of his plan to draw them in before they came."

Again, the creature coughed. It grinned. "They know nothing. Nothing. No human . . . is as clever as . . . an eternal wyrm. Plans. Plans. Plans within plans."

The yellow in the goblin's eyes began to fade. Connor shook the crook planted in its arm to wake the creature up. He deepened his voice, and his ghostly silver armor brightened. "What plans? Speak, corruption. I command you to speak."

The creature writhed against his order. Its face contorted with malice. "Your friends will die. Die, they will! They're walking into his trap!"

The dim yellow glow of its eyes faded to a dull, lifeless brown.

51

KARA
SIL SHADATH

AFTER MUCH ARGUMENT, INGARU HAD RELENTED–IN part thanks to Kara's pleading. She could not save Keir without Ioanu's help. Kara supposed that deep down, the older bear still held a blood-borne loyalty to the decimated House Arkelon.

Ioanu led them across a short swath of bleak hills north of the Tagamoor. "This is the narrowest stretch of the Bezik Hills," she said, "where Sil Shadath runs closest to the moor. The dragons planned their breach of the canyon wall here so that the greatest share of the moor vapors would flow up the Phantom River into their favorite forest. Since then, they have used the resulting mist and the rot from the forest floor to fashion their most nightmarish corruptions."

"Oh good." Tiran jumped from one hilltop to the next with his Suvoroth daggers out, riding on the vapors. "We have much to look forward to."

The bear did not seem to appreciate his dry humor. "Watch yourself, Wartroot. Stay alert. The forest is their home, but those terrible creatures are not bound to it. From here in, we may encounter them at any time."

Tiran paused on a hilltop and squinted ahead. "Darkness is coming, and the best defense against nightmares is daylight. What if we wait until sunrise?"

"We can't," Kara said. "Keir's time is short. To let him die now is to commit him to eternal death."

Tiran leapt down to land beside her and sheathed the daggers. "You're right. And so I'll soldier on with you and give my last breath to save–" He gasped and seized his head. "Look out!"

A glowing apparition floated out before them on a thick wisp of mist.

The creature took the form of an old woman, bare feet hanging below the hem of her tattered dress. "Return. Return! I was once as you are. Flesh and free. Enter not this forest, lest it claim your spirit as it claimed mine!"

Ioanu growled. "Be gone, corruption. Untruth. You were never as them, and you never had a spirit to lose."

At the voice of the bear, the apparition's face twisted. Double fangs hung from each side of its mouth. "Havarra abomination! Valshadox will hear of this!"

Tiran drew his sword and lunged. "Kill this ghost before it flees!"

The blade passed through the apparition, and the creature turned and bore down on him, jaw opening wide and clawed hands reaching.

"Your daggers, Wartroot!" Ioanu bellowed. "In the hands of a lightraider, Suvoroth steel will disrupt the mist that forms the creature."

He stabbed the sword into the earth, drew both Suvoroth daggers, and slashed upward to slice an *X* into the apparition's form. The mist shuddered. The creature screamed, one arm vanishing. With the other it clawed at his shield.

Kara tried to help, but a second apparition appeared between them, a child with two kitchen knives and a grin too wide for its face.

Ioanu swiped at it with her claws, and it shuddered and screamed like the other, slowing its advance. "Do you know the Verse of the Courageous," she asked, "from the Scrolls?"

Kara did. So did Tiran, she knew, because she'd heard him recite it during their lessons. They spoke it together.

"Stregov po asamav. Se stradov do letu strakov. Mi ke'Rumosh biyov shurnah. Ov se radeniond do ov rubeziond."

Be strong and courageous.

Don't be terrified or afraid.

For the High One will go with you.

He will not leave or abandon you.

Their Suvoroth-alloy weapons flashed blue green with every strike. In moments, the attacking creatures were no more.

"It's a good start, I suppose," Tiran said.

"Not so good as you think." Kara hurled a whirlknife at the tree line where another apparition drifted with the mist, an old man with a cane. Before the knife could hit its mark, the creature fled into the forest.

Kara ran after it, leaping to snatch her returning whirlknife from the air. "We mustn't let it escape!"

Only by Tiran's inventions and the grace of the High One did they stand a chance of catching the ghost. In two strides, Kara was at the forest with Tiran and Ioanu on her flanks.

The trees shortened their leaps. "Aim for the spaces between," Ioanu said. "Look two strides ahead, or you'll wind up impaled on a branch."

The apparition had no such limitation. The old man looked over his shoulder and smashed into a tree only to re-form on the other side and keep going. In almost comical fashion, his cane swept the air as if aiding his rapid, floating strides.

"We're losing him," Tiran said, flipping a Suvoroth dagger to hold it by the tip.

"Take care, Wartroot. You need that weapon for balance. Throw it now, and you'll fall out of the pursuit."

"If I don't, we'll lose the creature anyway." He landed in a crouch on a boulder and risked the toss.

The dagger sailed true. It pinned the ghost to a tree by its neck, and though it shuddered and wailed, gnashing its monstrous teeth, it could not break free. Kara reached it a beat later and finished the thing off with two slashes of her whirlknives. The old man dissolved into the fog.

"Thanks be to the Rescuer." Tiran walked up behind her and yanked his dagger from the pine. "See, Ioanu? There was no other way."

The bear made no answer.

Kara turned around to find her hanging back, sniffing the air. "Ioanu?"

"I have him. I smell your brother's blood. But there is no warmth to the scent." Ioanu's deep blue eyes locked with hers. "So much blood, but all of it is cold and dried."

52

WITH NO DARK CREATURE TO PURSUE, THE PARTY slowed their pace. Ioanu led the way, following her nose. In the darkness of the night forest, with the thick ground fog to carry her, the bear hardly disturbed the underbrush. Kara could see how she'd be mistaken for a wraith–at least by those Grenton villagers who'd never met one.

In the Forest of Believing and in the Highland Forest, where she'd lived with her brehnan, Kara had always moved like a ghost. But here, aided by Tiran's inventions and her whirlknives, stealth and quickness gained new meaning. She felt the temptation toward pride and power but remembered her lesson on the moor.

"For your glory, and yours alone," she whispered, and set her focus on watching the trees for threats. The creatures were coming for sure. They must have heard the apparition's wailing. It was only a matter of time.

"The blood scent is strong," Ioanu said. "Keir is close, but another is with him. Take care." With a nod, she directed the cadets toward a thick copse of pines.

Tiran winced, clearly pained by his lingering wound. "I sense dark creatures. Far more than we've yet encountered. Their numbers may be too great."

Kara could not see what lay on the other side of the copse, but she would not abandon Keir, no matter how many creatures they might face.

As they drew closer, she looked to Tiran, and he nodded, reading the thought in her gaze. He changed course to move left while she and Ioanu went right. If barkhides or dark creatures had Keir, whatever the odds, their small party would fall upon them from both flanks.

Shouting reached Kara's ears. Not Keir, but the voice was oddly familiar. "Leave me alone! I will suffer your torment no longer."

Lee? That made no sense.

Kara crept to the last pine on her side of the copse and saw a man swinging a black scimitar to keep a crowd of dark creatures at bay. Not Keir. Not Lee, either, but one who could easily have come from his village.

The odds were not in his favor—nor in the favor of her party, should they intervene. The besieged man, dressed in the dirty wool pants and tunic of a prisoner, faced a small platoon of orcs, goblins, and ghosts commanded by the same wraith she'd seen through Keir's eyes. She saw the green fire in the wraith's eye sockets and more under the black orc ribs visible through its ragged cloak. How the prisoner could even stand in its terrifying presence, she did not know. She felt for him, but if her party tried to save him, none might survive to find Keir.

"Be gone!" the man shouted in growing desperation. "Leave me be, I beg you! I won't go back!"

A grunt reached her ears, and she looked to see Ioanu vying for her attention. The bear lifted her nose, then nodded toward the prisoner. Dried blood covered his tunic. He was the source of the blood smell. Keir's smell. But Keir was not with him.

Kara closed her eyes. To find her brehna, they'd have to free this man. They had no choice.

Ioanu seemed eager for the fight—poised like a bolt ready to spring from a crossbow.

Tiran showed more caution. He answered Kara's gaze with a tilt of his head as if to say, *Your call.*

She made it. Kara leapt high, near to the top of the pines, with her whirlknives open. "For the Rescuer!"

CONNOR
ABOVE SIL SHADATH

ZEL WORKED THE RUDDER WHILE THE CADETS STARED over the rails on each side. "Plans within plans," she said. "What do you suppose the creature meant?"

"What does a goblin ever mean?" Connor resisted the urge to glance back at her, keeping his eyes on the black forest below. "Most of what spills from their vile mouths is gibberish."

"If that's what you think," Lee said. "Then why have we turned from our mission?"

"I didn't say what the creature said was useless. Master Jairun told us Kara and Tiran are headed for a dragon's stronghold. The dragon lured them, but until now, I sought comfort in the idea that Kara could block him out. I hoped they might approach in secret. The goblin's babbling changed that. Dark creatures likely follow our friends as they followed us. They may be preparing an ambush. We must warn them."

The tenor of Lee's voice changed. "Connor. Over here."

"Do you see them?" Connor switched rails to join him.

"Not Kara or Tiran." The scribe held Faelin's journal in the moonlight, open to the page Connor had noted in the tomb. "But that looks like the Aropha haven Faelin drew–the one he calls Emen Kar." He lowered the text, and Connor saw the ruin, tucked in a valley at the southern border of the forest. The trio of long, round-peaked structures and the glade on the south side were an indisputable match to Faelin's drawing.

"Emen Kar looks far better preserved than Ras Heval," Lee said. "If that is where Kaliphan went to live out his last days, the Rapha Key may still be in there."

Connor returned to the north rail and resumed his search. "If so, the key has been safe for centuries. It'll keep for a few more hours. Once we find Kara and deal with the dragon's trap, we can come back."

He felt Lee's eyes on him. "You mean once we find Kara *and Tiran*."

"Yes. Of course, I do."

Zel let out a quiet huff from her place at the rudder. "This seems a vain endeavor, and one that may prove our undoing. I told you, I'm running low on my father's fuel. A long search will leave us stranded–not just in Tanelethar, but here, in this Forest of Horrors. And we stand little chance of finding your friends in the night. We're risking too much."

"We're risking what we must."

Connor had more to say, but his eyes fell on something that sent waves of hope and dread through his heart. "Turn north. Now."

Despite the misgivings she'd expressed, Zel made the correction. "What have you found?"

"Spires. A dragon gate." Connor waved to call Lee to the bow and pointed. "Beyond that rise. The pyranium spires are black, but the steel chains catch the light."

Lee lowered matching lenses over both eyes, the ones Connor had often seen him use for seeing long distances. "That's a dragon stronghold, all right–a diamond pyramid topped with a domed dragon gate. But the pyramid is too small to be the whole fortress. The rest may be underground." He raised his lenses and glanced at his friend. "Up here, we can see much, but so can the dragon. If he comes at us in the air, *The Starling* stands no chance."

"You're right. Zel, bring us lower. Kara's headed for that stronghold, or somewhere close to it. We must trust the Rescuer has brought us near enough to find her."

Lee coughed.

Connor sighed. "*Her and Tiran*. Yes. I get it. Thank you."

The Starling began her descent, but the bow also turned west.

"Zel, hold your course!" Connor kept his eyes off the starboard rail, trying to maintain sight of the dragon gate spires. "We need to keep heading toward the dragon's stronghold."

"*Or* we could go that way."

The spires fell out of his sight, and he looked back to see her pointing off the port bow.

Lee was already there. "Flashes in the trees, Connor. Indigo. Green. Dark blue. They look like–"

"Keledan armor." Connor turned to Zel. "It's Kara and Tiran, and they're under attack. Take us down."

53

CONNOR HAD ZEL BRING *THE STARLING* IN AT TREETOP level, canted against the northern breeze. They saw no dragon, but the crowd of dark creatures surrounding their friends looked bad enough. Orcs. Goblins. Ethereal creatures he'd never seen flitted about on the fog. Connor could only describe them as ghosts. But these were not the most frightening enemies in the fight.

"What is that big thing in the shroud?" Lee asked, holding an arrow on his string. "It wields both a scimitar and a halberd."

"I don't know. But it hangs in the fog like those ghost creatures. Stranger than that, I think that creature is . . . is . . ." He trailed off.

Zel finished the statement for him, shaking her head as if she couldn't believe her own words. "That creature is fighting a floating bear."

The oddities of the battle did not hold them at bay. Connor dropped his hand, and Lee loosed the first arrow, killing a goblin. He felled two more, eliminating all the enemies carrying bows, before any of the combatants looked up.

Zel held *The Starling* steady, wicker brushing the tops of the pines, and aimed her crossbow over the rail while Connor and Lee descended on the rope. To speed his drop, Connor let the line slide through his gloved hands until he felt its heat. He landed next to

Tiran and raised his shield to deflect an orc's halberd. "Where's Kara?"

"Nice to see you too. Look up."

Connor followed the point of Tiran's sword and saw Kara leaping at half the height of the tall pines. On her way down, she jabbed her whirlknives into one of the ghosts, causing it to shudder and wail before dissipating into the mist.

Tiran finished off the orc, then traded his sword for a pair of green daggers and leapt after her, soaring high. "Connor, watch your feet!"

In the distraction of seeing his friends' strange movements, Connor had almost missed a pair of bulbous spiders crawling out of the brush. He stomped them into the forest floor, causing sparks from his silver armor. "How are you able to—"

"Talk later!"

Tiran and Kara's effort seemed focused around protecting an Aladoth in drab wool garb swinging a scimitar to keep the orcs at bay. The big, shrouded creature was moving that way too, slowed but not stopped by the bear's attacks. She took more blows from its dual weapons on her dark blue armor than she was dealing out. Brave, but it was only a matter of time before the creature's strikes got through.

Fighting his way through the orcs with his crook and sword, aided by crossbow bolts from above, Connor caught a glimpse of the man's face. He could not possibly have been Keir. Yet he might have been Lee. Very much so. A little taller, perhaps. Harder in aspect. But an uncanny resemblance.

Connor used his crook to yank an orc's legs from under it, adding momentum to its fall with a shield bash. He drove his sword down through its chest and risked a glance at Lee. In the melee, the scribe did not appear to have seen the Aladoth.

"Die, Lightraider!"

The shrouded creature had almost reached the Aladoth, with only Kara standing between them. From his new angle, Connor saw a black gargoyle skull under the hood and green fire in its eyes. More green fire flared within the ribs under its shroud.

Three orcs had surrounded the bear, taking all her attention, and others kept Tiran and Lee busy. Kara stood alone.

Connor hacked at an orc's neck to clear his path and ran to her side. He uttered a prayer on the way, the same prayer he'd spoken in the crystal cave, and his sword, Revornosh, shone with white light. "Get away from her!"

The creature shot him a blazing glare. "Hide that light, Keledan. You've no authority over me. You're as tainted as the Suvor traitors from whose ashes I rose."

"Not my authority, but the Rescuer's. His sovereignty. His righteousness. Your nights tarnishing his creation are over."

Connor swung Revornosh, and the creature countered with its halberd. Lightraider steel met some alloy of pyranium and sent up green sparks. The impact scored a nick on the creature's blade, but nothing more.

It laughed. "You stand no chance against the centuries of my existence. I roamed the land long before you. I'll roam it long after you're gone."

"I don't think so!" Kara had used the breathing space Connor bought her to speak the same prayer, so that her whirlknives shone like his sword. She slashed at the creature, forcing it to defend with both the scimitar and the halberd. To Connor's astonishment, the knives cut deeper into the pyranium weapons than Revornosh.

He followed her attack by driving the spike of his crook into the creature's ribcage. The green flames sparked and flared. The creature screamed. Kara stepped in with her knives crossed and slashed outward to scissor its neck. The blades passed through the ore spine, and the fire under the black bones went out.

The orc's shrouded skeleton made a slow, reluctant fall through the gray forest vapors and settled into the brush.

Connor and Kara turned, ready for more fighting, but their friends and the bear had finished the rest.

Lee stood with mouth hanging, staring at the Aladoth they'd all fought to protect. Anger overcame the shock in his brow. "Shan?"

54

"IT SEEMS I FOUND THE WRONG BROTHER."

Ioanu, the name Kara had used when she introduced the bear to Connor, watched with ears forward as Lee and Shan traded harsh words and sharp hand gestures at the edge of the clearing.

"Taller," Tiran said, "older, with no spectacles or red paste in his hair. But otherwise, he could be Lee. Strange."

Connor shot him a glance. "Strange? You do remember you're a twin, right?"

"Not an identical one. And Lee has no twin. I didn't even know he had a brehna."

Kara tugged at Connor's sleeve. "Whatever their relationship, we need to find out what this man knows about Keir and move on. We cannot linger here after the noise of the battle. Your . . . airship may be seen as well."

Connor nodded and started toward the arguing pair, but made it only two paces before he felt her grip on his arm. She pushed close and lowered her voice. "I heard you. When I was fighting the wraith, that shrouded orc we killed, I heard your call. You commanded it to get away from me."

"I didn't mean to imply you couldn't defend yourself."

Kara pulled her head back a bit and narrowed her indigo eyes at him. "I never said I was offended." She gave him a quick smile. "I'm glad you came."

He let out a quiet laugh, about to speak, when he sensed someone else had joined the conversation. The two turned to find Ioanu right behind them. She wasn't sneaking, not that Connor could tell. But the way her mass moved in the ground fog made no sound.

Ioanu gazed back at them, looking from one to the other, then sniffed in Connor's direction. "Huh. Interesting."

Connor suddenly felt as if he should check the scent of his tunic. "What's interesting?"

"Nothing," the bear said. "Sorry to intrude."

The argument between Lee and Shan had settled to a quiet simmer by the time Connor approached. "Are you ready to introduce us?" he asked Lee.

"This is Lee Shan, my brother, who took the ships." The manner of his introduction earned a frown from Shan, but Lee ignored it. "He was kept by barkhides and orcs in a camp in this forest with many others. The prisoners are being tortured and terrorized–"

"To make us ready to slaughter the Keledan," Shan said, interrupting him.

Connor had suspected as much, but he needed to be sure. "Are you certain?"

"Oh yes. I am certain." The darkness in Shan's gaze sent chills through him. What horrors had this man suffered?

Kara, still hanging back, lifted her chin. "How did you come to have Keir's blood all over your clothes–so much that my bear friend tracked you instead of him?"

Shan looked down and lifted the hem of his tunic. "This is your brother's blood?" He laughed. "He was as my brother too, though the terror of our prison stripped him of his name. I know him as Hosal. We escaped together. The orcs wounded him with many cuts during their torture, but then I helped him out of the camp."

Kara's hand went to her sword and twitched. "If you helped him, where is he now?"

"We were separated by dragon fire. Lord Valshadox attacked. But he aimed at me, not Hosa–not Keir, I mean." Shan showed her charred fabric at his shoulder and a burn underneath. "I ducked behind a boulder in time to escape most of the blast. The dragon flew on, attacking other prisoners, not your brother." He nodded toward the thickening forest to the east. "We set a meeting point, a tower to the southeast. I was on my way there when the wraith and his creatures found me."

"Show us the way."

"Wait," Connor said to Kara, lowering his voice a touch. "We were beset by a pack of goblins in the Bezik hills, also to the southeast. They knew about you and Tiran. We questioned one, and it said you were walking into a trap."

Behind him, Tiran sighed. "We've always been walking into a trap. That was the point of letting the dragon send Kara visions of her tortured brehna."

"I know. Master Jairun told me. But there's something more. The goblin said Valshadox has plans within plans. The dragon may have steered Shan and Keir. Herded them. Allowed them to escape."

Shan began to protest, but Lee held up a hand. "This meeting point of yours. Is it a landmark, easy to spot within this forest of darkness?"

"Yes. It is, but you cannot think–"

"Connor's right. The dragon has set some plot in motion to capture Keir."

"Keir and I both," Kara said. "Or all of us. What a boon for a dragon to hold a pack of lightraiders in its clutches, even cadets. We must find my brehna before he reaches this landmark and change his course. Can we use the airship?"

Connor shook his head. "*The Starling* is low on fuel, and I doubt it can handle Ioanu."

"Then Lee should use it to get his brehna out of here. He's endured enough. The rest of us will go on foot."

Lee began to argue, but Connor pulled him aside. "Kara's right. You and Zel take Shan and head for Emen Kar. Seek the key. Talk to Shan on the way. He may have left Keledev years ago, but I believe you can still rescue him–an answer to your mehma's prayers. We'll find Keir and meet you at the ruin. And then we'll all go home to celebrate two brehnan saved instead of one."

55

TEEGAN
KELEDEV
UNDER PELLION'S FLOW

THE LAST CHAMBER OUTSIDE THE GOBLIN DEN WAS quiet when the party arrived, much as Teegan and Dag had found it before the iceblade attacked. "Careful," she said. "This may be another ambush." She stretched out her trident toward the opening in the opposite wall. "The entrance to the main den is over there."

The party advanced slowly and in silence–watching and ready–until they passed the middle of the chamber. There were no grunts, breathing, or shifting from the enemy–only the steady *drip, drip* of ice melt.

Dag, near the front with Master Jairun, let his twin axes rest. "I suppose they've truly all gone out to the flow."

"Gaah!" Goblins camouflaged in grit and brandishing ice knives and scimitars jumped out from the chamber walls.

"Hold fast!" Master Jairun shouted. "Keep them on the rim!"

Called by his command, Pedrig, who'd hung back in the previous passage, appeared behind them in full armor. His set his claws in the stone floor, silver fur rising to a ridge on his back, and unleashed his terrible bark. The undulating pine-green sphere, which Teegan had seen bounce over goblins in the straight crevice the day before, rolled around the edge of the chamber like a child's ball in a pail.

The goblins, held in place by the guardians, melted one by one into boiling lichen as the sphere passed over them.

Dag looked back at Teegan and grinned. "Looks like our plan wor–"

A screech interrupted him. More goblins rose from the floor among the party, camouflaged in the same way as their comrades. One wrapped a clawed hand around Paskin's throat and plunged an ice knife into his body. Paskin screamed.

Dag crossed the chamber in a single stride and grabbed the goblin by its pale shoulders. He ripped the creature away from the younger cadet and threw it against the wall, cracking its brittleknit skull.

Others finished two more off in short order, and Teegan rushed to catch Paskin as he fell.

He gazed up at her, eyes wide. "It's cold, so cold it burns!"

She pulled his cloak aside and cut away a bloody patch of his tunic to find the wound. "It's your shoulder. If we can stop the bleeding, you'll stay with us in this life. I promise." Even as she said it, Teegan knew she was breaking a rule Master Jairun had taught them in their renewer classes–never make a promise you're not sure you can keep. She chewed a wad of black tea leaves from her manykit and stuffed them into the wound. "This will slow the bleeding. But the infection needs prayer."

Paskin nodded, and though she could see that even breathing pained him, he spoke the words to the Rescuer with her–the same prayer Pedrig had taught Teegan when the goblin ice scratched her during the scouting expedition.

The lichen growing in the wound receded. Teegan began wrapping it with a dressing. "Yes. You'll be all right. I'm sure of it."

Together, Dag and Teegan carried Paskin as the party ventured into the main goblin den. It was a risk, but to escort the wounded back through the tunnels now seemed a greater one. Paskin's safest path now was forward.

Dag walked in a low stoop to match Paskin's height. "I'm

grateful for your father's advice, Teegan. Without his knowledge of that goblin tactic—hiding in the walls—we might have taken greater casualties than this. Thanks to him, we were prepared."

"We were," she said. "I hope he's prepared his watchmen just as well."

According to Teegan's tehpa, the companies had taken many losses in their trek north through the tunnels. Half the strength of Thousand Falls and the Windhold had come from the west. The same portion of Ravencrest and Orvyn's Vow had marched from the east through another set of tunnels they'd found. Both groups had suffered casualties in the fighting on the way, and they'd taken more after meeting up where the tunnels joined south of Pellion's Flow.

The watchmaster of Thousand Falls, struck down but not killed during a brutal attack at the intersection of six passages, had passed command of the full contingent to Sireth. Together, he and Master Jairun had concocted a new plan to defeat the dark creature army. Teegan had overheard only a little.

"Your losses show me your contingent lacks confidence in their Keledan armor," Master Jairun had said to her tehpa. "Speak to them. Lead them. Remind them the armor is as much a weapon as it is a defense—a lesson vital to our success."

56

THE PARTY ENCOUNTERED A FEW STRAGGLERS IN THE main goblin den and wiped them out in short order.

The den looked like a natural cavern, with smooth, toothy formations hanging from the ceiling and pockets of age-old ice in every corner. The party lit their torches and split to scour every nook and alcove to be sure no other attacks would come.

During the search, Teegan stayed with Paskin on a shelf in the north wall, where a sloping passage looked to be an exit to the surface. While she waited, she fitted him with a new air bladder from the extra stores Dag had brought. The warm air it supplied did little to aid his labored breaths. She glanced up at Master Jairun as he and the others came together again on the shelf. "He's feverish, and his breathing is thin. Should we leave him down here? Won't he be safer far from the battle?"

Master Jairun shook his head. "None of us are safe down here, and that will be doubly true within the hour. Best to get him out of this dark and up into the light of the moons and stars."

As the headmaster finished this reply, Quinton returned and directed his torch at the northwest corner of the cavern. "Over there, we found a tunnel leadin' downward. If we follow it, we may learn how they breached the barrier."

"Later," Master Jairun said. "Right now, we must deal with the dark army up there on the ice flow." He ducked to enter the passage to the surface. "Our watchmen are waiting. We must act now, lest they become impatient and spoil the plan."

Teegan bristled at the idea her tehpa's men might spoil anything, but as she and Dag helped Paskin up, she realized the headmaster was not wrong. Her tehpa, a hunter from the coastal forest of Sil Tymest, was now leading two hundred or more men and women of the foothill companies. They'd suffered casualties. With fear and rage pushing through their ranks, how long could he keep them under control?

AARON
SOUTH OF PELLION'S FLOW

"WHO ARE WE?" SIRETH SHOUTED, RAISING THE watchmaster's oversize war hammer high.

Aaron answered him with the others in the strongest voice he could muster. "We are the watchmen!"

"Who are we?

"We are the wall!"

The rocks south of the ice flow echoed with the chorus of the watchmen. Upslope, the creatures–many carrying frost-green torches and some with the same frost-green glow in their eyes and joints–shifted about. Restless.

They weren't the only ones.

"When will we show ourselves?" Aaron asked, tugging at the dressing where he'd burned one of the black worms away from his neck. "When will we avenge our comrades?"

"At the signal, lad. Not before. And the vengeance will be the High One's, not ours. We will shine with his armor, and he will do the rest."

"His armor." Aaron looked down at his hands and arms, as if expecting to see more than wool and leather. "What if I have no armor?"

"In truth, I might have asked the same not long ago. But my behlna and sehna and their friends at Ras Telesar showed me the way. The armor is a gift for all Keledan. We all carry it."

"How will I call it up when the creatures come at us?"

"By leaning on him, lad. By knowing his word is true and resting on his promises."

Aaron had heard similar words too often in his village chapel without a deeper explanation.

Sireth seemed to sense this and took him by the shoulders. "Shout your belief *here*." He laid a hand upon Aaron's chest, over his heart. "Shout that his word is true. And neither man nor creature, neither height nor depth, neither sword nor ice will separate you from his love and gift." Sireth released him. "When the goblins come at us, lean on that with all your being."

Aaron nodded, calmer now. But if he'd been struggling, perhaps so had others. "I think the rest need to hear the same."

Sireth gave him a grim smile and turned to a young woman he'd chosen as a lieutenant. "Pass the words I've spoken. Quietly. And remind them that no matter what happens, not one soul is to move until we see the fire. Make sure they understand."

Once she'd started her work, Sireth thrust the watchmaster's hammer high again. "Who are we?"

"We are the watchmen!"

"Who are we?"

"We are the wall!"

Upslope on the ice flow, the creatures squirmed.

Aaron gritted his teeth. "Come on, Master Jairun. Show us that fire."

57

LEE
TANELETHAR
ABOVE SIL SHADATH

LEE SAT ON *THE STARLING*'S AFT BENCH, WATCHING Shan, who stood with elbows resting on the rail, looking out over the forest. Kara had come to Tanelethar in search of her brother, and the Havarra bear the Rescuer sent to aid her in this quest had found Lee's brother instead. How strange and unfathomable was the High One's design?

"I forgive you," he said after a time.

Shan lifted his head and glanced over his shoulder. "I never asked for your forgiveness."

"You have it all the same. All these years, I've harbored anger for what your leaving did to Mother and Father–what it did to me. But now that we're together, the anger fades. I want you to come home. The Rescuer wants you to come home too."

Shan turned and rested his back against the wicker. "Trang, you know I–"

"It's Lee now, Brother."

This earned him a flat look. "We are all Lee. Our whole family."

"True, but that is what they called me in the Scribes, and I've grown accustomed to it. Even Father calls me Lee now."

"Oh. Well. If Father permits it." Shan rolled his eyes.

"Don't speak of him with disrespect. It broke his heart when you left. He loves you."

"Strange. I remember only the shouting."

"Perhaps if you hadn't bucked against his every word–challenged him at every turn because of your lack of . . ." Lee stopped and sighed. He was growing harsh, and he didn't want to.

But the damage was done. He felt heat in Shan's reply. "My lack of what, Brother?

"Your lack of faith." Lee lowered his gaze to the talanium ring, larger than the ringlets he'd earned in the Five Quests, and turned it about his finger. He expected a rebuke but received none, and when he lifted his gaze again, he found Shan waiting, expectant.

"Go on." The words were a plea rather than a dare. "Convince me of the faith I've forgotten."

Was this the moment Lee's mother had prayed for? "You know the Scrolls as well as I. In our youth, you helped me learn them. No knowledge I can share will help you unless you acknowledge their authority–the High One's authority."

"I don't know that I can."

"Can't you?" Lee spread his hands. "Look now what you've seen. This ship, for one thing."

"Man's handiwork, not the High One's. A wicker basket under an overlarge festival toy."

Lee frowned. "Without the High One, this toy could not have passed the barrier."

"You forget, I came here in a ship that passed the barrier. Storm portals are a natural wonder–a strange feature of our world. Nothing more."

"Then what of the Keledan armor you saw in our battle against the wraith and its creatures?"

This gave Shan pause.

After a moment, he opened his mouth, but Lee cut him off with a wave. "Don't say sorcery. You know better than any Aladoth that there is no Keledan sorcery. We depend upon the power of the High One and his Rescuer."

Shan furrowed his brow. "All right. I saw his power. I'll acknowledge that. And your armor is something I never witnessed nor could have witnessed deep in the shelter of the Liberated Land. What else?"

"Must I also mention you met a talking bear—a Havarra shepherd that most here would deny could ever exist?"

Zel, quietly observing from her usual place by the rudder, stifled a laugh.

"A talking bear." Shan turned away from them. "Score another point for the lightraider cadets. But if—" He seemed to spot something in the forest and leaned over the rail, staring down. "Brother, come here!"

Lee ran to join him, and he pointed. "More prisoners in the forest. Ten at least. I didn't know any others escaped during the revolt."

Looking straight down, Lee saw only trees, fog, and darkness. "I don't see them."

"They've passed under us." Shan pushed off the rail and ran to the other side. "Over here."

This time, when Lee joined him, he lowered his best lens into place. Thanks to Belen's invention, he could count the needles on every black pine, yet he could not find the prisoners Shan spoke of. "I still can't see them."

Shan sighed and sat on the bow bench. "Me either. Not anymore. Perhaps they hid. They must have seen our shadow in the moonlight and mistaken us for a dragon passing over. We should land and convince them otherwise." He looked up at Lee. "You could rescue them too."

You could rescue them too.

Too.

Lee's heart thumped in his chest. "What are you saying, Brother? Are you convinced?"

Shan took a long moment before answering, then smiled—the softest smile Lee had ever seen from him. "I am. The way you and the others fought off the dragon's creatures showed me my folly. I want to come home."

"If you want to go home," Zel said, interjecting for the first time, "there'll be no landing to rescue more prisoners. I'm sorry. There's no good place, and we don't have the fuel. Besides," she nodded off the port side, "we're here. Emen Kar lies there, to our south."

Shan would not be denied. Lee did not even get the chance to pray with him. As soon as Zel landed in the glade on the south side of the long ruin, Shan vaulted over the side. "I can reach those prisoners, Lee. I'm one of them."

"You'll never find them, Brother."

"I will. I escaped the dragon's camp, didn't I? Found my way through the forest until your bear sniffed me out. Those feats were nothing compared to this. Pray for me, and I'll succeed."

Zel watched him with a cautious eye. "Succeed in doing what?"

"Bringing them here, where you two can share the Great Rescue. With me on your side, they'll listen. I know it. What a glory it will be to bring a dozen brothers home to Keledev instead of one or two." Shan ran off without allowing any further argument. "I'll be back before the others reach this place. I promise!"

He disappeared around the corner of the ruin.

58

CONNOR
SIL SHADATH

"NOTHING QUITE LIKE IT, IS THERE?" TIRAN ASKED, flying at breakneck speed beside Connor, daggers held out.

Connor gripped Ioanu's fur tighter. "Eyes on the forest, please. Or do you want to snap your spine by running into a tree?"

They hit the underbrush beneath the ground fog for another leaping stride, and Tiran laughed. "A funny thing to say, Brehna, since your eyes have been shut for most of this run."

Connor had considered Zel's wicker airship the most frightening form of transport possible. He'd been wrong. Riding a bear capable of leaping long distances and rushing headlong through a thick forest of mist and black pines was much worse.

The bear had explained the strange properties of the vapors and how they interacted with the alloys and creatures from the Tagamoor. But that knowledge didn't assuage his fear. He'd have preferred to walk, especially given the terrors of Sil Shadath.

"The scent is growing strong," Ioanu said. "Keir is close. This time I'm sure. The other Aladoth is no longer here to muddy the trail, and now warm queensblood mingles with the cold and dry. Your brother still has open wounds."

The bear slowed to a stop, prompting Kara and Tiran to do the same.

Connor dismounted. “Where is he?”

“Ahead, my Keledan friend. A hundred of your human paces or so. But as before, our objective is not alone.”

Did this smaller party have the numbers for another fight?

“How many?”

“Three”—Ioanu sniffed the air—“no, four others. Three forest goblins and an Aladoth. The Aladoth smells of rotten breath and old burns.”

“Old burns.” Kara tapped her whirlknives against her legs, chin lowered, glaring in the direction Ioanu had sniffed. “A barkhide.”

Connor heard as much growl in her voice as he’d heard in the bear’s. “Take it easy, Kara.”

“I’ll take it easy once I have my brehna back.”

KARA

KARA CREPT THROUGH THE FOREST ON THE MIST, AS lightly as Ioanu. The four had formed a line for their advance, each separated by ten paces. She and Ioanu took the center, and they were the first to spot Keir. Kara halted and held up a fist to signal the others.

Ioanu’s nose had missed two of Keir’s tormentors. Apparitions—a young man and woman in wedding clothes like those Kara had seen in Charlotte’s boutique in Trader’s Knoll. The ghostly woman’s dress was not rich but not one for peasants either.

“What a happy couple we are,” the woman moaned in mock glee, hovering near Keir. “Together forever. And you, too, will be with us”—her mournful frown became a wicked sneer—“forever!”

Keir strained against the barkhide’s hold and lurched at the creature. She lurched back at him with a hiss and a wide mouth filled with sharp teeth.

"Leave him," the barkhide said. "He's mine. My catch. I want the credit from General Moach."

Kara wondered if the barkhides who first took Keir from the Highland Forest had thought the same—that they might earn some favor or rank by his capture. Perhaps they had. But this barkhide would get nothing.

"Keir!"

Without a sign to the others, she rushed into the open. The apparitions stood no chance. The ghostly woman had hardly extended her long claws before a flying whirlknife passed through her. She shuddered, frozen in place, and then dissipated into the fog when the knife sliced through her again on its return.

Her ghost husband tried to run, but the second whirlknife did the same to him.

In her fervor, Kara had forgotten about the goblins. She sensed a presence bearing down and turned her indigo shield just as a long knife came stabbing at her neck.

With a flash, the blade glanced away, and in the next instant, the goblin vanished under a flurry of claws and blue-gray fur.

Ioanu growled. "Watch yourself, Queensblood."

Two other goblins fell to Connor and Tiran's swords, leaving only the barkhide. He pushed Keir to the foggy ground and squared off against Kara. "Who is this? A feisty creature to add to our ranks?"

"No!" Keir sprang up and rushed at them. Connor grabbed him and spun him away, sparing him a blow from the spike the barkhide had driven through his own arm. In the next beat, Keir had gained his footing, and he rushed the man again. Connor and Tiran needed their combined strength to restrain him. "It's you," Keir kept saying, staring wild-eyed at Kara. "It's you!"

"Hold my brehna fast," she said. "I must deal with this one." Ioanu stood beside her, fur bristling, but Kara motioned her away with her sword. "I must deal with him alone."

She'd faced this test before, in the Arena with Swordmaster

Quinton. And she'd failed. She'd thought then that the failure cost her dearly, but the cost of failure this time would be far greater.

"Are you certain?" Ioanu asked.

"Very much so."

The barkhide chuckled. "I'll not argue. I'm happy to take you one at a time. Makes my work easier. What are you? Devotees of Lord Valshadox's rivals?"

Kara matched his stare. "Lightraiders."

The half-beat that preceded his overloud laughter told her the very word frightened him. News of Vorax's death had traveled—the first defeated dragon in two generations.

"Come and kill me then, Lightraider," the barkhide said. "Destroy a dragon's creature. Is that not your calling? Is that not your mission in holy zeal for your Overlord?"

He circled, as Quinton had done in the Arena, and Kara countered in the same way. "You are not a dragon's creature. You belong to the High One. He is your creator." She spoke the first verse of the Great Rescue, *The One and Only*, in the Elder Tongue—a prayer and preparation for her effort. Then tried to explain its meaning to the Aladoth. "Because you're his, the High One sent his son the Rescuer to die for you. Won't you see that?"

"Lies!" The barkhide drew a whip from his belt and slung it at her neck.

On instinct, Kara leapt out of the way, forgetting the Suvoroth gear she wore or the fact that she had one hand already occupied with her sword. Her flight reached the tips of the pines. On the way down, she whipped one whirlknife open, but it could not stop the growing speed of her descent.

Protect me. You are a shield about me.

Her armor glowed bright, sending a pulse of indigo through the mist from her hard landing.

The barkhide backed away, eyes shifting from side to side, no longer hiding his fear. "Sorcerers. You're all sorcerers, as the dragons tell us. Kill me, then. I am an abomination to you and your

Maker, like my master Moach."

Kara heard Quinton's voice from the Arena, what he'd said moments before she'd almost delivered a killing blow. *Admit it. Ya see me as an abomination.*

She did. Still. She saw the barkhides that way even more now that she was faced with a real one. And again, she could not lie by denying it.

As if fighting were his only hope for survival, the barkhide came at her with whip and sword.

Kara fought off his blows. "He's *our* Maker, yours as much as mine." Had those same words not fallen from her lips during the failed quest? "Twisting yourself away from what he made you, mutilating your body to be something you were never created to be *is* an abomination. The Scrolls say so."

The barkhide smashed his sword against her shield in repeated, futile blows. "Your Scrolls mean nothing to me."

"They should. Don't you see? They were written in love–love for all his creations." She spoke the second verse to the High One, *Not One is Perfect*, and tried to rephrase it in a way the barkhide would understand. "All of us are corrupted, in need of restoration. That's why the Rescuer had to sacrifice himself." She followed quickly with the *Perfect Sacrifice* verse. "He made the one who did not know sin to be sin for us, so that in him we might become his righteousness. That sacrifice proves his love. Why can't you see that?"

Kara's own words echoed off the pines, and echoed off the walls of the Arena back at Ras Telesar. *Love! Can't you see? That's why I'm fighting you!*

This was the moment her failure had reached its peak. But what had come after the failure? What had Master Quinton told her?

If ya ever hope ta lead a real barkhide ta the High One's forgiveness, lass, you'll have ta forgive him first.

How could she forgive what she saw here? A mocktree acolyte–one who desired to be a soulless dragon corruption, and one of those who'd cost her Liam and caused Keir's suffering?

With unconscious motions, she continued circling and fending off the barkhide's blows. The attacks no longer angered her. They were just something the poor man did because a terrible infection had taken hold of him. A distant voice called to her. "Kara! Should we take him for you? Kara!"

She saw Quinton in the Arena, with her clunker blades at his throat–the tunic with the oak symbol, the leather gauntlet with the spike through it. In the Arena, she'd seen only the barkhide Quinton pretended to be, and it had enraged her. But under the trappings of that corruption, she'd been fighting a fellow Keledan.

Wasn't this fight the same, at least in potential? Behind the mutilations, was this man not Aladoth, to be rescued and shown the path to Keledev?

"I see you," she said.

The barkhide stumbled back, breathing hard. "What did you say?"

"I see you as the Maker sees you–as a child he loves and desires to heal." Kara lowered her sword, holding back tears. "And I see those who took Keir and Liam from me in the same way. I forgive them. I forgive you for these attacks."

If nothing else, the man seemed grateful for the rest. His arm, the one with the spike driven through it, hung at his side. He couldn't keep this up much longer. More than that, he seemed to be listening. His resolve to oppose the Rescuer was fading. "You really aren't going to kill me, are you?"

"No." Kara shook her head. "I don't want to. I'm not angry with you anymore. I forgive you, and so will your Creator." She glanced up and spoke the *Liberation* verse in the Elder Tongue, then locked eyes with the Aladoth. "Proclaim the Rescuer. Claim him as your lord instead of that mocktree corruption. Declare that he lives, and you will too."

The man met her gaze for a long time, then looked down at his hands and dropped his sword and whip as if they were poison. He fell to his knees in the fog. "I do. He lives, and I want him as my lord."

Kara's shield faded. She knelt with the man, and together they prayed.

When she opened her eyes, she found Keir kneeling with them, tears streaming down. His hand trembled as he lifted the bear pendant from her tunic.

"Kara."

She nodded, and he let the pendant fall against her. "I could not protect you. Can you forgive me?"

"There's no need. You were never meant to protect me. The Rescuer had me in his hands all along."

Keir let out a sob. "I see that now. And I see him in you." He took her hand in his, and with the other, he took the hand of the man she'd been fighting. He raised it up so that their forearms were pressed together, showing her the same barkhide burn scars in his own skin. "See? I am like him. And like him, I believe."

59

TEEGAN
KELEDEV
PELLION'S FLOW

A MURMUR PASSED ALONG RAS TELESAR'S RAID PARTY as they climbed the goblin tunnel to the surface. The cadet in front of Teegan turned to whisper in her ear. "Dame Silvana says you are to join her at the column's front. Immediately."

With a nod, Teegan began working her way up the line, and soon reached Silvana, two paces from the tunnel's outlet. "You sent for me?"

"Time to put your huntress skills to the test, my girl."

"I left Aethia at the fortress. Master Jairun would not let me bring her."

"Not falconry. Stealth. How close can you sneak to the enemy without alerting them?" She glanced down at Teegan's boots. "Remove those spikes."

Once Teegan was ready, Silvana set off in a crouch and held a hand low near her heels—a command for Teegan to stay close. The guardian ranger moved across the ice flow without a sound. Her feet left no impressions. Teegan could not say the same, although without the spikes, her footprints were light, and she avoided the *crunch* of punching through the packed snow.

Silvana stopped after ten paces and pointed two fingers at her eyes. Then she pointed ahead. A pair of goblins—guards, perhaps, left behind to watch the tunnel outlet. But goblins have notoriously short attention spans, and they were now watching the main force downslope.

The ranger drew her knife, and Teegan did the same. She knew the job that had to be done. They'd need this kill to be silent–no screeching. This was likely why Silvana had not dispatched them with her bow.

The two snuck up behind their quarries, and they slit both goblins' throats in the same moment. No sound escaped either creature beyond a rattling rush of air.

A quick scout of the area showed no other foes. "The party's path is clear now," Silvana said, drawing close to Teegan.

"Yes, but what path, exactly?"

The ranger pointed east and slightly up. There, extending out at a sharp angle over the small army of goblins, trolls, and golmogs, was an ice formation loosely resembling a giant bovine figure. A corner of Teegan's mouth curled upward into a half smile. "The ox Pedrig spoke of."

"A beast that has graced these Celestial Peaks as long as the Order. But I think his time to shed his icy bonds and roam free has finally come. Let's get the others."

The lightraiders made the short climb to the ox's back without incident. Shouts from the rocks far downslope held the goblins' focus and covered the noise of the party's footfalls. Teegan felt a touch of pride. Her tehpa was making good use of the companies.

The ox's back sloped upward toward the moons, blocking the lightraiders' view of the army below, but Teegan knew they were down there.

"Is it time, Avner," Quinton asked.

The headmaster nodded. "Take your posts."

Teegan moved upslope into the rocks behind the ox while every lightraider with a blade lined up along the crease where its back met the slope. Their weapons chipped away at the ice in what seemed a futile effort. But during the climb, Master Jairun had told them they needed only a few fingers of depth. They achieved this quickly.

With this shallow furrow finished, most of the party moved into the rocks with Teegan, leaving only Dag, Quinton, Baldomar, and the headmaster on the ox. Dag and Quinton stood at either end with their axes. Baldomar stood at the center, with his greatsword raised, tip pointed down. Master Jairun stood behind him, a hand on his shoulder.

The headmaster lifted his face skyward, eyes closed. "These are your words, High One. Let your will be done." Then he prayed, and they all joined him.

Kelas osana po lelom krafana.
Thrivam beregana po morgom krafana.
Anah, ke'Rumosh, pal koth oltim mahesoth.
I form the light and create darkness,
I bring prosperity and create disaster;
I, the Lord, do all these things.

Teegan opened her eyes to see the axes and Baldomar's greatsword burning white as if they'd just been pulled from a blazing forge.

"Now," Master Jairun said, and the three men struck the ice as one.

A great rending *crack* shook the mountainside. The guardians and Dag leapt back, and the ox tore free from its bonds. The massive formation slid downslope.

Quinton did not sit idle. He dropped his axes and lit a torch from one of the still white-hot blades. With the flame burning, he twisted his body, ready for a mighty toss. "Say the word, Avner."

"Hold, my friend. Show me your patience."

AARON

"HOLD!" SIRETH SHOUTED.

Aaron doubted the companies could hear him anymore, not with the deep crackling and thundering of the giant ice block tumbling down the flow. It had already crushed many of the creatures. The rest fled before it, heading straight for the watchmen. But the signal still had not come.

"Hold!"

"Are you sure?" Aaron asked.

"Don't question me, lad. Keep those feet still until I say."

A long breath later, he saw it. The torch flew high over the battlefield. No watchman could have missed it.

Sireth lowered his war hammer. "Go!"

Aaron jumped out into the open beside his friend, gratified to see the long line of the companies, and Sireth seemed to put all the voice he had left into the next command, drawing out the cry. "Shields!"

Every man and woman crouched and raised a forearm parallel to the ground. The line lit up with radiant armor in a hundred colors. The dark creatures, blinded and terrified, let out a chorus of earsplitting screeches.

In the next instant, the first of them crashed into the shield line. So much was their speed, and so firm the wall of watchmen, that the first wave of goblins obliterated themselves upon it, bursting into snowy dust. The next sizzled and hissed at their impact and fell dead.

Not until the first troll reached the line, did a single watchman move. Two went down under the force of the iceblade's hit, but the creature took the greater damage. Others fell upon it and finished it off with sword, axe, and hammer. Aaron saw similar engagements all down the line. These were short by necessity. The ox ran close upon the enemy's heels.

Sireth pointed behind him with the hammer. "Into the rocks!"

The wall collapsed downslope into the terrain from which it had sprung, followed closely by the last of the dark creatures and the ox that pursued them. The ice block had broken up in the fall and gave itself completely when it struck the rocks. More creatures died under this final blow. The rest fell into the blades and shields of the waiting companies.

Aaron found himself nose to nose with a disgusting golmog–a rotund, lumbering blob almost twice his height with a wide mouth and horns. He ducked the creature's three-fingered fist while Sireth smashed his hammer into its leg. The golmog buckled and fell.

Aaron finished it off with his axe. Watery gray fluid seeped into the gravel at their feet, sending up a horrible stench. "Disgusting," Aaron said, holding a wrist to his nose. "What are these things made of?"

"Fear and sickness, or so Tiran tells me from his studies, held together with everything unsavory you might find in a Taneletharian cave. Best to stay clear of the remains."

The golmog was the last of the creatures their section encountered. The two climbed up upon a high rock to survey the rest of the line. Sireth's wall had held. Many were raising their blades in victory, armor still shining.

The sight brought joy to Aaron's heart. "For the Rescuer!" he shouted, raising his axe high, and all the companies answered.

"For the Rescuer!"

60

LEE
TANELETHAR
EMEN KAR

"WELL, YOUR FATHER GOT WHAT HE WANTED," LEE said as he and Zel walked up the steps to the ruin.

She gazed up at the high statues guarding the entrance, both Rapha, one holding a breadbasket and the other a pitcher. "How do you mean?"

"The quest for the Rapha Key and Lef Amunrel is no longer in the hands of an Enarian. The first part falls to you and me."

Zel gave him a frown. "My father's words are not mine. Nor are his opinions. To my eyes, Connor"–she glanced down at the journal Lee carried–"*and* his grandfather have proven their worth."

Three long, joined buildings formed the Aropha haven–a large central hall with smaller structures on either side. According to what Lee had read in Faelin's journal, this place served as a resting point for Lisropha warriors and Rapha servants in their journeys across Talania.

"The hilltop temples were centers of worship," he said when Zel asked the difference between Emen Kar and Ras Heval. "And don't be confused by the sanctuary we found in the Fading Mountains. That was built from the remains of Ras Heval after the dragon scourge began." He waved the journal at rows of stone tables and benches rising from the floor–what might have been a dining hall. "Think of this place as a way station."

"Where in this way station might the key be hidden? If Faelin failed to find it, what hope do we have?"

"Ah." Lee raised a finger. "I don't think Faelin came here. He wrote about this place–included a map, even–but only because he'd learned our magician-thief Kaliphan had sold a relic from Emen Kar to a nobleman. Faelin was looking for Kaliphan's final resting place, not some ruin he'd robbed."

"Yet now we think they may be one and the same?"

"That's what the parchment we found at his treasure hold implied."

They started with the item Kaliphan stole. Lee read the journal as they walked, with Zel steering him on occasion to keep him from running into tables or columns. "The thief sold the item as a talisman to ward off goblin looters. Goblins were a new threat in those days–an annoyance for a nobleman with cattle or sheep to protect. But Aropha do not carry talismans, so Faelin believes what Kaliphan stole was actually a decoration."

He looked up from his reading to survey the walls. The Aropha had spared no space. Every surface seemed to be a canvas for works of praise to the Maker.

"Well," Zel said. "That narrows it down. Is there a description?"

"The item was too large to wear and hung over the nobleman's hearth." He showed her the book, tapping the page with his finger. "This drawing, here. A diamond shape formed of water above and fire below."

"You do realize we're looking for an object that is no longer here, right? We're looking for the empty space where it was before Kaliphan stole it."

"Or are we?" Lee closed the book over his finger and lowered a lens to his eye. He quickened his steps. "This way. I think Kaliphan tried to make amends in his final days."

They found the ornament placed among the carved murals

on the north wall of the great hall. The rest of the mural was smooth and seamless–one continuous piece. But Kaliphan had clearly cut his diamond-shaped prize out with a hammer and chisel, then put it back sometime later.

"I think he tried to repair the damage," Lee said, taking a closer look at the grout around the diamond. "That would mean Kaliphan found the noble he'd tricked into buying this piece and bought it back, probably at great risk."

Zel looked from the restored artwork to the rest of the hall, scrunching her brow. "But why?"

"As I said. He wanted to make amends. From his note, we know our thief repented of his ways." Lee stared at the carving, with its flames below and fountain above, then frowned. "But I think we're dealing with something more. I think when he came back here to live, the broken space where he'd cut out this piece became a reminder of his past, and he could no longer bear the shame. That is what drove him to return it. That would mean he walked by this spot often."

He left the restored artwork and walked along the mural.

Zel followed. "You mean Kaliphan made his final home nearby?"

"Correct. Emen Kar is vast. Had he made his residence in one of the other two buildings, he might have lived out his years never looking again upon this mural. But I think he walked the very pavers under our feet daily."

He turned to pass under an open arch, looking up at its rippled stonework border. "I've walked under an arch like this a hundred times or more to enter the kitchens at Ras Telesar."

"The kitchens?" Zel had to double her steps to keep up with him, hurrying between gaping cavities, still blackened from their ancient work. "You think Kaliphan took up residence in one of these giant ovens?"

"Not the ovens." Lee stopped at the far end where he'd found another image of a Rapha servant holding a breadbasket. "The cupboard."

61

CONNOR
SIL SHADATH

THE GHOULS HAD NOT LET UP DURING THE PARTY'S flight south toward Emen Kar. But neither had Kara and Tiran nor the bear who walked with them. Ioanu's claws seemed specially purposed for destroying apparitions. The attacks centered around Keir and the former barkhide, who called himself Peram. It was as if the creatures sensed the frailty of these newly rescued Keledan. But Connor and the others defended them with passion.

The insects bothered Connor most. Bulbous spiders leapt at him from the pine boughs, worse than giant cave spiders because their size made them hard to hit with Revornosh or his crook. Droning horned beetles fluttered at his face. These exploded into burning goo against his Keledan shield and helmet.

They'd finally experienced a stretch of peace, with no attacks for at least a quarter of a league, when Tiran halted his bounding gait and gasped. He pressed a hand to his forehead.

Connor had learned early in their search for Keir that Tiran's old wound flared up when evil approached. "Where?" he asked, placing an arm around his friend to support him.

Tiran aimed his sword at the trees to the southwest. "It's strong. A single presence, I think, but dark. Very dark. A wraith, perhaps–or the dragon. I've not learned enough about this sense to say."

Kara started toward the threat without waiting for Connor or the others, and glanced over her shoulder at Ioanu. "Stay with the new Keledan, Keir and Peram. Keep them safe. We'll handle this."

The bear lowered her snout in something between a nod and a bow to Kara as Connor and Tiran rushed to catch up. Together, the three cadets ran into the next clearing to confront the new enemy.

Connor jogged to a stop, as did the others, confused by what they'd found. There was no wraith, as Tiran suggested. And no dragon. "Shan?"

Lee's brehna stood as if in shock with his stolen orc scimitar held up in a guard position. The approach of the lightraiders stirred him to life. "I killed them," he said in a whisper. "I destroyed them both."

Connor helped him lower the orc weapon. "Killed who?"

"The ghouls. Two of them. They came at me, so I shouted the name of the Rescuer and struck them down. They burst into mist and drifted away."

Connor and Kara exchanged a look. The guardians had taught them that Aladoth did not have the strength to destroy dark creatures on their own. For that, any human needed the aid of the Helper.

"Does that mean . . ." Connor asked, not finishing the question.

"I believed. My brother spoke with me, and I believed."

Connor stood amazed. Three new brehnan for the Keledan. Three lives the Rescuer had entrusted to him and the other cadets to bring safely to the Liberated Land.

"But where *is* your brother?" Ioanu asked, approaching with Keir and Peram. She bore a strange look in her midnight blue eyes. "How did you come to be separated from him? I would not have thought he'd let such a thing happen after years of waiting for your restoration."

"I gave him no choice. I saw other prisoners from that ship of the sky. I wanted to save them too, and once we touched earth and grass again, I ran off to find them before my brother could stop me."

The bear held that odd look in her gaze. "And where are these prisoners now?"

"Gone. I never found them. In my searching, I was accosted by ghouls."

They did not linger for more explanations, but started south once again. Tiran, who'd been helping them hold their course with his compass, now spent more time holding his old rag to his wound.

Connor walked with him. "Talk to me, Brehna."

"The burning will not stop. My head is a flame."

"What do you expect in this forest, filled with so much evil?"

"That was not my experience before. I have other suspicions. One suspicion, I will not speak yet. The other is that this pain is a warning."

"What sort of warning?"

"A warning that the greatest evil we've yet faced is heading our way."

62

LEE
EMEN KAR

"IT'S ONLY A WALL, LEE. ANOTHER MURAL."

The scribe glanced back at Zel with a look that said, *Oh really?* "Did you learn nothing from our time at the underground sanctuary? Aropha minds do not work like our own. What seem to us like puzzles and mysteries were part of their everyday life here on Dastan."

He walked to the corner between the ovens and the wall and reached into a recess. His fingers found a cool metal rod. He grinned. "Watch."

Lee pulled the lever, and the wall sank into the floor as quietly as the slate door they'd encountered at the sanctuary. A steep stone incline lay beyond, carved with waving lines and set with footholds like recessed steps. He tilted his head. "Follow me."

They climbed the incline, and not long after they passed the midpoint, it began to move, reversing its slope. Zel held on to Lee as the rising edge behind them cut off their exit to the kitchen. "What's happening? Is this a trap?"

He laughed. "What use would the Rapha have for a trap? This is a storehouse." The platform eased to a stop with a light *clunk*, revealing another chamber opposite the kitchen. "Ras Telesar has one like this, though we hardly use it at the moment. Master Belen thinks it provides a barrier between the heat of the kitchen and stores that must stay cool and dry." He held his lantern out into the chamber ahead of them. "But for our thief, I think it offered the perfect hideout."

Lee had guessed right. Someone, most likely Kaliphan, had converted the storehouse into a simple home. There were no treasures here, no chests of gold and jewels or fine clothes and pottery. The magician-thief had dug a hearth into the far wall and built a simple bed, chair, and table. That was all.

"He really did give up his former ways for a life of reflection and poverty," Zel said, looking around.

"One man's poverty is another's wealth. According to his note, our thief traded the treasures of this world for those of the next." Lee's gaze settled on the wall above the bed, and he walked over. "Kaliphan vowed to serve the Maker as the Rapha had done." A disc of what looked like pure garnet hung from a carved stone peg by a thick silver chain. On the face of the disc was carved the *perot*, an Aropha letter and the symbol for both bread and life.

Reverently, Lee lifted the artifact down from its resting place and held it out for Zel to see. "This is what inspired him. This artifact became the beacon that led him from an alliance with the first traitor king to a life dedicated to the Maker. *This* is the Rapha Key."

Zel shook her head in disbelief. "We did it. We found the key that opens the lost Bread Gate of Ras Pyras. You hold in your hand a way to sneak into–"

"Shh!" Lee held up his hand. "Can you hear that?"

In the quiet, the tone became clearer, but no louder. It seemed like the ring of a bell far away.

Zel looked down at his hands. "It's coming from the disc. What does that mean?"

"I think it means we'd better get out of here."

CONNOR

CONNOR AND HIS PARTY RACED OUT OF THE WOODS north of the Aropha ruin. He altered course to make for a corner of the structure. “They’ll be in the glade on the south side. That’s the only place with room enough to land *The Starling.*”

They didn’t need to run far. Lee and Zel rushed out from behind the ruin. The scribe held an object high—a disc. Connor recognized it from his patehpa’s journal. They’d found the Rapha Key.

A mix of elation and worry hit him. Either they’d brought the Keledan one step closer to ending dragon rule over Tanelethar, or he was about to continue the Enarian pattern of failure in this quest. His party may have led the enemy straight to an artifact that otherwise had stayed safely hidden for centuries.

Connor waved his arm back and forth, trying to signal Lee to stop and turn around. But the scribe already shared his worried expression and shouted what Connor was thinking.

“The dragon is coming!”

63

"HOW DID HE FIND US?" LEE ASKED WHEN THE TWO groups met.

Connor turned and set his gaze on the sky to their north. "I don't know, but Tiran can sense him coming."

"As can this." Lee showed him the disc. "Do you hear its ring?"

He did. And the tone seemed to be deepening. "I think our time grows short."

"I hear it too," Kara said. "You and Lee must take the group overland to the hollow tree that brought Tiran and me into Tanelethar. Tiran and his compass can help you find it. Zel and I will use *The Starling* to gain the dragon's attention and draw him away."

Zel spun to face her. "I'm sorry. Zel and you will do what?"

"You heard me. It's the only way to save the larger portion of our party and get the artifact home to Keledev."

"It won't work." The argument came from Ioanu. The bear inclined her head, calling their small group away from the others. "The dragon wants Kara. Though my heart wishes it were not so, she is right to take *The Starling* and risk the dragon to save the others. But there is one more who must join her."

"You mean Keir," Kara said. "The two queensbloods must

draw the dragon away together."

"Not Keir." The bear shifted her gaze to Connor. "Him. Keir was a lure for you—or perhaps you both. The dragon wants you and Connor, and he'll try to take you alive, which gives you a fighting chance."

Connor scrunched his brow. "Why would Valshadox want me?"

"We've no time for explanations. Trust me." The bear lifted her snout toward Zel. "Get your flying ship ready to sail."

A sickening hollow opened in Connor's gut. He hadn't come this far to put Kara in danger again. But his spirit overcame that fear, and he saw the same reaction in her.

Kara met his gaze and nodded. "This is the right path." She raised her voice to the others. "Zel, Connor, and I will distract the dragon in *The Starling*. The rest of you make for the hollow tree on foot."

As she spoke, Connor shot Lee a glance with one additional order, and the scribe answered with a nod of understanding, tucking the disc under his cloak. He would protect that hope at all costs.

The Starling waited in the glade. Once they'd climbed aboard, it took Zel only the pull of a rope and the flick of a lever to make her ready to sail. The stormrider held up a pouch and two vials. "This is the last of my father's fuel. We'll escape the dragon or we won't. Either way, this will be *The Starling*'s last flight for this mission. Say when."

"When!"

She dumped the fuel into the lamps and added, "Or this may be her last flight ever."

As *The Starling* rose above the rounded rooftops of Emen Kar, dragon fire flared from the dark mass of the trees to their north. "Find the wind, Zel," Connor said. "He's coming!"

Kara looked over her shoulder. "I feel him searching with his mind. He's trying to find me—trying to decide which group to follow." Before Connor could tell her to hold the dragon's mind at bay with *The Sleeper's Hope,* she drew in a sharp breath and dropped to a knee. "That's it. He knows. He knows we're both here."

In the distance, the dragon turned, making a straight line for them.

"Zel!" Connor shouted, eyes locked on the dragon.

"Working on it! Do you think I can outclimb one of Heleyor's wyrms?"

"How should I know?"

Kara regained her feet. "I hope you two aren't planning to argue like this until he captures us." She reached for the crossbow hanging from Zel's belt. "Do you mind?"

"Not at all."

Kara set herself up with a knee on the stern bench and the crossbow braced on the rail. Connor stood beside her. "Don't shoot until you know the bolts will reach him."

She elbowed him in the chest. "Thanks. I think I know what I'm doing. Concern yourself with this mad plan. What are we to do? Crash into the hills and make a run for it? Fly over the Celestial Peaks, days to the south?"

"You'll see. For now, I'll just say I'm glad we found you."

She reached over and squeezed his hand. "As am I. Let's hope we live long enough to share our full tales with each other and the guardians."

In the next moment, Zel cried out, holding her head in both hands. "The dragon is calling to me. He says you led me here to die. He asks what sort of friend would do that."

"Mind speech," Connor said. "Dragon lies. They're subtle. He's probing. He wants to know how we came into Tanelethar. Block him out. Sing *The Sleeper's Hope* in your head. Do you know it?"

Zel nodded, still wincing. "I'll try."

Connor moved to the bow, searching the night ahead. *Please, Rescuer. You know our needs before we ask. Provide us an escape.*

Lightning on the horizon told him his prayer had been

answered. "We have a storm cloud dead head."

"Wonderful." Zel's flat tone showed no gratefulness. "How far?"

"Pretty far."

"Then it may do us little good."

Connor saw what she meant. The storm and the horizon slowly rose in his view. *The Starling* was losing height, and there was no more fuel for the lamps–nothing to lift them up again.

"We're falling into the slower wind," Zel said. "He's gaining."

As Connor returned to the stern, he saw Kara let loose her first bolt. The dragon canted his wings and dodged. Connor put a hand on her shoulder. "Well done."

She frowned. "Don't celebrate yet. It only means he's close enough to engage."

As if he'd heard her, Valshadox unleashed a stream of flame. It fell short, but Connor got the feeling that was by design.

The dragon's voice in his head confirmed this suspicion a moment later. *We can be allies, you and I. You will be rich beyond your every dream. I'll give your spirit and body the strength to live for a dozen generations.*

Connor lifted his chin in defiance. *All the treasures I need, I already have. And my master has gifted me with eternal life. He prepared a table for me. I will dwell in his house forever. Your offer is nothing in comparison.*

The next stream of fire came much closer, blackening the starboard rail.

"Connor!" Zel shouted.

"I think I made him angry."

"Then perhaps you shouldn't do that."

Kara loosed another bolt, forcing the dragon to dodge.

Connor checked the bow. The storm was close. But the dragon was closer. "Zel, we need your tehpa's blaze–the very-bad-day-device."

"That's only for dire circumstances."

"Is this not dire enough?"

The dragon's fire came at them again. They all ducked the

attack, but one of the ropes caught flame. Zel patted the fire out with gloved hands. "Do it, Connor!"

"How does it work?"

"Just light the wick and pray!"

The dragon roared. The thunder ahead grew louder. Kara kept shooting as Connor crouched to open the stern hatch. She glanced down and shouted over the noise. "What are you doing?"

"I don't know! But I think you should hang on!" With that, he struck a flint and steel over the wick. It burned like no wick he'd ever seen, sputtering and sparking.

As he stared, Zel kicked the hatch closed. "Get away from the–"

She didn't get to finish. Flames shot behind them, throwing them against the stern. Up above, the envelopes rippled and snapped as if they might tear away from their trusses.

Connor crawled his way forward with a pouch of shairosite clutched in his fist, shouting over the wind rush, "*Howda'anu koth kolama vadsepah mi kerator ma aneth ava'od, ma aneth vi zamethod hal serend. Rumosh*, we put ourselves in your hands!"

He dumped the silver powder into the lamps.

Dark blue smoke spiraled around them until the whole ship was covered in its shroud. The dragon's deep, angry cry echoed in his mind and on the wind. "Nooooo!"

Lightning flashed in every color.

Sea spray broke over the bow.

The three Keledan fell again to the floor as the runners struck land, and a mix of sand and smoke flew up behind them.

The Starling came to rest, and they all groaned. Zel pulled herself up by the rail. Connor and Kara followed a moment later. Connor rubbed the back of his neck. "Where are we?"

The stormrider wore an odd smile on her lips, staring out along a stretch of moonlit beach. Following her gaze, Connor saw a barefoot child running at full speed to meet them. Bewildered parents chased after him. The couple looked as if they'd been out for a night stroll–one which had taken a very unexpected turn.

Zel gave them a tentative wave. “I’d say we’re home.”

64

LEE
TANELETHAR
DARKLING SHADE

WITH IOANU'S GUIDANCE, THE PARTY HAD SKIRTED the Bezik Hills, heading west along the southern edge of Sil Shadath and entered Darkling Shade. "This was once part of Sil Shadath," she told Lee, who walked with her at the head of their loose column. "It was the larger part, with beautiful hills covered in black pine and bristlecone. Many bears roamed here. But in the early days of the scourge, the ore creatures pillaged the shade's wood to build walled towns for the dragons' favored nobles. Only a narrow swath remains."

"But there is a hollow tree here," Lee said.

The bear nodded. "One our clan has known of for some time. I will recognize it by the description of sight and scent my mother handed down to me."

In a quiet counsel with Lee and Tiran after their first flight from Emen Kar, Ioanu had made it clear she would not return to the Tagamoor. "I will not move so much as one paw in that direction," she'd said. "I pledged to keep the bear clans hiding there safe, and I will do so."

The party had journeyed without rest into daylight and on to dusk, until they'd passed beyond all trace of the gray-green mists and the reach of Sil Shadath. They'd encountered little resistance–

some goblins and two wanderers. In each skirmish, Shan hung back, despite his claim of vanquishing two ghouls on his solo venture to find the other prisoners.

During the long march, Lee had also noticed Tiran and the bear keeping a close eye on his brother. Neither would say why, though it might have been Shan's frequent questions about the dragon. "Sil Shadath belongs to Valshadox," he'd say. "Are we not in danger of his mind, here?" Or, "I fear the dragon, Brother. I can't go back. How can you be certain we'll escape him?"

Each time, Lee assured him that dragons were not omniscient, even in their own domain. "Without a report from one of his creatures, he cannot find us, and we are keeping out of sight. As an added measure, Tiran and I are singing the song of the sleeper in our heads at all times. The ancient melody from the days of the Maker's pure creation keeps the dragon's mind at bay."

These assurances didn't help. Shan looked over his shoulder at every turn. He was so distracted that twice, Lee caught him falling behind. "You must stay with the party, Brother. If you are separated, you may be caught and expose us all. And if I fail to bring you home now, I might never forgive myself."

Lee needed to get Shan to the hollow tree–to the safety of Keledev–then all would be well.

By nightfall, they still had a half-day's journey before them, if Ioanu was right. The bear advised the cadets to make camp for the night. Lee took the first watch, sitting up with Shan. He tried to talk of their parents, of the celebration that waited for them.

"Don't speak of it yet, Brother," Shan said, quieting him. "Not until we're free of this place. Instead, teach me *The Sleeper's Hope*. I'm not sure I remember all the words."

They sang softly together while the fire dimmed. Lee could not remember a moment in the last several years when he'd been more content.

But his contentment did not last.

That night, during the second watch, a commotion roused him

from sleep. Lee shook off his exhaustion to find Shan facing down both Tiran and the bear. Tiran's sword was out. Shan's scimitar too. Ioanu's dark blue armor glowed.

"Tiran, what are you doing?"

Ioanu glanced Lee's way. "Stay back. Your brother is not well."

Shan laughed. "Not well? Is that what you call it? Is being free of delusion some kind of disease?"

Contrary to the bear's warning, Lee approached, hand out. "Shan, calm down. The fear of the dragon is troubling you. But we can help."

"He's not afraid," Tiran said, "not in that way. And your brehna is not what he claims. I'm sorry. But he's not Keledan."

The truth of Shan's lie stabbed into Lee like a dagger to the chest. He'd suspected it–wondered if Shan was hanging on to Tanelethar in some way. "Listen to us, Brother. You are the one caught in a delusion. Let us wake you from the nightmare. Let us bring you home."

"Nightmare? Oh, Trang. Poor deceived Trang. I am far from any nightmare. I have found my dream." With this, Shan's eyes took on a red hue. He slipped his left hand out from a pocket in his dirty prisoner's trousers. He wore three wide bands covered in runes on his thumb, middle, and ring finger–one pyranium with a ruby, one gold and silver with black gems, and one pure jade in the shape of a curled dragon. With a flick of his fingers, a ball of red flame appeared in his palm.

"Sorcerer!" Lee shouted. "Shan, no!"

Before they could stop him, Shan threw the fireball high above the trees, where it burst in a rippling pulse of red light. "If Lord Valshadox did not see that, his creatures will. They will come, and so will he." Another fireball appeared in his hand. "Stay where you are. You are my captives. My reward will be great."

Ioanu growled. "Like every sorcerer, you overestimate your power."

The look Lee and Tiran exchanged said everything. Sorrow

tore at their hearts, but they would do what was necessary. Lee drew his sikaria.

The lightraiders advanced, and Shan cast his fireball, but it shrank to nothing on their shields, extinguished. He cast two more with the same result, and then retreated, eyes shifting between opponents. They spread to envelop him.

"Calm yourself," Tiran said. "What we do now, we do in love. We need to bind you, but whether we knock you senseless is your choice."

Shan shook his head, still retreating. "You won't take me. I belong to him." He dropped the scimitar and threw both arms wide. A red flash lit the forest, forcing the lightraiders and the bear to shield their eyes. When it faded, he was gone.

"A portal?" Lee asked

Ioanu sniffed the air. "A distraction. He's running, and I do not think it wise to pursue him. He wants to lure us back to the dragon's domain." She turned to Lee. "Shan is your brother. What say you?"

"We run." Lee sheathed his knives, doing his best to stop the tremor in his voice. "My brother is gone. This is now a foot race—Shan to the dragon, and us to the tree. For the sake of Keir and Peram, the new Keledan, we cannot lose."

Within moments, the whole party was up and tearing at full speed through the night.

65

CONNOR
KELEDEV
RAS TELESAR

"WHERE ARE THEY?" KARA ASKED, LOOKING TOWARD Watchman's Gate from her favorite spot on the fourth rampart. "They should have come through by now."

Connor sat on the battlements beside her, feet hanging over the edge. "Have patience. They had far to travel, and they did not have the advantage Zel gave us."

The Starling rested on the glade outside the academy gates, where Zel was busy preparing it for the flight to the capital. They'd landed near Harbor Joy, not far from the place where the ship had first been pulled into the Storm Mists.

Connor had wanted to ride on horseback for Ras Telesar, noting he'd never been happier to have his feet on the ground. But Zel insisted the town would have all she needed to make her ship airworthy enough to reach Ras Telesar, where she could spend more time on her repairs. The two had argued until Kara added her vote on Zel's side. She wanted to be at the academy when her brehna arrived.

Aaron Ilmari, a young watchman who'd fought beside Teegan's tehpa, aided Zel in her preparations down on the glade. Connor tapped Kara's leg and motioned toward them with his elbow. "Look. The watchman follows Zel's every move, and I don't think his jaw has stopped moving in half a tick or more. He must be quite interested in the airship."

"Or in Zel," Kara said with a hint of a smile.

Connor watched them for a while longer. "Perhaps it's a little of both."

Dozens of men milled about in the lower courtyard, some hobbling on crutches or with bandages wrapping their heads. Dozens more were lying in Ras Telesar's long infirmary. Kara and Connor had learned of the Battle of Pellion's Flow from Teegan and Dag. The watchmen, led by Teegan's tehpa and aided by the Rescuer, the lightraiders, and a falling ox-shaped block of ice, had claimed their first victory.

Kara kept her gaze on the foothills to the south. "I heard Teegan telling you they discovered a tunnel in the goblin den, one which may shed light on how they breached the barrier. To my ear, that's excellent news."

"Then you didn't hear all of it. The quaking caused by the falling ice ox collapsed the den. With the thin air and the perils of the ice flow, it may take the miners months–perhaps a year–to uncover that tunnel."

They fell into silence until Kara grabbed his arm. "Connor, look!"

The fireglass at Watchman's Gate flashed once, then twice. The cadets manning the academy's glass waited for a time, and then answered with two flashes of their own.

"Two flashes," Kara said. "One for the lightraiders and one for the Keledan who've come through the portal with them." She wrapped Connor in a hug. "Keir."

KARA

WHILE THOSE AT THE ACADEMY WAITED FOR THE lightraiders who'd returned on foot to make the journey from the

Passage Lakes, Headmaster Jairun sent word for Kara to visit him at his ninth-level chambers. His message said to come when she was fully rested. She was not, but she welcomed anything that might occupy her mind.

"Enter," Master Jairun said when she knocked.

As soon as he saw her face, he smiled. "My girl. It makes my heart glad to see you home."

"Keir is coming. I can hardly think of anything else. We have so much to talk about. I . . . I never told him about Liam."

"There'll be plenty of time for that–sharing joy and grief. For now, set that burden down at the Rescuer's feet. You and I have academy business to discuss."

Business?

The spheres.

Before crossing the barrier to save her brehna, Kara had failed two of the Five Quests, with a third failure almost certain. And now she was truly out of time. The annual ceremony was too close upon them.

"Tinker, Vanguard, Navigator." Master Jairun laid a ringlet to match each sphere he mentioned on the desk before him–a blend of bronze, copper, and steel for the Tinkers' Sphere, the marbled black-and-white telesite ringlet for the Sphere of the Vanguard, and a swirled band of blue-and-silver lapis and gold pyrite for the Navigators' Sphere.

Kara lowered her gaze. "These are the quests I failed to complete."

The headmaster wrinkled his brow. "No, child. These are the quests you *did* complete. You finished them on your mission to Tanelethar."

Quinton and Belen entered the headmaster's chamber behind her. They each gave her an encouraging smile.

Belen lifted the metal ringlet of the Tinkers' Sphere from the desk. "The reports we guardians received from your fellow cadets, and even the bear who brought you home, were thorough.

In Tagamar, in the heat of a mission, you forged new blades for your whirlknives. I hear they served you well in battle." He held the ringlet out for her to take. "Congratulations. Your dreaded Tinker's Quest is over, and you've passed."

Once Kara had added the narrow metal band to the other two stacked on her finger, Master Jairun lifted the lapis ringlet. "In Grenton and Sil Shadath, and at Emen Kar, we're told you led your party well."

"I had help," she said.

"And you used that help with wisdom." He placed the ringlet in her hand. "You proved your leadership while a dragon rushed in to attack your party–when it counted most. Your Navigator's Quest is done."

Belen moved aside to give Quinton room, and the swordmaster lifted the telesite ringlet. "Ta hear Ioanu tell it, ya faced a real challenge I could only mimic in the Arena. An' from the bear's tale, ya faced it with love and courage." He set the ringlet in her open palm. "The Vanguard is honored ta declare you've passed our quest."

While Kara stacked the last two bands on a second finger, next to the one with the first three, Quinton and Belen retreated to the corner of the chamber. Master Jairun stood and cleared his throat. "Kara Orso. As headmaster of this Lightraider Academy and head of the Order, I'm pleased to inform you that you've passed all the quests required of a cadet scout. You may now enter the spheres with your class."

EPILOGUE

CONNOR

THE MARCH TO THE VALLEY OF SPHERES WAS bittersweet.

Lee said little.

The returning lightraiders had brought shock and sorrow with them—news that Shan had not only rejected the Rescuer again, but that he'd let the dragon make him a sorcerer. On the journey from the lakes, the party determined it was Shan who'd sent word to the dragon that they were heading for Emen Kar instead of the trap at the twisted tower. His solo venture to seek other prisoners had been a lie. Those other prisoners had never existed.

What comfort could Connor offer his friend? Lee had lost Shan all over again. And this time, any hope of saving him seemed lost.

When they were out of Lee's earshot, Kara leaned close to Connor. "Can one born in Keledev, who's given himself over to become a dragon's sorcerer, be saved?"

"It seems a hard thing," he replied. "But if I've learned anything since coming to Ras Telesar, it's that nothing is beyond the Rescuer's power."

Ioanu, who padded along beside Kara, grunted. "Hard, indeed." She added nothing else but seemed to focus on her breathing. Without the advantage of the moor vapors, Ioanu's every step had been labored these last few days.

Kara laid a hand in the deep fur of her neck. "How are you adjusting to Ras Telesar, good friend?"

"The food is excellent," the bear said between breaths, "especially the brambleberries. And I feel the Helper's presence all around me. But why must there be so many stairways?"

Connor smiled to himself, but did not let her see. "Time is all you need. Your muscles will strengthen, and we'll be glad to have you with us in our next battle with the dragons and their creatures." He hoped that would not come any time soon.

The party—all the guardians and advancing cadets with their guests—arrived at the ridge above the valley within a tick of the appointed time. The light of the setting sun would soon catch in a glass built into a notch in the ridgetop and shine a narrow ray down upon the platform of the spheres.

As their column descended from the pass, Connor marveled at the work of the early tinkers. "The ceremony platform is more ornate than I imagined," he told Kara. "More colorful."

"Have you never seen it before?"

"Initiates and cadet stalwarts, those who haven't entered the spheres, are not permitted here, even after passing the Five Quests."

The early tinkers of the Order had built rotating concentric rings on supports extending from the steep valley wall, so that they seemed almost to hover over the deep mountain valley. At the center was a collector much like the fireglasses on the watch towers. And on the five outer rings were globes made of agate, telesite, talanium, lapis, and the tinkers' blended metals, sculpted with figures representing the five Lightraider Spheres.

"How does it work?" Kara asked.

"Master Belen says the faceted glass at the center collects heat from the sunray passing through the lens in the ridge. The heat causes the rings with the globes to turn." Connor lowered his voice to be sure the guardian would not hear. "He said a lot more, but I didn't understand a word of it."

Master Jairun bid the party stand on a broad ledge cut into

the ridge and raised his staff for quiet. "The lens will catch the sun soon, as it does on this day at this hour each year, so I'll be brief. On this day, the Order's newest cadet scouts enter a lightraider sphere–the navigators, tinkers, rangers, comforters, or the Vanguard. This was our tradition before the disbandment. And we renew that tradition today."

He waved his staff at the guardians of the light, and they crossed a short bridge to the rings, each walking to one of the sculpted globes. While they took their positions, Master Jairun continued. "Make no mistake, this is a contraption and a ceremony of the Order's making. We lean on the Helper to choose the spheres for our cadets, but our lord is not bound by our timing or traditions. And our cadets are not bound here today. A change of spheres is rare, but not unheard of. That is between the Rescuer and his servants."

After waiting for the murmur of agreement to subside, the headmaster directed his staff at Connor. "Mister Enarian, please come forward."

As Connor approached, the sun hit the lens in the ridge. A beam of light shined down on the collector in the center circle, lighting it like a star. The five rings began to turn. They moved at different rates, so that the passage of the sculpted globes became a gauntlet.

"You may notice, my boy," Master Jairun said, loud enough for the whole party to hear, "that no guardian stands by the globe representing the navigators. That place belonged to your grandfather. The navigators are known for their discernment. They are trailblazers, helmsmen, and raidleaders. They hear the whisper of the Helper and choose the path. Since you first joined this class, that has been your gift. Spheres are by no means hereditary, but you are–like my dear friend Faelin–a Navigator."

Connor gave him a solemn nod and turned to make his way through the gauntlet to the sculpted lapis globe on the navigators' ring. But Master Jairun used his staff to block his path. "Not yet, Mister Enarian. You have work to do. By our traditions, the navigators listen to the Helper and choose the spheres in this ceremony. I made the first choice, but now the Order has a navigator once again. You must take over."

Connor swallowed. Master Jairun had given him no warning that he'd be choosing the spheres for his class. What if he chose wrong? What if he couldn't discern the voice of the Helper?

The headmaster offered no advice, but simply walked away, straight through the gauntlet to the globe representing the Sphere of Comforters. When Connor remained silent, staring after him, he scrunched his bushy eyebrows and mouthed, *Get on with it.*

"Right. Uh . . ."

Three of the choices were easy, and the Helper confirmed them in Connor's heart. He called Dag first, and sent him to the Vanguard's telesite globe, where Quinton welcomed him. The miner and the swordmaster bumped chests and embraced.

He called Teegan next. She was a ranger through and through–a knight of his creatures. When Connor made this declaration, she called Aethia to her arm and joined Silvana next to the sculpted globe of green agate.

Lee's place also, was no question in Connor's mind or anyone else's. "My friend," Connor said. "You belong in the Sphere of Comforters as a renewer. I only wish the rest of us could offer you comfort now. Hard as it is to bear, I expect your present suffering is preparing you to encourage many brehnan and shessan–brothers and sisters–in the hard days ahead."

Connor's last two choices were the hardest, and though he knew his time was limited before the light passed from the collector, he took a moment to silently pray and ask for guidance. When he opened his eyes again, he called Tiran forward.

"Tiran Yar, when you came here, you desired to walk with the Vanguard. Yet we know from experience that the bravado in you led only to pain. After your trial in the Dragon Lands, you decided to become a cleric of the comforters and never cross into Tanelethar again. The Rescuer had different plans. With his help, you designed tools that aided our work fighting the terrible creatures of Sil Shadath."

Connor glanced toward Sireth, who wore a beautiful pendant depicting a woman holding twins–the one Tiran had fashioned for him. "I see the spark of creation and the gift of knowledge in you. The same creative spark guides your sword in every duel on the lists, and knowledge of weapons and their use brings you much success in a fight. But these serve you more in the blacksmith's fire and at the crafter's bench. You, Brehna, are a Tinker."

Tiran did not argue, as Connor expected he might. Instead, he chuckled to himself and nodded, and walked the gauntlet to take his place beside Master Belen and the globe made from many metals.

Connor looked last to Kara, who stood with Ioanu, wringing her hands. He'd thought the choice would be difficult, but her sphere came to him even before he began to consider the options. He motioned for her to step forward.

"Kara Orso–the first Aladoth in two generations to accept the Rescuer's gift–I know where you are bound."

Facing him, and with her back to the others, she raised an eyebrow. Her message to Connor was clear. *Get this right, or you'll hear about it later, and you'll hear about it a lot.*

He cringed. "I know you desire to join the rangers as a knight of his creatures. Your skill with the wolf pup and the way Crumpet is drawn to you in the Forest of Believing tell me you'd do well in that sphere. But with the wolf pup, you were also a comforter, and in Tanelethar I saw you leap into battle with the faith of the Vanguard. So where do you belong?"

He turned to face the rotating platform with her, so that their gazes met each of their friends in turn–Dag next to Quinton and the globe representing the Vanguard, Lee with Master Jairun and the Sphere of Comforters, Teegan with Silvana joining the rangers, and Tiran with Belen, now among the Tinkers. Kara might succeed serving with any of them. But Connor knew there was only one sphere in which she'd thrive.

"On this choice, I hear the Helper's voice as clear as my own. Through Gloamwood, the Tagamoor, and Sil Shadath, you led the way to Keir's rescue. At the ruin of Emen Kar, you chose to sacrifice yourself for the party. You steered the course that saved us all from the dragon's fury, and because of you, your brehna Keir and Peram–a man most of us would have left forever to the barkhides–are safe in the Liberated Land."

Connor took her hand, and she whispered, "What are you doing?"

He whispered back without moving his lips. "Just wait."

He led her across the bridge to the rings, and they passed through the gauntlet to the lapis globe, where he turned so that they stood facing the others. "You and I are of the same sphere." Connor lifted her hand and raised his voice. "We are navigators."

ONCE THE SPHERES HAD STOPPED TURNING, THE PARTY made the short journey over the pass to the academy. The guardians and the younger cadet stalwarts celebrated with the now official cadet scouts and their guests in the Hall of Manna, enjoying Glimwick's cheeses, shortbreads, and brambleberry cider.

Connor heard little from Kara during the return, and she sat apart from him with only Ioanu as company. Connor brought her a mug of hot cider and sat with them. "Are you angry with me?"

She shook her head, raising the mug to her lips. "Stunned is more the word."

"No more than I."

Ioanu grunted. "I do not know why. Discernment is your gift from the Helper, but leadership is in your blood. And that applies to you both."

"It does?" Connor narrowed his eyes at the bear. "I think it's high time you tell us what you promised to share when we left Emen Kar. How did you know the dragon would follow Kara and I when we went with Zel in *The Starling*?"

"A better question," the bear said, dipping her snout in a bowl of fresh brambleberries, "is how did *you* not know?" She swallowed a mouthful before continuing. "How is it possible that humans do not know the scent of their own families?"

"You mean our ancestry?" Kara asked.

"Whatever you choose to call it. You are queensblood, of House Arkelon." Ioanu turned her snout toward Connor. "His blood is also of the north. He is one of the Leanders."

House Leander. Ancient kings of the far north and King's Cradle. The first to capitulate–second house of the traitor-kings.

Connor considered insisting he was an Enarian–shepherd folk. But in the short time he'd known her, he'd learned there was no arguing with the bear. Instead, he posed another question. "Why would our blood interest the dragons?"

"Why would it not? Many here in Keledev, I'm sure, hold dear the stories of the greatness of House Leander before its fall and remember the sacrifice of House Arkelon with fondness. A joined pair from those noble families might stabilize Keledev after an invasion."

"Joined pair." Kara put down her mug. "Are you saying the dragons want me to marry Connor?"

"Oh yes. And after they crush the Liberated Land, they'll want you to rule what remains as king and queen."

A long and uncomfortable silence followed, until Connor forced a laugh and stabbed a fork into a hunk of cheese. "Then it's a good thing no dragon will ever cross these peaks."

VALSHADOX
TANELETHAR
SIL SHADATH

THE SIX EYES GLARING AT VALSHADOX THROUGH THE transmitter's diamond window showed pure malice. Pain wracked his mind.

"I do not tolerate failure. You know this."

"Yes, my lord. I know. I am sorry."

The pain lessened. "You will have another chance. I'll see to it. Now tell me of my Aladoth army."

"The prisoners are recaptured. Their conditioning continues, as well as the culling. They will be as a plague upon the Keledan, destroying them in their homes and streets without a thought. But they will need a general, and I desire vengeance. I will go if you show me how to cross into Keledev."

A surge of new pain told Valshadox he was not worthy to lead the army he himself had built.

"You will not cross the barrier. Not yet. That honor, raised on a standard of blood and brimstone, belongs to another."

The image in the window wavered. Behind the six eyes, a pack of forest goblins pulled a cart along a dirt road. Though it was covered by a canvas tarp, Valshadox recognized the hexagonal shape of the large pyranium chest he'd seen the orcs pull from the fire of Ras Pyras several nights before.

The image of the goblins faded, leaving only the eyes of Heleyor. "The shaadsuth is moving south. Soon my creatures will lay it in the breech beneath the mountains. And once the life inside springs forth, my army will be unstoppable."

END

APPENDIX

NAMES

INDIVIDUALS AND FAMILIES

Advor (ĂD-vohr)
Aethia (Ā-thē-ə)
Arkelon (AHRK-ĕ-lahn)
Baldomar (BAHL-dō-mahr)
Belen (BĀ-lĕn)
Bordu (BOHR-dū)
Boreas (BOHR-ē-əs)
Enarian (En-ĀR-ē-ən)
Fulcor (FULL-kohr)
Ilmari (Il-MAHR-ē)
Ingaru (Ēn-GAHR-ū)
Ioanu (Eye-Ō-ə-nū)
Jairun (JEYE-rūn)
Kaivos (KEYE-vahs)
Leander (Lē-AN-dĕr)
Orso (OHR-sō)
Quinton (KWIN-tən)
Rumosh (RŪ-mŏsh) [Exalted One]
Silvana (Sil-VAH-nə)
Suvor (SŪ-vohr)
Yar (Yahr)

LOCATIONS

KELEDEV (KĔ-LĔ-DĔV)

Argallan's Maze – A series of deep gravelly ravines and boulder fields carved by winter ice and spring runoff southeast of the academy. The maze is an excellent place to test a cadet's navigation skills. Of course, there's always the chance of cadets getting lost and dying of starvation before they find their way out. After all, most lightraiders believe that's how Argallan himself vanished.

The Celestial Peaks – A barrier formed by a massive mountain range. Three days after a horde of dragons spent all their fire to vanquish him, the Rescuer returned, raising these impossibly high peaks. Together with the Storm Mists, the Celestial Peaks protect the peninsula of Keledev, the Liberated Land, so that the Rescuer's followers will never be subject to the dragon's wrath again.

The Clefts of Semajin – A network of clefts northeast of the academy. The colossal main fissure of these clefts on the upper slopes of the Celestial Peaks looks narrow because of its great height, but its base is far wider than the whole of Lightraider Academy. The interior shadow of this fissure hides a network of smaller clefts and caves. It is in the highest of these caves, in windswept caverns open to the interior of the clefts, that pale blue snowflowers grow—a powerful medicinal gift from the Rescuer. Some say that ancient ice-breathing *lashoroth* (paradragons) guard these flowers.

Dayspring Highlands – The high terrain from the foothills at the southern base of the Celestial Peaks stretching south to the rolling hills and dells on the northern border of the Central Plain. Dayspring Forest covers the northern half of the Dayspring Highlands.

"The five vales" – A colloquial term for the valley towns in the southern portion of the Dayspring Highlands. Spread among the grassy hills north of the Central Plain, the five vales are shepherding and farming villages. Pleasanton is the most populous town in the vales, and the region's center of trade, but it is by no means the largest in size in terms of land.

Harbor Joy – A coastal town on the northeast coast of Keledev. Harbor Joy spreads along a broad harbor protected by a narrow chain of islands and sandbars. It is not densely populated, but it is the main coastal Keledan town on the Gulf of Vows.

Lin Kelan (Lin KĔ-lən) – A coastal town on the northwest coast of Keledev. Resting at the mouth of the Ruames River, Lin Kelan is the primary coastal Keledan town on the Gulf of Stars. The fishing folk of Lin Kelan are known to rub red paste in their hair to keep the water from soaking their heads when swimming or diving in their daily work. In the Elder Tongue, Lin Kelan means Candle Sound. The town draws its name from sea candles—saltwater plants that shine with their own light. The Gulf of Stars is filled with huge sea candles, but the smaller plants dotting the protected sound of Lin Kelan glow brighter.

Orvyn's Vow (OHR-vin) – The easternmost outpost in Keledev's northern foothills. Orvyn's Vow and its fjord towers guard the eastern slopes of the Celestial Peaks where the mountain runoff enters the Gulf of Vows. A series of structures joined by wood, stone, steel, and talanium roads, bridges, lifts, and ferries, Orvyn's Vow is by far the largest of the highland outposts.

Pellion's Flow – Broad "rivers" of solid ice broken by small ridges and rock islands on the upper slopes of the Celestial Peaks. The flow sits well north of the academy, but not so far north as the Clefts of Semajin.

Pleasanton – The largest town in the five vales, positioned on the Anamturas River in the southern portion of the Dayspring Highlands. Pleasanton's water clock—powered by a large wheel that dips into the Anamturas—may not impress city dwellers from the capital at Sky Harbor, but for the shepherds and farmers in the five vales it is a sight worth seeing.

Ras Telesar (Rahss Tĕl-ĕ-SAHR) – The former Aropha worship and administration center that is now the jumbled fortress of Lightraider Academy. Translated as The Hill of the Fountain. This ancient structure was much transformed by the rising of the Celestial Peaks. Once it was a hilltop temple with four concentric walls, many towers, and a fountain chapel as its central jewel. During the rising of the peaks, those walls and towers shifted and jumbled to become the stepped, labyrinthian ramparts and passages of Lightraider Academy. Only the Rescuer could have taken them apart and put them back together again in this way as a new creation with new purpose. The original fountain chapel Nevethav still stands on an outcropping that forms the fifth level of the academy fortress.

Ravencrest – The second outpost from the east in Keledev's northern foothills. Connecting barracks on both sides of the Anamturas, the Black Feather outpost inn bridges a waterfall that pours down into Dayspring Forest. Thanks to its position as the closest outpost to Ras Telesar, Ravencrest serves as an important link between the academy and the rest of Keledev.

The Second Hall of the Assembly – The seat of government in Keledev's capital of Sky Harbor. This circular building with its great blue dome and high stained glass windows graces Sky Harbor's waterfront plaza. It is interesting to note that the first government hall built in the early days of Keledev, much smaller and made of timber and wattle, was also called the Second Hall.

Sky Harbor – The capital of Keledev. The Keledan built Sky Harbor at the mouth of the Anamturas where the river empties into Val Ratavel, the Sea of Goodness. The tranquil but busy harbor is sheltered by a crescent ridge extending into the sea from the White Ridge Mountains.

Stonyvale – One of the five vales. Stonyvale is a small shepherding town on the southern edge of Dayspring Forest between Pleasanton and Harbor Joy.

Thousand Falls – The westernmost outpost in Keledev's northern foothills. Perched on the sheer western cliffs of the Celestial Peaks, Thousand Falls houses its company of watchmen in long timber barracks. These are joined by wooden walkways with a central platform overlooking the Gulf of Stars. New recruits often think the outpost's name comes from the many cliff waterfalls visible from the platform, all pouring into the wind to feed the Storm Mists. They are wrong.

The Vales of the Passage Lakes – Long mountain valleys of portal lakes east and west of the academy. There are seven passage lakes in all, divided between the Eastern Vale and the Western Vale. These are the primary means by which the Rescuer chooses to send his lightraiders on missions through the barrier and into Tanelethar. The Vales of the Passage Lakes should not be confused with the five vales.

Val Pera (Văl PEHR-ah) – The largest farming town in Keledev. Val Pera means Sea of Bread, an apt name for this sprawling farming town positioned on the Anamturas River at the intersection of the Central Plain, the White Ridge Mountains, and the Eastern Hills. The farmers of Val Pera like to claim that without their fields, the Liberated Land would starve.

The Windhold – The second outpost from the west in Keledev's northern foothills. The Windhold outpost houses its watchmen in a series of caves above a crystal-clear lake. The Windhold is a natural water catch that snatches moisture from the wind blowing over the steep domed rim. Air blowing upward across the southern wall carved the honeycomb of caves that became the barracks for the company of watchmen. Most in Windhold Company describe the low tones of the wind blowing through the caves as the Rescuer's own music.

TANELETHAR (TĂ-NĔL-Ĕ-THAHR)

Barihav (BAHR-ē-hăv) – A village ruin in the Bezik Hills, all but lost to time. Barihav's history bears no great significance other than having been the home of a particular magician-thief who irked Heleyor early in his reign.

Bezik Hills (BĔ-zik) – The region between the Tagamoor and Sil Shadath, also known as the Bleak Hills. The Bezik Hills are shrouded in perpetual mist due to the vapors seeping out from the Tagamoor.

Darkling Shade – A narrow forest west of Sil Shadath and the Upland Wilds. Darkling Shade was once part of Sil Shadath, but shrank and became separated due to heavy logging in the early days of dragon rule.

Emen Kar (EH-mĕn Kahr) – An Aropha ruin on the southern edge of Sil Shadath. Emen Kar may have been a way station for the Aropha who roamed Talania before the dragon scourge.

The Fading Mountains – A mountain range on the east coast of Tanelethar, also known as the Muddled Mountains. This range seems to be constantly fading due to a clinging fog created by the vapors seeping from the Tagamoor.

Gloamwood – A dying forest in the central east of Tanelethar. Once the beautiful forest of Sil Belomar (Sil BEH-lō-mahr), meaning the Forest of Tranquility, Gloamwood has fallen to decay and rot under dragon rule. It lies southwest of the Tagamoor and northeast of the Tarlan Plains.

Grenton – A village on the northern edge of Gloamwood. The residents of Grenton may have been the first to begin calling the Tagamoor the Ghost Moor.

Highland Forest – A Taneletharian forest region north of the Celestial Peaks, bounded on either side by small mountain ranges known as The Eastlings and the Westlings.

Ras Heval (Rahss Hĕ-VAHL) – An Aropha temple ruin in eastern Tanelethar, at the northern extent of the Fading Mountains. Translated as The Hill of Grace. Though much smaller, the concentric walls surrounding Ras Heval's small chapel ruin offer a glimpse of what Ras Telesar may have looked like in the ancient days.

Ras Pyras (Rahss PEYE-rəss) – The former Aropha worship and administration center that became the seat of Heleyor's power. Translated as The Hill of the Flame. This ancient Aropha temple still stands, but it no longer glorifies the Creator. The hill of Ras Pyras is crowned by four icy concentric walls and supported by many towers. A pillar of fire sprouting from the volcanic underbelly of the northern Frost Isles burns constantly in what was once the central chapel. Heleyor, the Great Red Dragon, made that chapel his throne room.

Sil Shadath (Sil SHĂ-dăth) – A dark forest in eastern Tanelethar. In the Common Tongue, its name means the Black Forest. Sil Shadath is the home of Valshadox, a dragon lord. Ever since the ancient battle between House Suvor and the dragons, its shaggy black pines have held a heavy gray-green mist. Terrible creatures both large and small make their home there, and strange lights wander and flash in the mists. The Aladoth call it the Forest of Horrors.

Tagamar (TĂG-ə-mahr) – A forgotten city in the Tagamoor, on the Phantom River. The ruin of the once great city of Tagamar is a reminder that dragons cannot be trusted. The Suvoroth kings who lived there learned this the hard way. Gray-green vapors seep from the surrounding canyon moor and billow from a broken dome in the city center to cover the whole region in a shroud.

The Tagamoor – A moor canyon in eastern Tanelethar. This canyon moor was the ancient home of House Suvor who were said to fly in battle. Others live there now—creatures that move silently in the mist.

Trader's Knoll – A hilltop village in the Highland Forest. Trader's Knoll became the adopted home of Faelin Enarian during his long, self-imposed exile in Tanelethar. We are not yet certain why, but we believe it has something to do with Kara Orso.

TERMS

Aropha – Also known as the Elder Folk. The Aropha walked Talania before the dragon scourge, serving the High One by caring for and protecting his creations and acting as arbiters between the great houses. In those days, no one in Talania starved or thirsted. The peoples of the Aropha are the Rapha servants, the Lisropha warriors and arbiters, and the tiny Dynapha worshipers. Their artistry is visible in the smooth walls of Ras Telesar, the stairways of Sil Elamar, and in the jeweled trees at the southern gate of Vy Asterlas.

The Aropha and the Dragon Scourge – Heleyor, chief among the Lisropha, betrayed the High One and took many followers of his own kind with him, stealing and corrupting the form of the *lashoroth* into monstrous dragons. He took Ras Pyras as his throne—a fiery crown at the northern tip of the continent. Over time, most of the great human houses fell to Heleyor's deceptions, increasing the size of his armies. Although the High One's victory against Heleyor was never in question, a war between Ras Pyras and the remaining Aropha would surely have destroyed Talania. The Aropha withdrew and have not been seen since.

The Assembly – The government of Keledev. Councilors from all over Keledev meet and debate at the Second Hall in Sky Harbor to decide the laws of the land. The Assembly is overseen by members of the Prime Council who prayerfully seek the will of the High One.

Colloquial family terms – Talanians in much of Keledev and Tanelethar use these terms, though not as much in the cities or wealthier households.

- **Behlna** – Daughter
- **Brehna** – Brother
- **Mamehma** - Grandmother

- **Mehma** – Mother
- **Patehpa** – Grandfather
- **Sehna** – Son
- **Shessa** – Sister
- **Tehpa** – Father

Councilor – A member of the Assembly. Councilors serve their cities and villages by representing their hopes and concerns at the seat of government in Sky Harbor.

The Five Quests – Cadet missions that serve as the tests required for promotion from cadet stalwart to cadet scout. Most cadets endure these quests as a class, working together like a lightraider raid party. Each of the Five Quests is named for and overseen by one of the five lightraider spheres.

Dark Creatures – Monsters cobbled together from corrupted natural elements and animated by the dragons. Some dark creatures use "song sorcery," a form of rhythmic music from within their bodies, to charm their victims. Messages unique to the victim are often heard in the undertones. Many dark creatures employ poisons or infections.

- **Apparition/Ghost** – a dragon corruption formed from rot and mist, designed to deceive mankind into believing they are the risen dead.
- **Giant** – A huge dark creature formed using elements from its environment. Sand giants are blocky creatures of sandstone and desert foliage. Forest giants appear as beings of twisted roots, vines, and clay. Giants may be eight times the height of a man or more and are known to employ song sorcery. Once a giant links itself to a human or group of humans, it demands more and more of them and can be extremely difficult to get rid of. A common jest among lightraiders states that "Giants make terrible houseguests."

- **Goblin** – Goblins come in many forms and sizes. Frost goblins are formed of northern lichen. Cave goblins appear to have flesh formed from cave fungus. Spore goblins are terrifyingly small and toothy and known to inhabit Taneletharian deserts. All goblins are vindictive and delight in torturing humans and animals in many ways.
- **Golmog** – A foul-smelling dark creature a little taller and much heavier than a grown man. Fat and lumbering, golmogs serve the dragons most in manual labor but can be terrible foes in battle.
- **Granog** – A winged dark creature that looks like it shares dragon and human heritage, a littler larger than a grown man. The appearance of granogs is a dragon deception and likely a poor attempt at making creatures that look like the ancient Lisropha warriors. Granogs serve as dragon administrators in Tanelethar.
- **Mudslinger/Muk** – A slimy mud creature found in Taneletharian swamps and wetlands. Muks are known to moan at their victims, luring them into a sense of despair. Spines may grow from their bodies and fling poisonous slime that burns through clothing.
- **Orcs** – "Ore creatures" formed from various minerals. Iron orcs and coal orcs are the most common. Quicksilver orcs are considered the most dangerous, able to shift form at will. The dragons filled their orcs with burning rage, often exhibited by fire blazing behind their eyes, within their joints, and from the runes carved into their hides.
- **Rime Runner** – a long black worm found in ice tunnels where frost goblins live. Rime runners attack in great numbers and attempt to burrow into their victims' flesh.
- **Spider** – Giant arachnids used to terrorize and deceive mankind. They are known to share the influence of the same dragons that control giants. Where giants

are found, the caves and burrows are usually infested with spiders.

- **Sprite** – A creature formed to mimic the ancient Dynapha, which many remember today as faeries. Sprites employ insect-like stings that inject their poisons. As with goblins, there are several forms.
- **Troll** – Four forms of troll are currently known in Tanelenthar—wood troll (mocktree), water or river troll (rattlefish), stone troll (rumblefoot), and north troll (iceblade). Trolls are known to employ both song sorcery and infections/poisons.
- **Wanderer** – A wan and withering human-like thing designed, like ghosts, to deceive mankind into believing it is a form of lingering dead. Wanderers carry lanterns and are known to roam Sil Shadath and Gloamwood.
- **Wraith** – Although this term may be used throughout Talania to describe different and often imagined creatures, an actual wraith is a specific form of orc made in the ancient days from Suvoroth ore by the dragon lord Valshadox. They may be found in Sil Shadath, where they float on the mists flowing from the Tagamoor.

Lightraider Academy (Ras Telesar) – The seat of the Lightraider Order and the fortress where they live and train, including training new recruits.

Lightraider Order – A knightly order in Keledev, commissioned for service by the Rescuer himself when he appeared to his people after he raised the Celestial Peaks and the Storm Mists.

Lightraider Spheres – The primary divisions of the Lightraider Order. The five spheres include the Navigators' Sphere, the Tinkers' Sphere, the Rangers' Sphere, the Comforters' Sphere, and the Vanguard. Members of each sphere may choose additional specialties such as becoming a knight of his creatures, a renewer, or even a lightraider bard. Some specialties are unique to certain spheres, but not all.

Manykit – A leather harness with many pouches, buckles, and sheaths for carrying kit and weapons. Lightraiders prefer to wear manykit in place of carrying packs. Manykit harnesses come in a number of forms, with broad and narrow bands of pouches and sheaths that may strap to the chest, waist, arms, legs, or any combination thereof. Large lightraiders like Dagram Kaivos may wear manykit with spikes on the shoulders. These look imposing in battle, but they are designed as hooks from which to hang additional satchels filled with supplies for the party.

Queensblood – A Taneletharian term for a member of the matriarchal Arkelian bloodline. House Arkelon never bowed to the dragons, and was decimated. A queensblood will often have identifying traits like hair so silver it appears blue and blue freckles that form flourishes on her arms, feet, wrists, or face. The granogs fueled hatred of queensbloods in Tanelethar with the rumor that their ancestors invaded from Arkelia, a separate continent, to become one of the prominent houses of Talania.

Starlot – A jewel formed from crystalized dragon fire. Starlots are the tokens of the Lightraider Order, symbolizing a lightraider's willingness to venture north of the barrier on missions to rescue the Aladoth. Starlots formed when the dragons blasted their fire against freezing winds at the start of the Great Rescue, amid the rising of the Celestial Peaks.

The Turning of the Spheres – The ceremony during which newly promoted cadet scouts are assigned to their sphere. Spheres are chosen for cadets by the headmaster or the head of the Navigators' Sphere, who prayerfully listens to the Helper. Lightraiders rarely change spheres, but it is not unheard-of.

HOW TO PLAY VANQUISH

HISTORY

Vanquish began in the manor houses of Talania, first played by northern nobles, who quickly refined it from a raucous game of knocking wooden balls off a table to a respectable game of battlefield honor. Popular knowledge credits a Fulcor duchess with the single biggest change to the game. A tinker by nature, she crafted padded leather rails and woven "pots" and added them to her dining table to stop the intolerable noise of wooden balls crashing to her floor.

Common folk soon adopted the game, and it remains a favored Talanian pastime, especially during the winter months. The colors and patterns of the balls are generally the same throughout the land. Most Vanquish sets include an army painted with stripes and an army painted with whirls (Fig. 1). The "commander" is a white ball used by both players to control the soldiers. The "dragon" is a solid black ball. Thanks to a jest about his top general by one of the first nobles to play, the commander must be spurred to motion by "poking him with a stick."

Rules vary slightly from region to region, and on Tarlan Plains and in the Eagle Peaks, the game is called Captains and Corporals. What follows here are the rules used by lightraiders who have added the use of a starlot to bring additional strategic choices to the game.

FIG. 1

GAME BASICS

Vanquish is a battle between two armies. To win, one player or team must vanquish all the other player's soldiers followed by the dragon (black ball). Each army includes four corporals and three captains. Vanquish balls in Talania have no numbers. However, in our world, the game may be played with a standard pocket billiards sixteen-ball set (pool set), and the numbers make it easy to remember which colors are the captains and which are the corporals.

GAME TERMS

The Armies (based on a standard pocket billiards set)

Solids (representing Whirls)

- Corporals – Yellow (1), Blue (2), Red (3), Purple (4)
- Captains – Orange (5), Green (6), Burgundy (7)

Stripes

- Corporals – Yellow (9), Blue (10), Red (11), Purple (12)
- Captains – Orange (13), Green (14), Burgundy (15)

Dragon – Black (8)

Commander – White (cue ball)

Sticks – What we call "cues."

Challenge – The act of casting a starlot onto the field of battle.

Pot – A side or corner pocket.

Pot (verb) – To send a ball into one of the pots.

Vanquish – The name of the game.

Vanquish (verb) – To send a soldier or the dragon legally into a pot, thus removing it from the battlefield for the remainder of the game.

Getting Roasted – Losing the game by potting the dragon early.

Battle Line – The imaginary line joining the second diamonds from a player's end of the table (Fig. 2).

Territory – The area behind a player's battle line (Fig. 2).

Botch – (verb or noun) A foul or mistake such as striking an opposing captain with the commander before the opposing corporals have been vanquished, striking your own soldier first, or missing entirely.

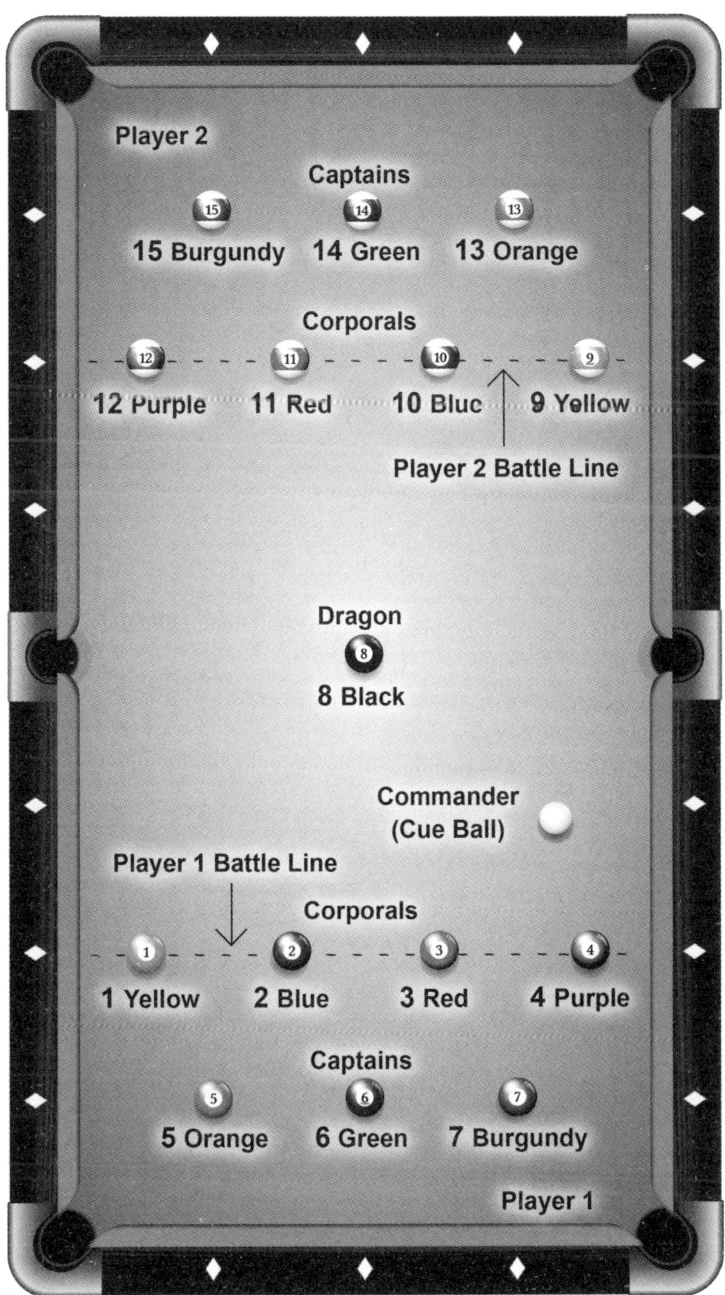
Player 2
Captains
15 Burgundy
14 Green
13 Orange
Corporals
12 Purple
11 Red
10 Bluc
9 Yellow
Player 2 Battle Line
Dragon
8 Black
Commander
(Cue Ball)
Player 1 Battle Line
Corporals
1 Yellow
2 Blue
3 Red
4 Purple
Captains
5 Orange
6 Green
7 Burgundy
Player 1

FIG. 2

GAME SETUP (FIG. 2)

Picture the table as a battlefield. Each player takes one end of the table for his or her "territory." An imaginary line connecting the second diamonds from the end is a player's "battle line."

The four corporals of each army are lined up on their own battle line, evenly spaced. The three captains are lined up behind the corporals, evenly spaced, on an imaginary line connecting the first diamonds from the end. The dragon starts in the exact middle of the table.

GAME START

Roll a starlot. The player with the highest roll chooses who starts first. The starting player must take the first shot with the commander ball (cue ball) from behind his or her battle line—meaning anywhere in his or her territory, behind the corporals.

The starting player may only target the opposing army's corporals.

After the first shot, the commander (cue ball) is played from wherever it lands unless a botch is committed.

GENERAL RULES

Targeting Order – Players must target the opposing soldiers and the dragon in this order.

- Corporals
- Captains
- Dragon
- Captains may not be targeted until all corporals in their army are vanquished. The dragon may not be targeted until the entire opposing army is vanquished.
- This order applies only to the first soldier struck by the commander during each shot.
- Chain reaction shots are legal even if accidental. Soldiers vanquished by accident or design remain van-

quished as long as the first ball struck in the sequence was a legal target. The dragon may also be used in chain reactions after it is awake.

The Dragon – The dragon must be vanquished after the entire opposing army is vanquished. The dragon starts at the center of the table and is "asleep." A sleeping dragon may only be struck if it is the player's last legal target. If inadvertently struck, the dragon is considered "awake" and dangerous. Waking the dragon is bad, and is therefore a botched shot (see Botch or Botched Shot). If a player pots the dragon before vanquishing the rest of the opposing army, the player is "roasted" and loses the game. Players are not required to "call the pot" into which they intend to send the dragon (see below).

Calling Pots – The fog of battle and its consequences are recognized throughout Talania. A soldier struck in the leg by an arrow who then trips and falls into a ravine is still dead, and the archer, though he missed the heart, may still claim a victory. In no region, including Keledev, are Vanquish players required to "call pots," meaning to designate the pot into which they intend to send a soldier or the dragon. While newer games that employ the same table include variations of this rule, in Tanelethar, those who suggest calling pots in a game of Vanquish are traditionally locked in the town stocks and pelted with rotten vegetables. In Keledev, a person who suggests calling pots in Vanquish is quietly reminded that if not for the Rescuer and the core strengths of love, joy, peace, patience, kindness, goodness, faithfulness, gentleness, and self-control, they too would be locked in the town stocks and pelted with rotten vegetables.

Challenge – A starlot may be thrown onto the table as a challenge before an opposing player's shot. The challenge may be thrown at any time before the opposing player begins the motion of striking the commander with the stick tip. A successful challenger may move one soldier anywhere within an area between the imaginary lines joining the two nearest pairs of diamonds (Fig. 3). A moved soldier must be at least one index finger width away from the rail and other soldiers, the dragon, or the commander. Players are granted only one successful challenge during a game, but may challenge as many shots as desired until a challenge is successful. Players may not challenge a shot that legally targets the dragon.

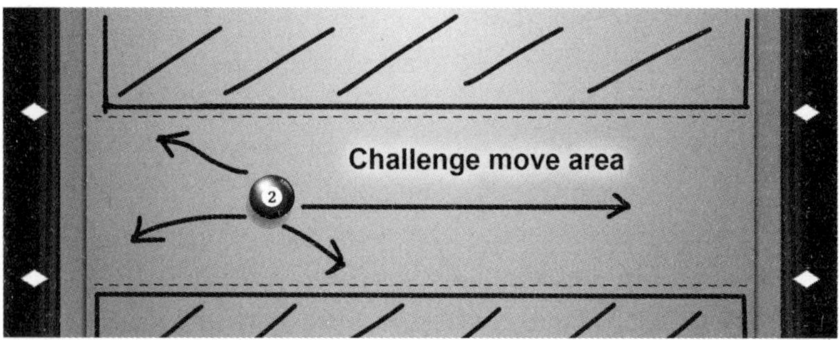

FIG. 3

Challenge steps

- Throw the starlot onto the table and declare “Challenge” followed by a declaration of the soldier you intend to protect.
- A seven (7) or higher is a success (see Challenge above).
- With a result of two (2) to six (6), nothing happens. Remove the starlot from the battlefield, and play continues.
- A one (1) is a “mishap.” The soldier that the challenging player hoped to move is vanquished and potted. If the player mistakenly tried to protect a captain while any of his or her corporals remained on the field, one of the corporals must be vanquished instead. Player’s choice.
- A ten (0 on the starlot) is an “achievement.” The

opposing player's turn is over without taking the shot, and the challenger has the option of either moving the threatened ball or leaving it in place. The challenger begins his or her turn.

- No matter the results of the challenge roll, the commander remains where it is.
- Note – To challenge after a botch, the challenging player must wait for the opposing player to place the commander and remove his or her hand.

Botch or Botched Shot – All possible botches are listed below. When a player botches a shot, control of the commander moves to the other player. The controlling player moves the commander to any spot behind his or her battle line (his or her "territory"). This player may target any legal ball on the table (see Targeting Order), no matter where the ball sits relative to the battle line. Thus, if an enemy soldier has wandered into your territory, you may place the commander near it and vanquish it. Once you remove your hand from the commander, the ball is considered placed and may not be moved again. Any opposing soldier potted during a botch must be returned to that soldier's game-starting position or as close to that position as possible (a finger width away from other soldiers, the dragon, or the commander). Any of the botching player's own soldiers who are vanquished during a botch remain vanquished.

List of Botches

- Striking any soldier or the dragon out of order (see Targeting Order).
- Missing all soldiers entirely (must at least contact a legal target).
- Vanquishing your own soldier (such soldiers remain vanquished).
- Potting the commander.

- Pushing the commander (as opposed to striking the commander).
- Striking the commander with anything other than the stick tip.
- "Startling" the commander—causing the commander to jump. The commander may not be intentionally jumped off the table surface.
- Intentionally delaying the game by challenging every shot (subjective).
- Waking the dragon (occurs only once per game; once the dragon is awake, striking the dragon after striking a legal target is allowed).
- Double hit (hitting the commander twice with the stick).
- Taking a shot without keeping at least one foot on the floor.
- Throwing a starlot to challenge a shot after the commander is struck.
- Bumping any soldier, dragon, or the commander with any part of the body and causing that ball to move more than an index finger width.
- Unsportsmanlike conduct (acting contrary to what is just and good according to the Sacred Scrolls, or in our case, God's Word).
- Knocking any soldier, the dragon, or the commander completely off the table (this is known as the Duchess Rule).

AUTHOR'S NOTE

THE LAST YEAR SINCE THE RELEASE OF *WOLF SOLDIER* and the first new games in the Lightraiders Realm (Starlots and First Watch) has been exciting to say the least. Other adjectives might be chaotic, crazy, and blessed. God has added wonderful people to our team, and as I write this, the new full Lightraiders Adventure Bible Study system is nearly ready for launch.

With *Bear Knight* releasing so close to the launch of the Lightraiders system, I wanted to reiterate a few points noted in the *Wolf Soldier* author's note and elsewhere.

First, as I've said before, don't get bogged down in allegory. The Rescuer represents Christ, and the Keledan represent the Church, but the Rescuer is *not* Christ, and the Keledan are *not* His Church. With that said, I did intend for the themes in these stories to apply in allegorical ways.

Second, sacred verses in our realm are designed to teach Scripture memory and application. Lightraiders declare these verses, resulting in fantasy effects that relate to real-life applications. Neither the characters in the stories nor the players in the games are using these verses as "magic spells." Battle in the fantasy world represents spiritual battle in our world. Physical effects there represent spiritual applications here. In the fantasy realm, sacred verses are prayers and declarations of the Rescuer's power, not that of the lightraiders. The Rescuer, as the Christ figure, may or may not apply his power according to his own will.

Third, I want to address the question of "Why are Keledan forbidden from killing Aladoth?" This returns us to the idea that the physical in the fantasy world often represents the spiritual in our world. Try relating a wounded lightraider stabbing an Aladoth in the gut to a hurt believer lashing out in anger at a non-believer on social media. Love is not the absence of offense, but offense for its own sake is not love. We don't hide God's truth during spiritual debates (or ever), but like the lightraiders, we are not to strike with killing blows when debating those we were commissioned to rescue.

Finally, some thanks. Thank You, Lord, for Your blessings and this opportunity. Thanks to my wife, Cindy, for her love, support, and hard work on this book and all things Lightraiders. Thanks to James R. Brown for his hard work and inspiration in developing the Lightraiders Realm. Thanks to my agent, Harvey, for letting me make this leap and helping make it happen. And thank you to John, David, Kerry, Jennifer, Julian, and all the Lightraiders teens for their hard work, patience, and constant encouragement. I'm so grateful for all of you.

ABOUT THE AUTHOR

AS A FORMER FIGHTER PILOT, STEALTH PILOT, AND tactical deception officer, James R. Hannibal is no stranger to secrets and adventure. He is the award-winning author of thrillers, mysteries, and fantasies for adults and children, and he is the developer of Lightraider Academy games. As a pastor's kid in Colorado Springs, he guinea-pigged every youth discipleship program of the 1980s, but the one that engaged him and shaped him most as a Christ-follower and Kingdom warrior was *DragonRaid*, by Dick Wulf–the genesis of the Lightraider world.